Caballero

Jovita González, San Antonio, Texas, 1931. *Courtesy E. E. Mireles and Jovita González de Mireles Papers, Special Collections and Archives, Texas A&M University–Corpus Christi Bell Library.*

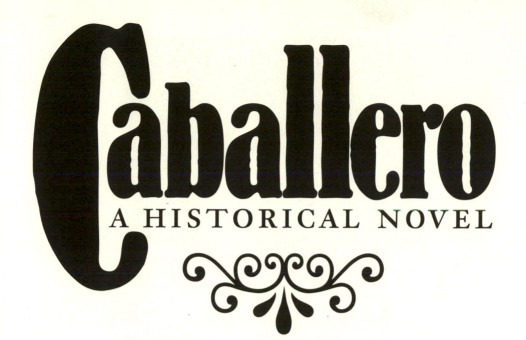

Caballero

A HISTORICAL NOVEL

BY

Jovita González
& Eve Raleigh

Edited by José E. Limón and María Cotera
Foreword by Thomas H. Kreneck

TEXAS A&M UNIVERSITY PRESS
College Station

The paper used in this book meets the minimum requirements
of the American National Standard for Permanence
of Paper for Printed Library Materials, Z39.48-1984.
Binding materials have been chosen for durability.

Library of Congress Cataloging-in-Publication Data

Mireles, Jovita González, 1904–1983.
    Caballero : a historical novel / by Jovita González and Eve Raleigh ; edited by
José E. Limón and María Cotera ; foreword by Thomas H. Kreneck. — 1st ed.
      p. cm.
    Includes bibliographical references.
    ISBN 0-89096-701-6 (cloth). —ISBN 0-89096-700-8 (pbk.)
    1. Mexican American families—Texas—History—19th century—
Fiction. 2. Mexican Americans—Texas—History—19th century—Fiction.
3. Landowners—Texas—History—19th century—Fiction. I. Raleigh, Eve.
d. 1978. II. Limón, José Eduardo. III. Cotera, María, 1944- . IV. Title.
PS3563.I6947C33   1996
813'.54—dc20   95-45525
                                                                CIP

For the *mexicanas* of Texas

Contents

Illustrations

Foreword

The publication of *Caballero* represents a milestone in the literature by and about Mexican Americans in Texas. Written during the 1930s and 1940s by Jovita González (de Mireles) and Margaret Eimer (pseudonym Eve Raleigh) about events in 1846–48, this historical novel has remained unprinted and unavailable to the public until now. As coeditor José E. Limón points out in the introduction to this book, *Caballero* significantly revises the emerging canon of Mexican-American letters and will be welcomed by a broad readership.

Its publication also serves as an important example of the efforts of the Special Collections and Archives Department of the Mary and Jeff Bell Library, Texas A&M University–Corpus Christi to preserve the history of Mexican Americans in South Texas. The original manuscript of *Caballero*—more than five hundred typed pages yellowed and tattered with age—is part of the E. E. Mireles and Jovita González de Mireles Papers in the Department's permanent research holdings. The Mireles Papers consist of a voluminous number of documents reflecting the life and work of these two prominent mid-twentieth century Corpus Christi educators. Their papers were generously donated to the TAMU–CC Library in 1992 by Isabel Cruz, longtime friend and employee of the Mireleses and heir to the papers upon their deaths. Local historian Ray J. García assisted Cruz in deciding where to deposit these valuable materials, as he shared her desire to preserve the contributions of the Mireleses for future generations. When the manuscript of *Caballero* came to TAMU–CC, it was tied with a simple twine string in a bundle of other documents, probably exactly as the Mireleses had stored it. Its importance was immediately apparent. Housed in the archives and made available to researchers, the manuscript was sought out and conclusively identified by Professor Limón, readied for publication by him and María Cotera, and is now accessible to the widest possible audience.

For any archival program or scholar to find an unpublished manuscript of such merit as *Caballero* is rare; to have it printed represents an exciting opportunity to allow the public to benefit from its recovery. From a South Texas perspective, it is especially gratifying to introduce a manuscript co-authored by Jovita González de Mireles—educator, folklorist, and historian—whose writing has increasingly received scholarly attention. We hope that other such publications will emanate from materials at TAMU–CC's Special Collections and Archives, deepening our understanding of Mexican-American history.

This publication is a tribute to the desire of Isabel Cruz and Ray J. García to ensure that the many labors of the Mireles couple be remembered. Scholarship owes them much gratitude. Their efforts to save the Mireles Papers exemplify the potential within every community to document its history with the assistance of committed archival programs.

Scholarship likewise owes a great deal to Dr. José E. Limón and María Cotera for bringing to fruition the publication of this worthy piece of Texana. Their initiative as well as their previous research on Jovita González de Mireles make them the logical choice to edit and explain the manuscript. Their expertise allows them to place *Caballero* in its proper literary and historical contexts. Professor Limón, with his vast knowledge, unflagging interest, and collegiality, has been central to the project.

I would like to extend thanks to Drs. Cynthia Orozco and Arnoldo De León who originally urged our archival program to locate and acquire the papers of the Mireles couple and whose preliminary examination of the manuscript enhanced our appreciation of its possible significance; Dr. Clotilde P. García and the membership of the Spanish American Genealogical Association (SAGA) for their help in searching for these and other Mexican American–related documents; and Corpus Christi residents Vicente N. Carranza and Mel G. Lemos for their assistance in documenting the lives of the Mireleses. Archives assistants María L. Martínez, Alva Neer, and Norman Zimmerman deserve commendation for their help with the administration of the Mireles Papers. Zimmerman and Neer, along with Deanna O. Solomon of the Library's Systems Department, were especially helpful with final preparation of *Caballero*.

I hope that this publication contributes to the spirit of cooperation among archival programs, scholars, community people, and organizations, as well as university presses, to preserve and make available the documents of Mexican-American history. It is through such efforts that we will further develop this important field of study.

Thomas H. Kreneck
Special Collections Librarian/Archivist
Texas A&M University–Corpus Christi

Editors' Acknowledgments

What follows in these pages—a first-time edition of a novel written in the 1930s and 40s by two women in Texas—is the result of a cooperative and collegial effort among yet other Texans today. Although we are principally responsible for this edition of *Caballero: A Historical Novel,* a work that speaks centrally to the Texas experience, many other persons and institutions in Texas society have had their strong positive influence on this book about the United States–Mexico border.

Originally from Karnes County, Texas, Dr. Thomas H. Kreneck, along with other Texans named in his foreword, played a critical role in retrieving the almost lost manuscript of *Caballero* and placing it safely in the Special Collections and Archives of Texas A&M University–Corpus Christi, where he ably serves as chief archivist.

Our border heritage is inescapably bound up in this book. We ourselves are native-born and Texas-raised and represent very different parts of the state: Cotera from El Paso and Austin, Limón from Laredo and Corpus Christi. Both of us were also centrally educated at the University of Texas at Austin, where Limón now serves as a faculty member (Cotera is temporarily doing graduate work at Stanford University, although we await her return to Texas).

Finally, belying its very title, *Caballero* deals centrally with the historical experience of Mexican women in Texas, so we think it wholly appropriate to dedicate this book to this often-neglected sector of Texas society. But, as with many other aspects of Texas, we believe that this book will be of great national and international significance, and it is in this larger sense that we offer it to the public.

José E. Limón
María Cotera

Introduction

BY JOSÉ E. LIMÓN

At present the recovery of a Mexican-American literary heritage has become an important project for literary critics and historians.[1] Several such efforts are now completed or under way, and two of these—both novels— may serve to introduce and contextualize our own contribution to this recovery effort as we bring before the reading public the previously unpublished work, *Caballero: A Historical Novel* by Jovita González (1904– 83) and Eve Raleigh (1903–78).

Like María Amparo Ruiz de Burton's *The Squatter and the Don* (1885), *Caballero*, though written in the 1930s and 40s, is also a woman-authored historical romance that inscribes and interprets the impact of U.S. power and culture on the former Mexican northern provinces as they were being politically redefined into the American Southwest in the mid-nineteenth century.[2] *Caballero* also centers on a fictive Mexican land-owning family, as does *The Squatter and the Don*. In *Caballero*'s case, the Mendoza y Soria family possesses its extensive land-holdings in the heart of South Texas as war and social change descend upon them. For *Caballero* does shift us from Ruiz de Burton's California and New York settings to South Texas as does the regional identity of one of its coauthors, Jovita González. And, rather than the relatively peaceful though coercive legal disputation over land in the California of the 1870s that forms the narrative substance of *The Squatter and the Don*, the González-Raleigh project and its romances between various young lovers is centrally situated in the military conflict of the U.S.–Mexico War of 1846–48 and the concomitant ethnic tensions that continued after 1848 in South Texas. Because this warfare is so central to the novel, a brief review of this conflict may be in order as a guide to the work's military and political context.

In 1845 the United States was embarked on an imperial expansionist policy aimed at eventually acquiring from Mexico what is now the Southwest, with California and Texas as the principal prizes. Texas facilitated matters by declaring itself an independent republic in 1836 after the defeat of Santa Anna at San Jacinto following the fall of the Alamo, an event recalled early in *Caballero*. Agitation for the annexation of Texas, both in

Texas and in the United States, soon followed but not without Mexican opposition. Mexico refused to concede the loss of Texas in 1836, especially that territory generally between the Río Grande and the Nueces River (see map), or what is now South Texas. For it was this territory, including San Antonio, north of the Nueces, that had been the principal area of Spanish settlement in "Texas" in the mid-eighteenth century in the last major Spanish expansion in the Americas, a settlement *Caballero* recalls for us. Following Mexico's independence from Spain in 1821, the territory continued as a Mexican population base settled in ranching communities, and *ranchos*, as well as in towns such as San Antonio to the north and Matamoros near the mouth of the Río Grande on the south side of a river not yet a national boundary. Matamoros, across the river from present-day Brownsville, the fictive *rancho* de la Palma of the Mendoza y Soría, San Antonio, rural south Texas and northern Mexico are the settings for most of *Caballero*'s narrative action. Indeed, the novel's foreword locates the *rancho* for us in the middle of South Texas, from whence the greater Mexican world and the United States are narratively interpreted.

South Texas became the immediate objective of a U.S. army that had been ordered to Corpus Christi near the Nueces in the fall of 1845 to lend force to the American position. By spring of 1846, after diplomatic negotiations had failed, and with the Mexican government in disarray, this army, under the command of Zachary Taylor, was ordered to advance across South Texas to the Río Grande at Matamoros. The goal was not only to establish an American claim to the South Texas area following the passage of the annexation legislation but also to position this force for a penetration of interior Mexico. But here we must take particular critical note, as *Caballero* does, of the paramilitary units of Texas Rangers—veterans of the Texas war for independence—assigned to assist Taylor's troops with their special talent for the indiscriminate killing of Mexicans, a talent acquired since 1836. Mexico responded to this provocation by bringing up its own troops to Matamoros and crossing the river to engage the Americans. War soon followed. Taylor defeated the Mexican armies under Mariano Arista at Palo Alto and Resaca de la Palma on the north bank of the Río Grande. He then took Matamoros and advanced to Monterrey and Mexico City with the continuing ill-disciplined assistance of the Texas Rangers. Even as he did so, other American armies entered California and New Mexico. The final result, of course, was the Treaty of Guadalupe Hidalgo which officially ended the war in 1848 and called for Mexico to relinquish all of

Map of Texas, 1846–48.

its northern territories, including the disputed Mexican border country of South Texas, to the United States.[3]

This South Texas border country most immediately and directly experienced this militarized imposition of American power and culture, the manifest subject of *Caballero*. Américo Paredes has noted in his classic, *"With His Pistol in His Hand": A Border Ballad and Its Hero:*

> With Taylor's advance across the Nueces the Lower Rio Grande became even more of a battleground. Rio Grande rancheros formed part of the Mexican cavalry at Palo Alto and Resaca. After these

American victories the rancheros neither surrendered nor retreated, as did the Mexican regulars. They remained on Taylor's flanks as guerrillas all the way to Monterrey, often causing more trouble than Santa Anna's armies. Consequently the Rio Grande ranchero did not endear himself to Taylor's men, many of whom later settled along the Rio Grande.[4]

These terms of nonendearment are carefully noted in *Caballero* as some actual male historical personages, men such as the Río Grande *ranchero* and warrior-hero Juan Nepomuceno Cortina, make appearances in the novel. But as the reader will soon discover, *Caballero's* story does not confine itself to these male landowners, and therein we find the novel's special strengths. For soon after we read of the American military occupation of South Texas, countervailing terms of romantic endearment begin to flow across this new and tense ethnic border as *Caballero's* leading young protagonists fall in love. These are romances that in rich detailed fashion set in motion a complicated articulation of race, class, gender, and sexual contradictions—contradictions, by the way, that place the Mexican world of *Caballero* at some interesting distance from what Carl Gutiérrez-Jones has most recently called the pre-1848 "utopian" vision of the South Texas–Mexican social sphere in Paredes's *"With His Pistol in His Hand"*.[5]

Even as we have turned to Américo Paredes, the primary scholar of Mexican-American South Texas, and his classic historical ethnography of this area, we can also now place *Caballero* in conjunction with yet another recently recovered novel, *George Washington Gómez*, by the same Américo Paredes.[6] Though both novels were written at about the same time and less than two hundred miles from each other—Paredes in Brownsville, González-Raleigh in San Antonio, Del Rio, and Corpus Christi—*Caballero* can now be envisioned as a kind of precursory text for *George Washington Gómez*, as González and Raleigh represent in fiction a nineteenth century–generated political culture into which Paredes's central South Texas Mexican protagonist, Gualinto, will be born some years later. Even as he is being born in 1915, ethnic violence, led yet again by the Texas Rangers, reaches a crescendo at the end of the "long" nineteenth century of South Texas history when armed, organized bands of Mexican Americans, *los sediciosos* (seditionists), rose up in armed revolt against American domination. Gualinto's narrative development is then carried forward in time to the Second World War, and it is as if these three authors—Ra-

South Texas *ranchero* Salome Guerra. Photograph by E. C. Olivares. This picture may have served as an inspiration or model for *Caballero. Courtesy E. E. Mireles and Jovita González de Mireles Papers, Special Collections and Archives, Texas A&M University–Corpus Christi Bell Library.*

leigh, González, and Paredes—have worked together to narratively span the Euro-American history of South Texas from its mid-eighteenth century Spanish settlement, vividly recollected in *Caballero*'s foreword, through the crisis period from 1846 to 1915, and on to Gualinto's maturity during the Second World War and his own exogamous political border-crossing into American culture, signified by his marriage to an Anglo-American woman.[7]

But before we fully knew Paredes as novelist, we knew him better as Professor Paredes, native South Texas Mexican-American folklorist and cultural historian, from the publication of his first major scholarly article in 1942 to the present.[8] Yet, so was Jovita González, also a Mexican-American folklorist and cultural historian, native to the South Texas area. González was born in 1904 and spent her early years in Roma upriver from Paredes's Brownsville. She traced her own heritage to the eighteenth-century Spanish settlement of South Texas and to its landed, relatively affluent, *hidalgo* and *ranchero* class, such as that represented in *Caballero* and from which it takes its very title. Nonetheless, the record shows that she was to spend most of her life in financially constrained circumstances. In 1910 she moved with her family to San Antonio, where she received a B.A. in Spanish from Our Lady of the Lake College in 1927 and subsequently a M.A. in history in 1930 from the University of Texas at Austin. During these years of higher education, she was influenced and encouraged to write about her native culture by the famous Texas professor and folklorist J. Frank Dobie. This she did in a master's thesis on the social history of South Texas and in a series of published articles on folklore— folklore work which, as I have argued elsewhere, offers an overwhelmingly male-centered and ethnically complicated interpretive sense of the Mexican world of South Texas.[9] In 1930 she returned to San Antonio to teach high school Spanish, although in 1934 she received a one-year fellowship from the Rockefeller Foundation, relieving her of teaching duties to research and write a book on South Texas history and culture. The ultimate result was two books: one, *Caballero*; the other, a largely unpublished series of folkloristic sketches in the form of another novel she called *Dew on the Thorn*, although *Caballero* is also a literary ethnography of South Texas–Mexican folklore customs and traditions.

Between 1935 and 1937, as she was beginning the writing of these books, González made two critical decisions, both bearing on *Caballero* and her writing career. In 1935 she married Edmundo E. Mireles from San Antonio, a former fellow student at the University of Texas and then a fellow teacher of Spanish. They moved from San Antonio, first to Del Rio, Texas, and then to Corpus Christi. Further information on this marriage follows later. Then sometime around 1937 she invited one Margaret Eimer, pen name Eve Raleigh, to coauthor *Caballero* with her.[10]

At this time I regret to report that we know very little about Eimer, although it has not been for lack of effort.[11] Born in 1903 in Missouri, she died in 1978 in St. Louis, alone, a ward of the State of Missouri, with no relatives claiming her remains. Clearly, however, for some considerable part of her life she lived in Texas, where she met González, probably in Del Rio. The record yields little else about her other than she obviously participated in some sustained fashion in the production of *Caballero*. Indeed, González's obvious assent to giving Eimer (Raleigh) first-author credit on the manuscript's title page would seem to imply a full and equal participation.

The perplexing question that must be answered is: why did González, already a published writer, feel the need to take on *any* coauthor at all, especially a non–Mexican American, non–South Texan, to write a book which deals so substantially with González's native community and is so clearly based on her own Rockefeller grant research?

In the 1970s she and her husband, E. E. Mireles, granted an interview to Marta Cotera, a leading Mexican-American feminist, archivist, and historian. Cotera was seeking to recover their papers, but particularly González's, on behalf of the Mexican-American Library Project at the University of Texas at Austin. Mireles would not permit a formal tape recording, so we have only Cotera's recollection of what transpired.[12] As Cotera reports it, the discussion got around to the book that González had worked on with her 1934 grant, which Cotera knew about because it was reported in progress in the author's biographical sketches for the several articles González had published in *Southwest Review* and the *Publications of the Texas Folklore Society*. With Mireles doing most of the talking, the couple confirmed that such a book had indeed been written, but, Mireles said, it no longer existed; it had been destroyed. I shall return to this denial in a moment. Mireles went on to make two other points about the presumably destroyed manuscript: first, the racial-political climate in the 1940s would have made the novel's publication controversial for them as public school teachers in Corpus Christi, and, second, as a strategy for dealing with this local problem as well as appealing to publishers, his wife had asked Eimer (Raleigh) to lend her surname to the project and to type the manuscript.[13] González said nothing to correct or dissent from her husband's comments other than to note that Margaret Eimer was a "nice woman."

The final word on the subject, however, appears to be more complex and speaks to a relatively equal co-authorship but one in which González's contribution is decisive. In 1938–39 González and Eimer finished their work and sent it to three major publishers, Macmillan, Houghton-Mifflin and Bobbs-Merrill, only to have it rejected.[14] A letter of August 28, 1939 from González to one John Joseph Gorrell—at this time unidentified— reveals her exasperation about these rejections even as she describes the novel and its co-authorship:

> All of these publishers have admitted that the background is in-teresting, the plot stirring, the characters alive and yet they reject it. The period is 1848–49, and we have pictured life as it existed in those days, material which has taken me twelve years to compile from memoirs, traditions and of course historical sources into which I have delved at the Garcia Collection of the University of Texas. . . . It is the only book of its kind, the Mexican side of the war of 1848 has never been given. We are not partial. We picture the Mexican hidalgos with their faults as well as their virtues, with their racial and reli-gious pride, their love of tradition and of the land which they inher-ited from their ancestors. We also picture the American officers, their kindness to the conquered race, but we also picture the vandals who followed on the trail of the army, hating anything and every-thing that was Catholic and Mexican, and who used the battle cry Remember the Alamo as an excuse to pillage and steal. It has a beau-tiful love story, that of the beautiful daughter of the hero of the novel, and of a young American officer, a Virginian . . . it is a good book. It is a book that is needed.[15]

The repeated *we* in this description of the project clearly implies a co-authorship without distinction although González is also intent on not-ing her own historical contribution. Three other letters in the Mireles Papers also suggest a stronger role for Eimer than E. E. Mireles implied in his conversation with Cotera. These suggest that Eimer may have done the initial crafting of González's contribution into the form of the romance novel, although undoubtedly such a contribution would have included González's specific narrative delineation of at least the Mexican characters—by far the great majority—in the novel and likely the Anglos as well. In the development of these characters González is clearly drawing on composites and fictive renditions of actual Mexican personages from her familial-ancestral background and, in the case of the Anglos, drawing on her intimate knowledge of mainstream Texas history as a professionally trained Texas historian. By the way of male Anglo-Texas speech patterns and mannerisms, she also would have had the benefit of a considerable amount of time spent in the company of J. Frank Dobie and the members of the Texas Folklore Society, a "privilege" then allowed to few Mexicans. While it is clear that Eimer had some large role probably in crafting the overall romantic narrative development of the plot, it is not clear that the idea of a romance that overcomes social divisions was hers alone. González had also trained in Spanish as well as history; like other well-educated Mexican-Americans at the time, she would have been familiar with the literary-intellectual currents then flowing from Mexico to San Antonio especially in the Spanish-language newspapers and publishing houses in the city; and, she also traveled extensively in Mexico and lectured at its universities including the UNAM. It therefore seems impossible to me that she would not have known Mexico's most famous romance novel and its revered author—Ignacio Altamirano's *El Zarco: Episodes of Mexican Life in 1861–1863*—published in 1901 and extremely popular in Mexico in these formative years of González's literary life. Indeed *El Zarco* was republished in San Antonio in the early 1920s. Like *Caballero* Altamirano's work has as its theme the overcoming of deep social divisions through romance and it foregrounds war, guerrillas, and young lovers of opposed racial backgrounds.[16]

During their relationship in a late letter dated June 29, 1946, Eimer acknowledges that, in what she calls the "original" version of the manuscript, González's name appears first on the title page but then informs González that a publisher has advised her as the "author," to place her name, "Eve Raleigh," first. She trusts that this new arrangement will be acceptable to González: "It matters not to me personally, particularly as I am still trying for more humility, *etc.* It is of small importance and I only mention it so you won't think I seek aggrandizement or something above you." In the rest of the letter she speaks of her active role in the construction of the manuscript so as to produce what appears to be the last version on record sent to González for her reading and presumed approval. I believe this to be the recovered manuscript we have at hand for it does show Eve Raleigh as first author, but we have no record that González necessarily accepted this new arrangement.

I strongly believe that Eimer had a strong authorial hand in shaping the romantic plot development of *Caballero* but always with the active participation of González in the crafting process. I have no doubts that the historical data and events and, perhaps more importantly, the development of the novel's characters were largely González's contribution to the project. She reasonably could have conceived the idea of a historical romance itself based on Alamirano's possible influence, although I cannot prove this point. Although Eimer identifies herself as "author" in this letter, I also believe that her claim and role in the construction of the work are outweighed by González's far larger role in the genesis and overall execution of the project. Thus, and in keeping with the early recognition of the authors themselves, in this finally published edition of *Caballero*, my co-editor and I wish to restore Jovita González's name to the first-author status affirming what we see as her primary role in the production of *Caballero*.

By the late 1940s, no doubt discouraged by rejections, the two women decided to set the project aside and go their separate ways, with Eimer now headed to Missouri. At this time González apparently ended all of her creative literary and folkloristic work and dedicated herself wholly to teaching high school Spanish and to writing several Spanish-language textbooks with her husband. She and her husband also became respected figures in Corpus Christi society and its educational community. She and her husband died in 1983 and 1986, respectively, leaving no children or close relatives. From conversations with her friends and associates, such as Lemos, in Corpus Christi, it appears that in this later part of her life she told no one in Corpus Christi about her manuscripts or her life as a creative writer.

As I draw to a close in these introductory remarks, let me return to the critical interview Marta Cotera conducted with González and Mireles in the mid-1970s. Let us recall Mireles's control of the conversation and his concern for what he feared would be the repercussions of publishing *Caballero* with a single Spanish-surnamed author in the still volatile South Texas racial climate of the 1930s and 40s. According to Cotera, Mireles also said that, even if it existed, he would not have wanted the manuscript published *then* in the 1970s, as he feared for its reception in the Chicano literary nationalist ambience of the period. For these reasons, Mireles announced to Cotera that the manuscript had been destroyed. According to Cotera, at the precise moment Mireles announced *Caballero's* destruction, Jovita González, unobserved by her husband, made a brief wagging gesture with her hand to Cotera, clearly *negating* her husband's statement. She then reinforced her negation with her eyes intently gazing upon Cotera.

Let me propose that in Cotera's interview we have a hermeneutics for approaching the novel itself, a hermeneutics consonant with the lived experience of González and Mireles as wife and husband in their lifetime. As Marta Cotera noted in my follow-up interview with her, the couple was very sensitive to the Anglo racial and racist presence in their lives and their tenuous status as middle-class Mexican-American public school teachers. But Mireles also indicated that the couple was sensitive to the nationalist Chicano politics and literary culture of the sixties and seventies—those writers of our own time whom Alurista, in a revealing metaphor, described as "warriors of the pen"—and their reception of *Caballero* had it been published then.[17] That González and Mireles would be concerned about the reaction of both Anglo bigots *and* Chicano nationalists speaks to *Caballero's* complex representation.

The production of culture in a mid-nineteenth century South Texas Mexican world, historically first fraught with issues of racism and countervailing masculinized nationalism, is at the heart of *Caballero*, especially as culture is deeply embedded in questions of class, patriarchy, and gender. Living with these issues in his own time and marriage, Mireles, like Don Santiago, the leading male protagonist in the novel, exercised his culturally chartered dominant role as the "Mexican man" and unilaterally announced *Caballero's* destruction in what he felt to be the defense of his family, even as González, like many of the women in *Caballero*, publicly assented. But, like them, only publicly. With a wag of a finger and a steady gaze, Jovita González ultimately dissented surreptitiously and subversively, as do her women characters in *Caballero*. And in so doing she let it be known to another Mexican-American woman—Marta Cotera—that a continuing later search for *Caballero* would bear fruit. By all accounts a solid citizen, Mireles did what he believed he had to do, given his place and circumstances. It is easy to imagine, however, that Jovita would have wanted her novel published, posthumously if necessary, as it represented the fruit of so many years of her labor and her major literary statement. It expressed too much to be relegated to oblivion.

In his foreword to this volume, Dr. Thomas Kreneck has told us about the circumstances through which the González de Mireles Papers, including *Caballero*, were placed in the archives of Texas A&M University–Corpus Christi. But it might be of interest and value to know something of the circumstances under which I and my coeditor came to the project. In the mid-1980s I began to work on a book about Mexican-American folklore in South Texas.[18] Like many socially marginalized areas, such as northern New Mexico, South Texas historically has generated and drawn its share of anthropologists and folklorists. In what first started as an obligatory review of the literature, for the first time, I fully read the whole of González's folklore work. Along with that of John Gregory Bourke, J. Frank Dobie, and Américo Paredes, her writings proved so fascinating as cultural representation that I converted this review into part one of *Dancing with the Devil*, in effect to an intellectual history of the scholarship. But as I examined González's published work, I, like Marta Cotera, kept picking up the references to her book in progress based on her Rockefeller grant. Thinking it then to be a work of folklore scholarship, I fruitlessly continued to search for it until finally *Dancing with the Devil* had to go to press. But my interest in the manuscript remained strong.

My coeditor, María Eugenia Cotera, is the daughter of Marta Cotera. It is appropriate and poetic that the active presence of the Cotera women be continued in this project through María's participation. Our shared interest in Jovita González intersected in the fall of 1992 when she entered the graduate program in English at the University of Texas at Austin after working with her mother on a variety of women's archival and documentary projects. When I learned of her background and interest in González, I asked her to collaborate with me in this continuing search for González's work. It was she, of course, who first told me of her mother's interview, and it was she who, through her extensive archival research in the university's J. Frank Dobie Collection, first determined that the still missing manuscript was indeed a novel—a fact unclear until then. Detective work, chance, and a suggestion from my good friend Victor Nelson-Cisneros, assistant dean of Colorado College, led me to locate and conclusively identify the manuscript. But it could just as easily have been María.[19] She has been a full colleague, collaborator, and friend in this recovery process. With her superior knowledge of issues in feminist criticism, she offers a critical essay on the novel in these terms. It has been placed at the end of the novel so as not to delay or critically mediate the encounter between the reader and the text anymore than necessary.[20] We trust that this analytical ending will be but the beginning of a sustained critical discussion of this important work that we now place in your hands.

Notes

1. The leadership and motivation for much of this recovery effort comes from Professor Nicolás Kanellos, Arte Público Press and the Recovering U.S. Hispanic Literary Heritage Project. María Cotera and I are deeply grateful for a grant-in-aid from the Project for this work. Limón also thanks the U.S.–Mexico Fund for Culture for a research grant that made this book possible. The editors also wish to acknowledge and thank the Special Collections and Archives Department of Texas A&M University–Corpus Christi Bell Library for making the manuscript available for publication.

2. María Amparo Ruiz de Burton, *The Squatter and the Don*, eds. Rosaura Sánchez and Beatrice Pita (Houston: Arte Público Press, 1992. Original edition, 1885. For a thorough discussion of the historical romance novel in Latin America see Doris Sommer, *Foundational Fictions: The National Romances of Latin America* (Berkeley and Los Angeles: University of California Press, 1991).

3. K. Jack Bauer, *The Mexican War: 1846–1848* (Lincoln: University of Nebraska Press, 1974).

4. Américo Paredes, *"With His Pistol in His Hand": A Border Ballad and Its Hero* (Austin: University of Texas Press, 1958, 1971), p. 133. See also David Montejano for a rich comprehensive analysis of the American economic and political motivations for the incorporation of South Texas in his *Anglos and Mexicans in the Making of Texas, 1836–1986* (Austin: University of Texas Press, 1987).

5. Carl Gutiérrez-Jones, *Rethinking the Borderlands: Between Chicano Culture and Legal Discourse* (Berkeley: University of California Press, 1995), pp. 103–105.

6. Américo Paredes, *George Washington Gómez: A Mexicotexan Novel* (Houston: Arte Público Press, 1990).

7. It could then be reasonably argued that yet another South Texas writer, the distinguished Rolando Hinojosa, brings this historical project into our own time with his Klail City Death Trip series.

Caballero can also be placed in another literary lineage, that of Mexican fiction which deals with the war from Payno's *El fistol del diablo* (1846) to Robles's *Cuando el águila perdió sus alas* (1951) as well as that of the Latin American romance novel.

8. For a critical review of Professor Paredes's folklore scholarship, see my *Dancing with the Devil: Society and Cultural Poetics in Mexican American South Texas* (Madison: University of Wisconsin Press, 1994), chapter 4.

9. For a critical review of González's folklore work, see my *Dancing with the Devil*, chapter 3. We should also take special note of González's master's thesis in history, "Social Life in Cameron, Starr, and Zapata Counties" (University of Texas at Austin, 1930), which clearly informs *Caballero*.

10. Hereafter, for purposes of clarity, I shall refer to E. E. Mireles as "Mireles" and to Jovita as "González," although after marriage she identified herself as Jovita González de Mireles. Interestingly, she does not do so on the post-1935 title page. This account is based largely on a brief autobiographical sketch González left us in the Mireles–González de Mireles Papers at Texas A&M University–Corpus Christi Bell Library.

11. Since my discovery of the novel in February of 1993, its publication has been held up chiefly because of our extensive and largely fruitless search for more information on Margaret Eimer. Having now exhausted every possible lead, we feel obligated to bring *Caballero* before the public without further delay.

12. Interview with Marta Cotera, Austin, Texas, June 14, 1994.

13. Later in their career González and her husband coauthored two Spanish language textbooks with R. B. Fisher, superintendent of Corpus Christi public schools and a friend, although he had no particular specialty in this field. According to Mel Lemos, González's long-time friend and colleague, Mireles and González only used Fisher's name to give the book greater "acceptability" in Corpus Christi, where Mireles was trying to implement bilingual education programs against great opposition. Interview with Mel Lemos, Corpus Christi, Texas, February 12, 1994.

14. These publishers have maintained no records of these transactions.

15. Letter to Gorrell, as well as the others cited below, are in the unprocessed correspondence, E. E. Mireles and Jovita González de Mireles

Papers, Special Collections and Archives, Texas A&M University–Corpus Christi Bell Library.

16. Ingacio Altamirano, *El Zarco: Episodios de la Vida Mexicana en 1861–63.* Prologo de Carlos Monsivais, (Mexico, D. F.: Ediciones Oceano, SA., 1986). Originally published in 1901. The San Antonio, Texas edition that González could have easily read was published by the Libreria de Quiroga in an undated edition. However, in their list of their other books available for purchase on the back cover of *El Zarco*, we find a book on the Mexican Revolution in 1916. Allowing for writing time and publication of the latter, I estimate *El Zarco*'s publication in the early twenties just as González was coming of age as a teenager active in cultural and political circles in the city.

17. Alurista, F. A. Cervantes, Juan Gomez-Quiñones, Mary Ann Pacheco, and Gustavo Segade, eds., *Festival de Flor y Canto: An Anthology of Chicano Literature* (Los Angeles: University of Southern California Press, 1976), p. xi. We should also note that a well-publicized *Festival de Flor y Canto* of Chicano literature was held in Corpus Christi, Texas, in the mid-1970s while González and Mireles lived there.

18. Limón, *Dancing with the Devil.*

19. As we go to press with *Caballero*, I have also identified and edited González's solely authored *Dew on the Thorn*, which will be published by Arte Público Press in 1996. I am also writing an intellectual biography of González and Mireles entitled *"Our Life's Work": Jovita González, E. E. Mireles, and the Mexican-American Politics of Self, Society, and Culture in Texas, 1748–2000*, under contract to the University of Texas Press.

20. Having completed her M.A. at the University of Texas with a fine master's thesis on *Caballero*, María Cotera is now pursuing doctoral studies in modern thought and literature at Stanford University. Her closing critical essay in this volume is a version of one of her master's thesis chapters. See also my own independent interpretive analysis of *Caballero* forthcoming in *Modern Language Quarterly* (1996).

Editing Notes

The E. E. Mireles and Jovita González de Mireles Papers at Texas A&M University–Corpus Christi contain two versions of *Caballero*, hereafter referred to as MS-1 and MS-2. MS-1 lacks approximately three concluding chapters and was found in a state of great disarray, pages out of order, in a pile, as if it had been discarded. It also reads like an early version of the novel. By comparison, MS-2 is almost fully complete in both senses. First, it contains the three final chapters, giving the work a clear ending. Second, its characters and scenes are more fully developed, and the plot has greater coherence. Finally, MS-2 was found in a neat orderly stack and tied with twine, as Dr. Kreneck has noted. For these reasons what we offer here is substantially MS-2 with the following editorial changes: (1) MS-1 does have a foreword not found in MS-2, and although the authors may have intended its deletion, in the absence of any such expressed intention, we have taken the liberty of adding it to MS-2 in the belief that it greatly enhances the novel's chronological range and narrative fullness; (2) pages 4, 5, and 6 are missing in MS-2; although they are not a perfect match, we have substituted the approximate pages taken from MS-1; and (3) MS-2 has a few occasional illegible phrases caused, it would seem, by faulty typing. Wherever possible we have turned to MS-1 to clarify these places and have noted them. Certain words in MS-2 were clearly marked out by the authors and we have respected these deletions, since they do not impair the narrative movement of the story. However, MS-2 has a few long passages marked "Omit"; however, if omitted the narrative loses its coherence, as the authors left nothing to replace the passages. The syntax, grammar, and spelling of MS-2 have been largely preserved with only the most minimal of corrections to a very few obvious errors or typos. Our editorial notes are footnoted by number for each individual chapter. However, the authors also have some footnotes and these are denoted by asterisks. In the interest of providing the fullest manuscript possible, we have kept these footnotes.

We also call your attention to the authors' own editorial notes where they refer to MS-2 as a "carbon copy" with "trivial" mistakes corrected in the "finished book." This final version, presumably the version sent to publishers, now appears to be lost. All publishers contacted inform us that they do not maintain archival records for this period. (Is this the manuscript that Mireles destroyed, if indeed he destroyed anything at all? Did González covertly keep this carbon? We can only speculate.)

Submitted by
Margaret Eimer
817 Maiden Lane
Joplin, Missouri
(Pseudonym Eve Raleigh)

CABALLERO
An historical novel by
Eve Raleigh
and
Jovita Gonzalez

Suggested titles:
The Hacienda.
Eyes to See.
Heritage.
"Mea Culpa."
Dew On The Thorn.
This My House.
Mine, Mine!

Facsimile of the original title page from the manuscript. *Original courtesy E. E. Mireles and Jovita González de Mireles Papers, Special Collections and Archives, Texas A&M University–Corpus Christi Bell Library.*

Authors' Notes

It is uncorrected. All flagrant mistakes in punctuation have been corrected in the original, many words changed and sentences bettered, to further the smooth flow. So if your mind "bumps" now and then, read on, secure in the knowledge that it is not there in the finished book. (We got so sick of the thing and had worked so hard to finish and get it on the market while the set-up is timely, that we could not bear the thought of correcting carbons.) In the main the mistakes are trivial and obvious.

The personnel of Fort Brown as well as all other characters, except those obviously historical, are purely fictional.

The Spanish—and the American—surnames used have no connection with similar existing names, either in Mexico or the Southwest. Names fairly common were deliberately used so that, in covering the many, no individual is touched. Any events that coincide with actual happenings are accidental and unknown to the authors.

This book is neither biographical nor autobiographical, but it gives a correct and exact atmosphere of the people and the period it deals with. If at times the speech seems stilted it is because the formality of speech used at the time has been retained and translated as faithfully as possible.

Without prejudice or palliation for race or religion, seeing the need to cover a phase of history and customs heretofore unrecorded, this book is offered.

The Authors

Characters

Don Santiago de Mendoza y Soría	patriarch, owner of Rancho La Palma
Doña María Petronill	his wife
Alvaro	oldest son
Luis Gonzaga	second son
María de los Angeles	older daughter
Susanita	youngest child
Doña Dolores	Don Santiago's widowed sister
Paz	old family nurse and housekeeper
Robert Davis Warrener	a Virginian, officer in the American army stationed at Fort Brown
Alfred "Red" McLane	politician and promoter
Captain Devlin	doctor at Fort Brown
Gabriel del Lago	neighbor and friend of Don Santiago
Inez Sánchez	friend of Susanita
Johnny White	a Ranger, adventurer
Padre Pierre	Catholic priest of the church at Matamoros
Major Fortesby	officer at Fort Brown
Captain Ross	officer at Fort Brown
Coley	private at Fort Brown
Shane	private at Fort Brown
Kelly	private at Fort Brown
René de la Ferriére	Mexican young man
José Luis Carbajal	Mexican young man
Monico de Deza	Mexican young man
Felix Cadena	Mexican young man
Leon Mora	Mexican young man
Juan Cortina	Mexican young man (historical)
Manuel	great-grandson of Paz, the old nurse
Don Eulalio and Doña Juana Sánchez y Argensola	parents of Inez
Clara	friend of Susanita and Inez

CHARACTERS

José Antonio Carbajal
Juan Monico Robles
Gáspar de la Guerra
Pablo de Olivares
Domingo Viscaya
Fernando del Valle
Hermilio Márquez
Juan de Cisneros

General Antonio Canales	*leader of guerillas (historical)*
Bony	*proprietor of The Skeleton*
Tomás	*overseer of Rancho La Palma*
Estéban	*second overseer at the hacienda*
José and Tecla	*servants in charge of the sheep headquarters*
Nicolasa	*house servant at Rancho La Palma*
Eulalia	*house servant at Rancho La Palma*
Luciana	*house servant at Rancho La Palma*
Josefa	*house servant at Rancho La Palma*
Narcisa	*house servant at Rancho La Palma*
Gregoria	*orchardist*
Simón	*vaquero*
Pedro	*vaquero*
Chonita	*nurse of Inez*
Ike	*companion of Red McLane*

Glossary

Alabado, El. *Evening prayer. Literally, a hymn of praise.*
alcalde. *Chief executive of a Mexican town; a sort of mayor.*
arroyo. *Gully.*
baile. *Dance.*
caballero. *Gentleman.*
calabozo. *Jail.*
caporal. *Overseer.*
chaparejos. *Leather leggings, chaps.*
con diez mil demonios. *With ten thousand devils; a favorite expression synony-
    mous with speed.*
donas. *The groom's gift to his prospective bride.*
don, doña. *A title given to persons of high degree, used only with the first name
    and never omitted outside of family circles. Equivalent to "Sir Santiago." In
    modern times the usage has been corrupted and is used indiscriminately.*
escopeta. *Shotgun.*
guisado. *A fricassee.*
hermano, hermana. *Brother, sister.*
hijo, hija. *Son, daughter.*
hidalgo. *Nobly born.*
huarache. *Rawhide sandals.*
-ito, -ita. *Diminutive; used in affection, as "hijito," little son.*
jacal. *Thatched-roof hut.*
jaras. *Shrub.*
ladrón. *Robber, thief.*
los diablos Tejanos. *The devil Texans.*
la Virgen me socorra. *May the Virgen protect me.*
marica. *Milksop, an effeminate man.*
maleta. *Saddle bags.*
merienda. *Afternoon coffee.*
muchacho, muchacha. *Boy, girl.*
Madre de Dios y todos los santos. *Mother of God and all the Saints.*

niño, niña. *A title of endearment, also baby.*

palomita. *Little dove.*

patio. *Inner courtyard around which the house was built.*

peon. *Lowest class of worker.*

perdóneme. *Pardon me.*

pita. *Spanish dagger plant.*

pobrecita. *Poor little one.*

posadas. *Literally, an inn. As used: Services which are held from the sixteenth of December through the twenty-fourth in commemoration of the birth of Christ.*

pulicos. *Pigs.*

querida. *Dear, darling.*

¿quien sabe? *Who knows?*

¡quien vive! *Who goes there?*

¿qué va aquí? *What goes on here?*

rebozo. *Shawl worn by the Mexican women of the peon class.*

reata. *Lariat.*

sala. *Sitting room.*

¡sálganse! *Get out!*

seguidilla. *A Spanish dance.*

sangre de Cristo. *Blood of Christ.*

siesta. *After-dinner nap.*

sí. *Yes.*

triste. *Disheartened.*

tipichil. *A hard floor of earth. Method: The earth was dug up to at least a foot in depth (generally two feet), mixed with fine gravel; water, preferably hot, was poured on it, then it was packed down with heavy tampers made of wood blocks. Sometimes covered with a sort of varnish.*

váyanse. *Go.*

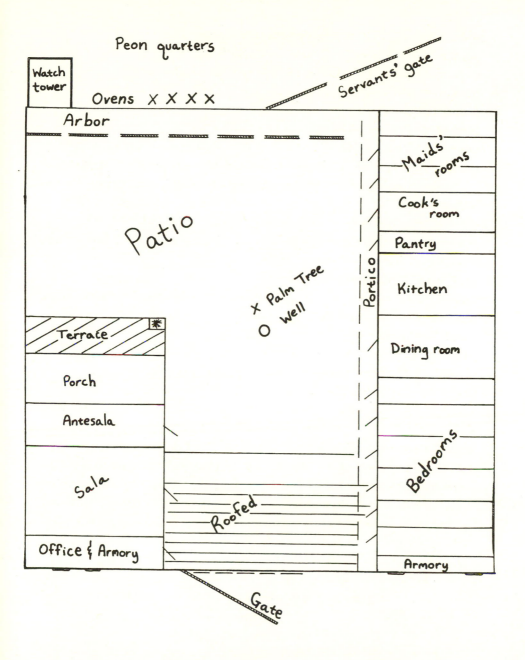

Sketch of the floor plan of the House of Mendoza y Soría. *Original courtesy E. E. Mireles and Jovita González de Mireles Papers, Special Collections and Archives, Texas A&M University–Corpus Christi Bell Library. Adapted by Boomer Cardinale.*

Foreword

Palm Sunday of the year of our Lord 1748.

Don José Ramón de Mendoza y Robles guided his horse to the top of the bluff that looked like a fragment of a great wall, and there stood at its edge and looked westward where mile overlapped mile into eternity itself, and only God could span it. To the north the grass-matted, undulating prairies along the Río Nueces, to the south the brush covered land of the Río Grande, and beyond it a home in Mexico already as nebulous as the horizon before him in the sharply etched desire for this new, this untrodden, unconquered land.

Here was the place for his home. In the months of travel as surveyor for the Crown, with the exploratory expedition sent by the viceroy of New Spain, he had ridden over much land that lay fair, camped at many a spring and river, yet nowhere had a place beckoned and smiled. None of it had whispered, so softly that only he could hear, "I have been waiting for you." Before his eyes a ranch took shape. Ahead, a little to the right, the gentle swell of plain broke against a smooth circle that was like a huge tabletop. In its middle the magic of the mind saw a palm tree. La Palma de Cristo, he mused. Yes, that would be the name for his ranch. A glorious triumphant name—Rancho La Palma de Cristo! Hadn't he first seen his dream home on this Palm Sunday? La Palma, for short, and it would be known all over the countryside. Beside the palm tree would be a well, flowers and shrubs, and space in the sun, and around this patio a house. Not a little home, but a great *hacienda* worthy of his name. Before his eyes cattle took shape on the deserted plain and moved in large dark herds, sheep and goats made white patches on the green, in the garden and the fields toiled *peons*. There were children and guests and the laughter and sorrow and joy and grief that is life.

Here he would create a new empire, and his place the finest of them all. Here he could rear his family and keep the old ways and traditions, safely away from the perfidious influence of Mexico City and the infiltration of foreign doctrines; not only for himself but for the generations to come.

Returning to Mexico City he laid his plans before the viceroy. Without cost to the Crown he and a number of his friends, all rich landowners of the north, would colonize the Indian-infested region just explored in exchange for all the grazing land they could hold. The bankrupt, tottering vice-regal government which saw in this movement the holding of the land for Spain consented, and the colonization of the new land began. They came. Men of courage, of fortitude and of daring, men of wealth in whom was innate the culture of the mother country Spain. Men of vision. Bringing small armies of *peons*, herds of cattle and sheep, they crossed the Río Grande in search of the flower-covered plains which their leader Don José de Mendoza y Robles had seen. And so they established themselves in the land between the Nueces and the Río Grande and there built homes for themselves, their children, and their children's children.

Don José Ramón took his retainers to the spot which he had seen and marked that Palm Sunday a year before—thirty miles north of the Río Grande and some sixty miles west of the Gulf of Mexico.

Sword on high, standing on the site where he would build, he claimed the land thirty miles to the east, the north, the west, and south to the river, for himself and his descendants. In the name of God and his Most Catholic Majesty, Ferdinand, King of Spain.

He built well and strong.

In the center of the huge grass-covered tabletop his *peons* dug for water and found it in plenty, pure and cold. That was good, for he had not wanted to build at the spring three miles below, in bottomland. That would make headquarters for the sheep and goats and keep the smell and complaint of them away from him. Then he stepped off dimensions for the thick stone wall against which the rooms of his house would be built through the years, with doors facing the patio, the outdoor living room centered with the well. With a wide, heavy gate on one side for the use of family and guests, a small gate on the other for the servants and *peons*, whose quarters would be outside the wall. Leaving instructions with his *caporal*, an overseer of prized efficiency, he rode to Cerralvo, made arrangements there for a place to bring his bride, and went on to Mexico City to be married.

No longer young, Don José Ramón had eschewed marriage until, the year before when having had to pay respect to his ruler, he had seen Susanita Ulloa curtsying to the viceroy. With him love had come as a flame, and as soon as decorum would allow he had asked for her hand. Susana's father, noting the sensation which his daughter's golden hair and limpid green eyes and oval face was creating, fearing she would succumb to the wiles of one of the dissolute scions of nobility who were parasites of the court, felt that it would be best for her soul's good to be taken to the new land as the wife of a God-fearing elderly man. A pure blood strain had been equally a pride of the Ulloa family as that of the Mendoza's—a thing of greatest importance to them both. The suitor was accepted and sent away with the promise that his bride would be waiting.

Poor Susana! Bitter against the fate that had given her the rare blond beauty only to move her where it would shine unseen, and wither in the sun and endless winds; bitter against the father who had not even asked her wishes and sent her away from the balls and clothes and admiration she loved; bitter against the husband old enough to have fathered her! Still Susana bore her burden bravely and well. To the man she never came to love she gave six sons, and her green eyes became dimmed by the incessant tears when, one by one, all of them died but the youngest, Francisco.

One son or six of them, Don José Ramón's dream of a great *hacienda* had to come true. Year by year rooms were added until they filled all of the great wall. The armory with loopholes beside the gate, many bedrooms, dining room, kitchen, pantry, rooms for the cook and the housemaids, which could be turned into more bedrooms when the guests were many. On the other side another armory and his office, a huge *sala*, an *antesala*, a roofed porch, an open terrace like a platform. This filled half of the left side, leaving a square for the most important of all rooms, the outdoor living room called the patio. The palm tree was set beside the well, precious grape roots were brought to form an arbor. Tile by mule back across the mountains from Puebla for the *sala* floor, sabine wood for the other rooms and the porch and terrace, from the Río Sabinas. A bell from the old ranch in Mexico which his father had brought from Spain, to swing in the high arch above the well, a sundial above the big gate. Seeds and flowers and vines, to make the patio a cool retreat in the summer. A long portico against the rooms, part of the gangway inside the gate roofed over, where saddles and other riding gear could be conveniently hung.

The building was an obsession with Don José Ramón, and he loved every bit of mortar and every wooden pin that bound it. It was his conviction that, after celebrating a great *fiesta* to celebrate its completion, he would die. But he lived on and, abandoning the poor winter home at Mier, built one in the newer town of Matamoros. By now the group of *rancheros* were a tightly knit unit, their ranches built and thriving, a winter social season in the small towns developing. "Marry a woman from the old families at Cerralvo or Monclova," Don José Ramón, dying, gave advice to his son. "A strong woman used to hardships who can bear you many children that will live, to fill the house that I have built for them."

Francisco married Amalia Soría. Strong, ugly of face, silent, with a beauty of soul and intelligence that only Susana saw, and loved. Amalia sickened after the first child, Santiago, bore a daughter Dolores, and died with the third, Ramón. When Francisco selfishly refused to marry a second time, Susana became the matriarch. She softened the once fine skin with mutton tallow and olive oil, curled the hair whitened this many a year, bought new cloth for dresses, brought out the jewelry she had laid away with her memories. Disappointed that the girl Dolores had taken after her mother and had not inherited her own blond beauty, she encouraged the signs of an independent spirit which the child showed early in life. "A girl is cursed when her face and figure are homely and awkward," she excused herself. "With independence she can still get something out of living."

Religion, traditions, the ways that had survived centuries and received permanence through that survival, gentility—all those Susana inculcated in her grandchildren. If she was stern almost to harshness, it was because only duty upheld her. Her spirit had become old so many, many years before. When the children were growing to marriageable age and Death came for Susana, she met him unprotesting, gladly.

"You will some day be master of Rancho La Palma de Cristo," she told the eldest, Santiago. "It was your grandfather's dream, which he built into reality. It was my entire life. Santiago, be worthy of Rancho La Palma, and the things for which it stands."

They buried Susana beside her husband, in the church he had helped to build, in Matamoros. Later Don Francisco was laid beside them, and Santiago became the Don.

And now another spring had come, almost a hundred springs since that one when Don José Ramón had climbed the bluff and visioned his home. Spring in South Texas, in the year of our Lord 1846. . . .

Caballero

Chapter 1

Don Santiago de Mendoza y Soría strode through the wide gateway when the three clangs of the bell that hung in an arch above the well in the center of the patio had shattered into a chorus of notes against the house walls calling to each other.

His heart sang in harmony as the high boot heels, with their jingling roweled steel spurs, clipped across the *tipichil* floor to the raised terrace that extended out and was a vantage point from which both gates, all of the patio, and all doorways could be observed. This was the time he loved best, when the sun tipped to meet the nebulous skyline and leave a blaze of splendor over Rancho La Palma, and old Paz rang the bell for *El Alabado*, the ranchman's evening prayer. The household had orders to wait until the last thread of sound was scattered before the vespers assembly, so the master could have these heart filling moments alone.

A bas-relief of power and strength was Don Santiago, as he stood against the mat of dark green vine covering the wall behind him. The concha-trimmed suit of buckskin covering the flexible body and fitting tight at the ankles over soft leather boots, the black sash wrapped about a waist only slightly corpulent, and the broad-brimmed hat heavy with silver braid, proclaimed the wealthy *ranchero.* The clear-cut features, hawklike high-bridged nose, eyes like polished coal under the protecting lintel of eyebrows straight as the firm, thin-lipped mouth, could only be chiseled by generations of noble forebears. Arrogance sat on the high flung head and squared shoulders and moved in the long-fingered narrow hand that now lifted the hat from the black hair and dropped it on the terrace beside him.

Such was Don Santiago, lord of land many miles beyond what his eye could compass, master of this *hacienda* and all those that would soon gather before him.

He ran a right forefinger inside the wide sash, a habit he had when, like now, the sky seemed more blue, the wind softer. Life itself, a wine cask filled to the brim. For life was good, here in Texas in the spring of 1846.

All these rumors that Texas no longer belonged to Mexico was the talk of fools easily frightened who gave significance to the rout of the braggart Santa Ana. Because these blue-eyed strangers trespassing here had made a flag with one star—what did that mean? (Only that they were blindly ignorant, like a child cutting out patches of cloth and pretending they were gowns.) The fools! Making a flag and thinking this made a nation! It would not be long before they would be gone again, back to their own country. He moved a hand before his face to rid his mind of the thought of them, as one would a bothersome fly, and turned his face towards the rustlings heralding his family.

His wife, Doña María Petronilla, glided like a black ghost down the portico steps from her room, and Don Santiago felt that swift jerk of frustration which the sight of her so often gave him; as if the self-effacing meekness and the faded thinness of her were a personal insult to him. From his wife his eyes took up his daughter a step behind her with no more pleasure: María de los Angeles, also in black, but where the dress of her mother was of finely spun cloth that ballooned in the semblance of modishness from the tight waist, that of the daughter was coarsest wool gathered with a girdle of white cord. Where the dark hair of the older woman was covered with a mantilla of silk, the head and neck of the pretty young face were swathed in a cloth of white. María de los Angeles had wanted to go to the convent and, forbidden to do so by her father, had brought the convent to herself, inasmuch as she was able. [Rosaries, one of black beads in the mother's hand and one of large wooden balls hanging from the girdle of the daughter, clicked softly as the two women moved and Don Santiago bit a lip to stifle the involuntary "Pah!" that rose to it. (Enough of anything was enough. He had, he told himself, been patient with Angela far too long. When they went to the town house in Matamoros next winter that doleful nun's garb would be forbidden. This summer, but no longer.)][1]

The two gave him small smiles to his scowl and took places before him, staying on the patio so that his foot-high eminence on the terrace should not be dimmed. Servants came out of the rooms opposite, their flat *huaraches* making flapping sounds on the portico floor. *Peons* came on silent bare feet through the small gate from their quarters outside the wall; dozens of them, from naked infants suckling noisily at bare young breasts down to bent, old people. There was Martina the kitchen-maid, sweet with the curves of young womanhood, demurely modest beside her stern-faced, shapeless mother—keeping a slanted eye on the gateway for Fulgencio the[2]   aloof in the importance of his position; Juan Bautista; personal servant and coachman, carrying his double duty with the dignity becoming to his gray hair; Nicolasa the baker, witch-like with her stoop and peering eyes. There were children and more children, giggling, pinching each other. A few *vaqueros* from the range camps, burnt almost black by the daily sun and eternal winds, walked stiffly on bowed legs and stood, shy as strangers, just inside the gate, circling worn large hats in nervous fingers.

Don Santiago scowled. Alvaro would again be late. Luis Gonzaga would be late. In spite of daily admonitions these sons of his failed to be on time. But then, he secretly smiled, they would not be his if they had showed no defiance to rule. A son with too many virtues was nothing to be proud of. And where was Susanita? Before he could ask there was a flash of blue, the sound of tripping small feet, and his face softened as he watched his youngest and dearest child hurry to him. Pain at her flowering maturity gripped him anew, as it had gripped him for a year. Susanita should at least be a bride if not already a mother, and still he could not bear to let her go, had refused to even listen to proposals of marriage. He still insisted that the gorgeous hair be allowed to hang in braids like a child's, as if that would keep her a child a little longer. As she stopped to squeeze his hand and return his tender smile, he twisted the end of a braid round his finger, marveling anew at the spun-gold fineness and sheen of this heritage from his Asturian ancestors —already so rare among his people that it seemed a gift from heaven. Lovely was the cream skin, delicate the molding of the red lips. And her eyes were like limpid green water upon which a vagrant cloud had left a remembrance of gray.

Susanita, beautiful one. Susanita, beloved one.

Doña Dolores, dignity slowly propelling the full skirt of stiffest silk as if her feet were on rollers, took time to look at the flowers along the portico, quite as if she did not see them a dozen times a day. To aggravate him, he knew, because yesterday she had come sooner than he wished and he had told her so. Why, why, he asked Fate for the thousandth time, had this sister of his been widowed young and dropped back into her brother's household, a special cross for him to bear. Yes, why?

Alvaro's spurs clinking, swaggered past the servant women, lustful, possessive eyes on the youngest and prettiest ones. Slender but powerfully built, the muscles revealed by the tight-fitting suit of buckskin moved with the coordination of a creature of the woods. Don Santiago watched his firstborn with approval, greeted him with a slap on the shoulder and playfully shoved him beside his mother. He frowned again when slim, good-looking Luis Gonzaga walked quickly past him and took a place beside Susanita, a little to the left of the family group. Painting pictures like a woman, and he a Mendoza y Soría! An artist—insult to a father's manhood! A milksop, and his son!

They were all there, everything that supposedly had a soul and therefore had need of prayer. Old Paz, privileged in her position of housekeeper and family nurse moved close and clapped hands together impatiently. Faces turned to the master—faces branded with grief and sorrows, faces pitted with pox, faces bright with the faith and hopes of youth—and in a rich baritone that filled the patio and drifted over the walls, the master intoned *El Alabado,* the hymn to the Sacrament:

> *Alabado sea el Santísimo*
> *Sacramento del altar*
> *Y la Virgen concebida*
> *Sin pecado original.*

The chorus, full in its unreserve, surged in harmonious rhythm and Don Santiago, leading and commanding them, felt a kinship with God. This evening particularly, with the sky a splendor of crimson and gold, it seemed as if the figure of Light were over them, spreading sacred hands in blessing. And why not, he asked himself. So had the Mendozas and the Sorías praised their God at the end of the day for ages, back to the beginnings of recorded family history, surely in the dimness beyond it. Why should the Lord not commend this His servant?

Into the echoes of the hymn he intoned the Angelus: "The angel of the Lord declared unto Mary—"

"And she was conceived by the Holy Ghost," came answer.[3] Then somewhat unctuously he prayed alone: "Hail, Mary, full of grace, the Lord is with thee, blessed art thou amongst women and blessed is the fruit of thy womb, Jesus."

The chorus: "Holy Mary, Mother of God, pray for us sinners, now and at the hour of our death, amen." A chorus of one mighty voice, lilting with the joy of hearts lifted and faith renewed.

So purely rose-color was the sky now that it painted the white plaster walls and changed the very air into tinted mother of pearl. [It seemed to Don Santiago that a part of heaven opened over this patio this evening. He would not have been surprised, so carried away was he for the moment, if the Virgin herself in her robe of blue had come floating over the gateway, hands stretched out to them, praying with them.]⁴

["Behold the handmaid of the Lord—" Heads bowed humbly with the answer: "Be done unto me according to Thy Word."]⁵

"Hail Mary—" Could that be hoofbeats? A guest, at this time of day? Ah yes, that was the way the Master visited those on earth, by sending a fellowman. In such manner came He to His own. Exultantly he sang out after the amen: "The Word was made flesh—"

Hoofbeats without a doubt, like a drum backgrounding the response: "And dwelt among us." The old dog, Tigre, came from his wanderings and tore past the wall outside in a ferocity of barking. Heads turned gateward, obediently faced Don Santiago again when he prayed on, loudly. Excitement crowded out religious feeling, curiosity broke the even tenor of the familiar words; the Lord momentarily forgotten in that welcome rarity and diversion—a guest. Tigre came back, yelping high in his new role of herald. Galloping hoofs, plain now. Then a horseman was at the gate, leaping to the ground before the running hostler, Silvestre, could catch the flung reins.

Through the lane made for him the newcomer hurried, and Don Santiago, forgetting all prayer, rushed to meet him. His neighbor and dear friend, Gabriel del Lago! Arms around him to support a suddenly reeling body, he brought him to the terrace. "Gabriel! *Por Dios*, what brings you here like this? Alvaro, bring a chair, Luis, a glass of wine—"

Old Paz had turned to face the retainers and valiantly continued the prayers which they dutifully followed to the end, eyes popping with curiosity. Alvaro lifted an arm at the last "Amen," snapped his fingers and ordered them out with a terse "*¡Váyanse!*" Like sheep turned by a dog they scurried away without a backward glance to the safety of their quarters, there to babble with wonder and speculation. What could it be? Why should a man who was an *hidalgo* ride a horse to his knees when he had a hundred *vaqueros* to command? What was the world coming to, here in this Texas? Could it be that the *Americanos* were coming, or even worse, the terrible Rangers? Perhaps they had destroyed the *hacienda* and killed everyone and only Gabriel, by riding like the wind, escaped. They had heard that things like that were happening and surely it was true, for were not the Rangers spawned in Hell itself, devoting their lives to evil? Santa María, San José, protect us!

Completely exhausted, Don Gabriel slumped in the rawhide-and-stave chair, opening his eyes to sip at the wine, closing them again, paying no heed to Don Santiago's anxious questions. Until Doña Dolores unceremoniously shoved her brother aside and crisply commanded: "Come, come Gabriel, if you are too tired to talk you can at least assure us that you are not riding ahead of doom to warn us—or are you? You have been sick, what business have you riding before you are strong? One would think you did not have a *peon* on the place!" The two had been children together and more than once Doña Dolores had taken him down with her tongue when she thought it necessary. "Is it the Indians, or is it war again?"

"In a moment, my friends. I am weaker than I had thought. Then I galloped most of the way—" He smiled at them and his round face took on some of its natural pinkness again. "Why is it that one always hurries to bring bad news? Young Carlos del Valle brought it to me and rode his horse down in his haste. Have patience, Dolores, until this trembling in my legs ceases so I can stand." The smile left him and pain laced the whispered, "I must stand, when I tell you. Perhaps I do ride ahead of—doom."

They were all on the terrace now, and Susanita and Luis Gonzaga moved to inconspicuousness against the vine covered wall, all curiosity. Angela and her mother stood back of the visitor's chair, Alvaro, Doña Dolores, and Don Santiago before it. Waiting politely, wondering, fearing.

Don Gabriel drained his wine glass, slapped his thighs punishingly, and rose to his feet. All his comic short roundness of figure and moonlike face submerged in a new dignity as he raised his hand and said slowly, tragically.

"Yes, what I have to say must be given standing, and taken so. One stands, to receive a blow. Brace yourselves, for my message strikes through our pride, our hearts; even our destinies, if *El Señor Dios* does not help." Suddenly weariness and sadness vanished and his hands clenched as he shouted, "We have been betrayed! Heaven's wrath is upon us in truth!"

Susanita reached for the hand of Luis Gonzaga and held it tightly, frightened at this neighbor she had known only as a pleasant man of happy moods—and not the blazing-eyed figure of volatile passions that clenched hands at an unseen enemy, then flung them open as if throwing his despair at their feet. The intensity of his torn emotions shook his voice and transfixed all of them. He swung his arms in a wide, embracing circle. "¡Los Americanos! All this land has been taken by them—all of it, everything!"

"*Por Cristo*, that cannot be!" Don Santiago shook his head like a charging bull. He dug his fingers in the buckskin-covered arm of his friend as he implored, "No, no, no, Gabriel, not that. You cannot be telling the truth! Someone has lied to you . . . ah no, no. . . ."

"But," Alvaro sputtered, "that means that . . . what does that mean? If they have taken our land are we then . . . to be driven off like cattle and killed?"

Don Gabriel gave him a bitter smile. "It is worse than that, Alvaro. Many things are worse than death. This our Texas has been taken into the union of their states, and, according to their law, we who live in it become *Americanos.*" The smile changed to mocking laughter as he slapped a hand on Don Santiago's shoulder. "You and I, and del Valle, and all our friends—can't you laugh? Is it not something to laugh at? We are *Americanos!*"

"What nonsense, and stop that crazy laughing, Gabriel!" The wart on the right cheek of Doña Dolores turned red, as it always did when she became agitated or angry. "We do not choose to be [dirty] *Americanos.*[6] We are Mexicans, our mother land was Spain. Not all of their laws can change us, for we are not them. *Americanos,* indeed!"

The tension was broken. They were again a family, rather than figures in a drama. "Your reasoning is as foolish as that of all women," Don Santiago told her sharply. "Certainly it will make a difference. But, Gabriel, is this truly a fact? Are you sure it is not just another rumor? You know the wind whispers many things variable as itself."

Fresh exhaustion dropped Gabriel back into the chair and he shook his head as he answered sadly, "We should have seen it before. It has been coming a long time. It was already done when Santa Anna surrendered to that infidel, squaw-loving Samuel Houston. We called Santa Anna a traitor then and looked for—what did we look for? Saint Michael with his sword of flames? It would have taken him and all his army of fighting angels to keep back those devils. We lived too much in our world, I see that now. Do you remember when it was rumored that Texas wanted to join with the other states, more than a year ago? When we heard, what did we do? We merely shrugged our shoulders as if it did not concern us. We thought—no, we did not wish to see or hear. Yes, it is true. A missionary priest from San Antonio stopped at the *hacienda* of Señor del Valle and he said it happened last year. He saw papers and it is an accepted fact everywhere."

"*Americanos.*" Alvaro repeated the word, as if it were something tangible held in his hands. "We are then *Americanos.*"

The pronouncement was as tragic as if he had said, "We are lepers." Luis Gonzaga brought a chair for his mother and she sank into it as if she were ready to faint. What little color her face held drained away. Not at the news, for that was too vague a thing to have meaning to her, but at the new glitter in her husband's eyes. When Santiago's eyes looked like two discs taken from the polished jet necklace which Doña Dolores treasured, it boded evil for all of them. Particularly for her, his wife, buffer of his wrath.

María de los Angeles fingered her beads and prayed for them all, vaguely and scatteringly. "They are not even Catholics, these *Americanos*," she put in. "I cannot understand how God allowed them here in our country at all, seeing He is Catholic like we are. Is it a scourge, do you think, for our sins?"

Susanita, now back of her mother's chair, suppressed a giggle. Angela was always so funny. As if the good God cared if one were Mexican or something else; why it was the same as saying he would care if one's hair were yellow or black. To Susanita there were no frontiers in God's love, for surely He loved everybody, everything He created. Looking up, she caught the twinkle of the first evening star, pale silver against a sky still blue, and nodded to it as one greets a friend. That was part of God, that star and it was there for everyone to see and love. Would being an *Americano*, she wondered, take some of the dullness out of life? It had been really stupid lately, since they came back from Matamoros. She had never seen a young man of the hated race—*papá* was always so strict when they were in town—but she had heard that sometimes they were handsome and all of them very tall. Not of course, she quickly quieted a small voice of conscience, that a Mendoza y Soría could look at one. Not more than a tiny, safe peek. . . .

"Our sins, Angela?" Don Gabriel smiled. "Then we would need to have been sinners indeed to meet the punishment. I have not told you all; there is again war. This Zacarías Taylor who was at the Nueces with his army last summer is now in Matamoros, building a camp in the *chaparral* on this side of the Río Bravo. Our army is with Arista but what of that? I have not heard of a battle, news comes to us slowly. This is May and Taylor only went to the Río Bravo last month. What can Arista do? He has too small an army, and if Texas now belongs to the United States what would be the sense of fighting? So many have already been killed, and if we are already *Americanos* it—"

Don Santiago's face brightened. "We aren't though! All our fright was for nothing, Gabriel. When you mentioned the Nueces—have you changed your mind that the Río Nueces is the boundary, and our land still in Mexico after all?"

"That is our talk because we like to think so." Don Gabriel shrugged in depredation. "When Santa Anna surrendered, the boundary line was set at the Río Bravo. They wrote it Río Grande, and call it so, but the change of name does not change the river. Be assured they will see that the boundary stays there, for their greed knows no end; they will fight until the river runs red with blood for the land above it. We laughed at their Republic of Texas and the flag they made and turned our backs to it and said 'We are in Mexico,' as if the saying of it was enough. You delude yourself, *amigo*. It is time for us to open our eyes."

"This Taylor, can he fight?" Alvaro wanted to know.

"That remains to be seen. They can all fight like devils. It is believed by many that the Evil One gives them power, but knowing neither Taylor nor El Diablo I could not speak of their partnership."

"You are ill and have talked too long." Don Santiago lifted his guest to his feet, paused a moment before leading him away to say to Doña María Petronilla, "Have food sent to Gabriel at once in his room, he will rest better on a stomach less empty. When he has rested, then we will meet later in the sala." His eyes flicked over them all. "I scarcely need to remind you that before the servants all is as before, and I expect you to act at the dinner table as if Gabriel had come only to give us a neighborly greeting. We may be *Americanos* now, but nothing can change the fact that we are always—*hidalgos.*"

Doña Dolores, with an audible sniff that covered much unspoken—and caustic—comment, followed the men in dignified retreat. Angela took her mother's arm, the two rushing ahead to see about the tray of food. Alvaro, heels clacking and spurs ringing, strode across the patio like the hero he already saw himself to be, and leaped spectacularly into the saddle of his waiting horse for a last gallop before dinner. Only Susanita and Luis Gonzaga stayed, seated on the terrace edge, wondering and speculating with all the optimism and curiosity of sheltered, ignorant youth. More absorbed in the mysteries of Americanism than in its menace and humiliation.

They were barbarians, thought the boy, so they would know nothing of art, and he could not learn from them the things about painting he wished to know. And for that, Luis sighed.

It would be nice to dance with a man who was so much taller that you had to hurt your neck to look up at him, but if they were uncouth, like *papá* said, then they could not dance gracefully. If they could, it was unthinkable that she dance with them, naturally. And for that Susanita sighed.

Old Paz, whose hearing had been honed by many years of listening took the news to her kitchen crony, Nicolasa. Estéban, in hiding at the gate, had stretched his receptive ears and had lost no time getting to the square of pounded adobe outside the wall, around which clustered the quarters of the peons.

Americanos. Well then, if Don Gabriel said they were not to be driven off and killed, what was it going to mean? Would they still be *peons*—what do you think Isidro? *Peons*—why, fool, what else could we ever be, when we were born so. A *peon* is a *peon*, from birth to death, as the master remains the master . . . Would they have to learn the bastard language? They had heard that one could not pronounce it, the tongue refusing its harshness . . . *Ay de mí*, their lot in life would be no easier, be assured of that . . . They should pray—and what for, Clarita? Prayer would not keep back the *Americanos*, if they came to Rancho La Palma . . . Woe to the women, then! Ha ha, ho ho, listen to old Amanda! Don't you be afraid, Amanda, they'll leave you alone after just one look at you; you are safe, old woman . . .

Americanos, a dread word, which held nothing of good. One crossed one's self, name of the Father, Son, and Holy Ghost, when one heard it.

Chapter 2

Don Santiago slowly circled the *sala*, then stood in its center. How long, he wondered would this great living room with its family background and tradition remain as it was? The fireplace was a black maw against half of the north wall. Against the white wall above it hung a large black and silver crucifix flanked by massive silver candelabra resting on the wide mantel. He took a blazing splinter from the tiny fire, and touched the candle tips, watching the play of light and shadow against the polished metal. Would the *Americanos* dare to take these symbols of his faith and change them to silver dollars? Would they dare to rip the paintings of the Immaculate and the Ecce Homo from their pegs and cast them into the fire?

There were weapons in heterogeneous display, in corners, on the walls, each with a legend. The broad sword with gold inlay to form a cross on the hilt, nicks along the blade and a broken tip, was a proud heritage of the first Mendoza who had come to the new world, had a place beside a long spear upon which many a Moor had been impaled. Rapiers, lances, knives, long-barreled *pistolas*, an *escopeta* with a brass bell-opening at the muzzle, bits of old armor, spoke anew of wars and blood. A Mendoza glared, thick lipped and ugly, through the patina of cracks and gloom age brings to oil on canvas. There were mahogany chairs and tables finely carved and a great harp of gilt, relics of a former splendor in Spain. And opposite there were products of the ranch land, chairs, stools, benches, and a couch of stave and rawhide tied firmly with thongs. In a corner hung spurs and quirts and bridles of leather exquisitely tooled and trimmed with silver, on the floor a reata of rawhide coiled like a snake beside a string of bells. Candles were yellow in sconces against the wall, in sticks of beaten metal on the tables. Great beams of sabine wood supported the ceiling and on the middle one was carved the motto, in gold and purple Gothic letters:

Dios es Señor de esta casa.*

The room had a pleasing odor, from years of wood smoke, perfumes, leather, tobacco cured with cognac, which had been impregnated into the walls like incense in old churches. And over it all was the spirit compounded of the emotions of living: music and dancing and laughter, and judgments and tears and deaths; prayers, the chants of Mass; quarrels and heartaches, loves and hatreds—each leaving a bit of itself to haunt the room forever.

Don Santiago flung out his arms and brought them together again against his breast, as if he were scooping up the life that had been here and holding it close. He had never seen an *Americano* closely or talked to one, but it was to him a dread word symbolizing barbarism, destruction, evil.

"God of my ancestors," he whispered, "Have mercy on us."

The family and guests came and Don Santiago sat in the throne-like, high carved chair in the middle of a long wall. The seat of the master and a throne, in fact, for in the patriarchalism of custom he was king and his word law. His emotions had calmed and his long hands on the chair arm lay still. Alvaro stood at his father's right, but the rest of the family grouped themselves near the fire which was now burning brightly. Don Gabriel on the cushions of the couch, Doña María Petronilla and Angela (almost non-entities) on a bench, Luis Gonzaga hidden in the corner behind them. Susanita, flowerlike in a dress of coral and blue silk, sat beside the harp but did not lift her lovely bare arms to its strings. Only Doña Dolores, scorning chairs for the backless stool over which her billowing taffeta skirts spread like an open umbrella, showed no tenseness. In her code of self-possession and assurance were the fixed attributes of the true lady, which no disaster either real or rumored could change. With jet comb glittering above high-piled hair, hands folded in her lap, lively dark eyes on her brother, she was completely mistress of herself.

Don Santiago spoke quickly before the silence could thicken. "Don Gabriel, what do you think of the news you bring?"

Don Gabriel sat up and sighed softly. "I have given it careful thought, Santiago, but I find it difficult to say what one should do. It seems to me there is a choice of three things before us: First, we can move to Mexico and look to the charity of relatives who have forgotten us or depend on the generosity of a government which betrayed us. Secondly, we can meet these *Americanos* halfway, learn their language, and try to assimilate. How much or how little of this is needed to have us keep both our possessions and our dignity I could not say, knowing so little of them. I have heard that in East Texas and even in San Antonio Mexicans have given their daughters to them in marriage, but if such a shocking thing could be I would not know what came of it. Our last resource is to fight them always, be ourselves, and keep ourselves against them."

"Fight!" Alvaro shouted, hitting a palm with a fist. "Fight them until we kill them all or they kill us all. The blood of conquerors runs through our veins—the Mendozas, the Sorías, know no defeat! Fight, I say!"

Don Santiago leaped to his feet and flung his arms around his son, flame in his cheeks and his voice as he cried, "My son, our ancestors have spoken through you. So shall it be; we fight them to the end; whatever end that may be!"

Alvaro ran to the wall opposite the fireplace, ripped the sword from the ring holding it, leaped back to a place in front of his father's chair, and dramatically raised the sword on high with the words:

"By the cross on the hilt of this sword I swear death to all invaders of our land. Death—death to all *Americanos!*"

It was the spark needed to disrupt their disturbed emotions, and all ran forward while Don Santiago cried, "Death to all foreigners who set foot on Rancho La Palma de Cristo! *¡Muerte, muerte!*"

At these words, Angela struck at the sword and sent it clattering onto the tiled floor. Her voice cried out, "No, no! When you swear by the Cross, Alvaro, it must be for a holy cause, and we do not know whether we have the right to kill just because another may be infidel. We must love our enemies, our Lord said, we must not hate. It would be murder to kill anyone even on our land unless he attacks us. Surely there is some good in the Americans or the Lord would not have made them. *Papá*, you say Santa Anna is a wicked man, and he is Mexican." She stepped back and raised her right hand, pronouncing solemnly: "I call upon the Cross to give our hearts *love*."

And before the paternal storm could break María de los Angeles lifted the nun's robe and curtsied to her father, with a charm and graciousness a queen could have envied. After a soft "*Buena noche,*[1] Don Gabriel, *papá*, *mamá*—with your permission," she walked quickly from the room, head high as if it were carrying the golden crown of Truth. Angela—Angela the meek one!

They were so astonished that Doña Dolores was able to quickly inject her stout common sense. She picked up the sword and handed it to Luis Gonzaga, commanding: "Put it away. There is too much emotion and not enough reason this evening; let us put away further talk till tomorrow. After all, as yet nothing threatens us. I shall sleep whether I am called a Mexican, Texan, or *Americano*, and be quite ready for chocolate in the morning. With your permission, Santiago, I retire."

"You speak sense, I must admit," said Don Gabriel. "I too shall retire, I find I am weaker than I thought."

Only Don Santiago sat still in the high-backed chair, giving scant replies to their goodnights as they all hurried away—away from a brewing tempest diverted by Angela, away, for awhile, from this new trouble and what it threatened to bring. When the house was silent Don Santiago snuffed out the candles with a hooded rod, then from a chair back he lifted his *poncho,* a rug-like scarf of finest wool—black with a border of white above its fringed ends—and dropped it over his head through the square opening in the middle. Then from the *sala*'s blackness he passed to the portico and down the steps to the patio.

There the darkness was lifted by the star-packed ceiling of sky. The air pleasantly touched with oncoming summer's warmth, the silence like a blessed hand over the night. Hands behind him, he paced slowly across the floor, hard packed as stone by the countless tread of master, guest, and prolific generations of servant and *peon*.

This was his own, this trusted heritage from his father. As deeply rooted as the majestic palm tree beside the well, now a black column in the patio's very center: as fragrant as the gardenias for which tall hibiscus served as background, against the wall between the terrace and grape arbor. In his mind's eye he could see the flaming splash of hibiscus, the rare tropical potted plants along the portico, the baskets of vine and bloom hanging everywhere. A whiff of earthen *olla* hanging in the rattan frame from the roof by the gate came to him, wet and cool. It had hung there always, offering welcome refreshment. Before a clump of shrubbery the rawhide chairs held the presence of the many who had relaxed in them, in family intimacy. Little things—dear, familiar things. It seemed as if they came and touched him caressingly, each one in turn, and then went back to their places to keep the pattern built for them.

And now from the turmoil of his soul came the past. Came a night like this one, the air vibrant with the promise of growing things singing spring's song. Eleven years ago—yes, that was when the *Americanos* started their destruction. How could they have imagined then that this battle of El Alamo was but a passing thing in their destinies, just one more battle of many? He stepped to the palm tree and ran a hand down its rough bark.

"Now I am glad," he whispered, "that my father is dead."

Eleven years, yet he could see and hear everything as distinctly as if it were happening now. Don Santiago wondered again how his father Don Francisco could have loved his family so dearly yet at times be so unbendingly harsh that the family fled him in fear. Only with Ramón, his youngest, had he been indulgent to the point of allowing him to beg off marriage—even though Santiago had but four children and Dolores none at all, a dearth indeed of grandchildren in a home designed for many. When the adventurous youth joined the forces of Santa Anna, his father merely shrugged and spent his time building his son into a hero and planning the fiesta for his homecoming.

Then one bright morning, when the waiting had become an almost unendurable burden, a rider brought the message that Ramón was coming home. There had been, the messenger related, a battle with a great victory at which the *Americanos* had been killed to the last man, led by the man who styled himself the conqueror and savior of Texas and the great Napoleon of the West, Santa Anna. Oh *sí*, a battle *muy grande!*—the messenger told them. Even the bodies had been piled in the square and burned, so that the memory of the battle should be its victory. The *padres* had gathered the bones and buried them in the church, it was said, but if that were true he could not say. Though the *padres* did strange things like that.

There followed two days of excitement. Dozens of times eleven-year-old Alvaro ran up the steps of the watchtower in a corner of the wall by the arbor, looking for a rider. Many riders, Don Francisco told him. "Your uncle will come properly escorted as befits his position." The *don* was at times an erupting volcano spewing the fires of his impatience upon all, at others he wore down horses galloping down the trail. The third day came, the fourth. "Doubtless his commander had need of him," Don Francisco consoled himself. Over and over he had pictured the homecoming: Ramón riding ahead of his escort when the turn of the road at the cottonwoods brought the *hacienda* into full view and the clack of his horse's hooves on the stones heralded his coming. Ramón would gallop to the very steps of the portico, standing in his stirrups, triumph a living thing unfurling like a banner streaming in the wind. He would leap from his saddle, laughing, rushing to the extended arms held out to him. He would be dressed in a fine, flashing uniform, and he would be handsomer than ever.

Another day, and he had not come. Dinner was over and the family sat in the *sala*, waiting for him. Sitting in the *sala* with the gloom-shrouded old man in the big chair was a trying ordeal. Doña Dolores and Doña María Petronilla had risen to say goodnight—then slowly, without prelude of sound, startling as a ghost, Ramón walked into the room.

"Wine," he begged when eager hands seized him and excited questions tumbled over him. "I am a little weak."

They clustered around him, wondering at the torn and dirty uniform, staring at the strangeness of him, rebuffed a little by his queer withdrawment. Don Francisco, overwhelmed with joy at seeing his beloved son again, attached no significance to the wanness of the face under the bristle of new black beard, and kept tilting the wine bottle as he babbled.

"You killed them all, my brave son. The messenger told us not one was left from the battle at the Alamo." He embraced Ramón lovingly. "Our men showed the cowards who is master of Texas, eh, Ramón? Cowards all of them!"

"Certainly they are cowards," Don Santiago echoed, squeezing his brother's hand. "We know that."

"No."

Ramón handed Santiago the empty glass. Suddenly his face shone as if a light were turned on it from within, and the pupils of his eyes spread and shone like coal. He threw out his hands as he breathed, "It was wonderful, their bravery. No, Santiago, the *Americanos* are not cowards."

He closed his eyes awhile, and then went on, throwing jerky, excited sentences into the shocked silence, telling his story in a queer fervor. "They were a handful, only a hundred and fifty. We were an army, there were thousands of us. Thousands, *papá*, to less than two hundred, was that fair? We tried to get over the walls—is it not strange that it took us so long? Twelve days. Yes, twelve days. Santa Anna cursed like a madman and swore that—If I could have a little more wine—No, Dolores, no food now, a little later, perhaps. You see I must—I must say these things—now—while I can. I must tell—"

He gulped the wine while they stood and watched him, uneasy before his strangeness. They had never known him as other than boasting or laughing, had never seen him except as a dashing *caballero*. They could scarcely believe that this man stamped with a solemn maturity could be

Ramón. That he could praise an enemy and invader amounted to blasphemy, and Don Francisco's face darkened with displeasure, though he kept silent and let Ramón finish what he might have to say.

Ramón rose. His lips spread wide in a smile, and black shinning eyes looked beyond the walls, away from this room and all that was in it. "Ah, they were great," he whispered, as if to himself.

(Or as if to that small heroic band, their ghosts had taken flesh before him.)

Then his voice rang out. "They were great! I wished, when I fought them, that I were one of them. I wished that I were there with them, fighting gloriously against a swarming horde, refusing to surrender. By San Pablo, but I wished to be with them! So could a man die in glory, his soul free forever! So could he die and leave a name that could never die!"

His eyes scorched them, so wild in the flame-swept young face. "They had something wonderful, the *Americanos*." He leaned against the chair and his voice was a whisper's echo.

"We, not they, were the cowards, *papá*."

Don Francisco de Mendoza y Ulloa struck his son on the mouth, so that he fell to the floor. And blood gushed from his opened lips and ran in a bright small stream onto the tiles.

Don Santiago stood by the palm tree. He could see his brother's young body now as if it were lying before him, could feel again his father's anguish when he knew his son's life went out with the blood staining the tiles. Anguish, which was never freed from reproach or abated when it was found that Ramón had been wounded, and internal bleeding started from the long ride home. Ramón was dying when he walked into the *sala* and asked for wine. They had been so happy to see him that it had not even occurred to any of them that he might not be well.

For the dreadful blow he gave his son, Don Francisco blamed Americans. As he held it against them, in the gathering bitterness of memory, that they could incite admiration in a man whose father was a Mendoza and his mother a Soría. When a year of heartbreak brought him to his deathbed, he adjured Santiago, who would now become the owner of the ranch.

"Allow no *Americanos* on this land. Have nothing to do with them, ever, build a wall between them and what is yours. Remember always that Ramón was killed because he defended his country against them. Fight them—fight them to the end!"

All night long Don Santiago paced the patio. Hatred—he wondered whether Angela's "maudlin woman talk" was so wrong after all, as he remembered that last corroding year when his father nursed his hatred until hate alone possessed his heart. Don Francisco's face retained its black bitterness to the end, too strong for the prayers of the family kneeling around his bed, for the crucifix in his hand, to break. Doña Dolores put her arms around her brother's neck and sobbed: "Santiago, let us never be like that, never!"

A wind rustled the leaves of the palm tree, and Don Santiago leaned against it, crossing his arms over the poncho. [A trust had been given to him which he had to guard. Given of the land by the Crown for its colonization, a group of rancheros had moved their small armies of *peons*, their herds of cattle and sheep, to the flower decked plain between the Nueces and the Río Grande, in the year 1748. They were men of vision and of courage innate with the culture of the mother country Spain, and Don José Ramón de Mendoza y Robles was their leader. And the reason they had come to this Indian-infested new land was to preserve the old ways and traditions of family life, safely away from the perfidious influence of Mexico City and the infiltration of foreign doctrine.

For that had Don José Ramón built this *hacienda*, and built it well and strong so generations would rear families in it and keep it without change. A thick stone wall was built around an acre of ground, and rooms built against it through the years, with doors facing the outdoor living room centered by the palm and the well. Because he had first visioned his home on Palm Sunday, he had planted the palm and dramatically named his domain Rancho La Palma de Cristo. When he built the *hacienda*, he built strong and well, to make it a shrine for the old ways. A thick stone wall was erected around approximately an acre of ground and rooms built against it through the years, opening into the outdoor living room, the patio. The best, for the *hacienda*: tile from Puebla for the *sala* floor, sabine wood for the rooms and portico from the Río Sabinas; precious seeds, grapes, vines, and flowers laboriously kept alive on long treks from Mexico, for the patio.

Susana Ulloa, golden-haired and green-eyed, was the first bride, but of the six children she bore José Ramón, only one, Francisco, lived. Amelia Soría, plain of face and gentle of heart, gave Francisco three children and died, leaving Susana to raise them. Susana, married against her will to the elderly Don José Ramón, had mended her broken heart by devoting her-

20

self to the *hacienda*, and had done much to knit the ranchers into a tight group. She inculcated the doctrine of traditionalism in the children—religion, gentility, family rank, patriarchalism—those were the good things, the only ones.

On her deathbed she told the first-born Santiago: "You will some day be master of Rancho La Palma. It is your grandfather's dream built into reality. It was my entire life. Here I buried my heart and my dreams, and they came to flower in love of it. Santiago, it is your heritage. Be worthy of Ranch La Palma de Cristo and the things for which it stands."][2]

Don Santiago put his hands against the rough bark of the palm tree, and it felt strong against his back, like a firm pillar, for it was a symbol.

There could be no compromise, neither for himself nor for those over whom he was master. What he had was his and his it would remain. Only so could the good things be preserved. He would have to hate the *Americanos*, for they were evil. "I need not hate as did my father," he murmured. "His was a lash curling around the throats of all who were near him. But I can hate as befits me: with the dignity and pride of my position, with all the contempt a Mendoza has for the infidel and the barbarian."

The leaves of the palm rustled softly, the night held him gently. There was no one there to tell him that hatred feeds upon itself and lives but to destroy. No one to remind him that the Christ who rode in a procession of palms came to earth to preach the gospel of love.

Chapter 3

Trouble rode in Texas, on a fresh mount. It galloped over the plains, lay at ambush in the hills, stalked the mesquite thickets, camped at the water holes, swaggered and strutted in the towns. Trouble whispered to the domineering Anglo, to the marauding Indian, to the mercurial, high-tempered Mexican. Trouble kindled the fire beneath a pot where simmered racial antagonisms, religious fanaticisms, wrongs fancied and wrongs real—and brought it from the simmer to boiling, up to the edge and spilling over. The adventurer, the outlaw, the siftings of the East, came to the new state, and each took what suited his individual fancy. Mexicans were killed for a cow or horse, for no reason at all. The Texans, grabbing the spoils, fixed the southern boundary of the state at the Río Grande and marked it down with the black of gunpowder and the red of blood. The Mexicans marked it the Río Nueces and harassed the invaders of what they considered Mexican territory. The Rangers, formed of dire necessity and recruited, too often, with men whose sole virtue was a daring courage, were reluctantly recognized by the army units which came now by water and by land, and were rewarded for their hardships and courage by penurious dribbles from a niggardly nonunderstanding government. The Rangers hated the Mexicans, who hated and feared them in return. Politics stretched out its tenuous fingers and drew in the weak, the ignorant, and those lusting for power.

There was turmoil and strife unending.

There was blood. Texas dipped a pen deeply in it, and wrote its history with it.

Yet slowly, relentlessly as Time, the indomitableness of the Americans laid its foundations for permanency and order and built firmly upon them. The Mexican *hidalgo* and the high-bred *ranchero*, by nature slow to recognize the logic of events, failed to gauge the future by happenings of the past. Serene in the belief that his heritage of conquest was a sort of superbravery which must, inevitably, conquer again, he built a wall against the Americans—against everything American—and excluded himself within it.[1]

If trouble did not actually come to Rancho La Palma it nevertheless flung its shadow across it. A stray rider, asking food and a night's shelter, brought the news that Arista had not only been defeated at Resaca de la Palma and Palo Alto but had been run into Mexico with his utterly demoralized army. Zachary Taylor was preparing to go to Mexico after Santa Anna. The Rangers had built a camp at Reynosa and "*Señor*, under *el diablo*'s guidance they are riding up and down the Río Bravo and doing what they wish in Matamoros"; the rider reported dramatically and in detail that three wagons and a band of riders went past one of the *vaquero* camps, going west. Tomás, the *caporal*, braved Don Santiago's disapproval—and got it in a contemptuous lift of lip—by saying, "I could see the men had guns, and, as they went their way and molested nothing, I did not see the need of attacking them, and the *vaqueros* agreed with me. One must use a certain amount of discretion in life, as you yourself have often told me." There was also, Tomás reported, a pestiferous small band of Indians riding about, and they had strengthened the fence around the camp. Estéban, whose duty it was to see that the *peons* did not shirk their tasks and that the horses of the family were always in trim for riding—Estéban had found a large flat hat such as the invaders wore, doubtless blown many miles by the wind, for it was impregnated with dust. This hat Estéban put on his head, only to have Alvaro jerk it off, rip the brim, and pass it to his father, who tossed it under his horse's hooves. "The next time," Don Santiago told Estéban, "the whip will be laid on one who flaunts anything of the *gringo* before my eyes."

And Estéban never forgot the feel of the fine felt of the hat that was rightfully his and taken from him so arbitrarily.

The pastor, old Victorino, left the sheep long enough to bring his tale of woe. Lovingly called "Tío" by all, the old man had given so long and loyal service that he was privileged to drop the title *don* in addressing his master. To Victorino went the cast-off suits of Don Santiago and, larger and taller than most, he presented a comical scarecrow appearance now as he entered the patio. A waist-long white beard curled from a ruddy round face, and the big hat with remnants of braid clinging to it was tied firmly over long snowy hair. The dirty braid-trimmed suit, loosened to fit with cord and riding high above horny bare feet thrust into *huaraches* of rawhide, was worn as proudly as ever it had been worn by its master when new. A personal servant in his youth, he had deeply loved Paz, but too shy to voice it, he had let his heart break to see her marry the man her mistress selected for her. He asked his master to let him go to the pastures and there, alone with Nature, he evolved a mystic belief in the Creator and built stories around all creatures and growing things. Now he made a small obeisance to his master, at ease in a chair in the shade of the portico. "*Buenos días te dé Dios,*" he greeted.

"Your face proclaims bad news, Victorino. What now?"

"*Sí,* Santiago. God reminded us once again that we are nothing and He is all things. The lightning struck and thirty of the sheep lie dead, over in the valley of the *pitas.*"

Don Santiago started to retort that, while God was Master of the elements, He scarcely sat in a chair to direct the lightning where to strike, but quickly restrained himself. These *peons* had too limited an intelligence, and Victorino was like a trusting child. Surely his beliefs did more good than harm. They talked awhile about the pastures and the old man's charges, and soon he left again, walking slowly in the hope that Paz might see him and pass the time of day with him. A faithful servant indeed was Tío Victorino.

José came chunking in an ox cart, his young wife Tecla beside him. They lived in a *jacal,* built as a headquarters and provision depot for herders, about three miles from the *hacienda.* The fertile brown land around the *jacal* and the strong spring which watered it was a valuable adjunct to the ranch, and José and Tecla tended it well. José also brought news, moving a large straw hat nervously from one hand to the other. The gophers must have rained from the sky as numerous as raindrops, and half the corn was destroyed before it could take root. The rats and mice—José wondered, in his simple ways, whether such a thing as a sterile rat had ever lived. "Is this because the *Americanos* are in the land?" José asked. "Is it a curse put upon us, do you think?"

Don Gabriel came again, perturbed, and told what more he knew of the invaders, and left further unease behind him. All in all, it was a summer of clouds for the *hacienda.*

"Twenty pesos for wax, twenty for a new dress, coins for mass and the responses," counted Doña Dolores softly, in a shady nook of the patio. "Needles, a *mantilla—*"

"Time sweeps by like the flight of a swallow," murmured Doña María

Petronilla. "Here it is October, and to town we must go to do our duty to our dead, visit the living, get new—"

"The way you say that," snapped her sister-in-law, "one would think your very soul had left you."

"Perhaps it is only tired, Dolores. Santiago is in a mood to remain here for the winter, and a wife's duty—"

"A thousand evil spirits take away wifely duty!" Doña Dolores crushed a hibiscus bloom and threw it away. "That's all you can talk about, duty, duty, duty, to all but yourself! A wife has rights too and if I were in your place, Petronilla, the orders would not come from only *one* pair of lips, I can tell you that!"

"What's this now?" asked Don Santiago, spurs clinking as he came across the patio floor. "What is it, Dolores?"

"I am merely counting the money I shall spend on All Souls Day, brother. Wax candles to burn for my poor Anselm, may his soul rest in peace for he was a good man."

"Not any candles will he need, my sister," Don Santiago laughed, turning back to the roof by the gateway to tip the *olla* and pour cold water into a gourd dipper. "He had enough purgatory in the two years of his married life, it seems to me."

The wart on Doña Dolores' cheek burst into bloom. "Santiago, if you mean that I, your sister—"

"It is no secret that you helped him get to the other world with your independence and sharp tongue, my dear Dolores." He took a chair facing them. "Our dead will have to manage with prayers from the ranch. We are not going to Matamoros."

"Now . . . what?" She put a hand on his arm and shook it. "Have you lost your senses, are you turning into a heathen? The *padre* has not been here all summer, and certainly it is time to be shriven from our sins. What do you mean?"

"What I said. We are staying here. As for our sins, I know I can bear mine easily awhile longer if you women cannot."

Doña María Petronilla crossed herself at this presumption, but Dolores sprang to her feet [with a snort]², the pouch of coins clinking to the floor as she crossed arms over the full bosom. "Eldest born and only living son of your father, you will refuse the respects to the dead?" she stormed. "Your sainted—"

"My sainted mother would have taught you more submission had she lived!" He stood opposite her, glaring at her. "I command you to be silent! Sit down!"

"Command all you wish, I shall not obey. I do not cringe before you as your wife does, I shall not blindly do your wish as does Angela, I shall refuse the abuse you heap upon Luis Gonzaga. I am a Mendoza and a Soría also and worthy of the name if you are not, and though a woman, I know my duty!"

It was always so between these two when their wishes crossed. Don Santiago raised a hand, dropped it with a muttered curse. "Silence!" he thundered. "I command your respect if not your obedience. I am master here!"

"So? Go into the *sala* and read what your grandfather carved on the rafter, that the Lord is the master here. His things come first. Why did your grandfather build the house in Matamoros? So we could renew our souls by going to church and give due respect to the souls of the faithful departed. Respect—you overwork the word, my brother. First have some before you preach it!" She swept past him close enough so her stiff skirts could slap against him, carrying the triumph of victory away with her in this unanswerable retort.

He watched her disappear into the house, words choking his throat, furious at himself as well as her, that he let her whip him into such a rage. When words came, he piled them upon his wife, tramping back and forth before her. Ha! So Dolores went to town each winter to renew her soul, did she, and who believed that? To renew her wardrobe and get new finery, to deck herself in jewels and be the *gran señora;* to go to parties and gossip and renew her vanity, that was the renewing she did. Respect—he had too much respect for his family to take them to a town polluted with alien soldiers and Rangers.

Doña María Petronilla folded her hands over the crocheting and sat still till the storm wore itself out. In the twenty-five years of marriage to this man, she had fashioned only the armor of meekness to meet his dominance, and it gave her no protection. For she still shrank under the lash of his words even when, as now, she was the handy recipient and not the target of them. She did not resent it. Such was the law according to her mother's teaching and example, and, implanted into a nature innately timid, it could not make her other than she was—an obedient, dutiful wife. When shouts and laughter rode into the patio on a light breeze, she sighed in relief. He would, she knew, join his children and ride with them until they

❧

were all tired, returning in a good humor. In truth, Don Santiago welcomed the excuse to get away from the diatribe which was wearing thin and swung into the saddle with alacrity. He was one of the few ranchers who allowed his daughters to ride. When Angela had decided to forego the saddle in her desire to pattern her life after that of a nun, a year ago, he had ordered that she should ride some every day. It would, he hoped, help to break up what Angela saw as a vocation.

Why, the wife left in the patio wondered, had the dashing young Santiago ever selected her? Family, for one. Inordinately proud of their unadulterated lineage, the Mendozas demanded a family tree as select as their own, and she had been a de la Garza. Having small knowledge of genealogy, her delicacy had been taken for extremity of refinement instead of what it was: deterioration from generations of unmixed, thinning blood. Don Francisco had railed that there were only four children, not knowing that the bearing of four was close to being a miracle. Then young, Santiago, having strangely enough never been in love except fleetingly, had enough of authoritative women who leaned to independence—as was the grandmother who raised him and the sister so quickly widowed. Santiago had not wanted the taming of a woman, subservience seeming to him the sweeter fruit. And Petronilla had been so sweetly shy and pretty. His father's choice of her had suited him exactly, so he thought then. Yet always silently blaming her, in those years to come, that she was not the full-blooded mate of moods and passions to meet his own—the only kind of woman with whom he could have found true happiness.

Poor María Petronilla never suspected that. Even that one winter in town when Dolores told her he had a mistress, she thought him merely male and effaced herself the more. Foreboding laid a heavy hand on her now as she thought of her children, and what the changing conditions that would inevitably follow the war and fresh invasions would do to them. They would suffer, shut away from the gaiety of the winter season, yet there was foundation for Santiago's fears. True, it might be the same happy season as always and yet—yet—

"Something will happen," she whispered. And whatever happened, she would suffer most. "But I have learned to bear it," she smiled a little. "I can bear it so much better than they."

Doña Dolores tried again the next day, while they were waiting for afternoon coffee in the patio. "Have you forgotten the day of the first anniversary of our dear mother's death, my brother?" she asked softly, bringing in a poignant note of sadness. "We were so young, you and me, and Ramón a baby. Grandmother took us to church, first to the high altar where we knelt and prayed, then to the side altar before which our grandfather was buried. There was a glory around her as she said, 'My dear ones, you tread upon holy ground. Here lies one who fought for his God and his King, who helped build this church, who lived and built not for himself but for those who would come after him. Keep his name and memory stainless.' Do you remember, my brother, how we kissed, our tears falling? Or have you forgotten?"

"Forgotten, Dolores?" He laughed harshly. "It is that I remember. My heart has burned enough all summer without searing it the more by going there to see a new flag, hearing an unknown language, and perhaps having humiliation forced upon me by men as beneath me as one of my *peons.*"

"You talk like a woman," she answered. "For shame, Santiago! We must show these *Americanos* that we are not defeated. Can you imagine any of them humiliating me?"

Before he could retort that sensitivity was needed first for humiliation, Susanita came waltzing down the portico. "Look, *papá*," she sang, "See, I am practicing for the balls in town—"

"Balls in town—humph!" Doña Dolores snorted, disgusted that her ruse of sentimentality had failed. "You'll have to do your dancing by yourself for your father is keeping us here all winter. Make up your mind to marry a ranch hand. Pablo the ditch man, like as not. Or an unwashed *vaquero.*"

"Oh no!" seeing the truth of the news in her mother's shrinking figure, the flame of her aunt's wart, the set line of her father's mouth, Susanita wasted no time. She let the pressing tears make pools of her lovely eyes, smiling cajolingly as she pressed her father's hand. "Why, *papacito*, don't you want to show the *Americanos* what a handsome *caballero* looks like— why in your Sunday suit you are the handsomest man in the world! And you want to see me in my pretty clothes—"

"¡*Americanos, Americanos!*" Don Santiago jerked his hand away in anger, his voice thundering so that old Paz, bringing the coffee, fled back to the kitchen. "I hate them! For the last time I say we shall not go, and I forbid the subject to be mentioned again. Dolores, you can burn a candle for your dear Anselm at home; Susanita, it is time you were thinking of more serious things. Go to Angela, perhaps she can console you with her platitudes. She and her convent, you and your vanity and cavaliers, Dolores with her vanity and candles, Luis Gonzaga with his crayons—pah! I suppose even Alvaro—" he kicked at a chair, slammed the large braided hat on his head and stamped away.

Women! Why God ever made the creatures the way they were was beyond comprehension. Women, with their loose reasonings, their . . . their . . . *por Lucifer*, what a man had to endure! He leaped into the saddle of the horse always ready for him at the gate, and spurred the animal so violently it reared and pitched and tore away into the plains.

In all truth, the master felt his own punishment. He loved conviviality, the renewed familiarities of old friends and faces, the *fiestas* and religious services. Most of all, he liked to see his family happy. His heart was heavy when daily he saw Angela's tear-washed eyes, María Petronilla's silent reproach, Dolores's glumness, Susanita's unhappy small smile. Alvaro took to the camps of the *vaqueros*, sullen and arrogant beyond endurance when at home. Only Luis Gonzaga was happy, for he had discovered a flair for caricatures and practiced it among the *peons*, much to their delight. And this, the sole compliance with his wishes, angered Don Santiago almost beyond endurance.

The father's greatest fear was that his beloved, his beautiful one, might see and fall in love with one of the invaders. He had used every means to keep Susanita a child, yet he knew that the door holding back her womanhood no longer had hasp or hinge. When it fell away and her impassioned nature had full sway—what then? Gabriel del Lago, on a visit in the summer, had relayed what he heard of the ways of the tall newcomers with women. "Some had their wives with them in San Antonio," Don Gabriel had said, "and I am told that they treat them like equals, even like queens, and actually defer to them. These men have an ease and a manner about them which, mark well my words, *amigo*, will strike to the heart of more than one of our girls. There will be trouble, Santiago."

Yes, there would be trouble. "Rather would I bury my girls," he had told his friend, "than see them married to an *Americano*." And he had meant it.

He fed his hatred and it filled him with fears.

Two weeks of submission. Silent, resentful submission that darkened the *hacienda* and set old Paz to ceaseless grumblings and scoldings. Then, when it was on the verge of eruption, a rider came to the patio gate just after the household dispersed after the last "amen" of *El Alabado*. A dusty, tired messenger from Rancho San Juan, the Olivares's stronghold.[3] There had been a meeting at the rancho of Mexican landowners, and they had sent this note to Don Santiago. It read:

It has been decided that strong action is needed if we are to keep from being swallowed by the hordes of infidels moving in our direction. Those of us who have winter homes in Camargo and Mier will come to Matamoros, inconveniencing themselves by crowding with relatives and friends. Not only because travel along the Río Bravo is no longer safe, but so we can decide, at fuller meetings, what is best to be done. It is to be hoped that you, Don Santiago, will not fail us now in this crisis.

The note struck a patriotic zeal, the fire of it sweeping through his mind and burning the fears from his heart. He dismissed the messenger to the servant's quarters, crushed the note, called his wife, and gave orders to prepare for their leaving—for once grateful for her meekness which forebore to ask any questions. "Do what must be done, but see that there is no unnecessary delay."

"As you wish, Santiago," she answered simply.

Calves were killed, the meat cut into sheets and strips, salted and spiced, and hung on rawhide rope lines to dry. Roasted on coals and shredded, or chopped with heavy machetes, it would be the foundation for varieties of soups, hash, and vegetable combinations: *caldillo, picadillo,* the delicious omelet *albondiga.* For days the women were busy roasting and grinding cocoa beans that would make foamy cups of the favorite spiced chocolate. Corn was shelled and sacked ready for the oxcarts; boiled and ground over the *metate,* it would be made into *tortillas, tamales, enchiladas.* Doña María Petronilla was everywhere, supervising the work, while Doña Dolores, like a general, gave orders and commands. Between them they finally managed to get old Paz out from under foot by flattering her into overseeing the soap making. "You have the secret, Paz. Your lye soap is always whitest and best and the amole and roseleaf—Susanita's hair is always more shiny when you make that complexion soap, and the perfume is exactly right."

Two days before departure the baking began, where Nicolasa took charge. Juan and Pedro kept the fires under the rounded earthen ovens outside the wall burning day and night, looking like red-faced, half-naked demons. While Nicolasa measured and her helpers mixed and kneaded and shaped, endlessly. There were *polvorones:* flour, cream, and sugar rolled into little balls, dipped in cinnamon and sugar, set on orange or lemon leaf, and laid on huge sheets of hammered copper. A luxury, these flat trays, and only a few *rancheros* were fortunate enough to own them. There were *empanadas:* a syrupy pumpkin mixture heavily spiced and baked into small hard-crusted pies. *Semitas:* yeast bread mixed with toasted flour and brown sugar and formed into round cakes. There were hundreds of *biscochos*. For this, corn was soaked in lye, the points removed, and the kernel dried into flour, then mixed with lard and cheese and made into patties with a dimple in the center, or into balls with fluted edges. Baked hard and brown, crisp, crackling, and absorbing as a sponge, they would be a favorite to dip into coffee. There were long loaves of white bread made with flour brought from the wheat fields of Monclova, shorter loaves made with bran.

With the personal maids pressed into service in the kitchen, Angela and Susanita had the task of sorting and packing clothes. Don Santiago and the boys rode to the camps with Tomás, the *caporal*, looking over the long-horned stock, giving orders regarding marauders. And if *Americanos* came they were to be run off the ranch, given no food or water, did Tomás understand? At the sheep camp Victorino listened to orders about his fleeced charges with silent respect, quite as if he did not know far more about them than the master.

There was hurry and worry and work unending, to gain a few days on the time lost. Grumblings, sighs, imprecations—to which no one paid attention. But finally all was ready. Three ox carts were loaded high with food and baggage, boards laid over a wagon for seats for the house servants. The pick of the *peons*, wearing jean trousers, clean shirts of domestic, huge straw hats, *huaraches* on bare feet, formed a guard in front and behind the carts. They were armed with muskets, several even carried the old Spanish musketoon, and all had knives of varied lengths. Starting days ahead of the family, a sizable, slow-moving caravan, it would barely be in town before the arrival of the coach. Don Santiago called the leader, a swarthy Mexican Indian named Tirso, to him and said, "You may meet some of these *hombres* called Rangers. You will know them because they are shabbily dressed and have no wagons, but they ride good horses and are most presumptuous in manner. If they molest you or wish to uncover the carts—" Don Santiago snapped his fingers—"one dies but once, Tirso, in bed like an old woman or in glory of righteous battle for what is one's own."

Tirso's eyes glinted. "*Sí, señor,*" he agreed, smiling.

At the very last as they were ready to start, old Paz disregarded her aged bones and leaped from the wagon. "I will not go without Manuel," she asserted firmly. "I know I agreed to leave him but I cannot do so. He must go with me."

Argument was of no avail. Manuel, great-grandson of Paz, was the joy of her heart, and with both his mother and grandmother dead he was altogether her own. Small for his nine years, he had an ingenuity and self-reliance far beyond them, was petted and spoiled by Paz, and in general was such a nuisance that orders were firm that he remain on the ranch. But there were times when Don Santiago was not master. When Paz was really firm, he was a small boy and she his disciplinarian. To save his face before the interested watchers, he let Doña Dolores do the arguing—knowing, as they all knew, that Paz would have her way. Paz made solemn promises. "*Sí, señora*, I will see to it that he behaves, he will be like an angel this time. If need be, I will lock him up, you know I will."

When Manuel came at call, he was scrubbed and in his best, Don Santiago burst into laughter. Susanita leaned down to kiss the shining brown cheek, and the little imp ran to the first cart and climbed on a sack of corn. Paz took her seat, Tirso called "*Arre, arre*" as he cracked his long whip, and the caravan started. Those left behind scattered to their quarters, consoling themselves that, if they were denied the diversions of town, neither did they have the extra burden of labor there.

Doña Dolores sighed. "We might as well get at the clothes, Petronilla, you know we will have to sort everything over again. What with the cleaning and packing we will be plenty busy until we start. Sometimes I wonder if it is worth all the work and worry. I ache as if I were ninety."

Doña María Petronilla echoed the sigh. To her it was not at all worth it. Particularly now, for the foreboding which would not die was a heavy weight on her heart.

On the eve of the departure Don Santiago mounted a gentle brown mare, forked across a small grassy valley below the *hacienda*, and followed a trail which led to the foot of a high bluff that was like a fragment of an ancient huge stone wall. There the trail zigzagged for footing and lay like a great pale snake against the bush-covered steep side. The mare took it with the ease of custom, found her favorite resting place, and dropped her head. The top was about twenty feet in diameter and flat, with a cross of stones in the center, at its base a bench made from a sandstone slab.

It was a rendezvous beloved by the master of Rancho La Palma. Here pride could have a man's stature, here he was on a throne. He stood beside the cross, monarch of all he surveyed. To the north, the east, the south, pastures dipped and rolled and swelled in a mighty sea of green, finally to break into mists of blue against infinity of space. To the west the land lay flat as if pressed smooth by a mighty palm, a long limitless plain running into a reddening, gold-painted sky to catch the fireball of sun. As enchanting, as beckoning and beautiful this evening as it had been nearly a hundred years ago, when Don José Ramón had stood here and felt its call. Here he had envisioned the ranch, and later built the dream into actuality. Like a romantic dream was the huge *hacienda* with its watchtower now, the patio a brilliant jewel in the setting of white, the figure in it like small gnomes. Outside the wall the *peons* were bits of animated color, busy in this their own small village. The white thread of a stream blocked off gardens, orchards, fields of ripening maize like oddly striped aprons of green and brown and yellow.

Don Santiago's pride spread and burst in his chest, and he flung his arms wide. "Mine," he murmured. "All this that I can see, and far beyond, is mine and only mine."

"Mine!" He brought his hands together, and cupped them into a bowl, and flung them wide again. And he stood there so, watching the flame of the sky give way to rose and violet-orange and spread its glory over the land. Power was wine in his veins. Power was a figure that touched him, and pointed, and whispered. Those dots on the plain, cattle, sheep, horses, were his to kill or let live. The *peons*, down there, were his to discipline at any time with the lash, to punish by death if he so chose. His wife, his sister, sons, and daughters bowed to his wishes and came or went as he decreed.

"Yours," said Power, pointing, "All yours!"

He dropped his arms and circled the place slowly, his eyes following the line of an imaginary wall springing around Rancho La Palma. For so it would ever be, as if a wall were around him and what was his, and the key to its door held only in his hand.

Like distant beautiful chimes came the call to *El Alabado*, and Don Santiago mounted the patient mare. So, he thought, would the bell ring at close of day for generation upon generation, the old songs and prayers led by the lord of the household. After him by Alvaro, and his sons, and their sons. Let the world whirl in madness. Rancho La Palma would never change. The Mendoza line never die.

The household was bustling while the morning star still beckoned. Don Santiago, patience long fled, rode to the corrals, around the house wall and in and out of the patio gate, finally leaping from his horse in exasperation. "These women, these women!" he fumed, the boot heels on the *tipichil* floor like small explosions of his impatience. "So it was in my father's day, so it is year after year—we wait for the women!"

☙❧

Alvaro and Luis Gonzaga, appropriating *machetes* from the workers, moved out of earshot and played knight, running dangerously at each other with their high strung, eager mounts. Servants rushed about excitedly, scuttling for cover when the glowering master came near them.

The coach, Juan Bautista, stiff and important on the box, drove up to the gate—silver-trimmed harness glinting in the first rays of the morning sun, bright tassels swinging on the heads of the six matching white mules; like dancers with their slender legs and clean black hooves. Don Santiago rushed to the portico steps and shouted. He took a knife from his sash and threw it at the palm tree, jerked it out, and threw it again. "Women! Petronilla is doubtless still making the rounds of the rooms, finding something useless to pile on our already heavy load. God knows Angela can tell her beads in the coach, but she has to be on her knees asking blessings on a journey which will never so much as start. Susanita is flirting with her looking glass and Dolores—You gave them to me, Lord," he burst out, raising hands to heaven, "give me the patience to bear with them!"

A door opened and Doña Dolores swept past him, in her fullest, stiffest dress, carrying a wicker cage with a canary.

"*Dios de Dios*, Dolores, haven't we enough baggage without that miserable chirping thing?" he shouted at her.

Doña Dolores, deigning neither to see nor hear him, took a seat in the coach with all the dignity of a queen, the cage on her lap.

"Here we are, *papá*," sang Susanita, pirouetting the tight-bodiced, full-skirted dark dress of thin wool before him. "Don't you think I look nice in my traveling suit?"

"Get in the coach," he snapped, unmollified even by his darling one. "Here we are an hour late because of your primping, so the cows along the road can admire you! Where is Angela, your mother—where is— your—mother?"

Her mother slunk down the steps [5] of Don Santiago's over an arm, carrying a headless two-foot-high image of a saint which, evidently, was to be restored to life by some craftsman in town. At the sight of it Don Santiago choked on a growl, words failing him. He jerked the saint from her and flung it down on the steps, where it sprawled like a deflated drunken man. Angela ducked past him, keeping the box she was holding intact as she scurried inside the coach. The master shoved his wife impatiently after her and slammed the door.

The boys pranced forward, Luis Gonzaga on a slim-legged dun with black mane and tail, name Tabasco; Alvaro on a rangy, full-chested reed roan conspicuous for its taffy-colored mane and tail. Don Santiago mounted his special pride, a glistening black named Negro. All three were dressed in their best, dark flaring trousers and short jackets elaborate with white braid and hung with silver buttons. Don Santiago wore a wide felt *sombrero* of black embroidered with silver braid, the boys wore tan with gold braid. Inlaid, fitted boots of exquisite Moroccan leather held large-roweled silver spurs augmented with tiny chains to make a ceaseless jingle and draw the eye to the small feet. The best was worn on these journeys, so that anyone seeing them would know they were quality, of a house accustomed to the best. Particularly was this important when they came into town, with many eyes upon them.

"Alvaro," called Don Santiago sharply, "come back here. I ride ahead, you and Luis stay in the rear with the guard." He looked over the twenty hard-bitten, lean *vaqueros* as they came forward, each with a gun hung under a leg in a scabbard looped to the saddle. He nodded approval. A good guard against Indians—or now, *Americanos.* Outriders took positions on each side of the coach, the rest fell into place in the rear.

"Ready, Juan Bautista?" he called to the driver. "*¡Con diez mil demonios! Go!*"

Juan Bautista needed but the word to crack the long whip, shout "*Arre, arre,*" grasp the reins tightly, and leap into the lead after the lunging black of his master. The coach lurched, then bumped into steadiness. The women crossed themselves, called on a favorite saint to protect them. Alvaro and Luis shouted, rearing their horses with those of the *vaqueros* in a spectacular act before they trotted after the coach.

Old Nicolasa watched the cavalcade until the road turned and a rise of ground took them from view. She picked up the saint and brushed it with a brown, work-twisted old hand. And without envy, grateful for her simple lot in life, went inside the empty *hacienda*.

Chapter 4

The Mendoza y Sorías came too late for the festivities of All Saints and the [1] of All Souls days, but were immediately showered with calls and invitations. The last to arrive, there was much gossip to be relayed. For if this year there was a grimmer purpose for the *rancheros* to gather in town it did not disturb the main object: daily conviviality, dances, dinners and parties, religious *fiestas*. It was for this the town houses had been built, small compared to the ranch homes but with a large *sala* and patio for entertaining. Made of stone and elaborate with grilled windows, arcades, and portals, all had a corral for the horses and quarters for the servants in the rear. In spite of the threatening war clouds and the blot of the army encampment across the river, they would enjoy their stay to the full. There would be a social gathering at the home of some *hidalgo* each evening, but care would be taken that all talk of the invaders would not be serious enough to disturb the gaiety. That was reserved for the secret meetings of the men, of which none but they would know.

This was also the time for love-making—under careful surveillance and strict chaperonage but expressive nonetheless. There would be match-making, betrothals. A wife for Alvaro, a husband for Susanita. A husband also for Angela, Don Santiago had determined. At their first town break-fast, he ordered that Angela should put aside her nun's garb.

"Not once do I wish to see those swathing bandages around your head, they have depressed me for too long a time. María Petronilla, I want no excuse that she has outgrown her old dresses and must wait until new ones are made for her—heaven knows Susanita has three times too many, and the girls are the same size. She is also to go to parties and dance and laugh. Ours is not a religion of sorrow, there is plenty of joy in it as Angela should know. I have said no to the convent, now I say no for the last time. Do you understand Angela?"

"*Papá*, not to dance, please, *papá*, please! No dresses with flowers and no jewels . . . I . . . ." Angela choked and burst into tears. Doña Dolores rose, handed her a handkerchief, and kissed her on the cheek, as much to reproach her brother as to comfort the girl.

The girl's distress struck him, for he did love his children. Also, now and then his conscience prodded him, reminding him that vocations for a secluded life were gifts from God and were not to be thwarted. Though this he quickly silenced with the belief that no daughter of his could be called away from him. In his opinion only weaklings went to convents, or those whom no man would marry. That the small group of nuns who had a house back of the church, teaching the children of the *hidalgos* in winter and doing missionary work in summer, had an intrepidity beyond that of any man in his entire group, Don Santiago had never stopped to consider. Besides, he felt that Angela's vocation was more of a notion on her part kept green by her mother. He finished his meal and rose, telling her:

"Go talk it over with Mother Gertrudis at the convent. I am sure she will tell you that obedience to your father is a virtue; you know there is a whole commandment on it. And unless I greatly mistake them, neither the Mother nor our Padre Pierre will see sin in dancing and wearing a bright dress. It is my wish, Angela. You have the grace and gentility of my grandmother even more than Susanita has, and I wish it to be noticed."

Angela managed a smile and lifted the wimple. Her beautiful full black hair dropped into a dip over each temple, giving the pretty face a charm so surprising that her father beamed with pleasure. "Very well, dear *papá*," she said, "but I would like to go to church a little while each day. After *siesta*. No one is in the church then and it is so peaceful. I would hurry back for the *merienda*."

"I am sure we could use the prayers, *hija*, that is not too much to ask." He turned to smile and say teasingly to his youngest: "Susanita can go with you, I am sure she would love to."

Doña Petronilla laughed in sheer relief that the storm and dictatorial commands she had expected had not materialized. "I fear Susanita will be far more concerned at four o'clock with the dressmaker and the chattering of her friends than with her rosary beads. *Mi chiquita* loves the gay life."

"So did I when I was young." Doña Dolores pulled the braid of her niece, the natural dignity of her face dissolved into a coyness which sat ludicrously upon it. "I fear we will get no rest at all these nights, for there will be much serenading under her window. I hear that young Carlos del Valle—"

"Oh him," Susanita pouted. "He is round like a keg, and his face is greasy, and he thinks he is handsome. He can serenade me but he will get no rose from me. Neither will Leon Mora nor that long-nosed Felix Cadena. I wish—may I have more chocolate, *mamá?*" Better not say what she wished, it was not ladylike to express her wishes, and *papá* might start preaching about respect and duty.

Divining her thought, Doña Dolores said, "One does not marry to have an ornament in the house, my child. One marries to have a husband, which is a different thing entirely. If women married for handsomeness only the *padres* would have few weddings to witness. As for love—"

"Weren't you ever in love, *tía*? Not even a tiny bit?" Susanita left the table and practiced a curtsy, put fingertips on the arm of an imaginary escort, and tripped beside him, melting eyes raised to supposedly adoring ones in a face far too vague of outline to satisfy her. She had already forgotten her question, for the very idea of the homely, proper Doña Dolores loving, or having been loved, seemed impossible.

No one noticed the sudden crimson in the wart on the doña's cheek as she quickly drained her cup. Don Santiago snorted, told Susanita sharply it was time for her to learn wifely duties, rather than perfecting the art of flirting, and left the room. Love—pah, what was love! He slammed the door as he stepped into the street, frustration again rising and jerking at his throat. He would select a husband for Susanita and she would marry him. Love! There would be none of it if he could avoid it, other things were more important. A man who had sown his wild oats, so that he could be the more true to the one he married. One who possessed a proud name and could be the father of strong sons. This time frustration broke and he muttered imprecations upon an unjust fate. He had been such a man— and had only Alvaro worthy to be called 'son.' Luis Gonzaga, the *marica!* Eighteen and without an affair, never even kissing the servant girls he sketched. He sighed. Perhaps Luis might still be a man, given time. But there would be no more indulgent waiting for Alvaro, nor for Susanita. Neither for Angela. Let them talk of love all they wanted to. He would let it be known, by discreet word here and there, by new clothes for the girls and Alvaro, that the house of Mendoza y Soría had an ear for proposals.

Head up, sure of himself once again, Don Santiago brushed a speck from the black suit and went to join his friends, gathering for gossip in the plaza. He had wealth, position, power. He gave the proper obeisance to his God. What could pluck the crayon from his hand when he mapped out the future of those over whom he was master?

Nothing, he thought. Nothing could.

Love. Beaux. It was the ceaseless, never tiring topic of the young. Susanita's closest friends, Inez Sánchez y Argensola and Clara Mora, came bursting with news and sat [like bright, multiple-petaled flowers][2] on the sofa in Susanita's room. Whispering excitedly, wary eyes on the door for an eavesdropper in the form of Paz or one of the two conscientious duennas of Inez and Clara. Clara, shiny black braids wrapped about her head, was ready and eager for marriage. "When *mamá* was my age, she already had me," she was wont to sigh wistfully. Inez also had braids, but they were a live, fiery red, looped high and forward to accentuate the heart-shaped, piquant face.

Inez had been betrothed to a man who could easily have been her grandfather but who, unwittingly gallant to a weeping bride-to-be, let a weak and overtaxed heart kill him two days before the wedding. Now, emerged from a period of "decorum," she found a great advantage for the approbation of the males and the envy of the girls to carry a brave sorrow, and had mastered a brooding detachment which she wore or flung aside as the occasion demanded. Alone with her friends she was the same Inez and a girl like they, eager to attain that rare thing—a marriage of mutual love.

There was real news this time, and Inez moved close and opened brown eyes wide. "You know there are *Americanos* in a camp but oh, Susanita!" She clasped her hands and sighed ecstatically. "There are officers, and there is one so tall and so nice looking, with black hair that curls and gray eyes—gray, Susanita, it's true, and an impudent mouth and—"

"We met them when we went shopping with our *mamás*," Clara interrupted eagerly. "The street was narrow, and they stood aside and held their hats in their hands and were most polite, and our *mamás* walked quickly without looking, and we put down our heads most decorously—oh, we did! *Mamá* commended us later." She giggled. "But we managed a very good look. Inez, she looked twice."

Susanita, all eager ears, was dutifully shocked. "I admit I would like to see one but I would not look twice, never. They are bad men and have no education. Tell me more, Inez, tell it all."

Inez needed no encouragement, first going to the door to make sure no one was eavesdropping, excitement painted her cheeks, and her useless little white hands fluttered like caged wild birds, now and then touching Susanita for emphasis. "Yes, you would look, and three times. They were both so divinely tall—you know how we have wished that we could once dance with a man higher than we are—ooooh, it would stretch one's neck so deliciously to look at their faces and in their eyes! The one in the blue uniform was the handsomest, and his hair was pale brown and his eyes so blue you could scarcely believe it, but the other one—I don't know why, because his clothes were not so fine, and one eyebrow is higher than the other, and his mouth is stretched kind of flat, and there was a boldness about him but I—I pray that I may see him again. I do, Susanita. And they were not crude at all like *papá* says, and I am sure they do not kill babies and do dreadful things."

Inez suddenly burst into tears and burrowed her face in the shirred silk of Susanita's blouse. "I don't care if he is *Americano*, I could—love him like everything, and if *papá* finds out he will betroth me to another old goat who is so tough he will never die—and I'll be d-d-dutiful like *mamá* and always wear black and get—fat and never have any fun and—get pious—"

A dramatic deluge of weeping at this awful picture racked her for a full minute. Then she was smiling again, the present being too full to weep long over an imaginary future. "Chonita, my duenna, has heard that they love wonderfully, these *Americanos*, and marry for love, and let their women ride a horse after marriage and give them things. I would like a husband who makes love to me after marriage, too."

"You would *marry* one of them? Oh, Inez!"

"If this one loved me as much as his eyes said he could,—oh, those gray eyes!" Inez sighed. "At least I would like to see him again and talk to him. But *papá* can see no good in them. He hates them."

Clara nodded. "So does my *papá*. I am sure they are all faithless, I would not trust one at all, though I would like, just once, to dance with one. What do you think, Susanita?"

Susanita, pleating a pink ruffle with slim fingers, did not answer. Impulses old as life but new to her were stirring. Don Santiago had done his utmost to keep his baby from maturing and, lighthearted and joyous by nature, her home life had been happy and sufficient for her. A popular belle, she had arrived at seventeen with her heart intact, a rare thing among a people where it was not unusual to betroth a girl at thirteen, and girlhood leaped from tight bud to full flower without the slow, sweet unfolding of the petals. Inez's boldness, her shocking wish to have a lover after marriage, the tantalization of the unknown exemplified by them, brought the upheaval Don Santiago believed his mere talk of marriage would accomplish. She creased pleats and smoothed them out again. Welcoming this strange heart-fluttering, again shying away from it.

"I do not know," she answered slowly. "Except that of course I shall obey *papá* in whatever he orders."

Inez sniffed. "Obeying has been easy for you; he has never ordered you to do anything that hurt inside. Wait until he tells you to marry some old widower like Señor Montoya, you'll cry as much as I did."

"I wouldn't." Clara sat up primly. "I would marry anyone if he were not too loathsome. I'd be happy and have ten children at least. Naturally I'd like to marry for love, but as that never comes true why even think about it."

A sad maturity lay oddly over the piquant face of Inez as she said, "Then you are more blessed than we. Being a wife and mother and being called *doña* is everything to you, and so you cannot help but be happy. You see a man as something to bring you these things and not really as something personal at all; and you'll get married and be so busy with your babies and waiting on your husband you won't have time to worry about love later. I am not that way." She struck her breast. "I am *me*, inside here. Chonita says I am like my red hair but I don't know—Adelita Cadena has red hair too and she isn't at all like me."

"Pooh, she's too stupid to be anything," Clara put in. "And her skin isn't pearls like yours is, Inez. Her face always looks dirty and yours always so sweet and clean."

"Then how am I different?" Susanita asked, knowing she was different, glad she was.

"Oh, your eyes. Nobody has green eyes. You can't have something nobody else has and not be different. And when Rosario de Deza died that left you the only one with golden hair. And you're—you are—oh, I don't know—"

"I am exactly like my *papá*'s grandmother and her name was Susana. *Papá* says she was a great beauty and Mexico City was at her feet. But Tía Dolores says she was always sad and wore black and was kind of cranky."

Inez nodded knowingly. "I'll bet anything the reason was because she loved someone very much and had to give him up. But I can't imagine dying of love for any of the boys we know, can you? I could for the *Americano* with the gray eyes. Imagine it, I mean. I don't know about the dying, just yet."

Clara gave the sign which meant "someone coming" and immediately they broke into laughter and chatter. Susanita said brightly, "Tía Dolores said I should have a dress of green velvet for the dance on the feast of Our Lady of Guadalupe, and *mamá* says she will ask if I may wear the emeralds and—"

"Never!" Inez shrieked, for the benefit of the ears outside the door. "If you wear the emeralds and green velvet not a man will look at the rest of us."

Then more whispers, when retreating footsteps told them they were alone again. Whispers of the new men, these tall, so grandly tall, *Americanos*, until there was the smell of coffee and a call from Paz that their elders were having *merienda*. And so, masks of laughter on their young faces, they curtsied at the dining room door.

Trouble rode the land. Trouble laughed at chaperones and barred windows, and traditions and customs. Trouble laid fingers on the old, and on the young.

The Mexican *caballero* wore his finery and walked in the plaza, and had to leap out of the way of horses ridden by the uniformed dragoons of the army of a conquering race. He went to the brothel to forget his worries and found his favorite on the lap of the invader, his gold in her hand. He lifted his voice in song and had it drowned by the strident tones of a language unmusical to his ears. He gathered in a carefree group to relay his jokes, and had Rangers strut past him—tall lean men towering above him and making him conscious of his small stature and paunchiness. He put on his best and went to his church.

"Even there, in our churches built to honor our God," Don Santiago complained, pacing the floor of the *sala* before his wife and his sister. "One of them has been going to Mass on Sundays. I would not have believed it, but Gabriel was there last Sunday and saw him and I do not doubt Gabriel's word. It seemed Gabriel came late, and while standing in the rear a moment he saw this soldier, before the little altar of San Antonio, which you know is near the door. I had thought all of them were Protestant or infidel, but Gabriel says this one knelt and crossed himself with the familiarity of habit, and his devotion and attention at Mass were not assumed. Others saw him too and someone told me later the man is a doctor at their camp across the river. They invade even our churches! I have been thinking of keeping you women—"

"Away from Sunday Mass because an *Americano* is there? What nonsense!" Doña Dolores's embroidery slipped to the floor and she did not reach to pick it up. "Do we—*we*—hide from inferiors? What did we come here for if not to go to church? You talk like both a coward and a fool, Santiago, shaking at a wind moving the leaves. Is he young and good-looking? I ask merely out of curiosity, of course."

His lip twisted scornfully. "Yes, your curiosity, my sister, I wonder at my patience with it. Gabriel says he is not so young but what has that to do with it? Eyes to see women have no age. To me their very gaze upon a woman is a desecration of them, and I will not have my daughters stared at by them. Padre Pierre is French and has not the proper distrust of the *Americanos*. These French priests are too liberal. They are too much the missionaries. I understand he is very firm that they be allowed in church, and he has even heard this one's confession. In the summer several soldiers came with him and the *padre* allowed them there also. It is an insult to our fathers in their graves."

"I do think," Doña María Petronilla ventured adroitly, keeping her face bent over the lace she was mending, "that Susanita's hair should be taken up on the head. She is no longer a child, and it draws attention to her this way."

"As if she could escape attention, Petronilla! You talk about me shaking at wind in the leaves and I ask you, Dolores, would an *Americano* see her golden beauty and not look again?"

"Let him. Then he can go back to his people and tell them what beautiful women we have. You wouldn't want them to see only women as homely as I and take that opinion home, would you?"

Don Santiago stamped a heel hard on the floor, annoyed that as always his sister got the best of an argument with him. Gabriel had said there was no harm in this one who went to Mass; he was middle-aged, unobtrusive, and walked with a cane, limping. Surely no girl would look at him except with the merest curiosity. "Yes, take her hair up, Petronilla," he told his wife. "I want you also to make her understand that I will seriously consider all proposals made to me for her. Do not mention this *Americano* and the girls will not look for him. Dress Angela's hair also and see that her *mantilla* lies loosely and becomingly. It will be our first Sunday and I wish everyone to look their best."

So he can think "these are my women," thought Doña Dolores. So he can thump his chest and lord it over his friends. Then quick tears sprang to her eyes as she bent to pick up the embroidery. Poor Santiago, who hurt himself so. Poor brother, who had never learned that a little tolerance was ease to many a heartache. Poor man, who acknowledged God as Master yet refused to stand below Him. "Poor Santiago," she said aloud when he left.

Doña María Petronilla did not answer.

In the rectory of the church Captain Devlin shook the hand of Padre Pierre and introduced the man with him, speaking in hesitant, none too good Spanish. "Lieutenant Warrener, Padre, of Virginia, a state not far from the capital of Washington. Robert Davis Warrener, to be exact."

"The family black sheep," the officer answered, offering a hand, speaking in quite good Spanish. "Not exactly booted out of the family mansion but not implored to return. The captain reported that you wished to see Major Fortesby, and he sent me to say he is sorry he cannot come and will be gratified if you will relay the message through me, inasmuch as it would be possible to do so."

"Yes, yes, that is quite all right and I am glad to meet you. Will you have chairs, please, while I get a glass of wine?" Padre Pierre left the rather bare office to resort to a trick he despised as being dishonorable but which he had found to have too many advantages to be scrupulous about it. His people were prone to bring their troubles to him and expect him to be a Solomon in solving them. This peephole in the wall frequently showed another side withheld from him, coming to their faces when he left them alone.

These invaders were something new to him as their faces were difficult to read, and a few minutes at the peephole was really a necessity to him. Devlin, the lame doctor, he knew well and liked. The stranger—hmmm, here was an *hidalgo* if ever he had seen one. The face was much too long and the mouth too large, neatly missing being handsome yet keeping the essence of it. Young, perhaps a little headstrong. The *padre* decided he might like him, at least he would not resent him. Not any more than he resented any of these men of an alien race who made his position so difficult. He smiled ruefully at himself that he should resent their courteous silence, took up a tray holding a wine bottle with a label of excellence and contents of inferiority, set two glasses upon it, and went back to the office. Ah, blue were the eyes of the newcomer, and clear and clean.

❧

He had thought to see them brown, to match the crinkly chestnut hair.

The priest himself was small, the full cassock hiding a wiry suppleness of body that could outride many a young horseman. At Mass, or under the cowl, the thin face would have been taken for ascetic instead of what it now revealed itself to be, that of a scholar and perpetual student. While his callers sipped wine he took a high-backed chair opposite them and told them:

"If you had not come but recently, lieutenant, you would know that the Rangers, last summer, and the soldiers of General Taylor—a fine man and we were friends—did nothing to make the people of Matamoros love them. It was a great relief when the old soldiers left and the new and more restrained ones arrived at Fort Brown. And more than a relief, I assure you, when the Rangers went and left less than a dozen of their numbers behind, fortunately too ill to get around. You know all these things, lieutenant?"

"Major Fortesby has not approved them, Father."

"So I understand. What I wished to impress upon the major was the necessity of prudence. It is the *rancheros*. He does not know about them nor do either of you. They are a compact group and rather provincial, if I may use the word, and they will not take kindly to the presence of the *gringos* here in this their town. I do not use the word *gringos* in a personal sense, I assure you, *señores*. However, the *rancheros* will talk much and do little and it is possible that, if friction can be avoided, they will go again with at least the sharp edge of their hatred blunted. Tell your major that I ask for peace, for these few months." He rose suddenly and threw out his hands in a gesture of futility. "I babble like a fool. Of what use is it to ask for peace?"

The lieutenant shrugged. "We have no jurisdiction whatever over the Rangers, sir, and I fear our friend the doctor here has cured most of them. Our men will behave well enough if the Mexicans do not provoke them. We all ask for peace, but these wild young bloods—"

"Yes, and I know several who bear watching." The *padre* sighed and sat down again. "It is a time of tension and only *El Señor Dios* knows what will happen. Tell me of yourself, lieutenant. I have a deep interest in these United States and hope some day to travel in them."

The talk was restrained at first until Warrener described the Virginia plantation and the life there. Black slaves! Padre Pierre did not like that and voiced his sentiments. "A man should be a slave only if he wishes it. Slavery as such does not exist here, but we have peonage which is almost as bad. If your nation is so progressive, why does it not free its slaves? Only freedom of the individual is progress."

❦

Water did not rise above its level, Devlin argued. There would be chaos if the blacks were freed unless they were sent back from where they came. Freedom—who then was free? Was anyone, ever? In argument and counterargument they forgot themselves and parted finally in an agreeable mood. The *padre* thanked them for coming but did not ask them to come again. They were aware of his thought, that it would be wisest to show no friendship to the enemies of the congregation of which he was in charge.

He watched them mount and ride across the plaza, their length of leg still incongruous to him. When they were out of sight, he closed the door, shaking his head. There would be some trouble this winter, perhaps even tragedy. He wished the *rancheros* had not come to town.

The two officers walked their horses through what seemed a deserted town, for *siesta* time was not yet over. Devlin grinned as he said, "I rather think *El Padre* wanted to say he hoped none of us would start trouble by looking at the girls now come to town. At least he had more on his mind than he gave voice to. Well, in my opinion, it's easier to win this war than it is to get even a good look at the girls. You, being young and having, therefore, an aura of romance about you, might have them maneuver to get a look, at least to see whether you might react to their charms, but I with my lame leg and advanced age get small attention. Except, of course, out of curiosity."

Warrener laughed. "The *papás* can feel safe as far as I am concerned. You know why I am down here. With both families and the lady herself determined I should marry sweet Mary-Belle, this seemed the only way out. No love affairs for me. Did I tell you Johnny White and I passed two girls some days ago? I thought all Mexicans were more or less dark, but this one had hair like fire and a skin like milk. Johnny mooned about her all the way back, but you know Johnny—he loves the ladies."

"And forgets them. Bob, I wish that parcel of Rangers was in Mexico, way, way down in Mexico. First they were too sick to either go with Hays or go home, and now that I got them well they won't go home, and Hays mistakenly told them to wait for orders here if they didn't go home. I wish Johnny would really fall in love with a Mexican girl, maybe he'd forget that his friend drew a black bean at Mier. The girl with the red hair — one of the high class, was she? *Mamá* and duenna and all?"[3]

"Yes indeed. Two very dumpy *mamás* who grew ten feet tall when they passed us, all of it outrage." Warrener chuckled at the memory of their faces. "Not that I blame them, understand. The one girl was just another girl, but the firehead would put my pretty sister in the background. They have stolen glances down to an art, doctor. With the *mamás* in front and the duenna behind them and maidenly reserve written all over them, they managed to get a good look at us. And somehow the redhead got one deep enough to tell Johnny she found him mighty good to look at too, and I am sure she was able to describe me rather accurately to her friends. My beauty did not make any impression, neither did my fine figure in its nice uniform and shiny buttons. The little dark one pulled up her nose at me, and the other one had eyes only for Johnny. They were new, doubtless some of these *rancheros'* daughters because we've seen all the regular residents."

"We have, and not a pretty one in the lot," Devlin sighed. "I'll watch for her in church Sunday. Why don't you come to church with me Sunday, Bob?"

The horses broke into a trot as the river and the familiar quarters of Fort Brown came into view. Warrener raised himself in the saddle to see whether the chaparral held lurking enemies and they reined in their horses. Orders were that no less than ten men should ride from the fort, but the officers had discovered that two commanded less notice and certainly aroused less hostility. Now and then someone threw a stone at them or called them a name from some safe hiding place, but in the main they rode unmolested. It was wisdom, however, to look over the chaparral. This was war, with wrongs and hatreds feeding upon each other, and ambush ever a probability.

"It would not be ethical," Warrener answered. "You profess the Catholic faith, and even if they resent your being in church, they admire your devotion and feel some kinship. The natives have accepted your presence, and the newcomers will also, in time. I am Episcopalian and that puts me close, but still—don't you see it would be like spying on people who have every right to be alone? A church isn't a theater. But I'll wait for you outside, if you want me to."

The doctor lifted an eyebrow as they trotted on. "My old Aunt Jane!" he thought. "A gentleman is in our midst. Our *hidalgos* here wouldn't believe it, I can scarcely believe it myself. Ethics, by all that's holy, in this place!" Aloud he said, "Do you see what I see, coming down the river? Must be the sons of the wealthy *rancheros*, by the look of the horses and all the silver and fitted buckskin suits and fancy hats. We'll about meet on the bank. Into the water, faithful steed."

The horses splashed into the shallow water of the sandy ford and would have met the riders at the opposite bank. But when the Americans were about twenty feet from shore, two of the riders spurred their horses into the water, throwing a head of spray before them and at the officers. It was deliberately, insultingly done. As they passed each other the faces of Warrener and one of the Mexicans were close, and their eyes clashed like sword blades. There was such an amused superciliousness on the face of the offender that Warrener's hand shot out to jerk him from his horse and throw him in the stream. Captain Devlin reached over in time to strike his companion's arm down, remarking in Spanish and loud enough for all to hear.

"Wait until they are weaned, lieutenant, I beg of you. We do not fight children and ill-mannered louts."

They rode on, their horses shaking their heads free of water. Six of the seven remaining riders came on and passed the officers quietly. The last one stayed on the bank, sheer curiosity in the searching look he gave the Americans. Devlin slowed to return it in kind, smiled, and stopped. He liked the long sensitive face, the arched eyebrows, the deep brown eyes that reminded him of one of El Greco's portraits. Surely this lad was no rancher. He looked like a poet or an artist should look—and so seldom did. And on the striking black-maned dun pony, sitting the elaborately trimmed saddle with the ease of long familiarity with it, he made a picture which thrilled Devlin through and through. He was about to speak to him when an insolent voice called, "Come on, Luis Gonzaga, can't you find anything better to look at than a *gringo*'s face?"

A blush suffused the sensitive face as he answered, "I'm coming, Alvaro." He gave Devlin a last glance after he turned, then spurred the dun into the water.

Later in the evening, when warming themselves by the fire the soldiers had built in the compound, Devlin remarked casually, "I hope I meet that boy again under more pleasant circumstances. I like him. Rather more than merely like him."

"I can't say the same about the other one," Warrener answered. "Unless it would be to slap his face. Yes, I would like to meet him again and teach him a few manners."

Devlin smiled. "No doubt you will. I hope it's for all our good, but I have my doubts. Don't let it bother you, Bob, and remember what the *padre* said."

A grunt which meant nothing, or could mean anything was his answer.

Chapter 5

It was night. A broken moon moved above the high hedge of the chaparral, flung ghostly light over the flat-topped stone house, and peered under the portal at the figure moving restlessly up and down its length. "Have the accursed Rangers got them?" he muttered. "Have they been stopped at the river, what has happened that they are so slow in coming?" There was no wind, and the silence of the night was so complete that the least sound would have been audible even at a distance. He had been waiting two hours, and heard only the whispering movement of wild creatures through the brush. He would wait another hour, then—ah, surely that was hoof against stone, at last. Yes, dark spots were looming in the lanes of light between the huisache trees beyond the chaparral, visible through a gap in the hedge. The riders came close, dismounted under trees and were still.

The man leaned over a branch upon which lay flint and steel, a tiny mound of lint, and a candle. He struck spark to the lint, lit the candle from the flame, and protected it with a copper dome slit on one side to allow for air. Presently a spark shone from the trees, was moved in one large and one small cross, to which he replied by lifting the dome from the candle and forming three small crosses.

"In the name of God and country," called one of the riders, and they all came close.

The host embraced them. "Gabriel del Lago, Ramón de los Olivares, José Antonio Carbajal. May the blessings of the newcomer and the welcome of the Robles house be yours. You come alone? Where are the others?"

"We left in small groups and singly, taking different paths. One cannot be too careful these days as you know. We heard today that a new bandit gang of our own people is not far away and with the *gringo* renegades everywhere we took no chances. Here comes—that is Don Santiago de Mendoza y Soría and his son."

Light signaled five times more before the expected sixteen men were ushered around the long table in the dining room of the house, and the time was close to midnight. The room was so large that the candles on the table were inadequate to light all of it, and gloom crouched like a menace in the corners. The stern faces and the silence of the men added to the ominous air, and soon boots were tapped nervously on the floor. A pack of naipes lay on the hand-hewn mesquite table, and when the last man was seated, the host shuffled and threw them face down on the center of the table saying, "Who draws the high card presides, though he may step back for the next man if he wishes. I beg to be excused."

Don Santiago had the high card, and there were nods of approval as he walked to the head of the table. The rest seated themselves on benches and waited for him to speak. He looked at the familiar faces and renewed affection for them welled in his heart. Two of the faces were bearded and aged, three had drooping gray mustaches, the rest were clean-shaven—an ordeal emanating from pride in their fine skins which differentiated them from the *mestizo* of mixed Spanish and Indian blood. Don Santiago thought of that pride now as he looked at the smooth cheeks, and he found it good. That they were on edge, keyed high, waiting but a chance to give their emotions full sway, he found not so good. He was remembering his resolve made under the palm tree, that his hatred would have dignity.

He ran a hand over his buckskin jacket. "*Amigos*," he began, "I note that you too have all come in the dress of the *ranchero* and not in the finery of the *hidalgo*. It is as such that we are here tonight, binding ourselves together, as our ancestors gathered in Mexico a century ago to bind themselves together for the move to the new land to the north, this our Texas. But where they were applauded and came as conquerors of wilderness we sneak here as felons, as if we were guilty of a crime. We are considered undesirable foreigners in this land which was won by the sweat and blood of those brave men and held against the Indians for a hundred years. It was theirs by right of royal grants, ours by right of inheritance.

"*Amigos*, we have come to discuss ways to save this land. Yet first we must find ways to preserve our self-respect, to strengthen our morale, to keep the banner of our pride floating high. What say you, friends and neighbors?"

From the foot of the table came harsh sobbing as a white-haired man rose and rested palms on the table to steady himself. "My son," he cried, "my only one, the last of our line, the defender of his aged parents, was shot like a dog because he refused the *gringos* the cattle they demanded. There were six of them—six huge men and my son alone, and they shot him dead. May the curse of an aged, half-blind father—of me, Juan de Cisneros, be forever upon them!"

"What say I?" Gray-bearded, wrinkled Gáspar de la Guerra shook clenched hands at unseen adversaries. "They confiscated my land, my horses, cattle, and sheep, because I am a Mexican. And now I am little more than a beggar in the country where the king of Spain deeded land to the Guerras. You ask, what say I—need anyone ask what I say?"

"Or I!" A tall, thin man with aristocratic features etched to a delicate fineness pounded the table with a fist. "The *gringos* forced me at the point of a pistol to sell my racehorses, and when I demanded my money, the leader of them struck me on the face with a quirt. 'This is good pay for a Mexican,' he jeered, and his friends laughed. Struck me on the face—me, Don Pablo de los Oliveros! Whose great-grandfather was knighted by the king of Spain, whose grandfather surveyed this territory for his Most Catholic Majesty, whose father was honored by the viceroy Revilla Gigedo." He lifted a hand and his voice dropped from its high pitch of indignation to one of deep solemnity. "I swear eternal vengeance on them and their descendants. I swear war to the death! Cursed be the Oliveros who befriends them, may the eyes who look on them without scorn be plucked out, may the heart of those who love them be devoured by wolves, may the mind of those who think well of them become soft, may . . . ah . . . ahhh. . . ." Overcome with the intensity of his emotions he sank to his seat, sobbing with a wretchedness painful to hear.

Embarrassment kept silence for a time. None had heard the door open while Don Santiago was speaking, nor did they now see the hooded figure standing in the shadows. They were ill at ease, none knowing what to say.

Alvaro leaped to his feet and shouted: "Death to the *gringo!* Why do we wait? Why do we gather and talk like women when we should be stalking and killing them?"

Before Don Santiago, shocked by his son's action, could intervene, there was an uproar. "He is right, we should be after them" . . . "I say death" . . . "Why do we take their insults" . . . they pounded on the table and shouted, their voices overlapping into wild discordancy.

The cloaked figure came from the shadows to the head of the table and stood beside Don Santiago, pushing the hood from his head and opening his cloak. He stood there waiting.

"Padre Pierre!" Don Santiago cried, and the name was passed down the table. It was like a rod striking each one into silence, and the host, Señor Robles, came up quickly to explain: "Miguel my watchman told me that Padre Pierre was outside and naturally I opened the door. We are glad you are here, *Padre*." Adding quickly, aware of the insincerity in his voice, "certainly we are glad, and honored."

The priest smiled as he said, "An uninvited guest is seldom welcome and I apologize for intruding. However, when I heard of this meeting I felt it my duty to come, on a most treacherous beast who threw me twice. Don Santiago, if I have your permission to usurp your place for a little while—"

Don Santiago, glad to have another take charge after the tumult, stepped aside with a slight bow. "It is my privilege, *Padre*, and I am honored thereby."

"Thank you." The priest stepped forward, sternness hardening his naturally mobile features. He pointed a finger and said sharply, "Alvaro, sit down and be quiet; you talk like both a child and a fool, and I am ashamed of you, as I know your father is ashamed. All of you—is this a meeting to whip up your emotions? Let me first try to bring you sanity, calm—"

"Sanity, calm!" Another newcomer left the shadows and walked to the foot of the table beside Gáspar de la Guerra. His eyes flashed over the assemblage. "*Señores*, I also am an uninvited guest. I am a Spaniard, a merchant whom you all know, and your cause is mine also." He flung a hand to the priest. "The *Padre* can speak of calm, he who has no daughter! *Señores*, my beautiful Rosa, my little Rose, has been betrayed by one of these barbarians. I say, death to them all!" He ripped a dagger from his belt and threw it on the table so the point stuck in the wood. It quivered there, a diamond in the handle rainbowing facets of color in the circle of light from the iron candelabra. "I tore his heart open with that. And with these," he stretched long thin fingers before them, flexing them into his palm, "with these I shall strangle her child the minute it is born. Now what have you to say, Padre Pierre?"

The priest watched the diamond dancing in beauty in the quivering dagger. Could he tell this man to raise a bastard whose father had been, to him, the epitome of all that is evil? He wondered what he would have done had he been the father of that daughter? But he answered, levelly, "Was there no woman ever betrayed before the *Americanos* came? Were never any bastards born? Did you give him the chance to speak of marriage? They might have been happy together. Vengeance is mine, said the Lord—it is not your right, nor mine. Do you set yourself above God? Peace, my children. I beg of you, have peace. True, many injustices have visited you, war roils about us. I know you are thinking that I am French and so cannot feel as you do, but I can indeed. It is only that I have learned that one does not reason with the emotions, and that is what I am trying to impress upon you. There are laws, courts—"

"Where, *Padre?*" Don José Carbajal asked. "What laws are there, now that Texas gave up its independence? What laws are there for us from a nebulous stranger who is president of the United States? *Our* protector now, so we are told. I do not recall that any of us who built this wilderness were asked our wishes regarding this joining with their states. Laws, courts, Padre Pierre?"

The priest turned to Don Santiago. "Your place, *señor.* I do not ask that my cloth shall give me special privileges."

There were cries of "No, no," and Don Santiago bowed courteously. "I fear we need a balance wheel, *Padre,*" he said, "and you know more about these intruders than we do. It is true that nothing can be gained when emotion rules." He turned to the men to say, "I apologize for my son, *señores.*"

Padre Pierre inclined his head. "I thank you, Don Santiago, I thank all of you. It must be remembered, my friends, that these are troublous days for everyone. There has not yet been an adjustment to the laws of the union, and many are flouting the laws of the republic, excusing themselves that the laws no longer hold. There is strife among the *Americanos*, one holding this is law, another that, and the lawless take advantage of it. You, Don Gáspar, I will myself put in a protest against the stealing of your land to the proper authorities. There must be something you can do if you use your head. You, Don Pablo, the men who stole your racehorses were doubtless renegades and in ill repute. The Rangers will go after them and bring them to justice and—"

"Rangers, you speak of those devils?" . . . "You ask *us* to ask *them* for a favor or for justice?" The *Padre* had set fire to explosive powder when he mentioned the hated Rangers, and fifteen minutes passed before the blaze subsided.

He held up a restraining hand. "You see, my children? You think with your hearts and your passions, these *Americanos* think with their heads. Think, now, with *your* heads, and ask yourselves what you can gain by

53

opposing them. True, they are strong, powerful, fearless, and seem to have unlimited wealth, but most of them lack what we have: dignity, self-respect, pride, nobility, traditions, an old and sound religion. We—"

"Are you asking that we fold our hands and sit, among our traditions, like prayer-mumbling grandmothers?"

Padre Pierre scanned their faces. Long faces, hawk-nosed, browned, some of them gashed with deep lines, all of them molded in a pride fierce and profound. One topped with blond hair, the others black, graying, white. There was one other young man besides Alvaro, already stamped with a reckless daring that boded no good—Juan Nepomuceno Cortina. The priest decided to warn Don Santiago later against this friendship of his son and was about to ask what the slovenly unshaven Cortina was doing here when the young man pounded the table and said loudly, "They call the Río Bravo—or Río Grande, as they name it—the boundary. I myself shall do what I can to color the big river red—with their blood."

Squatty, red-headed, dirty, his appearance helped make his words repulsive rather than inflammatory. But Señor Robles, the host, put in quickly, "May we not expect a miracle, *Padre?* Just as our Blessed Mother descended to console the Indians at Tepeyac, may she not help us again? After all, God is Catholic."

The priest forebore to smile at this last naiveté and explained, "God is universal, not limited to us. As for miracles, they do not occur unless the heart is clean and then must be in accordance with God's Divine Plan. We see only the underside of His weaving, my friends, not the upper side that is before His eyes. I have a plan, and I ask that it be given careful thought." (And Thou, Lord, he prayed silently, open their minds so they will understand.) "You have your beautiful homes filled with many treasures; ordered households where courtesy reigns; food of the best, served graciously. Our dances and *fiestas* are entertaining and ruled by the charm and beauty of your women. Your clothes are of the finest and in good taste pleasing to the eye. I say this: Seek the *Americano* officials who have influence and invite them to your homes and entertainments. Show them that we have much to give them in culture, that we are not the ignorant people they take us to be, that to remain as we are will neither harm nor be a disgrace to their union of states. They are far too well acquainted with the lowest of the Mexicans and not at all with the best. It has seemed to me that what is done now will have a great influence upon the future. It is in your hands, *señores*. A bending now, a co-operation with the government which is ours no matter how much we may resent its being thrust upon us. A building of friendship with them. Wait, wait, until I am through with what I have to say. Calm yourself, *Señor de Deza*." He sighed, pushed both palms toward them for quiet. "I have met the commander of the fort, Major Fortesby, and I find him a fair and just man, if somewhat negative. You all have seen Captain Devlin in church, he is a doctor and a man of education and courtesy. I have been visited by the young lieutenant who, I presume, would represent his superior socially, and I found him a gentleman whom—"

"While their General Taylor is in Mexico fighting our people, smashing into and ruining our beautiful Monterrey," interrupted Domingo Viscaya, laughing harshly. He picked up the cards and let them fall and scatter like leaves over the table. "With all respect to you, Padre Pierre, but I trust you were not *honored* by this visit."

It was of small use to go on, the priest knew, but again he held up a hand for silence to finish what he had to say. The stir of emotions seemed to swirl bodily about him as if he were the center of an eddy, slapping against him. He could feel with them, remembering his first resentment and dislike of the invaders who had, all too often, treated the Mexican shamefully. He too had been insulted, and the wounds not yet completely healed. But he could not let them know that, had to let them think that his sympathy emanated from his position as spiritual advisor. He had to be the priest more than the man now regardless of what criticism it might bring, and speak from the head and not the heart. He ignored the interruption and went on.

"There are men here to restore order, and if we align ourselves with them, those who stole from us will be punished. General Taylor was disposed to peace and justice, and there are many others equally disposed. Always remember, my friends, that we are a conquered people and pride will need to suffer. You hate the Rangers, and it is true that you had reason to be incensed at them, but remember that they were met with enmity by you. Remember that, for it is an important factor. Travel for you has been safer because of them; they have driven away the Indians again and again. Consider this—when the Rangers saved you the plundering of a dozen cows by Indians, you refused them even one for food. Didn't you? Not one of you ever offered them anything but hatred, what should they show you in return? I think it of great importance that you learn the language of the *Am*—"

Jeers rained on him as they forgot his cloth in the audacity of this statement. "Learn it." one shouted, "Learn it when the tongue refuses it, and the sound of it is torture to the ears!"

Padre Pierre folded his arms and waited calmly until the commotion subsided, then continued, "They learn ours, and with amazing facility. They know what they are saying and have the advantage of us because we do not understand them. The man who needs an interpreter has already lost half the argument before it is begun. Cannot you see?" He held out imploring hands, newly aflame with the ideas which he was convinced were sound. "Invite them, offer them friendship, let them see our worth. Put our problems before them and ask their help. Show that it is your wish to be good *Americanos*, though the name was forced upon you."

"*¡Americano!* Rather would I cut off my right hand!"

"So?" the priest's eyes raked over Don Santiago, the speaker. "What then has Mexico done for you? She gave your fathers' land that was worthless to her, beset as it was with marauding Indians, and let you use your own money to build the towns and missions. 'Royal grants' sounds very fine, be assured you would have received not a foot of ground had it been worth anything to Spain or the viceroy. The land's worth was in the taxes the Mexican government could collect after you had built your ranches. It was because of greed for more taxes to bolster a rotten, tottering regime that she betrayed you by inviting American colonists into Texas, and gave them huge tracts of land. *Gave* it, *señores*. When was it? Twenty-five years or so ago.

"Now listen, all of you. After the Americans Mexico had invited into Texas had built their homes on the land given them, they were ordered out again—so that this improved land could be given again and a high tax charged upon it. The Americans did not go. Would you have done so, *señores?* Then Mexico declared war upon them and destroyed all the good will which had been built. There was good will, my friends.

"Cared Santa Anna for anything but his won glory and aggrandizement? Of a certainty he did us no good, and can you blame the *Americanos* if they believe that no Mexican honors his word? I ask again—you, Don Santiago, all the rest of you, what has Mexico then done for you? Might you not be better off, in the end, with a new government? A yoke can be padded until it no longer galls, or is lifted."

"Never!" . . . "Consort with them, we?" . . . "Throw away our pride" . . . Words were like hailstones against walls, echoing back from them in confusion, pouring over the priest. Only one, a small man named

Hermilio Márquez, still young, moved to the head of the table. "There is some truth in what Padre Pierre says," he shouted, pounding a fist on the table for attention. "At least we would do well to discuss it. Our good padre talks sense. Listen, *señores*—" But there was no listening, and they cast, each one, his stormy protest into the confusion of sound. Over all rode the high, excited young voices of Alvaro and Juan Cortina.

"Drench the land with their blood," screamed Cortina, waving a short sword. "Who will lead us? We can form our own band to cut them down, who will lead us?"

"Yes, who will lead us?" screamed Alvaro in return.

Don Santiago rapped for silence. "There will be none of that," he ordered sharply. "Juan Cortina, you were not invited here, and it is not your place to say even a word. You make it difficult for us to remember that your mother is a lady of the highest blood. Alvaro, I am far from proud of you, and I order you to keep your place. Certainly none of us are acting like the proud *hidalgos* we claim to be." He turned to his host. "Don Juan, you spoke of food being prepared. Perhaps if we eat now and plan for another meeting later it will be better for us all." He walked to where he could reach the dagger, took it from the wood, and handed it to the merchant without comment. Inclining his head courteously to Padre Pierre he said, "I think all my friends join me in thanking you for coming here, Padre. I agree with Señor Márquez that there is much truth in what you say, but, not being one of us, you cannot quite understand how sacred our traditions are."

Padre Pierre murmured a soft, "eyes to see and see not, ears to hear and hear not," nodded to Don Santiago, and pointed to Cortina. "You, Juan, will ride home with me now, as punishment for your wild talk. *Señores*, I bid you goodnight." And with the unwilling young man in his wake he left the room.

Servants came and laid a cloth, one brought a tray of wine. There was the soothing odor of food, of strong black coffee.

The eastern sky was paling when the first group headed for the river and home. The sun was a yellow ball peeping over the tops of the huisache trees when the last two guests of the night pressed their host's hand in farewell.

Trouble. Trouble danced along the Río Grande. Trouble played on old prides and on young enthusiasms with practiced fingers.

Trouble choked sanity, and trampled it in the fine brown dust of Texas.

Chapter 6

❧

Their first Sunday in town. And going to Mass dressed in their best was a ritual in itself to the Mendoza y Soría. The household rose early, and Doña Petronilla hurried to the girls' room to fix their hair. Bottled up tight inside her she had a passion for curls, and the night before, to Susanita's delight and Angela's tearful protest, she had wet their hair and rolled strands tightly on pieces of linen. "Let the discomfort of sleeping on them be your penance, Angela," she said shortly. Now she combed out the nubbins and combed them again over her fingers, as she had done when they were small. Angela's heavy hair had not taken well to the distortion of its smoothness, so her mother brought the natural dips further forward over the temples, pinned the two thick curls back of each ear and knotted the rest flat against the head at the neck. It was just the coiffure for Angela, for it left her dignity but added sweetness to it. The girl accepted it obediently, quickly stifled a small pleasure when she looked in the mirror, and hurried away to breakfast.

Susanita's fine tresses rioted like laughing imps. Her mother pinned them low, shook her head at the childish effect, then pinned them high. The curls caressed her neck and clustered over the ears, small tendrils danced on her forehead—and altogether, Susanita looked very much like an artful, lovely coquette. It was not the hairdress fashionable for marriageable girls, and it would single her out the more. By next Sunday most of the girls would have curls also, copying, but today she alone would. María Petronilla's heart knew fresh foreboding at the thought that someone, this morning, would fall deeply and completely in love with her, someone not approved of by her father. For a moment she considered wetting the curls and twisting the hair into a knot. No, it would be like killing something lovely, she could not do it. What would come could not be stemmed by her, nor would a curl matter in the end. She kissed her baby on the smooth, creamy cheek.

"Be good, *hijita*. Pray to Our Lady for your happiness. Pray especially for it today."

"Why, *mamá*, I have always been happy, I am happy."

The mother left the room quickly, to hide her tears. Worry was fresh again, over this, her beautiful, laughing baby. Why tell her that her girlhood would soon be gone, that before another year was past she would be married to a man chosen by her father regardless of her wishes. Let her have today.

When she saw Susanita later ready for church, she knew that the plain dress of black wool trimmed only with a white band at the throat and tiny satin buttons on the bodice, which she herself had laid out for her, had only enhanced her loveliness. One looked, now, not at the dress but all the more at the wearer of it. When Angela came Doña María Petronilla put a hand over her heart, as if to still the pain there. Angela had been given a dark red merino dress which Susanita had not liked and never worn, and it transformed her. The flared collar put color in the white cheeks, and the flared strips encircling the skirt to the belt gave her an air of grace so new that it surprised the family. The white lace *mantilla* fell softly over the smooth high forehead, the long single curls lay gently on each shoulder.

Angela, carrying her finery without vanity, wearing this obedience to her father's wishes with dignity, had a new and startling charm.

"No, no," Doña Petronilla told herself, a little wildly. "No, I do not like it, I wish she were back in her nun's garb. Something will come of this and it will not be good. O thou, her patron, Blessed Mother Mary, Queen of the Angels, look after my Angela."

Don Santiago approved of the curls, approved of Angela. Approved even of Luis Gonzaga, a handsome stripling in his braid and silver-trimmed suit of black velveteen. He bowed gallantly to the stiff imperiousness of Doña Dolores as she swept onto the portal over the street door; his wife took his arm, and they moved to the coach waiting in shiny black splendor, Juan Bautista rigid with pride on the box. Two horses replaced the white mules, their brushed black hides a gleaming background for the silver trappings of the harness. It was only a short distance to the church, but that did not matter; had they lived next door to it the coach would have been used. The *hidalgo* and his family drove to church, and as grandly as possible.

Doña María Petronilla did not ask for Alvaro. He would doubtless be at church with a group of young men as indulged and unrestrained as he.

Alvaro—what would become of her firstborn? Where would his uncurbed passions, his supercilious conceit, lead him?

At the church door they formed in procession. The girls first, eyes modestly downcast, then Doña Dolores, grandly decorous, with a hand on the arm of Luis Gonzaga. Last came Don Santiago, moving in the ego of his superior wealth and position and not even conscious of the wife by his side. They walked slowly, so that the servants and *peons* crouched on the floor from the front pews (for the *hidalgo*) to the door could see them in detail. They had come early to see their own and their fellow-servants' masters in all their pomp, and it would have been most ungentlemanly to hurry or walk in a disordered group.

Susanita got but a glimpse of the sun-browned face and the thin dark-blond hair of the *Americano* standing inside the door, but it was enough to keep her excited all during the service. Dutifully she knelt and stood and sat, simulating deep interest in the long sermon. If only she would get a close look at him after service, she so wanted to see an *Americano*. Our father who art in heaven—*papá* says they are barbarians—Thy kingdom come—I would like to see a barbarian—I wonder where it will show on him—as we forgive those—he is so tall—.

Holding on to Luis Gonzaga's hand, her mother beside her, she did not see him until they were outside. He had his back to them, quite a broad obscuring back, and he was moving slowly to the plaza. Slowly, because he was leaning on a cane. As Susanita came behind him, partly by adroit maneuvering and partly by the press of the people, she heard him say, "Ah, Bob, glad you're here. The leg is giving me the devil." It was the first English she had heard, and the excitement of it flushed her cheeks a delicate pink and put a sparkle in her wide eyes. Then the broad back moved aside. Just a step, but far enough to bring his waiting friend face to face with Susanita de Mendoza y Soría.

Eyes as blue as the still heaven above met eyes green as a summer sea. And the sun halted a moment. The world waited. The crowd melted away and disappeared and left only a vast silence wherein lived only these two.

Once to every man. Once to every woman.

If God is kind—.

Luis Gonzaga looked at the stranger and saw the ecstasy on the long fine face—as if the gates of heaven had opened and shown him a glory beyond man's ken. Luis looked at Susanita and felt faint and sick at the rapture on hers. And he almost spoke his thought aloud, "May *El Señor Dios* have mercy on us all."

"Come, *hermanita*," he said softly. He pulled her away. Laughing and talking to give her time to recover, maneuvering to stand between her and the tall stranger and break his entranced gaze on the golden curls beneath the lace *mantilla*, so that none but he would know.

One other knew. Doña María Petronilla, her nerves drawn taut by her worries, her mother instinct to the fore this day, was like a lyre set in a window for the winds to play upon. She had seen the quick stillness of the two bodies, the locking of eyes. She had felt the hush of breath, had been stunned by the profundity of emotion that enwrapped them.

When the coach stopped, she hurried into the house, thankful that no one had noticed her perturbation. It was characteristic of her that she kept thinking, "Poor Susanita. My poor Santiago." Not once "Poor me." Yet knowing that she would not turn against her child, knowing also that she was incapable of turning against her husband.

Susanita hurried to her room, refusing the help of Paz in changing from the too warm wool to one of gray silk patterned with flowers. She stood for a long time in front of the mirror in the large gilt frame, not seeing the reflection of herself in chemise of linen and petticoat elaborate with eyelet trimmed ruffles. "I love him," she whispered. "It seems as if I have always loved him and was only waiting for him. That is why I haven't wanted marriage nor cared for anyone, because he was waiting for me and I was waiting for him."

She looked into the mirror, and the face did not smile happily at her as of old. And she knew, without regret, that the child was gone. She slipped the gray dress over her head and buttoned it carefully. It was strange that she should be calm. She sat by the window with folded hands, glad of this beautiful peace within her which glowed so tenderly. Later there would be tumult and anguish, but now this perfect peace and sweet joy was hers to hold.

Angela came to announce that chocolate was ready, and impulsively went to Susanita and kissed her. Why, she wondered, did the curls and pretty dress seem right for her sister and were not the badge of vanity, yet she would feel sinful because she had noticed that the brown dress she was wearing matched her eyes. Why didn't it seem right to her?

"You are so lovely, little sister."

"So are you, Angela. Sit down a minute, *papá* will think I am still primping and he will only scold a little. Tell me, what did Sister Gertrudis say when you told her what *papá* ordered you to do?"

Angela sat on the sofa, happy that the old tenderness between them was coming alive again. She did not know that Susanita wanted a return to reality and was using this as a means. Susanita, she thought, did look exceptionally lovely this morning, but she was too engrossed in her own problem to ask the cause or remark about it. "Why," she sighed, "her answer was very peculiar. She said all things were God's plan if we did not get stubborn and try to force Him from His plans. She said I already had a jewel in my spiritual crown for obeying *papá*. Padre Pierre had forbidden me to make any vows in the past because he said it was not for a girl to direct her life when young, in these times. So, not being bound, Mother said it was most proper to join in the social life to which I was born if *papá* ordered it. She said my conscience was to be my staff and guide."

"That does not seem peculiar to me." Susanita rubbed her flushing cheeks, remarking that it seemed a bit warm. "What else was there for her to say, or for you to do?"

"Oh, that is not the peculiar part. Then Mother Gertrudis said I might have a more important role to play in life. She said I had a capacity for great things and that God had given me a profound ¹ and strength of faith—that is the way she said it—for perhaps a greater purpose than bringing it into the convent. She said I should watch for it and pray that I would know it when it came." Angela rose and moved to the door. "I have tried to humble myself and always remember that I am dust and shall return to dust. The good Mother disturbed me more than she knew."

As if, Susanita thought as they went to the dining room, you know anything about being disturbed, my Angela.

It was not a cheerful breakfast. Don Santiago was incensed anew at the presence of an invader in their church "—and an infidel waiting for him outside, it is an outrage. I myself shall go to the *padre* and have it stopped." He pulled angrily at an ear as his eyes swept their faces for approval. "Why, Susanita was close to them both, and I consider it an insult to have my daughter stared at by one of them. *Hijita*, were his insolent eyes on you?"

The test was here. Susanita braced herself and commanded all her forces of dissimulation and control. Unless *papá* could see the way her heart was flailing her breast—no, her dress was not moving. It lay quite smoothly, as if there were not even a heart under it. She felt the fire in her cheeks and hoped prayerfully that it would be taken for modest confusion at the thought of a stranger staring insolently at her. She kept eyes on her chocolate, lest the light in them betray her and commanded her voice to be steady and calm, her conscience not too stern.

"The lame man was ahead of me and I did not see his face, nor did I try to see it, *papá*. He had so very broad a back, it was like a wall, and there were so many people. Was there—another one?"

Luis Gonzaga, confused and shocked at what he knew, marveled at her clever evasion. He deliberately closed his throat and swallowed chocolate so that, choking and coughing, he had to leave the table. He would not betray his beloved sister by as much as a look. Doña María Petronilla closed her eyes. Only a woman, she thought, could have answered so. The child is gone. And she is in love; I wonder that not even Dolores sees the radiance of her. It is my secret and I shall not tell. "Mother of Perpetual Help," she whispered, "help me keep it secret, help me be strong."

"I believe she is lying," Alvaro said. "Every girl there saw him and stretched their necks like so many cranes. It isn't any of the suitors for their hands, their old friends and future husbands, who will be whispered about today by the girls. It will be the *gringo*, not us."

"Jealous?" Luis Gonzaga came back to the table and grasped this opportunity to turn attention away from his sister. "Confess it, Alvaro, you were jealous that the necks were not all stretched to see *you*, and whisper about *you* today."

"Who then was it?" asked Doña Dolores. "I was looking for our cousin Teresa, and I did not see anyone besides the lame one. He is very tall. What makes them so tall, Alvaro?"

"Probably the Evil One, *Tía*. They look as if their man's body had been taken and stretched out of its proportions, they look ugly to me. The one who waited in the plaza is a lieutenant in charge of the miserable camp across the river with its handful of soldiers too incompetent and cowardly to be fighting in Mexico. A very poor command, I would say." He flushed when he caught his brother's smile, knowing he was thinking of the humiliating episode at the river, and changed the subject: "I cannot understand how they have gained the good will of Padre Pierre, can you, *papá*? It is a pity that our spiritual advisor is a *gringo* lover."

"Oh no, Alvaro!" Angela shook her head. "It is wicked to speak slightingly of our *padre*. They must love all of God's creatures, else how could they be God-loving themselves? And you should not use the word *gringo*,

Alvaro, really you should not. It is a word of scorn and we should have only charity for them."

"Hmmm, I should have liked to have seen him," Doña Dolores commented calmly, taking one of the *polvorones* from a plate of delicate white china. "Whatever we may personally feel, it is the padre's duty to preach the gospels and the commandments. We do not go to church to have our anger stirred and ruin the Sunday for visiting and lovemaking for the young. We go for—um—spiritual flowers for the soul. What is his name, Alvaro? Is he handsome?"

"Anyone would think you were looking for a husband at your age," Don Santiago sneered. "A tall, handsome young *gringo*—ha!" he laughed uproariously, slapping a knee in mirth at the picture of the staid, homely, middle-aged widow with such a man. With, in fact, any man at all.

Susanita sipped chocolate daintily. How nice everything was coming out. Now she knew who *he* was and she would find out his name also. She hoped she was looking a trifle bored.

"Sometimes," Doña Dolores answered evenly, joyfully returning the jibe, "I feel certain that the indecency of a second marriage would be of small account when weighed with the position of subservience I must of necessity hold in your household, Santiago my brother. At the moment I can imagine that even an *Americano* husband would be less insulting to me. I hear that they make very indulgent husbands." She laughed at the rage gathering in her brother's face and reached to tap him on the shoulder, to remind him that an explosion on his part would be a concession of victory to her. He kept silent and Alvaro answered her question.

"The name is Roberto, and Warrener." He pronounced it *Vah-re-no*. "In their bastard language, the full name is Robert Davis Warrener. As we would say Roberto Vahreno y Davis, it seems they put the mother's name in the middle if they use it at all and do not separate it as we do. The lame one's name is Carl Devlin, from some place they call Baltimore. I think that *papá* is right about forbidding—"

"Enough, Alvaro." Doña María Petronilla asserted a seldom used authority. "This is Sunday and there will be no more talk of strife or ill will. Better for you to think of marriage, which has been put off too long. Now is a most auspicious time." She did not explain why but everyone knew. Alvaro was, this winter, the most eligible bachelor in town. It was almost certain that the parents of any girl he chose would give their consent. The eldest son of a man of wealth and position, good looking and personable, masterful, with the sowing of wild oats considered the proper thing in a young man, the best dancer, wearing the finest clothes with an enviable dash, the favorite of his father—yes indeed, Alvaro could choose. Many a girl had slanted eyes invitingly, many a *mamá* beamed.

"Yes, *mamá*," he answered, smirking with vanity. "The trouble is that there are so many lovely ones and too many ripe for the picking. A man is entitled to a certain amount of doubts and fears. Too many roses dropped from windows takes the rareness from them."

Luis Gonzaga laughed. "A minute ago he was telling us that all the girls' eyes followed the *Americano*. Are you certain you are not overestimating your charms, Juan Tenorio? Roses have thorns too, and not all ripe fruit is loose on the stem, *hermano mío*."

Susanita asked to be excused to feed the birds and quickly fled before the conversation could take a personal turn. The patio was serene and mistily cool, sweet with the scent of jasmine. She stood for awhile, dreams as hazy as the mist and delightful as the blossoms lifting her away into the land that has neither floor nor ceiling nor boundary—the unforgettable heaven of first love.

The pleading coo of a caged dove finally brought her to earth. Reaching through the bars, she stroked the silky gray feathers, murmuring, "*Pobrecita*, how sad you must be. They have taken you from your mate and put you in prison, but I will comfort you. Come kiss me, *mi palomita*." She put her lips to the bars and the bird pecked the red lips, then flung itself against the wicker and beat wings frantically against the bars. Tears ran down Susanita's cheeks as she whispered, "I am also imprisoned. Not in a cage like yours but in one of love from which I will never be free." Impulsively she reached inside and took the bird in her hands. "I shall set you free so you can join the mate who has been waiting for you. Go, fly over the soldier camp and tell him you have come from me."

The bird stretched its wings, fluttered uncertainly, then shot like an arrow through the mist and away.

Susanita debated whether to lie and say the door was open or tell the truth, a short debate for her frank nature. Doña Dolores, to whom the bird had been given, would understand when she told her how the poor wild thing had begged for freedom. "But I cannot tell her that I had to do something good today, it seemed that I had to." She went from cage to cage, twittering to the canaries, scolding the parakeets, whistling to the mockingbirds, who immediately imitated her, arguing with the bald old parrot named Pluthio Paz because he imitated the housekeeper's complaints and scolded everybody he saw.

Standing under an arch of the portico, her heart winging with the doves she fancied were circling over the camp, she wondered how this had come to her. It had seemed, when she looked at him, as though it were someone long known, long beloved. His hands had risen from his side towards her, and both of hers would have rushed to meet them if Luis Gonzaga had not been holding her fingers tightly. As if his hands had to touch her, hold her. It was as if he had shouted:

"You—you at last!""

And as if she had answered, "Yes, oh yes!"

Such a thing could not be, reason told her. It had been, her heart assured her.

Today would be hers, to wonder and dream. For tomorrow, the hopes and fears.

Chapter 7

When General Zachary Taylor moved into Mexico, a skeleton force of men consisting of a company of raw recruits from Ohio and a decimated company of dragoons were left at Fort Brown. With a dearth of officers, one Captain Fortesby, resigned from service and a dyspeptic, was recalled, commissioned a major, and put in charge. At his protest he was heartlessly told that he could sit around and take his pills at an inactive post as well as at home. Warrener, because of his background and education was put ahead to a lieutenancy. Captain Ross of the dragoons was recuperating from swamp fever contracted in Florida. Captain Devlin, the doctor, suffering from an old wound in the leg, was waiting for relief so he could go back to Baltimore. Johnny White, like Warrener, had a temporary captaincy slapped upon him, presumably to keep the disabled Rangers in hand when they got well.

"A most superior personnel," White had cynically remarked. To which Ross had answered, "You might be surprised at what we could do if we had to, Johnny." They were doing a great deal as it was: guarding the supplies, building adobe barracks to replace tents, re-enforcing the earth works, and, most of all, keeping the men out of mischief. There was not enough to do. Short scouting expeditions up the river to exercise the horses, crossing the river to a town that offered little besides enmity, writing the letters which piled up until someone came to take them further on. There were long days of ennui, nights of unrest.

One afternoon two strangers rode into camp on horses that would have enhanced a general on parade. As the riders swung off their saddles when Captain Ross came to meet them, even a lover of horses would have turned his eyes away from the beautiful blood bay and graceful sorrel to look at the men.

Ross stared, then said in amazement, "Red McLane and his shadow! What in the world are you doing here? There's no enterprise to further in this place, *amigo*. We've got so low we play poker for corn kernels and there's talk about taking up crocheting." He put on an eager expression. "Are you the instructor for the crocheting, sir?"

Laughter as large as the man boomed in answer. As tall as Ross, he was almost as wide as two of him. The feet, in the best boots money could buy, were large. The extended hand had blunt fingertips and was broad enough to hide the hand of the captain. It was the hand of a doer, arresting and strong. Most eye-filling was the short beard and hair that showed under the broad-brimmed flat black hat. It was red. A darkly glowing red which gave an illusion of purple in the shallow waves. There was a sense of movement about him difficult to define—until, knowing him, one learned it was Power. Power in the hard muscles under the long black coat and gray trousers which were tailored to a perfect fit, power in the swarthy face and flat mouth quirked up at the ends. And power in the small gray-blue eyes that saw far more than was laid out before them.

"How are you, Ike?" Ross shook hands with McLane's companion. Almost as large as McLane, he was distinguished only by the butter yellow beard of tight curls and the small fringe of curls below a hat he never removed unless he had to, because he was bald as an egg. A pleasant man, Ike Mullen, who asked of life only that he be allowed to follow McLane. A man people only remembered because of the one he served, and never for himself.

Captain Devlin came and shook hands cordially and even Major Fortesby, when McLane presented his respects and asked for a few days sustenance, unbent from his usual reserve to give the visitor a small smile.

"I should have said 'hospitality' in place of sustenance," McLane amended. "It covers a wider field and has the proper sound of courtesy."

"Sustenance is the correct word, sir, for it implies the bare necessities, and that is what you get here. Captain Ross, see to our guest's comfort—if I may say 'comfort.'"

Ross presented them to Warrener and took them to Devlin's room in the adobe barracks, callously turning the doctor out, who promptly moved in with Warrener, remarking as he hung his clothes on pegs in the wall, "I don't know whether it is you or me who is honored, lieutenant."

Later in the evening when the two officers were alone Warrener remarked, "A big brute of a man—somewhat repulsive, isn't he? Or is he, to you? I noticed you knew him rather well."

Devlin laughed and stretched out on the Mexican-style cot, laced strips of rawhide on a wooden frame. "That is usually one's first impression, but once you know him you will change your opinion as all of us have."

"Who is he? I've never seen anyone like him."

"How could you, in Virginia? Neither had I until I came to Texas. He is what I would call a product of the frontier and in its fullest meaning. You know I have been shunted all over the state from one army post to another and met McLane in the town nearest every one of them. I got to know him very well and pieced together quite a remarkable history." Then the captain, when Warrener had tipped back his rawhide-and-stave chair to comfortably settle his long legs, and pipes were lit, and a fresh candle put in the copper stick on the mesquite wood table, told what he knew of the man.

Christened Alfred Isaiah, the boy was the oldest of twelve children which came in multifold bounty to a Presbyterian minister in New York State. When his father announced one Sunday: "Next Sunday my son Alfred Isaiah, who will be trained to follow in my footsteps, will stand with me here in the pulpit"—young Red, then sixteen, stopped for nothing in his haste to leave for anywhere, anywhere at all, so it was far enough away from that pulpit. The place happened to be Tennessee when Sam Houston was its governor. The boy admired the brawny Houston, and, already having a flair for politics, young as he was, he became one of the governor's cohorts.

There was much talk of Texas, which the United States tried to buy and which was rapidly expanding with the Americans pouring into it. When Houston resigned his office to leave for the Southwest, Red McLane, who professed to be—and looked much older than his years, rode by his side. A sponge that absorbed every doctrine the verbose Houston was ever ready to expound.

"Texas is ours," Houston liked to say, repeating Jackson's words. "We are in Destiny bound to bring it under the flag."

Considering himself the Destiny, Red often thought, and he echoed the opinion loyally. Houston said, "I may make Texas my abiding place." When McLane saw Texas he said, "I will make Texas my abiding place. This is the place for Alfred Isaiah McLane, with the first two names buried deep and Red put in their place."

Beholding the vastness and the rawness of it, like a chunk of soft clay upon which a man might leave the impress of a hand, McLane knew that he had come into his own.

Red McLane met Stephen Austin and let the milder doctrines of the great man temper the harsher ones he harbored. Through Austin he was able to view the Mexicans in a different light, and soon found that Houston's way of lumping them all together was as fallacious as putting a Tennessee mountaineer beside a Bostonian and judging them the same. At San Felipe de Austin, McLane also met James Bowie and his lovely wife Ursula Veramendi, daughter of the Mexican governor, and for the first time was introduced to the graciousness of Mexican family life as it really was. Red was assembling his knowledge with a growing shrewdness, and noting the position and power Bowie had acquired through this marriage, he told himself:

"I am going to marry a woman like Doña Ursula: one who has good looks and charm and is of a high-class family."

Working himself into the good graces of Bowie, he went with him to San Antonio and let that part of Texas leave an impress on his mind. For by now he viewed all things in the light of a worth that might—*¿quien sabe?*—some day benefit Señor McLane. He was no longer the boy, following. He was the man, the rudder of his ship in his own hands.

Accompanying Houston to Nacogdoches, McLane acquired land and, the Mexican law requiring that all landowners be baptized Catholic, he acquiesced without protest, Rosine and Adolph Sterne acting as godparents. "That makes twice for me," he laughed, after the ceremony, "and neither one making much of a Christian out of me as yet." But he asked for a certificate of the baptism and put it carefully away. He would need it when he sought the hand of the Mexican girl he would choose. "Never overlook anything and you'll move right along in this world," he told Houston. "You can squeeze something to your good out of everything that happens to you." He would have learned to speak Spanish even if it had not been compulsory, and spent hour upon hour to perfect it both in speaking and in writing.

Then came the Texas revolt. War. Houston in the limelight as commander-in-chief, a role he loved. He sent McLane to Louisiana to gather funds for the war when the husky man refused to fight the Mexicans. Fighting the Mexicans, said McLane, would interfere with his future plans.

After the surrender of Santa Anna, McLane moved to San Antonio de Béxar, knowing that the capitol would be placed not too far from there. A man of vision, he saw that whoever controlled the Mexican vote would control politics for many, many years to come. He was positive Texas would be taken into the Union. "We've got the agitatingest agitators in the country here in Texas," he told Ike Mullen, whom he had picked up in Louisiana, "and they'll agitate the crowd at Washington until they won't know that they're getting nothing but a bunch of ornery Indians and resentful Mexicans and loud-mouthed, trouble-making Americans, in a land that'll take years and years to develop. They don't know, up there, that most of the reason we're yelling for union is because as an independency we're so poor we're done for if we don't get help." And that, he elucidated further, would make every resident of Texas an American citizen. "Citizens vote, Ike, and lots of them won't know how. They'll have to be told how, savvy? I aim to be an expert in telling."

Captain Devlin refilled his pipe, lifted the candle from the table to light it and set it back again. "I consider Red a true Texan," he went on with his narrative. "It is my belief that the country will develop a certain breed of men different from any other. Hard, in many cases ruthless, the men of that breed will have courage above the ordinary and the thing courage needs to bring it anywhere—vision. Those of us who know Red well have never been able to decide whether his ability to make money is an extraordinary shrewdness and foresight or that peculiar magnetism to draw money which seems to be a gift. Perhaps it's a little of both. He is about thirty-five or -six, and already wealthy, started most of the enterprises in the state and owns almost all of San Antonio. It took him a long time to gain the confidence of the Mexicans, after the dirty way Juan Seguín was treated by the Americans he befriended, but he finally succeeded.[1] He's honest, too. If you take your money to a gambling house Red owns, you know the games aren't fixed. Of course, in politics—well—"

"What about politics, *mi capitán?*" It was McLane, and he came inside and sat on a bench against the wall facing Warrener. He took an elaborately carved pipe from the pouch that hung from a shoulder under his coat, filled it with the tobacco Devlin handed him in a small leather sack, reached for the candle and lit it. Warrener watched him, both fascinated and repelled by this type so new to him. From the first he had felt that something was wrong with him and now he knew: McLane should be wearing diamonds, flashy clothes, a thick gold chain on a watch set with jewels. The restraint of his clothes was unexpected, and until one became acquainted with him they seemed somehow wrong. What Warrener did not know, but Devlin had long ago guessed, was that Red would have delighted in decking himself so—but was too shrewd to wear anything but the conservative, finding some compensation in getting the finest materials and tailoring. McLane chuckled. "Politics is a great game, captain, but not everybody can play it. You can even be honest—that is, you can't lean over backwards, you understand, you may have to lean forward a bit now and then. It's like chess, moving the right figure at the right time; using the pawns to advantage, if you can see what I mean."

"For instance?" Devlin asked.

"I can bring an example right to your door, *señores*. You'll be standing at attention one of these days to receive our General Winfield Scott—howdy, Ross, come on in and learn. Did you hear what I said?"

Captain Ross squatted on the floor beside Warrener and nodded. "I heard. How do you know, and why Scott?"

"It's my business to know. Now listen, my children: Those who don't like this Zachary Taylor-for-president movement that is on—and they're sitting in on this chess game and can make the moves—don't like his military success at all. Makes Old Zach a hero to the people and that's bad, because the dear people like heroes in the president's chair. So the anti-Taylorites sitting in the high places move Scott down here, order Taylor back, and discredit him and give the glory of marching into Mexico City to Scott, see? Politics, and only politics, is the reason why Scott will show up here." McLane laughed and the sound rolled in the room. "They're slighting the little pawns though. Sorry I can't tell you about that, I may have said too much already."

"Not you," Devlin answered, smiling. "You never say too much. You intimate that Old Zach will be president, then. Most interesting, when I go back to Baltimore next summer, to be able to wave a nonchalant hand"—he illustrated—"and say that I knew all about it. Indeed, sirs, we knew a great deal about politics on the border in Texas, had a little something to do with it. The little pawns, you know."

His imitation of a smug know-it-all was so good they all clapped applause, and Warrener pulled a wooden box from under a cot, took out a wicker-cased *olla* and china cups. "I suppose you get liquor as *is* liquor, Mr. McLane, but this is the best we have; *tequila*, and pretty good if you don't mind the earthen taste of the *olla*."

McLane took the cup brimming with the white liquor and said, "A true Texan, loot'nant, finds all liquor good regardless of its name and—ah, nationality. Lift your cups, *señores*, and drink to our next president, Zachary Taylor!"

They poured the fiery drink down throats long hardened to it, even

Warrener taking his without flinching. Devlin said then, "Time will tell, *amigo*. You didn't come here just to advise us where to lay our bets in the next election. Matamoros is in Mexico so the Matamorosians won't be voting. May we allow ourselves to feel honored that you rode down here for the pleasure of a visit with us, and to let us envy you these clothes?"

McLane rose and made a bow to each of the men. A very good bow, even if it lacked the flexible grace of that of the Mexican. "Perhaps, my dear Devlin, I need to commune with men who are gentlemen *per se*, if I may use the term and so mend again the veneer of it that I wear, which cracks too often. I have, alas, only the appurtenances of a gentleman." Receiving their deep—overly deep—bows in return he seated himself and became serious. "I hear that all the *rancheros* around here are in Matamoros this winter instead of scattered in the towns up and down the *río*, as many as can crowd into the homes here. They are all citizens, and I can guess them to be not at all in favor of it, and I want to look them over and feel out the sentiment inasmuch as I can. At least I can understand how they must feel, and I can sympathize with them. I am hoping I can help them, for they will need help."

"Confess that you're going to keep an eye open for that wife also," Devlin put in. "Can't you find any in the rest of Texas? Surely San Antonio has them."

As McLane had made no secret of that part of his ambitions, he did not resent the remark, merely shrugging a shoulder. "If you want a thing bad enough, and wait for it long enough, and watch for it constantly,—you'll find it my friends. She has to be more than just the daughter of an *hidalgo*. She must have good looks and something—I'll know it when I see it, though I can't describe it."

A hand reached inside Warrener's breast and squeezed his heart. (He'll see Her! And oh, she's mine, she's been mine for a thousand years.) Aloud he said, "You talk as if you were buying a racehorse. Don't you take love into consideration?"

"No. You are a romanticist and you'd be fool enough to marry for that thing called love, asking nothing more. I ask for too many other things that are important to me, and I have learned long ago not to ask for more than a scale can balance. I'll see a girl who has 'Señora McLane' written all over her and I'll make my plans to get her. Love—that's for men like you, Loot'nant."

Love. Red McLane had loved often, if passion that a certain woman alone could satisfy can be called love. Consuming itself with its own fires, leaving but the rank taste of dead ashes.

There was a rap on the door and a hesitant voice supplemented, "It's Coleman, Lieutenant Warrener."

"Come in, Coley." At the entrance of a very round, very dark-complexioned private carrying a violin, Warrener rose and told his guests, "Sorry, gentlemen, we have a little business here which might be painful to anyone not musically inclined. If you care to leave—"

But the three were already started in a new discussion of politics and did not even hear him. Devlin left his cot and took a seat beside McLane on the bench, Ross drew a stool close, and the isolation was complete. Warrener put musical scores on the table beside the candle, explaining,

"It's a few arias from a new opera called the *Bohemian Girl;* I was in London when it was first produced there three years ago. I managed to get a copy of parts of it and wrote down the less involved arias. I heard you play last night and thought you might give an accompaniment on this one even if it's only a chord or two. Captain and I, between us, did what we could to translate it into Spanish, these are the English words:

"Oh what sweet delight, through my bosom thrills. Bliss unfelt, unfelt before, hope without, without alloy. Speak with raptured, raptured tone, of my heart the joy.—I'll sing it first in English so you can get the swing of it. It's waltz time."

Softly, in a fine, trained baritone, Warrener went through the melody.

Coley swung in at the finish, then took up the beginning in an extravaganza of introduction, and this time the singer used the Spanish words; richer, more musical, filled with a sweeter tenderness. At the finish Coley added a magnificent flourish of octaves in ascending scale, and Warrener clapped his hands in delight.

"Bravo, bravo, that's the way it should end, Coley. Why you are a musician! Have you heard this before?"

The soldier flushed. "No sir, I haven't. It's—you can feel that it should be that way—you know what I mean." His small black eyes were alight with pleasure. Up to now Coley had played only tunes in the camp, keeping his musicianship hidden. As Warrener had not sung at all, fearing the implication of "show-off," their finding of each other was like finding a treasure. "You sing—pretty fine, sir," Coley added. "Would you tell me about the opera?"

Warrener sang bits to him; after the "I dreamt that I dwelt in marble halls," Coley asked him to repeat it. He built in a high octave accompaniment and Warrener, carried away, let out his voice. It was not until clapping, stamping applause came from within and outside of the room that they remembered where they were and what they were.

"Calls for a drink," Warrener said. Not that he wanted one, but to cover his self-consciousness and also to compliment Coley. "You refresh yourself now and then, I presume?"

McLane watched the two touch cups to a newborn friendship. He sighed, in a momentary envy of the young, good-looking lieutenant. So he was already in love. A serenade rehearsal? Undoubtedly. Well, the stripling from Virginia would fit neatly into a Mexican household, and McLane hoped the girl's father would remove the spectacles of prejudice from his eyes and see in him a desirable son-in-law; for Warrener had everything the *hidalgo* asked and looked for. Yes, and more.

(And good luck to you, loot'nant. The kind of girl you want isn't the kind I'd want, that I know, so we'll stay friends. Provided, of course, that we become friends.) McLane said to Coley, "If you're not going home when your time is up in the army, look me up in San Antonio. I can't as much as toot a whistle, but I can appreciate good music and want it in my town. I can use you somewhere." And to Warrener: "Roll that *r* when you say *corazón*, it's not pronounced as in apple core, not in Spanish. And I'd advise a Mexican costume when you—ah, use that song."

Devlin wanted to say, "Don't, Bob, it won't do either of you any good. Forget her and let her forget you." Instead he took up politics again with McLane. What he had seen on Sunday was none of his affair. He had not seen it.

Ike Mullen came, Coley left, and there was man-talk, far into the morning. Major Fortesby invited McLane to have breakfast with him, and, as they were finishing the meal, Johnny White came in. The major let White stand at the door and said sharply, without preliminary, "Captain, I must tolerate your men in my camp and, therefore, I assume some authority, at least some, is due me. I noticed the condition of you and the men with you when you came in yesterday evening. What happened?"

White lifted an eyebrow and smiled. "Nothing much, sir. We went into one of those dives they call *pulquerías* and had a little argument with a gang there. In deference to your wishes that we keep the peace till after Christmas anyhow, we didn't use our pistols, just showed them who was the better fighter of the two. It wasn't anything at all, sir."

"Not this time, perhaps," the Major grumbled; waved White away and said to McLane, "I can't keep my men prisoners here and these Rangers can tell me to go to hell if they choose—what can I do? I promised the *padre* peace."

"They're homesick more than anything else," McLane answered. "They can play cards and drink here, but if they do it in town they feel like they've been somewhere. A man has to go somewhere once in awhile. If they had a decent tavern like they have at home instead of that filthy dive one Bony runs—that gives me an idea—"

From this The Skeleton came to life. Captain Ross took up the idea immediately. "I've got just the men who can do it, Shane and Kelly. Only God who made the Irish knows why they get along with the Mexicans better than the rest of us, and these two can do anything. I'll call them."

"Sure and Saint Michael himself whispered to ye," Kelly said when the plan was presented to them. "Leave it all to Shane and me. Kin we have off r-right now, sir?"

"If you promise not to get drunk. I'm trusting you."

The two talked to Buenaventura, paunchy proprietor of a *pulquería* in town that bore the name of *El Toro* but looked more like a dirty, mangy old crow. Bony was a Basque, listened closely, and not being as simple as he looked, he set to work with them at once. Loafing Mexicans, glad to work a little while for the money held out to them, cleaned out the place and whitewashed the walls and ceiling. The dirt floor did not suit Kelly and flat white stones were gathered from the pastures below the town; set carefully into the earth, the cracks packed with moist sand and pounded smooth and hard, it gave a clean, pleasing floor. A long hand-hewn table was scrubbed to near-whiteness, set in the center of the room, and flanked with benches; more benches filled the corners. There were seats and small tables by the fireplace. The bar at the side was bright with polished bottles, candles were set in the walls, and a huge copper candelabra, found on a pile of debris, was cleaned and polished and stood on the bar. The effect was a somewhat peculiar imitation of an eastern tavern but the resemblance was there, and it was good.

"Has to have a name," Shane said, and Kelly replied, "I s'pose we'll just call it Bony's like we been doin." They had another drink of *mezcal* on that—and inspiration came.

"Bony!" Kelly banged the table. "Get it? Bony. Bones. Skeleton. We'll get Captain Devlin to draw a big skeleton on the wall over there opposite the door. What'd y'all think? Ain't that an idea *muy grande*, now ain't it?"

"With a bottle in one hand and the Mexican and American flags in the other. We're s'posed to bring order 'n peace 'n goodwill, ain't we? 'N the Texas flag too!" Shane wept into his cup, overcome with the glory of the picture. "Three flags together in peace 'n harmony."

Kelly lifted his cup. "*¡Viva Méjico! ¡Viva Texas!*"

"*¡Viva* Ireland!" Shane added, for completeness.

To which they had one more drink, staggered to the patio in the rear to their horses, and galloped back to camp to see Devlin about the painting, and show Captain Ross that they weren't drunk, having only wet their lips, you might say.

The skeleton was duly executed in charcoal according to instructions, a bottle high in the right hand and the left stiffly outstretched holding the flags. It was toasted at an open-house—which for once did not become a rough-house—paid for by McLane, and Bony metamorphosed, with the aid of soap and water and a stack of bleached homespun aprons, into a genial, almost lordly, host. *Caramba*, these *gringos* were not so bad! The big red one with the fine clothes and the money—San Patricio, as if money were stones!—and the yellow-bearded servant who was unlike a servant, was he some lord then, in that country across the river? A most peculiar people, where the soldier and the officer came to the same place, a lord drank with his servant and common soldiers—most peculiar. But lucrative. Bony counted his undreamed sudden wealth and buried his prejudice.

If Mexicans came to stare and puzzle over the intriguing game called poker, they were not molested as long as they did not come with belligerent intent. When they ventured a question they were answered civilly, and peace reigned.

"It will not last," Padre Pierre said to the brother who kept house for him. "I look for trouble, though I thank God for Bony and The Skeleton, and I fear this neutral ground will not long remain so with the *rancheros* in town."

There was no neutral ground in the year of 1846, in Texas and beyond the border. Trouble smiled, and stirred the pot, and brought fresh embers to burn below it.

Samuel Walker, a brave officer and beloved, was killed in battle in Mexico, and the Rangers wept in their beards when they buried him and vowed further vengeance on "the dirty greasers."

Lieutenant Colonel Nájera was killed at Monterrey—Nájera, both an officer and a gentleman—his fellow officers touched lancetips over his grave, and let the tears run down their cheeks into their elaborately trimmed uniforms. And swore vengeance on "the vile, barbarous *gringos.*"

Chapter 8

Don Santiago postponed the annual trip to New Orleans to dispose of the ranch products, wool, hides, tallow, horsehair, and bones, until the next year. Service was disrupted and he had felt he should be close to his friends and family this year. Also, word had come that the French merchant, with an eye for opportunity, was bringing goods to Texas and a boatload would arrive in Matamoros before the first of December.[1] "For which thank the Lord," Doña Dolores said. "Now of all times we need new clothes, and I have set my heart on green velvet for Susanita. I want her to look like Susana did when she appeared at court, and Angela must have wine-color to go with the garnets. Heaven knows I am shabby and almost in rags—"

Time moved relentlessly toward the twelfth, the feast of Our Lady of Guadalupe, with no trader. Then, when the women were sadly spreading out the contents of chests holding three generations of gowns and Susanita had wept a few tears, M. François La Rue arrived and sent word that he would bring some of his stock to the house the next morning. "Vanity," Don Santiago teased, "will be satisfied after all. One would have believed you women had only a heap of sacks for wardrobe."

Mantillas, laces, trimmings, fans, jewels, flowers, yards and yards of materials, all lay in brilliant array over the chairs, and tables of the *sala*, light from the flames in the high shallow fireplace in the corner adding allure to the fine fabrics. The trader's two sons, eyeing Susanita approvingly, withdrew discreetly after the wares were spread—though today she had little time for flirting, particularly with immature youths. She had seen velvet, held the roll against her and draped a green length over a shoulder, dancing to where her father and the trader stood by the fire. "*Papá*, you promised me a really beautiful gown, look—look at it—"

He pinched her cheek, well aware of the admiration in the Frenchmen's eyes. "For whose eyes, then, must you be beautiful, *hijita?* Velvet and emeralds, for whom?"

"For you, *papá.*" She kissed him and tripped back to the table. For whom? (Perhaps he will come to the door of the hall and get a glimpse of me, or hide in the shadows to see me get out of the coach. He might even dare to come inside; he will if he loves me as much as I do him, and cannot bear the days for hoping to see me as I cannot bear them. For *him, papá.*)

Doña Dolores was in heaven. Loving fine things, her creative mind building marvelous gowns as she fingered fabrics and trimmings, she moved entranced around the room; piling goods on a table for her brother's approval. For herself, plain black in silks and in wool for afternoon and evenings, figured calico for early mornings, a bolt of nun's veiling to be cut into *rebozos* for gifts for the servants. For Angela, fine striped material, black wool and shiny purple satin, upon which she resolutely turned her back a half dozen times but finally yielded to its allure and added it to the rest. The wine silk, a sprigged jasmine, self-stripe brown, maroon, in satin and silk and wool, for Angela. A third pile for Susanita. Half of it would go back again, but there was always a chance that Santiago would have a glass of wine too many with the trader and loosen his purse strings. Doña María Petronilla selected some calico. "For me a dress is something to cover me, the old as good as the new, and I shall not go to the ball."

When Don Santiago was called from the room, the trader opened a package and expertly threw its contents upon the table. Lace, richly black and intricate of design. His eyes upon Doña Dolores, he said, "This I imported for the governor's lady, and I promised I would not sell what was left to anyone she would meet. I intended taking it to San Antonio, but when I saw you, *señora*, I knew none would appreciate it more or wear it with the dignity necessary to it which you so admirably possess." He bowed deeply. "If the compliment is allowed me."

Doña correctly gauged the compliment and shrewdly hid her delight in the lace. If the price were not too high, Santiago would buy it, for he too loved the fine things. "Lace—I do not know if I want lace, *señor*. Perhaps." Then she asked eagerly, "The *Americanos* in New Orleans, do you speak to them, and do they go to your churches and stores?"

He raised eyebrows in surprise. He was a small man and very precise in speech and movement. "But certainly! They are our friends and neighbors, and we are Americans together. Is it then different here?"

Unexpectedly, Doña María Petronilla answered. "You have but come, *señor*, and do not know that they war upon us and destroy everything that we hold dear. It would be impossible for us to offer friendship, and *we are not Americanos*."

(I say that for you, Susanita. Tear this foreigner from your mind, from your heart, if you hold him there. Force yourself to think as we do and as your father demands).

He snapped his fingers. "Politics makes wars, we as a people need not foster enmities. My daughter is married to a man from the north whose ancestors came from England and he is a dear son to me. Wars—we had our war also, in 1812. We did not let it disrupt us."

Susanita said timidly, "*Papá* says none of them are gentlemen. Is he—good to her?"

The trader laughed at the thought of his very correct Bostonian son-in-law not being a gentleman. "Either your *papá* has not known any of them or views them with the eyes of prejudice. If pampering and deferring can be called good, then he is very good indeed to her. More than my French son-in-law."

"I confess curiosity claims me, *señor*," Doña Dolores said, smiling. "How do the women dress, do they make good wives and mothers; how do they run their households, are they pretty and polite? Are the men faithful?"

"One question at a time, *señora*! They dress much as you do but with more trimmings, I think, and the hair is worn flat—a style not in keeping with the Spanish type, except for the charming young ladies here. Your hairdress is most becoming, but for our women it is for the hats. Hats are worn where you wear *mantillas*, though I confess I like the *mantilla* better." He bowed to the ladies. "Some are pretty, some not, naturally. Certainly they have good manners and are good housekeepers. They are fine women. As for the men, they are taller than we, and run rather to the blond type. Faithful—my dear *señora*, men are the same everywhere, some are good, others not. It is to be regretted, Doña Dolores, that your brother stayed only with the buyer of the ranch products when he came to New Orleans and did not see the people and the life of the town."

Much to the women's relief—for this was forbidden talk and not good for the girls—Don Santiago came with Doña Juliana Sánchez y Argensola waddling beside him, Inez and her duenna, Chonita, behind them. Inez kissed Susanita, whispering that she wanted to see her alone.

"May we walk awhile in the patio?" Susanita asked, and Inez strengthened the request with: "I have a little headache and it is so warm in here.

Besides, I have the goods for my dress and I might know envy looking at all this."

Doña Juana assented, and Paz came from the kitchen after a few minutes to take the lurking Chonita inside for the latest exchange of gossip. The girls walked slowly between the flower beds, interspersing their whisperings with loud giggles and excited phrases about clothes and the coming ball, for the sharp ears of their watchful chaperones. But Inez was not the frivolous girl today that she pretended to be, and when she was certain they were alone, she said, "Susanita, I do not know what to do. The *Americano* of whom I told you is a Ranger, is it not terrible? *Papá* gets red with anger when someone mentions the word. You know the old woman who sells flowers at the church door—of course you do."

"Tía Dolores says she is a nasty old witch."

"So does *mamá*. Sunday she pretended she was giving me a flower and she—put a note in my hand. I couldn't pray a single word all during Mass, I was burning and freezing—you can imagine! Clara told me the blue-eyed one was in the plaza after church, did you see him?"

Susanita stifled the urge to share her secret and said calmly, "I was with Luis and *mamá*. Alvaro saw him and you can imagine all the things *he* said. What did the Ranger write? Oh, Inez, how dreadful!"

"My slippers are white, and Chonita is embroidering them with pink and blue forget-me-nots; you know she does the most *beautiful* embroidery." And when Paz and Chonita had taken their heads back in again and the door closed, she whispered, "*Papá* says they have no sentiment, but if *papá* could see this letter—he said my hair is gorgeous, really he did, he said *esplendoroso*—and that my sweet face had impressed itself on his heart, and he was longing to see me and assure himself that my voice is as beautiful as I am and—"

"O Inez, that sounds as if he had made love before!"

"—and I should give the flower woman a note, he had already paid her. He said he would come to my window late when everyone is in bed, he has noticed it is low enough so his face comes to the bar—just think, he is that tall! I should tell him if I wanted him to come." She tightened her arm around Susanita's waist. "What shall I do? I am a little—afraid."

Susanita pressed a hand over her heart. If *he* wrote her such a note, what would she do? "But you couldn't love him, not so soon." (*One* could, so soon.) "Don't you think it is the fascination of something new and dangerous for you, and for him because you are guarded so and forbidden to him? Of course he could love you, you're so lovely, but—"

"I have thought of all that. Yet—the blue-eyed one was handsome and better dressed and everything, and all I could see was the one with the gray eyes and impudent face. And it wasn't like just flirting at all. I—I want to see him and hear his voice and—I don't know what to do."

Susanita stamped a foot. "What do we know? Nothing but our own little world and the same things over and over, we can't even talk without listening ears." She repeated what the trader had said. "Imagine us being married to an *Americano*—Inez, it isn't fair! Yet, *papá* may be right. If you are caught whispering at the window with a Ranger you will—"

"Be sent to the convent at Mexico City where my aunt is." Inez laughed. "Perhaps he would come after me and rescue me like a knight after his lady. Wouldn't that be romantic? Why, our children's children would talk about it."

"It is serious. I—I am frightened for you." (And for me. If *he* writes me a note, what will I do?)

Old Paz came scolding, clapping her hands as she rushed them indoors. The Olivares twins, the Baca girls, and Clara were in the house, and no young hostess to greet them.

"Do not answer his note," she whispered to Inez later. "We must stay with our own, we must."

It was a night of mystery and of promise. Clouds scuttled across the moon, stars shone palely. Here and there a guitar twanged and a voice sang the flowery, impassioned words which convention forbade the man to speak to the lady of his favor. Carlos del Valle lifted a nasal tenor under Susanita's window and, receiving silence for his pains, strummed an abrupt chord in disgruntled farewell and moved on. Susanita giggled naughtily at his discomfiture, sighed, stared into the night awhile, and moved from the window.

Exquisite as a prayer from a heart that is pure, beautiful as the still night in which it hung like a golden thread, came melody from a violin. Not a sawing over strings, but the caress of a loved instrument by a master hand. And while Susanita listened entranced, hand over her heart, came a voice. A baritone that rounded the low notes and danced lightly to the high with an ease and proficiency that was sheer delight to the ear.

"Oh, what full delight through my bosom thrills, and a wilder glow in my heart instills—"

The violin soared, whispered, held a single high note while the voice poured ecstasy in a cadenza, then turned a triplet and held the note while the violin built chords up and up a magic ladder. There was a moment of vibrant silence, then the violin sobbed softly, was a wraith that sighed and was gone.

Susanita's hands were on the bars, eyes straining at the two figures just out of reach below. Gleam of silver pale filigree of white braid on black cloth—but she knew. No disguise of costume could bring even a small doubt. "Roberto," she was whispering. "I love you too, I love you—"

A token, quickly, before he should go. No, he was singing again. A second verse, so she should remember the song. Then a sprightly little Mexican song where the violin mocked the voice, ending with it in notes that were a shower of laughter. Softly then, a plaintive melody of farewell as the figures moved away.

The singer darted back to pick up the bit of white that fluttered from the window. A tall, a very tall singer. "Sweet dreams, my sweet, sweet dreams. Sweet dreams—"

The night closed like water over a cleft and was still.

Susanita slept on a cloud, if it could be said that she slept at all. Susanita forgot her resolve made that afternoon, to stay with her own people in everything.

Robert Warrener spread a square of linen on the table and moved the candle close. An open fan was embroidered in a corner, on each of its eight sticks an initial; and he put a finger on each letter in separate caress, "Susanita. That means Little Susan." Golden, sweet little Sue. "Oh, what sweet delight—" He sang the melody softly in English, all unaware that Devlin was awake. He held the handkerchief to his face and drank the intoxication of its rose perfume. He kissed the fan, unashamed of his tenderness.

Once to every man—.

There was a furor at breakfast. "Surely I know every voice, young and old," Doña Dolores said. "At least when one can sleep through them as I have been doing, it speaks of long familiarity. But Blessed Saints above, this one woke me—I thought I was dreaming and at the opera in Mexico City. Susanita, do you know who it was?"

Susanita dropped her eyes in pretense of modesty, hoping the flame in her cheeks would be so construed. "I am sure it was not for me. Don't you suppose it was someone from the boat—just being happy? I never knew a violin could be played like that, Tía."

Who could the violinist have been, they wondered, deciding finally that both men were from the boat. Believing firmly that Americans were uncouth, it did not even occur to them that it might have been someone from the camp; and the night was too dark to reveal half a leg protruding from the braid-trimmed trousers. Even Luis Gonzaga, his sensitive soul reveling in the music, had not connected it with the soldiers. They had no culture.

Now he knew. He had seen his sister's eyes when she came to the table, and her confusion confirmed what he had seen. There was a radiance about her—strange, that only he saw it so plainly. Yes, the blue-eyed *Americano* had had the air of an *hidalgo*, and they had the daring, these invaders. Well, he would not mention it if there was no need to do so. His little sister's secret was safe with him.

Don Santiago kept thinking, over and over again: "If I could find one so cultured for Susanita, one whose background fitted the voice, which I am sure this one did not, whoever he was. The young men of our group seem like water milk at times to me. Someone virile yet of good family, why can I not find him? *Madre de Dios,* but this one could sing and the other play! A man could wish it were more than just a serenade."

Only Doña María Petronilla had seen the handkerchief fall and noted that the man who picked it up was tall—too tall to be a Mexican or Frenchman for all his masquerade. She was surprised at the calm with which she was presiding at the breakfast table, more than surprised at the firmness with which she was telling her conscience that she would not tell her husband what she knew. She had been too frightened to show resentment against his domination in the early days of their marriage and had protected herself with the armor of meek submission. But the resentment had never died and now it came to give her strength.

"Ah well," she smiled, "it gave us a little excitement and pleasure. It might have been the trader's sons, after all he made a neat profit here today. Go feed your birds, Susanita, and stop looking so childishly silly."

Susanita kissed her mother, unaware of how much she had been protected by her. When the old parrot Pluthio Paz greeted with "Nothing but work, work, and no one but me to do it as it should be done," she burst into laughter. Everything would come out all right. And if it didn't, she would always have the memory of this beautiful serenade, locked in her heart like a precious jewel in a case. No one knew, and today she could dream once more.

Chapter 9[1]

❦

Mass on Sunday, and the lame *Americano* was there alone, kneeling and passing rosary beads through his fingers as the church emptied. No officer waited for him in the plaza, to Susanita's mingled relief and regret.

"Flowers, buy my flowers for the Virgin's altar," chanted the old witch, beady black eyes watching for flame-bright hair under a lace *mantilla*. "Here, Señorita Inez, you are so pretty this morning I will give you a blossom for your hair."

Withered, clawed fingers pressed a note into the soft white palm with the flower, received a note in exchange.

(*Ay*, if only I could read, what a tale I could tell. For many notes have I passed with flowers in the years I have stood here at the church. *¡Ay! ¡Ay!* Doña Juana Sánchez, I could pay you off for that glare at me. But the *Americano*'s silver is in my purse and I keep my secrets.)

"Flowers, buy my flowers for the Virgin and she will get you what you want—"

It was la Fiesta de Nuestra Señora de Guadalupe, and young and old, rich and poor, saint and sinner, obeyed the urging of the sonorous bells to come to Mass and do honor to the Blessed Lady who had appeared to a poor Indian boy, long ago at Tepeyac and left her image on his robe. As an act of humility many of the women walked today, including those of the Mendoza y Soría family; lace or hand-drawn silk *mantillas* on high-piled hair, rosary and prayer book in gloved hands, moving sedately past humble cotton-clad women who bowed *rebozo*-covered heads, past respectful *peons* in clean suits of white homespun. Street vendors brought their wares on huge trays, in small carts, in baskets and bowls, their cries vying with the call of the bells.

"*¡El pan caliente!*"—"*¡La barbacoa!*"—"Buy my bread, just out of the oven"—"*El amole*, to make your hair curl"—"*Mira, flores para la Virgen*, just a few cents for her favorite flowers, and she will reward you if you put them on her altar. She will give you a sweetheart—a tall and handsome sweetheart for only a few *centavos* to a poor old woman for flowers for *La Virgen*'s altar"—.

The Virgin must have smiled at the prayers offered her this day. For marriage, for love, most of them. And only Angela's heart wept that, tonight, a man might find her fair. Only Angela prayed that she might look plain, not beautiful. Only Angela asked forgiveness because she felt pleasure in the prospect of the ball. "Yet, Lord, whatever is Thy Will, behold Thy humble servant."

Indeed it was a trial for María de Los Angeles. After *siesta* Susanita put on a *mantilla* and said that she too would visit the church. "Not to pray for admirers tonight," old Paz mumbled, trotting after the girls, "you will have more than your share." Though in Paz's opinion none was good enough for either of her charges.

Then so quickly, the day was gone and it was time to dress. Old Paz, fondly imagining that unless she were everywhere nothing would be right, fluttered about like an excited mother hen. Had she not laid out Don Santiago's sainted mother? Who but Paz had helped Doña María Petronilla to remove her wedding dress and veil? Who had dressed the girl Dolores for this same *baile* year after year, and who had dressed her for her wedding and later set the widow's veil on her head? Who had dressed these two girls from babyhood? So she would have reminded anyone, had her presence been protested—which none would have dreamed of doing.

Doña María Petronilla had long before begged to be excused from the dance, and the wanness of her small face when she finished dressing the girls' hair lent proof to the assertion that she was not well enough to go.

At last Doña Dolores was ready. And very handsome in the black lace gown, her hair piled high and completed with a fanlike comb of jet and brilliants that enhanced her height and carriage. Jet winked from a close-fitting necklace, from the ears, from the links of a chain around a wrist from which swung a fan of black lace. Anticipation rouged the cheeks whitened with rice powder, put a sparkle in the dark eyes, and a smile on the generous mouth. Doña Dolores was in truth this evening the *gran señora,* moving in self-possession and just pride. She went to the girls' room to see if they were being properly dressed to the last detail—and stood in the doorway, speechless.

Although she had herself designed the dresses and fit them, she was not prepared for the transformation that met her eyes. Gone was the demure girl who had refused to remove the high chemise covering her perfect shoulders while fitting until sternly ordered to do so, who had wept at the vanities forced upon her. Gone was the María de los Angeles they had known. The full wine silk gown was like a regal robe on the erect, slim body, the beautiful shoulders rising exquisitely from the untrimmed tight bodice. Thick glossy curls, pinned back of the ears, fell softly against the slender neck. A dull gold chain with a garnet pendant and garnet earrings set off the creamy complexion, and a garnet ring glowed on the hand held gracefully against her waist.

"*Madre de Dios*, what have we done here?" Doña Dolores asked silently. "Perhaps it would have been best to leave the nun. And I had not even thought her pretty."

In Susanita Doña Dolores had another shock, for the girl might have been her own great-grandmother come to life and, like her, ready for presentation at court. The hair combed back from the high forehead was caught high with a wreath of gardenias, the golden curls falling in profusion to frame the lovely young face. Doña Dolores, while patterning the style of the old court gown, had expertly given it modish lines—though the skirt, falling smoothly, looked almost skimpy beside Angela's. The heavy cream lace taken from the original dress and carefully preserved, fell in a rich cascade from the straight line of the décolleté and covered the upper arm almost to the elbow. Emeralds glowed with a lambent light in a necklace set in gold filigree, in small earrings, in a narrow bracelet in each arm. The precious stones, purportedly a gift from Moctezuma, were an inheritance on the distaff side and so belonged to Doña Dolores, and Don Santiago had given his consent that Susanita wear them, so that the picture of his grandmother Susana might be complete. With her clear green eyes glowing brighter than the emeralds, Susanita was the queen of beauty, in a perfection of green and gold and cream.

"I don't know whether I like myself, Tía," Susanita said, unfolding a cream lace fan. "I look so different and I don't feel like me. I almost wish—"

"And this dress is indecently low," Angela protested.

"Well!" Doña Dolores' wart glowed. "Indecent, when low décolleté is the mode and your shoulders so perfect—be assured your mother would not have allowed it were it indecent. Susanita, you are frightened that you are a woman. Come, your father is waiting."

Don Santiago, looking dignified and strange in a formal evening suit of black with long-tailed coat and still, glistening white shirt front, approved them and praised his sister for her help in this achievement of beauty. "I have never seen you look so well," he complimented her. He would be very proud this evening of this, his family.

The large salon of the old *palacio de gobierno* in which this, the most brilliant of the pre-Christmas dances, was held was ablaze with light. The huge silver and crystal chandelier in the center of the hall scintillated with the light of dozens of candles, and candles burned in sconces against the walls. Festoons of greenery and flowers were everywhere, canaries and mockingbirds swayed in cages back of the orchestra and in the corners to help create an atmosphere of glamour and romance. It was considered shameful to be the first to arrive and the disgrace of it usually taken by the insignificant Zepedas—two stern spinsters and a shy brother—for the privilege of hanging on the fringe of society. The young men had to cool their heels until eleven o'clock before the first of the ladies came. Dressed somewhat self-consciously in conventional evening attire following the French mode, they stood in groups at the door.

Inez, her flaming hair like a torch among the dark-haired girls, was like a flame drawing most of the men to her. Deceptively fragile in the dress of then-soft cream silk embroidered with forget-me-nots, she resembled a delicate pale flower—of which she was well aware, and played upon it to her advantage and the chagrin of the rest of the grimly chaperoned girls. For a time at least, Inez was the reigning queen.

Close toward midnight the Mendoza y Soría family arrived, Don Santiago a most distinguished figure as he led them into the hall. A waltz was in full swing, yet when the girls came into view there was a lull, most of the players putting down their instruments the better to crane their necks. Two of the more daring of the young men took advantage of it and led their partners to their seats, much to the mortification of their *mamás*. Excusing themselves with a hurried bow, they rushed to the door where starry-eyed Susanita and blushing Angela stood, their father and aunt like flanking lions guarding them. Following the etiquette of the period, both young men ignored the girls completely and dedicated their bows and salutations to the father and aunt. Only after that was accomplished did they see the girls.

"May I, Don Santiago," said René de la Ferrière, son of the local French merchant, "have the honor of dancing with Susanita?" "May I," echoed José Luis Carbajal, "be honored by Angela's company?" Everyone was looking at them and it was plain to see that many of the young men regretted the politeness which had kept them with their partners. Doña Dolores tapped her large lace fan on her wrist and looked triumphantly at the assemblage, as though to say, "My nieces have the most coveted escorts, do you see?"

Don Santiago smiled and nodded assent, patting his sister's hand on his arm as they moved forward. "One feels almost young again, *hermana mía*. Look, there is Luis Gonzaga dancing with Clara, and he is better looking than many of the girls, do you notice? Alvaro, the rascal—do they not make a fine couple, he and Inez? Ah, he would be the one who could tame her!"

Rotund Gabriel del Lago claimed Doña Dolores, and Don Santiago bowed low before Señora Robles, one of his few relatives; distant, but an obligation remained, and though her dancing was a trial, he would not have dreamed of giving the first dance to another.

There was no doubt as to who was queen of the ball. Not even Inez could hold the young *caballeros* now, and they flocked around Susanita and begged the favor of a dance. "You do me such a great honor," she dimpled, curtsying charmingly, "but how can I dance with all of you?"

"I can arrange that very well," replied René. "She dances all of them with me, see how easy it is?"

"A nice girl cannot do that—for shame, René!" José Luis Carbajal took a guitar from one of the musicians, plucked a few notes, and then, eyes on Angela, began to sing. A song with which a courtier, in a far gone day, had hailed the appearance of his queen:

> *All light it dimmed by the radiance of thine,*
> *The stars pale, the moon hides in shame—*

Daringly, his dark eyes never leaving Angela, emotion throbbing through the melody, he sang two verses of the impassioned old song, ending with a soft ripple of supple fingers over the strings and a deep, heartfelt sigh.

"Bravo, bravo, José Luis!" There was clapping of hands and stamping of feet, as much in approval of the daring of this public serenade as the neat presentation of it.

Blushing, tears in her eyes, Angela tried to hide against Doña Dolores and got small comfort from her whisper, "What a triumph, Angelita *mía*, to have in your first dance acquired the most elusive and richest suitor in the land. Every girl here is dying with envy of you."

"But, Tía, I want no suitor, I . . . you know . . . I . . ."

Doña Dolores piloted her to a seat against the wall. "You do not know what you want, Angela. See that you do not offend him, and if he speaks to your father, I shall do my utmost to have him looked upon favorably."

The cries of "Alvaro, Inez" stopped the suitor hurrying to Angela, and all eyes turned to the couple standing in the middle of the room. Inez had changed to an Andalusian costume of black and green which turned her into a new, fascinating woman. The billowy black net skirt swirled with layers of ruffles iridescent with spangles, the green sash was tight around the slender waist of the low-cut ruffled blouse. A provocative costume which revealed by concealing. Alvaro stood in front of her, his slenderness accentuated by the bell-shaped trousers, red sash, and black bolero of the Andalusian.

The orchestra played the *seguidilla*, the merry, fast tune identified with the dance, and Inez, with a single click of the castanets, began the dance. Now slow and with undulating sway of the hips, leading him on—now whirling in the mad gyrations of a free and joyous soul, stamping her red slippers, caring for nothing but her own madness. Swaying again, coming close. Promising, melting. Fleeing. It was the dance of the provocative female calling her mate, and Alvaro followed her every movement with the ease and grace of one who carries the love of the dance in his blood. Cold to her, pursuing her, retreating. Catching her at last in a finale that was a spinning flash of brilliance and color, like wild souls twirled in ecstasy.

It was a superb example of the artistry of the dance that reached back to a homeland still beloved, and uncontrolled shouts and clappings applauded them. "More, more."—"Give me another one." Inez shook her head, and her fat little *mamá* hurried her to the dressing room to change again, fervently hoping the dance was a prophecy. A union with the Mendoza y Soría house was more than they had hoped for, for this, their somewhat too play-acting daughter. Doña Juana had always felt it most ungentlemanly for Inez's bridegroom to die before the wedding and deprive her of both the prestige of his name and the wealth that accompanied it. And what was as much to be deplored, leaving a problem on their hands in this daughter as restless as the flame of her hair. Did she dare hope it would be Alvaro? San Antonio, heavenly matchmaker, lend thy aid!

Alvaro, hurrying to the patio to still an inner agitation as well as get a breath of cool air, almost collided with a man in the buckskin suit of the *vaquero*. It was Juan Cortina, in the costume he loved and refused to change. "Cheno, what are you doing here?" Alvaro asked angrily. "You can't come in dressed that way, you know you can't." Cortina jerked a thumb contemptuously toward the doorway. "Do you think I'd hop around like that and look like a fool in one of those silly suits? There are other things to do when it is dark, and there is war, *amigo*." He drew his friend into the shadow of a shrub. "I have only come to warn you that an *Americano* will be here tonight."

"Are you dreaming, Cheno? That is impossible."

"Not at all, Alvaro *mío*. That fathead Juan de Leon, the *alcalde*, invited him personally and is bringing him here. I'd like to see a rope around his thick dirty neck!"

"But this *Americano*, who is he?"

"All I know is that the *alcalde*—curse the *gringo*-loving fat fool!—is bringing him as a guest. Don't tell anyone you saw me." He ducked through the shrubbery and was gone.

Alvaro changed to his formal suit and leaned against a pillar, watching old and young go through the intricacies of a *contradanza*. Doña Dolores giving coquettish glances to round little Gabriel del Lago, who mopped his shining red face with one hand and with the other held his partner's fingertips. Inez came into view, and his heart pulsed at the prospect of taming her. His wife? The idea pleased him. It would be soon, before some *Americano* saw her—it would be just like Inez to like the invaders if for no other reason than to defy the conventions she found so constricting. It would be like her to madly love one of them, and Inez, he thought, could love deeply indeed. Not himself, as yet. To her the dance had been figurative only. Cruelty pressed the warmth from his eyes. She would tell him she loved him whenever he wished her to, once she was his wife—*por Dios*, but he would tame her! And his wife she would be if he asked for her and her father approved, for she had no choice.

In this pleasurable contemplation he sought Inez for a dance. If such a thing could be that an *Americano* came, he could deal with him when the time came.

Gaiety was at its height, now that the older folks had enough of dancing, and many a *mamá* found her eyelids heavy. Occasionally a couple took the spotlight with a *jota*. Susanita, besieged by a dozen young men when the orchestra lured with a new, slower waltz, turned gratefully to René de la Ferrière when he fought his way to her side.

They glided to a corner, circled once around the hall, and were near the door—when René felt a stiffening of her supple body, and heard a sharp gasp of surprise. His partner had dropped her arms and was standing still, staring. Unannounced, the *alcalde* Juan de Leon and Robert Warrener entered the hall. Warrener, toweringly tall in correct evening dress and impeccably groomed, quite dwarfing the perspiring official beside him.

The music stopped as if a great hand had struck away the instruments, and with the stilling of the strings, the birds, too, ceased their trilling. The moment of silence that followed, with every dancing foot as if turned to stone, every face gaping as if beholding an apparition, might have been plucked from eternity and placed there, so utterly devoid of sound and movement was it.

Only a moment. Then the whisper of disapproval was a mounting wave from a muttering, angry sea, sweeping in a flood to the far corners of the hall. The *alcalde* dropped back a step, uncertain whether to present his companion or ignominiously to flee—which left Warrener standing alone. Poised, unconcerned.

No one moved. Generations of culture and breeding that made deference to a guest an obligation was a bar holding them. There was also the shock of seeing this member of what was considered an inferior people so far from uncouth, so at home in evening clothes better tailored than their own. None moved, though whispers swelled and the air was vibrant with tensed nerves and mounting angers.

The orchestra leader, knowing the *alcalde* well enough to expect the wrong move from him and fearful of what might happen, had his players break into a schottische, the new dance but lately introduced. And Robert Warrener walked forward to Susanita, took her hand in his and with a bow to her and a *perdóneme* to René de la Ferrière, led her to the empty middle of the dance floor.

Not a sound now, not a word, as the two danced alone. Too late Don Santiago realized what had happened was happening, before his own and his friends' unbelieving eyes. Yet he found himself helpless. To stop the girl in the middle of the dance was to act unlike a gentleman, a crime of which the head of the Mendoza y Soría house could not be found guilty. When Alvaro came to him, white with rage, his father put a restraining hand on his wrist. All they could do, he felt was stand and watch.

Scandalized *mamás* and outraged *papás* plucked their daughters from the dancing space where embarrassed escorts had been too bewildered to lead them to their seats. René, feeling the insult and blushing with shame at his impotence, could not move.

Susanita was not even aware that they were the only ones dancing and that all eyes were upon them. She was not, in truth, aware that she was dancing, that her feet were following a rhythm of steps in time to music. She only knew that music flowed from her to another, back from him to her, the touch of their fingers an ecstasy that built heavenly walls around them.

Reality came quickly. Scarcely had the last strain been played than Alvaro rushed to them, roughly grasped Susanita's hand and led her urgently to her father. He rushed back to Warrener and thrust a card at him. "I could kill you like a dog, *Americano*, but a Mexican *caballero* never does that. Here is my card, my seconds will see you—"

"But I assure you," Warrener interrupted calmly, glancing at the card, "that there is nothing to fight about." He looked about him, saw the hostile eyes of the men and the stark hatred in Don Santiago's face, and met them without flinching. "When Señor de Leon, the *alcalde* of this town, asked me to this ball I felt it an honor I could not belittle by refusing."

"So you felt it your privilege not only to come to an affair on a questionable invitation but dance with whom you choose without waiting for presentation."

Warrener could feel the finger of red moving into his cheeks as he realized what he had done. He could not voice the thoughts tumbling through his mind. He could not say: "Why, I have always known Susanita. She is why I left Virginia and home and came here. Don't you see, she was waiting for me to come to her—why, we knew each other that morning outside the church. I had to go to her this evening, I did not even remember that there were forms to go through before I could take her hand. She was there waiting, and I had to go."

"For that liberty, señor, I apologize." He bowed, adding gallantly. "Though I trust I will not be forced to lie and say that I regret it." He bit a lip to keep from adding "As I have always regretted that I did not dump you into the *río* the time you splashed water on me."

Warrener's poise was added fuel to flames for Alvaro. Also, the unspoken thought was in Warrener's eyes, and Alvaro read it and recalled the humiliation of that day. He swung an arm and slapped the American in the face.

Now there was commotion. Fathers, frightened at what their men might do, hustled their families out of the salon without ceremonies of farewell.

94

Some of the young men gathered around Alvaro, uncertain what to do, but the older ones went with their families or stood in groups, watching. Doña Dolores, like a hen gathering her chicks in a storm, took her nieces by the arm and by the very force of her going propelled Don Santiago ahead of her, Luis Gonzaga at his side. The music started again and Warrener, back on steady ground after the unexpected blow, yielded to the pulling at his sleeve by the *alcalde* and walked out of the hall, not even hearing the excited apologies of the little man, the tearful implorings and promises.

Red McLane intercepted the *alcalde*'s coach. "It was nice of you to send the carriage for the lieutenant, señor," he said, "but it won't matter if his fine pants get horse-hair on them now. You might get into trouble, señor. Come on loot'nant."

The town behind them, Red laughed. "The American army invaded Mexican territory and was routed, retreating in disgrace with as much dignity as it could muster."

"Disgrace is correct," Warrener threw back. "I should have slapped him back even if he was her brother. The—"

"Never mind the names, *amigo*, I know them all. Remember I warned you. You have to use more subtle means to win over an enemy. You got a lot to learn yet."

Warrener slowed his horse and twisted fingers in the mane. It seemed to him that he had acted the fool. "Were you peeking?" he asked abruptly.

"I was right behind the *alcalde*'s coach, leading your horse. Then I stayed in the shadow of the buildings opposite and I could see inside easily enough, with the doors open and all those lights. You had to have someone to look after you. I knew they wouldn't start anything, I know the Mexicans. Polite as hell even when they want to kill you. Was that girl—?"

"Yes, and you leave her alone, Mister McLane."

Red's amused chuckle stirred the doves in the chaparral that lived the river's edge. "My, my, loot'nant, but you're touchy. Can't blame you if that's the way you feel, and she is a beauty. You needn't worry, she won't do for me at all." The horses splashed into the water, now a silvery ribbon in the pale moonlight and quite believing its natural mud color, and were on the bank before Red spoke again. "I was surprised at the clothes and the exclusive air of the—er—assemblage. I might find Señora McLane here after all."

This time Warrener laughed. "A fine chance you'll have of getting her. They hated me, Red. I could feel their hatred like you can feel the wind."

"I told you what to expect before you started. This was a sort of ultra-exclusive affair with them, with match making one of the highlights even if kept in the background. There's more than one way to get the girl you want, *amigo*. If I do find Señora McLane here—I'll get her."

Warrener did not answer. He was not at all interested.

Chapter 10

Up and down the dining room tramped the master of the house, passions distorting his finely cut features and glittering blackly in the eyes. There had been argument and counterargument and now the breakfast chocolate was cold, Paz, worn with trotting to keep hot coffee at the head of the table; muttering and making as much noise as possible so the master's wrath would be turned on her who had weathered so many of them. Doña María Petronilla's hands were tightly clenched, Luis Gonzaga sat with downcast eyes, Susanita was weeping, Angela counting *Aves* on her fingers in lieu of a rosary, Alvaro pulled at a sullen lip. Only Doña Dolores was calm, submerging her emotions to keep her sharper wits a bulwark between her brother and his family.

Don Santiago stopped and struck a fist in an open palm. "There is only one thing to do. Alvaro, call Juan Bautista, tell him to get the coach and mules ready so we can leave tomorrow for Rancho La Palma. Well did I hesitate about coming to town, well did I know only grief would come of it. María Petronilla, we start at dawn, be packed and ready."

"Nonsense!" Doña Dolores rose. "Our friends would laugh at you fleeing from a lone *Americano* because he danced with Susanita, you who talk about fighting the many. And we are to hold the Christmas fiesta this year." She walked to him and put a hand on his arm. "Santiago, if you leave now you will be exposing Susanita to scandalous gossip, and I assure you plenty are waiting to build on it. They are not only jealous of last night's triumph—two girls as belles of the ball was too much—they are even jealous that the guest of the *alcalde* did not even see their homely daughters but selected your beautiful one. I heard more than one sigh and remark on his dancing and gentlemanly appearance. Really nothing has happened, brother, if you look at it sensibly. Just a dance, what is that?"

He pushed her away. "Just a dance, Dolores. A touch of the hand, a smile, a glance—tinder for the spark, and a *gringo* will steal the hearts of our girls. I had not known that they could be so personable, and I confess it was Alvaro of whom I was ashamed." Blood mounted darkly in his cheeks and his teeth bit cruelly in the lower lip.

Doña Dolores thought. Yes, that was it hitting his pride; that was the shame, that his son was the lesser man.

He walked to the table, gulped coffee and threw the cup on the table. It rolled in a half circle and crashed to the floor. He picked up a broken piece and threw it at his sister's feet. "That would be my daughter, married to one of them." He banged the table, raised his right hand, and in a voice which made Angela and Doña María Petronilla shrink with terror he proclaimed: "I swear by almighty God and by the souls of my ancestors that rather than see that happen I would wish them in their coffins. I curse the—"

But Angela, zeal overcoming fear, had run to him and was pulling at the raised arm, imploring: "No, no, *papá*, a curse comes back to the one who makes it, you cannot so call on God! Say a prayer quick—*papá*, you are not yourself—"

"I have had enough of all this nonsense." Doña Dolores's voice was like cold water thrown on them. "Never mind, Angela, God isn't listening to your father's playacting and you needn't work yourself up about it. Santiago, shame on you for frightening your family. Go hide, flee to your ranch like a scared rabbit, go spend your temper on your peons and those who fear you. We are women, yes, but we have our own souls. As for marrying— well, I can name you plenty I'd rather see Susanita dead than married to. Come, Petronilla, Angela, Susanita." She held out a hand to her sister-in-law, in majestic disdain of her glowering brother.

Doña María Petronilla rose and summoned the courage for which she had prayed in the early morning hours. "Santiago, I beg of you—" She could not go on. Worry, mental exhaustion, the shock of her husband's rage and cursing, the habit of bowing wordlessly to his will through the years, was too much. She gasped, reeled, and fell in a heap on the floor.

It was Luis Gonzaga who, glaring defiance at his father, lifted the frail body and followed Paz to his mother's room.

Don Santiago, his temper cooled, sauntered to the plaza where, he knew, most of the *rancheros* would be loitering. Sudden loud talk told him what had been the subject of conversation, and one Señor Zárate quickly made issue of it.

"A fine *baile*, Don Santiago. A pity we had to suffer the indignity of the presence of a gringo." When all looked at Don Santiago, who made no comment, he added, "*My* daughters would not have danced with a *gringo*."

Don Santiago did not like Zárate, who had his position in society not for the valued genteel blood and fine lineage but mainly for his wealth. Zárate's three daughters, noted as much for their stupidity as for their unattractiveness, were no longer young, and everyone knew that only the Zárate money could bring them a suitor. Don Santiago smiled amusedly at the faces turned to him and said, "Scarcely, señor. The *gringos* are not— ah—insensate to beauty and gentility. I have been told that they recognize it instantly."

Zárate bit a lip at the laughter aimed at him, then sneered, "You justify your daughter's dancing with one, then?"

Don Santiago took firm hold of the weapon Doña Dolores had given him, and with smiling composure answered, "He was the *alcalde*'s invited guest, therefore, our guest also. Good manners, Señor Zárate, if you did not know, are the attributes of a gentleman and his family, quite superseding personal feeling. My reproaches are for my too impetuous son and his breach of good manners; in sympathy with him as I might, possibly, have been."

Proud of the cleverness that exonerated Susanita or, at least, challenged opinion, Don Santiago moved on—somewhat disconcerted that he had also challenged himself. The *Americano* was a man of position, an officer, and the invitation from a public official like the *alcalde* did, in a way, obligate them. Yes, Susanita could well have been discourteous had she refused the dance. Nor had he moved from his position of enemy to all things American, rather had he given himself and Susanita a martyr's glow for their devotion to that yardstick of family—manners and courtesy. Even those who shrugged a shoulder would have to admit his cleverness and so still leave him triumphant.

Run away? He was Don Santiago de Mendoza y Soría. None ranked above him in family heritage. Pah—let them gossip, those that envied him.

By four o'clock, the coffee hour, he was composed almost to solemnity. With his wife still in bed, he told Doña Dolores, "See that the girls get the proper dresses for the *Posadas*, in keeping with our position for the Christmas festivities. We stay in Matamoros until Epiphany." He turned to the red-eyed, pale-cheeked Susanita. "On one condition, that Susanita promises she will not look at an *Americano* or speak to one, she must consider them as far beneath her. And you, Angela, thank God you have spared me worries in that direction."

"I promise, *papá*, and thank you." Susanita smiled wanly, grateful that her thoughts could not be read. (I did not promise not to think of Roberto, nor to write to him if he writes to me like Inez and the Ranger Juan, and I can think the soldiers and Rangers beneath me. Roberto is apart from them all.)

"Of course, *papá*," Angela agreed, "except that I cannot think anyone beneath me. We are equal in the sight of God. Even the *Americanos* are God's children, *papá*."

To this he disdained answer. But his heart was heavy with foreboding as he looked at his daughters. A smile, a handclasp, a spark—it could be. It could be possible for his girls to give their hearts to an *Americano*.

"This coffee is cold," he snapped at Doña Dolores, "and weak as water. See that I have some fit to drink. Angela, take off that black dress for something in color. Susanita, stop sniveling. Your hair is in disorder also. Must you all look like servants? Don't I spend enough money for clothes, and aren't there enough hands here to comb your hair if you cannot do it yourselves? Go to your room at once."

The trials of the day, however, were not yet over. Susanita had barely combed out the bedraggled curls and twisted them into a flat knot when she heard Paz' trembled voice:

"May all the angels of the celestial court protect me, blessed Saint James be my advocate—"

It was a duet of explosive oaths from Don Santiago and implorings that took in a generous number of the heavenly host from Paz by the time Susanita got to the patio. What in the world—Susanita stood and stared, speechless.

The thin black-robed buttocks of old Paz reared high from what looked like a posture of deep supplication to the portico. "You shameless one, you imp of Satan," came imprecation, "if you were not my dead child child's son I would—slap you until—"

"Enough, Paz!" Doña Dolores came bustling and put a hand on the slanted back. "Cannot anything be done calmly in this house? What are you doing—oh, its Manuel. What is he doing under the portico?"

"*Señora, perdóneme*." Groaning, the old woman pulled the squirming boy into view, got to her feet, and jerked him to his. "Look at the shameless *muchacho, señora*—look at him, is all I ask—look!"

"*La Virgen me socorra*!" Doña Dolores crossed herself. Susanita put a hand over her mouth to stop a giggle. "Oh, Manuel, where did you get that? Why Manuelito!"

Manuelito rolled dark eyes at her, grinning widely. A strange Manuel, indeed. Where the suit of domestic, badge of the *peon*, should have been, there were trousers of the brown jean which the Rangers wore and a coat of the blue of the enemy army. To say that the fit was crude was an understatement, but the smiling face shone with as much pride as if a king's tailor had turned him out.

"I wondered what he was doing all these days, out of sight from morning till night." Paz shook him angrily. "Gone right after Mass this morning and this is the way he comes back. When I tried to get these things off him he dived under the portico and I had to drag him out. Look at him."

Don Santiago took the boy by the ear and demanded, "Who gave you those clothes, Manuel? Where have you been? Answer me, or do I get the whip for you?"

"No sir, Manuel, no like. No whip, sir, *señor.*"

"*¡Dios de Dios!*" Paz clamped a hand over the boy's mouth. "The infidel's language! You hear it, the *inglés?*"

"A nice state of affairs," said Doña Dolores. "I knew something like this would happen when we gave in to you and let him come along. No wonder he hasn't been into things at home, you've let him run. It's your indulgence that has made him the Satan's imp he is."

"But he is all I have, *señora,*" wailed Paz. "*Manuelito mío,* why have you done this to me, aren't you ashamed?"

Manuel fixed impudent eyes on Don Santiago and chanted, again in the infidel's language: "Manuel like 'Mericans, like bacon and ham, damn it all. Hurry up, Bony, you old-poke, three of a kind beats two pair, the top o'morning to ye, holy Saint Michael. Manuel you little devil, bring me a drink, this is a helluva hole." The words came in confusion and highly accented, sounding like wild curses to the ears so new to them.[1]

Paz screamed as Don Santiago reached for a short whip lying on the portico and Manuel, with a quick jerk, freed himself and ran, the *huaraches* on the flying feet slap-slapping into silence before Don Santiago turned. He swept them all with rage-filled eyes and lashed out at Paz.

"He will remain at home hereafter or I lock the both of you up, you hear? This is a shame beyond enduring, Paz.

"I also feel the shame, Santiago. I will punish him." Calling mutteringly on more saints, Paz ran to the sanctuary of the servants' quarters, trying hard to kill the secret pride in her darling's latest accomplishments.

Don Santiago stalked away after a look at his sister which told her she was to blame for this, and Susanita went back to change her dress and safely release the pressing laughter. Doña Dolores dropped into a chair. What now, she asked, could anyone tell her, what else was going to happen?

Doña María Petronilla came from the shelter of a doorway, sighed as she took a chair, and folded her hands, looking at the serene sky. "Dolores, I am glad I do not know. I think God is kind, not letting us see the future. Kind."

Even as Doña Dolores was asking what else would happen, destiny picked another thread for the weaving. Luis Gonzaga, after sitting with his mother until driven away by his aunt, found the day strangely lonely. He rode awhile, took a siesta, then wandered about town. Finally he walked up one of the narrow side streets that spoked away from the hub of the plaza, quite by accident taking the one that went past The Skeleton. He knew, naturally, of the conversion of the dirty *pulquería*, but as it was so far beneath any gentleman to go there, he had no desire to see it; besides, his artistic peace-loving nature did not find saloons pleasant places. Had not candlelight beckoned from the open door he would not even have turned his head in going by—did not know he had turned until he saw a black skeleton grinning at him from a white wall. "The place looks clean," he argued to that part of him which urged him to go on. "And the drawing is a good one. It is necessary to me that I see it."

He walked halfway into the room, paying no attention to the two men sitting at the end of the long center table and facing him. He smiled at the skeleton with its grotesque salute of bottle and three flags, drew paper and crayon from his sash, and sketched in fast, sure strokes. With a change of angle here, a tilt of the skull, an added line or two, he made of the skeleton a crying drunkard, a dancing girl, a soldier, a mocking devil, laughing softly to himself the while. Then he drew it exactly as it was; yet not exactly, for it had a life which the other lacked.

Bony, eyes popping, black greased mustaches swinging out like horns, bustled forward and bowed as deeply as his paunch would allow. Fairly choking over his excited greeting: "*Señor*, I am too honored! What is your pleasure, *señor*, that I may hasten to accomplish it?"

An *hidalgo* here in his place. It was almost too much for simple Bony.

"A little wine, yes," Luis answered, letting the drawing drop on the table, absorbed again with his crayon. When Bony came with a glass on a tray, Luis showed him what he had done. It was the proprietor, cleverly made into a bull but with the horns above the mouth instead of on the forehead. A caricature without malice—and of the best.

Bony burst into laughter. "It is a creature most extraordinary, no? I would not ask that it be given me, *señor*, certainly not, if the young *señor* wished to keep it—"

Luis put it in his hand and quickly drew another. A flattering, a noble picture of Bony, important proprietor of an important place. At sight of it Bony drew himself up, swelled, bowed: with the proper deference, yet with the dignity of his position. If the noble *señor* saw him so, then he was so. "Your wine, *señor*, if you will honor me."

Then finally Luis Gonzaga saw the two men and felt a stir within him as the older man smiled, rose, and put a finger on the drawings lying on the table.

"May I have one of these?" Devlin asked. "It is more than mere pleasure to meet you for I also am an artist. But of sorts, for I can only draw the body and cannot breathe the soul into it. I, who drew the skeleton on the wall, bow my head in shame. May I congratulate your superb talent?"

The world rocked and shook for Luis Gonzaga. This man an *Americano?* But he had always been told that they were coarse, sometimes clever enough to simulate gentility but without the inner grace which was its true test. And to meet an artist at last—he had dreamed and hoped and prayed to some day meet a man who would understand the thing which drove him forever to crayons and paints. What a cruel jest, that he should be one of the enemy, and on the day that his father had cursed them. Even if Angela had stopped the words, it had been there. Then there was loyalty, to his father and to his people. Impulses urged and warred, beckoned and threatened, disrupted and confused him.

He stepped back and said stiffly. "*Gracias, señor*. The pictures I threw away and what one throws away become the property of whoever picks it up. I but amused myself for a moment." Regretting the coldness of his words he added, "I am not sure I could not have drawn your skeleton on the wall as well as you. It is very fine."

When Luis looked at Warrener, anger fled in a hot wave to his hair—that on this face too should be pressed the mark of a gentleman. Anger that his impulse had been to return the smile and friendliness upon it. Anger that those blue eyes had seen only Susanita that Sunday, and by some devil's magic struck through to her heart. (Do not lower yourself to speak to him, Pride whispered. Remember his presumptuousness in serenading her to flaunt his vocal gift. Remember how he forced himself upon her last night and disgraced all of you and brought trouble into the house. Remember who you are, and do not speak to him.)

Devlin was saying, "This is Lieutenant Warrener, *señor—señor—?*"

"Mendoza y Soría," Luis answered, holding his head high. Putting his name above them all, putting himself in a class that would be lowered by speaking to such as these. He turned from Warrener, bowed formally to Devlin, and wordlessly, ignoring the startled Bony, walked from the place.

He walked on until the street ended in a cowpath that wound through the chaparral and followed it slowly. The old loneliness within him was a new wound, torn open by a hand stretched to him in friendliness—a hand he had refused. Beyond his pride had been the urge to respond to the invitation in Warrener's eyes and sit and talk with him awhile. And the lame man who went to church, how he had wanted to take his hand. For a moment—a happy, expanding moment—he had had a feeling that he belonged. That he would not have been considered peculiar and effeminate, as his family and those his age saw him to be, he felt certain. Nor would he have been scorned for his artistry, as others scorned him.

Luis Gonzaga, had he followed his inclination, would have thrown himself upon the ground and wept like a child. Wept for the beautiful thing which had been laid in his hand and he had thrown away.

Chapter 11

Captain Devlin took the sketches to Padre Pierre and asked the priest to arrange a meeting with the boy for him. Padre Pierre pulled an ear lobe and said slowly, "It will require some thought. I have a deep affection for Luis, and it is I who have procured supplies for him and persuaded his father to let him use them. But his father's attitude toward all things American—yes, I must think a bit." He opened the door. "I am expecting callers, and your presence here might prove embarrassing. Come the day after tomorrow, at about three."

Padre Pierre decided against pretense, and when Luis came into the office, he lit a candle to lift the room's gloom and said simply, "Luis, it should be a pleasure to you to meet a fellow artist. Captain Devlin, this is Luis Gonzaga de Mendoza y Soría."

Devlin smiled and offered a hand. "Ah, the young man who put life into my skeleton. We have met, *Padre*, yet I might say we have not met; the circumstance was not favorable to further the acquaintance. I have wanted to know you further."

Luis, to his confusion, found his hand in that of the American; one of the army fighting his people. It was a terrible thing to do, the more so because it did not seem terrible at all. Also, Devlin's formality of speech and his adroit excusing of the boy's rudeness made the proper impression on Luis. He bowed and said, "I have regretted my rudeness to you, and it is most kind of you to overlook it."

"It was scarcely the place for extended amenities." Devlin thought it best not to mention Warrener, knowing it was because of him that Luis had left so abruptly. "You have a live quality in your drawings I would give much to possess."

Padre Pierre pushed them into chairs, pleasure warm in his brown eyes. "That is the trouble with Luis, Señor Devlin. I give him paints to create the saints—" he laughed so heartily his shoulders shook—"and they look most unsaintlike. He painted the funniest Saint Cecilia at the harp."

Luis laughed with him and told the American, "It was my sister Susanita, like she was playing her harp. She looked like a lovely *señorita* singing a love song."

"The halo—do you remember how the halo looked on her, Luis?" Padre Pierre asked, shaking with mirth.

"Personally," Devlin said, when their laughter had subsided, "I have always wondered why a saint is pictured as devoid of feeling, when to have achieved sainthood certainly required deepest character and deep feeling. Tell me, is painting important to you or is it just a fancy?"

"Important, *señor?*" His voice was eager, excited. "Do you mean the thing inside that makes you want to put everything beautiful on paper and keep it forever, that makes you see everyone first as someone to draw?" That at last he could tell this to someone! But to an alien—something, he felt, was wrong, but he did not know where.

"Yes. We call it the 'divine spark.' You and I and the good Padre here believe it is given to us by God." Devlin rose and walked around the office, scrutinizing the overly solemn pictures of saints on the walls. Padre Pierre had told him about the father's epithet of *marica* for his son, and the older brother and his companions who laughed at him. He turned and said impulsively, "I could teach you such things as I know, if you wanted to try colors and oils. You will eventually paint well without being taught, but—Lord, I wish you were in Baltimore! We have a portrait painter who is a master of—"

"Baltimore, is that in your country?" Luis asked. "I mean, that is I—I did not think there was any kind of art in the United States."

Devlin knew of the belief of the Mexicans that only they had culture, so he was not surprised. How could the boy have known the truth? He asked the priest, "Shall I tell our friend of us and our land?"

"Do." He motioned Devlin to his chair and drew up a stool for himself facing them. "Luis, Señor Devlin is with the soldiers because his wife died and the forgetting was hard. I thought you should know why he is so far from his home."

Slowly, to allow for his imperfect Spanish, Devlin told them of the cities of the East; of their art and music and fine homes and gentle, pampered women. He told Luis of Maryland—Mary's land, named after the same Blessed Virgin, Mary the Mother of Christ, whom the Mexicans venerated. Of Lord Baltimore who founded the colony so that, in a new land,

Catholics might worship free from persecution. "But we also believe that others may worship God as they choose, Luis. We do not think them evil because they are Protestant, do you understand?"

Luis listened, unbelieving, yet knowing it was true. He asked, hesitantly, "Your friend, *señor*, what family then has he? Is he a—gentleman, also?" (I must know, for Susanita. It will not change anything but I must know.)

"Robert Warrener?" Devlin laughed, thinking of what the older Warrener would say if he heard anyone ask whether his son was a gentleman. So he told them what a plantation in Virginia was like, of its fine horses and ordered living and entertainments, and the word pictures were as real as if they were on canvas. Time passed, and none of them knew of its passing, for to Padre Pierre much of this was new also.

"Then why did your people come here?" Luis asked. "Why do they take what is ours and force us to be citizens of a government we cannot endure?"

Shadow passed over the American's face. "That is not easy to answer, Luis. The mistake was for the Mexican government to invite settlers and give them land. Your vice-regal government did not play fair with anyone. If your people—but, no, there is too much that is wrong on the side of the Americans, much that is disgraceful. Let me simply say that we are a people who never are still. Shall we speak of what is more important, painting? Would it be possible for you to go back to Baltimore with me when I am relieved here, sometime next summer?"

It was long past *merienda* when Luis Gonzaga was again in the plaza and back to reality. Back, as it happened, to stern reality. From the door of The Skeleton up to the street came half dozen Mexicans and two tall, hefty Rangers. One of the Rangers lifted a large boot, and a Mexican pitched forward violently onto the ground. Mexicans spewed from doorways, there was a flash of a thrown knife blade; a pistol shot, running feet, a street suddenly deserted—except for a groaning form lying prone, another bending over it and cursing in a mixture of Spanish and English.

Bony came out, and he and the cursing Ranger lifted the other and carried him inside.

Nothing new, in Matamoros. Perhaps both were to blame, perhaps neither. Only the pot boiling over and spilling the fat of idleness and arrogance onto the coals of war. No, nothing new.

Luis Gonzaga hesitated. Devlin was still at the rectory and a doctor was needed. He struggled, move on. It was none of his affair, and besides he had seen nothing. Yes, that was best, not to have seen.

Don Santiago was having coffee at a small table with the father of René de la Ferrière when Luis came into the patio. That meant that the visiting *señor*, if not now asking for the hand of Susanita for his son, was leading up to it for a later presentation. Luis wanted to run to them and tell them "No, no, not René. Susanita and the *Americano* love each other, and he is an *hidalgo* in his country as we are here, and they have a *rancho* also and oh, *papá*, he is the kind of man you want for her and cannot find here. And they have a country named for Our Lady, and I want to go there and study painting, and you would be proud of me. *Papá*, let me tell you and you will see that we are blind—"

When he met the disapproval in the eyes of his father as they noted the bundle of artists' supplies under his arm, when he saw the same set, uncompromising jaw on the visitor's face as on that of his host, Luis knew nothing could be right. They believed only what they wished to believe, and no one under them dared even wish differently. Luis, looking at the two faces, felt a forlornness that was a sickening, spreading pain.

"To think, *amigo*," Señor de la Ferrière sighed, patting a huge paunch tenderly, "that I was once as slim as Luis Gonzaga here. When I wound my sash about my waist you could have taken your two hands, Don Santiago, and had the fingers of them meet around me." He sighed again and sipped at his coffee. "Ah, youth is so beautiful. So beautiful."

Luis Gonzaga bowed to the guest, bowed to his father, and hurried inside to look for Susanita. She was alone in the *sala*, a somewhat forlorn figure dutifully practicing scales on the harp. He drew a stool close, took her hands from the strings and held them.

"How much are you in love with the *Americano*? I know. I knew from the beginning, little sister."

"Luis!" She kissed him on the cheek and put his palms against her flushing cheeks. "You knew, and didn't tell—how I love you for that! Does anyone else know, or suspect?"

"I think *mamá* does, and since the *baile* I believe Tía Dolores—well, perhaps she only likes to think so; you know how romantic she really is deep inside. To me you betray yourself a dozen times a day. I asked you how much."

"There is no measure when it is real, *hermano*."

"Susanita, you know there is nothing for any of us except what *papá* wills, don't you?"

She nodded. "Unless God wills otherwise. I used to laugh at Angela, but now I see where she has something we do not have. So I—I just put it in Our Lady's hands and—and try not to worry too much."

He did not tell her what he had intended. Let her be happy while she could. He rumpled her hair, left the *sala*, and went to his mother's room. She was mending a lace *mantilla* by the light of two candles on a stand beside her, and he brought a footstool and sat close enough to lean against her knees. Perhaps they would both forget that he was eighteen and a man, and she would lift his face and kiss it as she did when he was small and assure him that everything would be bright again by the morrow's sunrise.

Doña María Petronilla, after a press of the hand on his shoulder, continued her mending. She wanted to ask him what was wrong but decided it would be best not to, for no matter what the problem, there could be but one answer at the present time—whatever Don Santiago wished. They were still under his displeasure and silence was the watchword. It came to her that Luis Gonzaga—she always thought of him by the full name—had been with Susanita that Sunday morning and must know of the love between her and the *Americano*. That it was love María Petronilla did not doubt. Those things were in song and story, and surely an instant love between His creatures was not impossible to God, who had created Love. What to do about it was another matter. To speak to her about it would be a shocking thing to do, for in their code a mother did not talk to her daughter about love and suitors and a husband. That was for servants, *peons*, the common rabble who had no culture, and was not done by people of pride. Nor could she ask Luis Gonzaga if he was aware of this love and possibly intrigue with him to bring her news of the *Americano*. It was not done.

For a short time Doña María Petronilla also beat hands against the wall of custom and traditions and the laws and rules that cemented them. For one hot rebelling moment she questioned the right of them, fashioned to make wife and child subservient even in thought, as much as this was possible, to the lord of the house. Then her world closed over her again; still without speaking, she pressed her son's shoulder once more. Whatever was worrying him could not, she felt certain, be of much importance.

Señor de la Ferrière took his leave when Alvaro came into the patio. The *señor* had carefully avoided the subject of marriage, but Don Santiago knew what the call portended, as his guest meant him to know. When the Christmas festivities were over, there would be a formal request of betrothal between the two families. So it was that Alvaro, in high good humor, found his father in like mood and took the guest's chair. It was past the coffee hour, but the rule did not hold for the spoiled oldest son, and Luciana came hurrying with a cup of the hot brew. When Alvaro ogled her, his father beamed in approval, pridefully.

"You have said, *papá*, that I must find a wife this winter," Alvaro sighed, "and of course that is my duty. I have made my choice, and, if it pleases you I would like to have you ask for her."

Don Santiago beamed. They were men together and at ease with each other. "That is good. Who is it, *hijo?*"

"Inez."

"Inez? You mean Inez Sánchez y Argensola?"

"You say that as if you did not approve, *papá*."

"I had not thought you would select her. Why did you?"

Alvaro's lower lip protruded stubbornly. He drained his cup and shoved it petulantly onto the center of the table.

"Because I want her."

A smile showed Don Santiago's white teeth and he lifted an eyebrow. "Wanting a woman is not a reason for marriage, Alvaro. That"—he snapped a finger "—can go again in a day. She provoked you in the *seguidilla* you danced with her and now you want her. That is for a mistress, not a wife, and the men of our family do not marry a mistress. If you would not marry Inez, if you could have her for mistress, then there is poor reason for choosing her to give her your name. Do you understand?"

"I understand. But I want her for a wife."

"She is not submissive. Quite the contrary."

Alvaro's eyes gleamed as he gave a short laugh. "Another reason why I want her. I want the joy of taming a woman and breaking her to my will."

"That has its points. And its dangers. Women are unpredictable creatures."

"I'll do the predicting as to what *my* wife will be. What other objections have you? The family is good."

"Both the Sánchez and the Argensola lines are good, yes. But Doña Juana bore seven children and only one lived; a thing to be considered when many children are needed to build up our family. And they are poor. They could not even spend the winters in town if Gabriel del Lago did not stay with them and pay them well."

"The children one has are also unpredictable, *papá*," Alvaro laughed, proud of his cleverness. "We are rich enough, I do not see that my wife must also have money."

Don Santiago became very serious. "Consider, Alvaro, what it would mean to have another strong-willed woman in the house rebelling against authority, for you will live with us. I will overlook the undesirable fact that she was so close to widowhood; we do not marry a woman who has belonged to another; that the two years of mourning make her now eighteen and far too knowing. You may tame her, but I wonder—and the process would be unbearable in a house accustomed to peace. That is, not considering your aunt Dolores, but then we are accustomed to her. Compare Inez with the Robles girl: not yet fourteen, decorous—"

Alvaro burst into laughter, folded his hands and mocked meekness. "Like this. Never her, *papá*. I want Inez."

"I will think about it. Wait until after Christmas, you may change your mind by then."

"*¿Quien sabe?*" Alvaro rose, remembered his manners and bowed deferentially. "With your permission I will leave to change my clothes and make myself presentable."

Don Santiago nodded assent, smiling indulgently at the spoiled selfishness and arrogance of his son. It had not occurred to either one of them to consider what Inez might think about the marriage.

Inez, who at the same time was sitting alone in her room, replying to a note that addressed her as "Beautiful lady of my heart."

Riding home after a scouting expedition up the river, Johnny White, too, was thinking of Inez, and wondering what he would do about it. The notes and the stolen visits to the window had been in most part to relieve the ennui of the long days, titillating because Inez belonged to the guarded and sheltered class forbidden to him. Now he found himself looking forward eagerly to the dark nights and soft whisper of her voice, and that was not so good. Marriage was all right for noble souls like Warrener, he assured himself again. Besides, where would he put her, how support her, if she would leave home? He shrugged. It was a pleasant episode, why not lengthen it? No harm would come from it. In Matamoros the warm sun kept winter at bay; soft winds were heavy with the perfume of blossoms from desert and garden; there was the song of birds, and music and laughter and dancing; there was love, and longings, and dreams. The things that would always be, whether man made peace or war.

Chapter 12

❧

Las Posadas. Beginning on the sixteenth, the spirit was prepared for the coming of the Holy Child. Families met each night at a different home to recite the litany of the Blessed Virgin and the Posadas, and all bickerings were put aside, enmities forgotten, too—serious discourse left for another day. After the prayers there was dancing and games for old and young— "*El Señor Dios* must weary of never-ending prayer," it was said, "surely he appreciates the joyous heart also." This year the coveted role of host for Christmas Eve was given to Don Santiago because as their leader it was fitting that his home symbolize their policy of isolation. Doña María Petronilla, both to please her husband and to be better able to submerge her worries, took charge. Meats, butter, fruit, and their complementary foods had to be ordered, the kitchen staff supervised, all details of the Midnight Mass mapped out well in advance so no confusion should mar their reputation of perfect hostship.

This suited Doña Dolores, who had been hungering to make up the black-and-purple-striped material, and with the excuse that her need for something festive was desperate, appropriated Isidora the household seamstress, and closed herself in her room to emerge only for meals. For which vanity the servants gave silent thanks, Paz going so far as to include the petition in her prayers at night that the dress be long in the making; the dear Lord knew there were troubles enough without her interventions.

This left the decoration of the *sala* to Susanita and Angela under the eye of Paz, who considered it her sacred duty and quite impossible of accomplishment without her. No one would have dreamed of telling her that she was only in the way, the girls even making a point of asking her advice. Susanita, dreaming of Roberto, dawdled over the wreaths she wove of the cedar and jasmine the boys had brought; Angela, preparing the crib, had a recurrence of her longings and doubts and let them slow her hands; old Paz, worn with work and excitement, napped whenever she took a seat. So that it was the day before Christmas when the last touches were done.

The *piñata*, an earthen pot filled with candy and nuts, was fitted in a clown suit and hung grinning from a rafter. A goodly part of a corner was taken by the crib, the *Nacimiento*. The waxen Mary and Joseph, highly treasured relics, were gaily dressed: Mary in a gown of white silk and crocheted blue mantle, Joseph in a robe of red satin. They knelt before a straw-filled cradle, where the Infant would be placed in ceremony later. Shepherds wore homespun and the Wise Men, one white, one yellow, one black, holding tiny pots heaped with their gifts of gold, frankincense and myrrh, wore elaborate costumes of satin and velvet. Flocks of sheep rested peacefully beside wolves, there were macaws beside ptarmigans, waxen green pines thrived with palms, tropical fruit grew on snow. Paper angels fluttered on invisible wires, a great star shone from above.

Doña Dolores came with her canary and set it beside the shepherds, cast an appraising eye at the room. "It took long enough, I declare I don't know what kind of wives you will make. Angela, go with me to the convent, I must see if the good nuns lack anything. I brought Manuel to bring the plants in from the portico—now where is the renegade?" She found him hiding behind the bombazine umbrella of her skirts and told him sternly, "Every one of the pots must be brought in, do you hear? Where is Paz? Susanita, you'll have to see to it, I'll arrange them when I get back."

As soon as they were alone Manuel put a finger to his lips, then held out a very dirty palm to show a silver coin. "Look, Susanita, from the *Americano* who sang at your window." Before she could ask him about it, he brought a folded handkerchief from inside his shirt. "There is a paper in it for you, for that he gave me the money."

Susanita hastily thrust the note in her tight bodice, kissed Manuel, and whispered, "You must never tell anyone, not even Grandmother Paz. You be a good boy and bring—"

Manuel kept on the single track of his mission. "He will give me money again if I bring him a paper from you. I will not tell. I made a cross over my heart for him that I would not tell."

"Then wait—no, bring in the pots and at least pretend you are being good while I am gone."

In the safety of her room, hands trembling and heart smothering her, she read: Beloved, tonight I will be at the Mass. Look for me near the door and try to come close enough so I can put something in your hand. Little Susana, you are so much a part of me that no waking or sleeping moment is without you. I will be at The Skeleton until noon, and I know you can trust Manuel. Will you write and tell me you love me? Robert.

Until noon. Manuel would have to hurry so as to get back again before Tía Dolores came. She finally found a crayon, tore a strip from the bottom of the note, and wrote: What your heart most wishes for is my answer.

She snipped off an end of curl and tied it with the bit of paper in one of her handkerchiefs and hurried to the *sala*, where Manuel in diligence was bringing in the plants. So now, she thought, I am a traitor. Yet I love him so that I am sick with it. I love an *Americano*, yet I am glad.

Don Santiago, a black cape lined with scarlet thrown over a shoulder, Doña María Petronilla fresh and young looking with the lace collar on the plain black dress, Susanita in gray, and Angela in brown silk, Doña Dolores in the splendor of the black and purple stripes—"through I do feel a bit gay," she confided—had not long to wait before their guests were at the door. There was laughter, strumming of instruments, then a man's voice intoned the words which were picked up in chorus:

> *In the name of heaven we ask lodging,*
> *My beloved wife can no longer walk.*

Alvaro and Luis Gonzaga came from the dining room and opened the door. A crowd of people stood waiting, carrying tapers whose flame burned high and steady in the crisp, still night air, and as Don Santiago and his wife came outside, they shifted into couples. Moving slowly, reverently, they marched along the portico which bordered the patio, servants coming from the kitchen and joining the procession and singing with the masters.

"*Mater de Cristi, ora pro nobis.*" As the loved litany had been sung for generations; would be sung for many more to come. Mystical rose. Tower of David. House of gold. Morning star. Refuge of sinners. Comforter of the afflicted. Queen of Angels. Titles to Mary, Beloved Lady, and the petition "pray for us, pray for us." (Ask thy Son for us, surely He cannot deny His mother's pleas.)

Four children in white robes carrying the *misterio*, a small shrine with figures of the Holy Family, stood by the host and sang with him the plaintive words of Joseph and Mary seeking lodging:

❧

> *Do not be inhuman, have a little charity,*
> *God in his mercy will come to reward you.*

Now came Inez's high soprano and Alvaro's baritone, refusing the door to the couple asking for shelter:

> *Continue your journey, do not molest us,*
> *If we lose our temper, we'll give you a beating.*

Again the plea:

> *We are very tired, we come from Nazareth,*
> *I am a carpenter, Joseph is my name.*

The answer:

> *We care not who you are, leave us in peace.*
> *We have told you we cannot let you in.*

The plea came again:

> *Beloved housekeeper, lodging for one night*
> *Is asked by the queen of heaven.*
> *If a queen is asking lodging for herself,*
> *Why does she wander so lonely at night?*
> *My wife Mary is the queen of heaven,*
> *For she is to be the mother of the Child Divine.*

Rejoicing at this news the chorus answered:

> *Is that you, Joseph, is that you, Mary?*
> *Enter the holy pilgrims, we knew not who you were.*

Now old Paz flung wide the door of the *sala* and said: "O blessed be this house which gives Thee shelter tonight."

The procession marched to the Crib. Two of the bearers took the Child from the *misterio*, swaddled it with a strip of cloth and placed it in the cradle, announcing:

❦

Good news to you, O shepherds, a virgin gave birth
To a child beautiful as the light of day.

That ended the religious part of the celebration. A child was blindfolded and given a stick to break the *piñata*, when at last one succeeded and scattered the sweets over the floor. After the children were put to bed, there was dancing. Old Alejo came and broke into the orchestra with his fiddle, stamping his boots in time with the fast rhythm of a quadrille. "*Ay Ay*, Alejo," shouted Don Santiago, laughing, "you want us people of discretion, to forget we are no longer young. *Bien*, you call the sets and we will follow. Ay, you fiddled for us when we were courting, old man."

It was too much for dignity. It was, for an hour, the turning back of the years. Even Doña Dolores flirted coyly with Gabriel del Lago and let the striped skirt swing out in full glory. They had, all of them, forgotten the *Americanos*. All too soon Angela's high thin voice, like a note on a flute, rose above the music and the dancing ceased. The children were brought from the beds, the servants from the kitchen, and Juan Bautista and his men came, and all together sang their joy that a Savior was born.

Come joyfully and adore the Holy Infant, new-born God,
The stars in heaven shine brightly because of Him.

In procession went old and young, master and servant, through the star-spangled, hushed night, to Mass. Beside the doors all over town a light flickered: candles in lanterns at the homes of the wealthy, a bit of wick in a bowl of oil at the doors of the poor, so that, if Mary and Joseph came by, they would know that there was room for them inside.

Susanita saw him standing beside the lame doctor at the little altar of San Antonio in the back of the church, when the family walked decorously forward to their pew. Here in church! That point had worried her, now it dissolved in a surge of joy. Perhaps *papá* would be approachable when he knew Roberto was not an enemy of the church. *Papá* was so happy this evening, he might have changed—.

Mass at midnight. Fingers of flame, in dozens of candles. Shine of silver and glitter of gold, on altar lace and vestment, chalice and paten, monstrance and candelabra; on men's jackets, on women's ears and throats and fingers. Fingers hiding the high carved altar and banking the statues. Incense swinging in a censor sending fragrant clouds upward. (Incense to me, for I am thy God.) Male voice chanting *"Kyrie eleison, eleison—"* Joyous bells ringing in the Gloria in Excelsis Deo.

Glory to God on high. Glory to Christ the newborn King.

Robert Warrener looked at the candles and saw the light in her eyes; he looked at the gold lace glistening beneath snowy altar linen, and saw her hair; he looked at the flowers and saw a face lovelier than they; he listened to the chanting and his heart sang to her.

To Susanita the familiar service was a wheel of light and color and sound that spilled over each other and ran together and made no pattern at all. Give us this day our daily bread—sweet Infant, give me Roberto, give me my love. Come close so I can put something in your hand—Mary, dear Lady, help me find him. The service was endless and then, when the last Amen sounded, it seemed as if it had but begun.

When Luis Gonzaga saw Devlin to the right of the church door when he came outside, an urge to speak to the American drew him that way. The men were beyond the light that streamed from the open church doors; nor did the glow of the lanterns on the posts in the plaza reach them, so Luis felt certain no one would see the encounter. This was the Good Eve when all was peace and all men brothers, and more than anything in the world Luis wanted to give this man greeting, and touch his hand.

All of Matamoros had been to the service, and it was easy for Luis to let himself be jostled to the right and work his way towards the two in the shadow; scarcely aware that his sister was clinging to his hand, for it was an odd habit of hers and by its very familiarity escaped notice. So happy was Luis to see his friend and so eager to greet him that he saw Warrener more as an object than a person, and when the fat Señor Montoya and his fatter wife moved so that they formed a screen, Luis hurried the few steps to be face to face with the man for whom he felt such deep affection. Thrilling to the furtive handclasp and the smile of joy on the older man's face—Luis had forgotten Susanita.

No one saw her hand in that of the American or knew that he was pressing something into the palm and closing her fingers over it. All their friends were too hungry for the fine supper waiting for them, too filled with good cheer, religious feeling and conviviality to pay any attention to the Americans or to resent them, if they saw them at all.

"May the Christ Child bring you good health, *señor,*" Luis Gonzaga murmured, using the Mexican Christmas greeting—and from the heart, with all his heart.

"Susanita, *te amo*," whispered Robert Warrener.

A minute of time. A fragment of eternity.

It seemed to Susanita that there were a thousand guests taking turn at the tables loaded with the traditional supper of tamales, turkey with *mole*—a secret blending of sauce for which Paz was famous—a salad of beets and lettuce, fruit, wines. The dancing and songs were forms to go through, the attentions of the young *caballeros* tiresome and flirting a bore. But at last dawn came and Don Santiago led his guests to the plaza, where in the opaline thin mist, they sang the song with which the *rancheros* salute the coming of day:

Forever Jesus be my guide
And the Flower which gave Him birth.

Susanita, pleading weariness, was allowed to take a candle to her room when the assemblage left for the plaza. Quickly, before Angela should come, she took the paper from the tight waist where it had burned into her heart for all these hours. It was a ring, and on the paper wrapped about it was written: "Keep this until I can give you a wedding ring in its place." The seal of the heavy gold ring was four exquisitely wrought stemmed lilies set stem to blossom to form the letter *W*, framed in a circle of over-lapping tiny rings. It seemed strange to Susanita, accustomed to seals and escutcheons of swords and lions, crosses, snakes, tigress, fisted arms, all the symbols of might and its right. Warrener could have told her that, many years ago, an ancestor had perfected a lily to honor his king, and had been knighted and enriched by the delighted sovereign—who him-self designed the simple seal and ordered his goldsmith to execute it. What matter now, if she had known. It could have a plain circlet of silver and it would have been as precious. Already it was her wedding ring and she slipped it on her finger.

And, tears washing it, she looped it on a ribbon and hung it around her neck so it could be hidden under a gown against her breast.

The Good Eve was gone. Susanita and Warrener had prayed that their love might find its attainment, knowing that only help from Above could bring it to pass. Luis Gonzaga and Carl Devlin prayed that they might go East together in summer, and prayed with the forlornness of one who dreams. María de los Angeles prayed that she might find and know her Destiny, adding a simple, "Jesus, I want so to stay here with the nuns when *papá* goes back to the ranch." Doña María Petronilla prayed for her children—sadly, knowing her own impotence. Don Santiago prayed that the invaders would be driven from Texas, righteously reminding God that the Mexicans were His people. Alvaro prayed—if it might be called prayer—that he might have Inez, and Inez prayed that Johnny White would take her away. Old Paz, her bones a misery with weariness, crouched against the wall and slept through the service, knowing that the Lord to whom she prayed for so many years would understand. Johnny White did not pray—it had been a long, long time since Johnny had remembered his God. Nor did Red McLane, in Camargo with General Scott for reasons of his own, pray. Red believed in prayer, but he did not ask a Supreme Being for anything which he himself could not accomplish. Red had known prayer only as he had to suffer it in his youth, in solemn long-faced sanctimoniousness of his dour father, the whining helplessness of his mother, the hypocrisy of the loudmouthed, and the whisperings of the meek. Red believed in the idea of prayer, and left it at that.

Padre Pierre turned a tired body on a hard bed. His soul had emptied itself of prayer. God, he was thinking, had given man free will—he wondered, sighing, how long God would be patient with man's use of it. The angel brought a message of peace to men of good will, and man refused good will to his fellowman—and railed at God because his hatreds, greed, and prejudices brought him war. Padre Pierre would have wept, had his heart not been empty of tears.

The Good Eve was gone.

Chapter 13

Señor Robles had sent the call for another meeting, stressing its importance and inviting the young men also. All had responded and were now grouped around the long table and beside the fireplace, the flames of the fire the only illumination of the large dining room, leaving the corners in darkness. There was desultory talk, most of it pointless.

"And I missed a good dance for this," René de la Ferrière told Alvaro, sighing. "I don't see why they can't have their stupid meeting without us, it's for the old ones anyhow."

"Tía Dolores's coffee parties have more life," Alvaro agreed. "Listen, they're talking about the redhaired *gringo*."

"Yes, he talked to me too," José Antonio Carbajal was saying. "I had to watch my speech, he talked Spanish so perfectly, and he was so courteous I couldn't refuse to listen to him. There is much in what he says, that we got nothing from our loyalty to Mexico and might at least try transferring them to the new government, seeing we are under its protection. When I laughed at the word 'protection,' he said it was ours if we asked for it and withdrew our enmity."

"One does not withdraw enmity," Don Santiago answered crisply. "It is a thing inside. You might as well ask that we withdraw our faith in God."

"It has been done," came a voice from behind clouds of *cigarillo* smoke. "Men have killed faith in God, Santiago. We could keep our contempt, for it can be covered where enmity shows itself. We are a conquered people, but that does not mean that we need give up our church and our customs and traditions, as Señor McLane says. I too have wondered whether it might not be better to show a seeming friendliness. I must admit the man had a certain honesty about him."

Voices ran over each other, some in protest, others in agreement, none in violence, even Don Santiago letting his anger, if not his indignation, remain dormant. "Don't let their smooth tongues convince you," said

Constantín de Deza. "If this McLane offers us friendship, be assured he wants something in exchange. However, if an *Americano* does not harm me and treats me courteously I will not kill him—though I will not embrace him."

Señor Robles, walking slowly back and forth, took no part in the conversation, and while many wondered why he had called the meeting, none questioned him. The young men, grouped at the end of the table, were plainly restless and whispered and laughed in a world of their own. Most of the men admitted having listened to McLane and his influence was evident. Then Juan de Cisneros sarcastically asked whether his friends were selling their souls to the invaders. Hermilo Márquez, still quite young, lean and blond, and clean-shaven, rose and made the first speech of the evening, slapping an open palm hard on the table. His voice was clear and unafraid, his face and demeanor calm.

"*Mis amigos:* When Padre Pierre spoke here at our first meeting, I saw much truth in what he said and have given it much thought. I have talked to the Señor McLane also, more than once. I am young and have many years before me and am the father of two sons. I have my land and shall follow the American's advice and have it recorded and the boundaries certified according to his directions. I shall teach my children loyalty to the new government, for it has also seemed to me, *señores*, that its shoe may not pinch more than the old—for God knows Mexico has betrayed us. I shall show these Americanos the best of me and I shall look for the best in them. Señor McLane is a sharp man, but I have heard that he deals honestly with our people, and I felt an honesty in him. I met the young man who came to the dance with the *alcalde*, and I could not see where he warranted enmity; in fact, I would say the contrary. Antagonisms and hatred and killings can avail us nothing, *amigos*. I say let us accept Señor McLane's offer to speak to us in a group and explain things. As has been said, we can keep our customs and traditions even though—"

"Ah, think you so, my young countryman?"

From a corner a heavy shadow detached itself and came swiftly forward to the table to a place opposite the fireplace, where the flames could light his face. He was a lean, powerfully built man with a long thin face the color of tanned leather topped by a head of almost white hair. The large, thin-lipped mouth was pressed firmly together, and above the aquiline nose small, piercing black eyes glanced quickly at the astonished faces turned to him. He wore the uniform of a Mexican general complete with heavy gold epaulettes, and when he lighted the gold-trimmed cap and set in on the table there was an awed, audible murmur:

"General Canales—it is General Canales!"[1]

Don Santiago rushed to him and embraced him, others crowded close and offered hands. The host, an arm around the general's shoulders beamed at the assemblage and said, "This is why I wanted you to come, *amigos*, and I trust I am forgiven."

"But, Antonio, should you be here?" Don Santiago asked anxiously. "How came you here, with every Ranger and soldier looking for you and wanting your head?"

Canales laughed. "I did not get the name 'The Fox' without reason, and you need not worry about my head." He took a step back to let them know he wanted them to take their places, then dramatically pointed a finger at Hermilo Márquez, and in a pulsing, modulated voice denounced him.

"With shame I listened to what you were saying. I had heard that some of my people were turning traitor to their pride, but I did not expect it of you *rancheros*. From a *peon*, yes, but not from an *hidalgo*. From some doddering old fool, perhaps, but not from a young man." His eyes went from face to face so intently that is seem like a physical raking, and he struck a fist against an open palm. "Most of you—has fat living put your manhood to sleep? While Mexico bleeds, while her men die to keep out the invaders, you feast and dance and listen to lying *Americanos* and talk about betraying your honor to them."

"Not I!" Don Santiago, fired with new zeal, pounded a fist on the table. "I have not changed, I will never change towards them!"

"Nor have I down in my heart," shouted one, and another, and another, until only Hermilo Márquez stood silent. All looked at him and waited for him to speak, but he stepped back to the fireplace and sat on a stool against the wall. Canales shrugged and the host hastened to fill in the awkward pause by asking,

"Tell us what you wish us to do, *señor*."

"I speak to the young men." Vehemence claimed him as he turned to the youths staring awesomely at him. "You who spend your time riding aimlessly to show what fine *caballeros* you are, thinking only of love making and the pleasures of life, while your country lies bleeding at your fine-booted feet. Torn and wounded she writhes in agony, trampled by the infamous avarice of the invaders who are never satisfied in their lust for wealth, while you—you—," he sobbed out the words, using his hands in passionate eloquence of expression. Zeal blazed from his small black eyes and flattened the thin lips against large teeth that shone milk white against his bronzed skin. "You content yourself with hating them, riding past their camp and spitting at it like children. Why didn't one of you kill the one who came to your dance, why haven't you young men taken it upon yourselves to kill this McLane whose devil tongue wins over your fathers?" He turned to Don Santiago. "And you, *amigo*, what have you been doing?"

Don Santiago struck his hands together and said deferentially, "You are right, we have been losing our manhood indeed. Show us what to do and I assure you that there will not be a man between Matamoros and Laredo who will not stand up in arms. Tell us what you want."

Gone was all lassitude. It was as if their passivity had held explosive which needed but a match. "I am with you, Canales," cried Olivares, and quickly there was assenting chorus, from all but the man on the stool by the fire; and he had been forgotten and was already an outcast.

Tears ran down Canales's cheeks, and this time he played on them with a warm, soft voice. "Not you heads of families, your place is at home to protect your families and deceive the enemy with your presence. When they see you in town and on your *ranchos*, they will not suspect that your sons are *guerrilleros*—yes, I want your sons in my army. That is why I am here. Let your sons go with me."

"I'll go," cried Alvaro, "and Chino here, we'll go!" But Pedro Mora, short and swarthy, shook a graying head. "No, general, I do not see that. I do not want my son a *guerrillero*. That is for the loafers in the plaza, the *peons* one must send away because they are unruly. It is not for the son of an *hidalgo*.

"There you are wrong, *amigo*." Canales had suspected that he must go deeper than a mere emotional appeal and now drew forth patriotism; letting his superb declamation and intensity of feeling blend and weld into a baton that commanded them as a leader commands an orchestra. "I know the *Americanos* better than you do, *señores*, and I know them for the sneaking, insidious, lying snakes that they are. In 1840 when I rebelled against Santa Anna, a number of them offered me their services to fight in defense of freedom and I, fool that I was, believed them. I even offered them twenty-five pesos, a league of land, and equal share in the spoils. And do you know what their motive was? To segregate the states of northern Mexico and join them with Texas. Engraved in my memory with letters of fire is still the letter I received from General Haines, proposing to take the land from Laredo to the mouth of the Río Grande and place the Texas flag on the Mexican side. Disgusted with this greed, knowing that I was to be used to give them more and more land rather than endanger the sovereignty of my country, I surrendered to Santa Anna. Since then my heart and my life have been embittered by the hatred I bear these people. Now that we have been betrayed once more by Santa Anna, sold to our enemy like so many head of cattle, I rebel again. I wish you could see our soldiers, our poor pitiful army. Hungry and in rags, they have no ammunition, and if they had it, would trade it for food as many have already traded their guns. What can we expect of a corrupt government whose very foundations are tottering? Look at Santa Anna, living in luxury, diamonds and jewels blazing in his sword and in his cane, gold on his uniform—my friends, he has a coat so heavy with gold trim he cannot wear it longer than an hour. He feasts and our soldiers starve; he wears diamonds and their nakedness kills them in the mountain cold. We *guerrilleros* are the only army keeping back the invaders, we are the army defending you and yours! You still think of the robber bands who were a scourge in the land, Pedro Mora, when you speak as you do."

He dropped his voice and the vibrancy of it whipped into coils that twisted round his throat and drew tight. They leaned toward him with lips open and faces taut, their eyes like black smoke veiling fire. Canales stretched out his hands and moved his facile fingers—and played on their hearts and minds as if he were plucking the strings of a harp. "We stalk the *gringos* in the mountain passes and are gone before they can avenge their comrades' deaths; we poison their drinking water; we lasso their messengers and pull them from their horses and kill them; we stab their sentries and disrupt their camps; we harass them and they cannot touch us. We can disrupt them completely if we have men enough. Young men of daring and courage. Young men who are loyal to their people, who hate invaders." He pounded his chest and raised his voice in magnificent drama of finale. "I—I—I can save Mexico! I can save the border on which you live if I have men! And then, the Republic of Mexico, freed from Spain! We can trample the invaders and trample Spain's corruption at the same time.[2] I want all the young men. If you give me these, others will follow, and victory will be ours. *¡Amigos, viva Mexico!*"

He had loosed thunder. The good seed McLane had sown had had no time to take deep root and was washed away. The shouts and stampings grew so loud that the host finally knocked on the table with a poker and called: "Order, for our safety sake, I beg quiet. Alvaro, Chino, Carlos—"

But order brought no cold sanity. Patriotism burned high and hatred had new life. Don Santiago's eyes looked like those of a madman as he and Canales embraced each other. Most of the youths were clamoring to follow their new hero, until Mora silenced his three sons by saying, "I would not let my sons go until I had talked to their mother. She is ill and would need to be soothed into their departure, surely I would not risk her death."

The burden was finally put upon Don Santiago. Canales had hoped to so inflame the fathers that he could take their sons with him at once, but the introduction of family ties checked him. Mora's stand reminded them that some of their sons were betrothed, that while the women had little to say, they needed to be considered, that they themselves wanted a more protracted farewell. Canales neatly hid his disappointment with the remark, "I see you are good family men and that is well. It is for our families we are fighting, for the families these your boys will have." He put an arm around Don Santiago. "I am promised Alvaro. Very well then, when Alvaro comes to me he will bring the rest of his friends. Seeing I must, I will agree to that. "I will leave my man in Matamoros, and he will lead the boys to me. Canales the Fox has many holes and all of them hidden. Inocente, come here!"

From a shadowy corner came a man to the side of Canales. An utterly repulsive man, badged with vices on his thick, leering lips, greasy dirty skin, mean little eyes and filth-encrusted thick fingers. From the stiff silk that swathed the loose belly protruded knife handles, and two pistols swung on fat hips. In lieu of shaving he cut his beard close to the skin leaving an ugly brush of bristles, and unkempt hair straggled beneath a large dark felt hat; an expensive hat with a high rolled brim edged with a row of gold coins that jingled when he moved his head, glinting when light from the flames touched them. In Rabelaisian humor Canales called him 'Inocente,' a name evidently enjoyed by him. "Look close at all these faces, Inocente, so you will remember them and safely bring the young men to me when they are ready."

"*Sí, señor.*" The evil eyes catalogued the faces carefully and slowly, and the man retreated again to the corner to wait for his master's command.

The arrangement was not to Canales's liking for he knew that not all who were now inclined to go with him would come later. Ah well, if there were only a half dozen they would bring good horses and money with them. He would whisper to Santiago again about the money—.

When the *rancheros* left the house, after food and wine were served, a hand touched Don Santiago's arm in the darkness as he was mounting his horse. A voice pleaded, "I beg of you, Don Santiago, take thought before you send your son. Canales is a master with his tongue, do not let him fool you. A *guerrillero* will not check the *Americanos, señor.* The boys will only learn cruelties and vices, and those who come back will never be as they should be. It will be bad for the girls they marry and the families they raise. Some will not come back at all, perhaps your son, and to what end would be his death? All Canales's fine words about building a republic, that is nothing to us whose land is here. I beg of you not to be hasty. If you say no, none of them will go. Keep them here, don't let their blood drain out in Mexico, or their manliness die. You saw that dreadful Inocente, and Canales is as bad, for all his gold braid and fine talk. Keep Alvaro and—"

Don Santiago spurred his horse. An epithet of contempt rose to his lips but he did not utter it. Better a silent scorn, for such as Hermilo Márquez.

The black night swallowed the riders, but it was not until the wind that howled through the huisache trees became the only sound that Canales and Inocente said farewell to their host.

Canales the Fox knew about betrayal. He trusted no man.

Doña María Petronilla flattened hands and back against the *sala* wall. What now—sweet Mother of Christ, what now? With the wall against her body, the heat of her husband's eyes a fire against her soul, the wild glitter of those of her son's a knife against her heart, she though that now, truly, she was to be crucified. Why had they called her, where had they been all night? Why this nervous tramping of Alvaro, in endless tap, tap, tap, on the floor, why Santiago's hands so tight on the chair arms?

"What did you wish, Santiago?" she asked softly, forcing her head high, driving courage into her heart. "What has happened and how does it concern me?"

Don Santiago leaped from his chair, put a hand on his son's shoulder so they both faced her. "This is a proud day for me, Petronilla. Alvaro leaves us to war against the enemy. He joins Canales the Fox, with all his father's blessing."

"Canales?" She dug into her memory. To war—to war—ah, the *guer-*

rillero! Determinedly she put the hand moving to her pumping heart, back flat against the wall, kept the tremor from her lips, stretched her body. A slight figure in black with a face of molded wax painted with lifeless dark eyes. A stiff figure, holding herself until she could feel a new will taking hold of her, forcing back the subordination of years, urging opposition to shape itself into words, and her throat to speak them.

"No. No, I will not have it, I will not!"

Had his wife rushed at him with a dagger, Don Santiago would not have been more shocked and surprised. Twenty-five years of passive humility and unquestioned obedience to all his moods and desires—now defiance. He had expected weak dissent and tears but not this. When she spoke again he was too stunned to stop her.

"I tell you, Alvaro, I will not hear of it." Her voice took on strength and rang out into the room. "I say you are not going. That is what comes of your running with Cheno Cortina—oh yes, I know all about it, Santiago, I am not utterly blind and deaf. Have you forgotten Ramón?"

Don Santiago laughed, and it was like the rattle of dry corn husks. "It is because I have not forgotten my brother Ramón that I wish Alvaro to go. Ramón would be a happy man with sons to carry on our proud name, were it not for the *Americanos*. It is time that I avenge my brother, and as my duty is to preserve Rancho La Palma I put the honor upon my son. You talk like a woman, Petronilla."

"Yes, I talk like a woman. As the mistress of this house, Santiago. Alvaro's place is at the ranch, with the wife it is his duty to take. Honorable war, if it comes to our door, yes, but a *guerrillero* stealing, killings, skulking in the hills, mixing with the lowest scum—no!"

"But, *mamá*," Alvaro protested, "my duty is to our country. You do not understand what Canales is doing."

His father nodded. "A Mendoza's honor is at stake, and you ask him to hide behind a woman's skirts. How can he face his friends? How can I face mine, when they know a woman is master in my house? He must, he will, go."

She took a step forward, head high. "Very well, Santiago, let him go. But if he has duty so have I, and I shall follow it. I go with him."

"Are you mad, Petronilla? That is impossible!"

"Oh no, no at all. Did not our Blessed Mother accompany her son to His death? So shall I follow mine through the chaparral, over the mountains, across the desert. I shall watch over him, I will be one of the women following the troops. Come, Santiago, call Juan Bautista to get horses ready; tell Paz to pack a *maleta* for me; tell Dolores to look after the house. Let us go at once. Alvaro."

"María Petronilla, stop this nonsense."

"Nonsense, to protect my child when he is in danger? It is no more out of place for me to be in Canales's camp than it is for Alvaro." Her lip curled in contempt. "Canales, who hasn't the courage to meet an enemy face to face—thief, murderer, cutthroat, is what he is. No, I will not let him take my son from me!" She flung her arms around Alvaro with a passion heretofore unknown to her, and shocking to these her men who had never seen her overstep decorum in even the smallest things.

Alvaro drew back in embarrassed confusion, Don Santiago stared. This creature of his will? To put herself against him and bare her emotions? "Petronilla, stop it," he ordered sharply, angrily. "You are insane!"

She drew back and laughed in his face. "I should have been insane many years ago, my husband. I give the orders today, and I order that Alvaro get married. Soon. Formalities can be set aside, you can use the war for an excuse, and I am sure the girl's father will agree. Select you a girl, Alvaro, and Santiago, see to the arrangements today. You have too long been free of obligations, Alvaro. If you refuse to listen to me and go to Canales, then I go also. The choice is yours."

And without another word, her slim body like a shaft of steel, she turned from them and walked out of the room.

Old Paz found a sobbing, broken wraith of a woman lying on the large bed. Old Paz brought her hot coffee, washed the bloodless face, held her in her thin strong arms, and whispered the sing-song prayer of a litany until sleep came.

"*Madre de Dios y todos los Santos*," murmured old Paz, "bring peace to this house." She did not add "and get to work at it," but something like it was in her mind. There were times when the saints were aggravatingly slow, she thought. She went to look for Don Santiago to give him at least a black look, but both he and Alvaro were gone.

Chapter 14

The awkward silence Doña María Petronilla left behind her in the *sala* did not last long. Father and son were too much alike to have embarrassment between them, though Don Santiago said quickly, "Your mother has not been well, Alvaro. You will have to wait a little while. You can tell your friends—I must think of a plausible excuse for naturally we cannot tell anyone we are letting a woman keep you back."

Alvaro slapped his thigh and laughed softly. "I know. What *mamá* said about my marrying is just the thing, and I'd like nothing better than to have Inez for awhile, and then I will have a reason to come back when I want to. If my wife agrees to my going, my mother will have to. Yes, this is much better because I want Inez. I want—"

"Yes, yes, I know about the wanting, we have discussed that before." Don Santiago flipped fingers impatiently. "I know Inez's father and mother are more than willing to marry into our house, but Inez is like your aunt, a thorn in a man's side forever if she is not willing to have him. I would suggest that you first find out what Inez thinks about it, and while that is contrary to our custom, it is the only thing to do. If Inez herself is willing to have you, I withdraw my objections and will immediately make arrangements with her father." He put an arm around Alvaro's shoulder and together they walked to the door. "Rest today, remember we have not slept since yesterday's *siesta* and our nerves are a little—ah, shaken by your mother's illness. Tomorrow close to noon go to see Inez; ask first for Don Eulalio's permission. I am sure he will allow it and remain carefully out of hearing also. Be sure to beg Inez's pardon for the informality; tell her you love her and wish to marry her and see what she says. Because she prefers dancing with you may mean only that you dance better than the rest; that she flirts with you means only that she is a normal girl. She flirts with all of them just like Susanita does."

Alvaro answered cockily that he was sure she would have him, his self-conceit too complete to even imagine a refusal of him. He smiled under-standingly at his father as they went to their rooms.

When Don Santiago saw his wife in bed with Paz crooning to her, he found his hat, and went to the plaza. It was the first time in his married life that he had left his home because he did not want to face its mistress.

Alvaro found the Señor Sánchez y Argensola and his round little wife enjoying the sun in the patio, with Inez on the sunny side of the portico sitting before a frame, doing drawnwork. Just as if it had been arranged for him, he thought; Inez properly in sight but out of hearing if he kept his voice low. He brought out his best manners,—and they were impec-cable—bowed to the two with the proper deference and asked if he might speak to Inez. Don Eulalio weighed the matter with the proper hesitancy and finally agreed.

Alvaro, having noted their pleasure, well knowing he was a matrimo-nial prize, walked with even more than his usual cocky arrogance to the portico, where he bowed silently to give Inez the privilege of greeting. She gave him a brief *"Buenos días,* Alvaro," kept on weaving her needle through the threads (   )[1] had she but known it, was tinder to his desire, roiling his blood so it beat like hammers in his pulses.

He wanted her. He wanted her as never in his indulged, licentious life had he wanted a woman.

When he seated himself on a stool at an angle from her and the frame, she had but to lift the corner of an eye to comprehend his glory. (I know, she was silently telling him, that the cloth in your suit is the finest that the French brought to New Orleans, the braid pattern on it the most intri-cate and most carefully sewn, your sash the stiffest and shiniest in town, the silver trim on your jacket the work of a craftsman. I know that is pure gold on your hat and there is gold in your pocket. I know you are slender and handsome and bear an honored name. And I know, Alvaro *mío*, what is in your thoughts now as you look at me.

I would give everything if one sat there in clothes that are cotton and patched and do not fit, so that his long legs and arms stick out from them; whose face is not handsome and his mouth unsmiling, except when he looks at me; whose eyes are hard—gray eyes. They are, Alvaro, like clouds—until they meet mine. They meet mine sometimes in the morn-ing when I go to Mass, and he rides toward me, and I can give him but one swift glance, and I can see them when he comes to my window, though the night is black. And I love him, and I would go anywhere with him and live in a *jacal*, so he lived in it also.)

"Can it be that you are thinking of me, Inez?"

"Perhaps." The word was cold, without the shyness which should have accompanied it. She knew why he was here and that the usual procedure of proposal was not being followed worried her. Her love for the Ranger had stripped Alvaro of his charm and now she saw frighteningly plain what manner of man he was. She kept on weaving threads, head bent, as if he were not there at all.

He said, imperiously, "Put the work aside, Inez, and listen. Look at me. My father will speak to your father because I want to marry you, and very soon. We will not wait for the usual time to elapse because I—" He checked himself; best not to mention Canales as yet. "Because I love you and want you for my wife."

She felt as if ropes were being thrown around her, tightening on her chest so she could scarcely breathe. She had expected something like this, yet the words were creatures of menace putting cold hands on her. "Why?" she finally asked. "Why very soon?"

"You don't seem pleased."

"It's disgraceful to marry quickly. I have no wedding dress, no trousseau, nothing." She laughed maliciously. "Unless you are willing to wear the sash I wove and the shirt I made for a former bridegroom and bring you the linens he paid for."

He waved that aside with a wide-flung palm. "Those things are of account only to the old folks. I am twenty-three and you eighteen, both of us a year too old already, why waste further time? Did you hear me say I love you?"

She was lovelier in the plain gray dress than he had ever seen her. Already he saw her as his bride, already he felt the cool pearly skin showing in the neck-square above her breasts on his lips. He edged close, reached for her hand, and brought it to his mouth in a hunger so vital that it spilled over and filled the space between them.

Anger flamed in her cheeks as she jerked the hand away and shoved the frame of linen between them. "You—you—" she wanted to scratch at the lewd eyes insulting her, leave the print of nails in red stripes on his clean smooth cheek, beat fists against the wet crimson lips. "I wish I could lower myself enough to call you the names I'd like to call you! Marry you? Not if I have to stay single the rest of my life, not if *papá* locks me up—"

"Inez, what is this, why should I lock you up?" Don Eulalio came to the portico, his wife waddling behind him, consternation on their faces. Anger had raised Inez's voice, and they had heard what she said. Doña Juana stood and looked at this daughter, wondering anew how this strange redhaired child could be hers; mentally beating hands together, berating herself that they had allowed the departure from form and allowed Alvaro to see Inez. Don Eulalio gathered up the wreckage of his hopes and rebuilt them, pretending he had no suspicion of what had been said, nor that he saw the mortification and anger of Alvaro flaming redly to his very ears. He smiled blandly as he said, "You have known each other all your lives, and it is natural that you quarrel a little. I am sure Alvaro—"

"I have been very bad and you must punish me, *papá*," Inez said penitently, artfully playing a naughty girl ashamed of herself. There must be peace, and if she could stave off marriage for awhile perhaps Juan would take her away. (She called Johnny White by his Spanish equivalent, Juan Blanco.) "If I may tell Alvaro I am sorry—"

Alvaro bowed to Doña Juana and murmured the he was grateful for having been allowed to overstay his time, and trusted he might present himself again sometime in the future, with their permission.

When the two discreetly turned their backs and moved away, Inez gave Alvaro a venomous look. "I meant every word of what I said. I despise you and nothing you can do or say will change me. Go away and don't ever come back."

With Don Eulalio's eyes on them again, Alvaro bowed low to Inez, turned, and hurried out to the patio. Inez called a plaintive "May I go to my room, *papá?*" and fled at his nod. Don Eulalio beamed at his wife and she beamed in return. By tomorrow they would have another caller: the master of the house of Mendoza y Soría, asking for the hand of their daughter.

Alvaro kicked at pebbles in the little street that ran crookedly from the plaza, on his way to see Rosa. A stale draught, the drink from Rosa's eager lips, but it might lull the turmoil inside him for a time. At the blue door of the narrow house he turned again,—oh, a curse on all women, good or bad!—spat on the ground, and stamped it with a heel.

"What troubles my so fine friend, dressed up as if he were going courting. Surely those fine clothes are not for Rosa—or is it Rosa?" came the mocking voice of Juan Cortina. Alvaro felt a momentary revulsion for the reddish stubble of beard, the soiled buckskin *vaquero* suit and scuffed plain hat Cortina always affected. But it passed quickly, and he jerked a thumb to the rutted road at the end of the street that lost itself in a thicket of scrubby mesquite. They walked silently side by side until they were out of sight, and then Alvaro told his troubles, leaving out such details as he did not wish to share; yet telling more than he would have had he been less upset, not noticing his companion's chuckles as he vented his anger on Inez in small explosions.

"I want her, and she puts me off. Me! I kiss her hand and she jerks it away. I tell her I want to marry her—I tell her that, and I could pick any girl in town. And she tells me she won't have me if she has to stay single all her life. I tell her I love her and she says she despises me. I tell you, Cheno, I wanted to take her by the hair and drag her away and—"

Cortina laughed so loudly that a dozen bright birds winged from a bush to the safety of the desert beyond. He slapped his leg in glee, slapped his friend on the back. "And you don't know why," he said softly, amusedly. "You don't know why your little dove won't come flying at your mating call. Now that is funny, very, very funny indeed."

"I suppose you know why, you know all about women! I'd have her anyhow, but *papá* says she must agree or he won't ask for her. Maybe I rushed her too fast, perhaps—"

"Still can't swallow the idea that a girl could refuse you. You have a big opinion of yourself, my handsome *caballero*." Cortina chuckled and slapped his leg again. "Yes, I do know why. She's in love with an *Americano* and worst of all, a Ranger. A good joke, don't you think?"

"You lie! You take that back or I—"

"Not so fast, not so fast." Cortina caught Alvaro's fists in his strong hands and held them. "You'd like to think it's a lie, *amigo*. Listen, and I'll tell you what I know. You know the window in Inez's room, just high enough so your face is below it. You ought to know it, seeing you've played the bear there more than once. Well, it's not too high for this *gringo-diablo*, they are as tall as trees, no?"

"Go on." The height of the Americans was another thing which irked Alvaro, for it had made him seem insignificant. Now he resented it anew, and doubly.

"I've followed him often, the last time only three nights ago. You may remember how black it was that night. I followed him and he didn't hear me because I know how to track a man—I spend my time learning things useful. It was late and the town still as a tomb and all the Sánchez family sleeping. Except her, she was there waiting."

"And then? What are you stopping for, what then?"

"Can't wait to be tortured, is that it? By that time I had cat's eyes and I saw his face against the bars. A tall man, Alvaro *mío*, can reach arms through the bars to a body inside, and he can put his mouth to where she can find it. They don't wait, these *gringos*, like we do to kiss a girl after marriage. Ha, 'tis not an unkissed bride you'll have if you take the redhaired Inez! *Por Dios*, I wanted to slip a knife between his ribs, but I was too amused. And I learned much about love making, it was a pity you weren't there to learn a little more, *amigo*. They can make love, these *gringos*, at least this one could. He told her—"

"Stop it, stop, I don't want to hear." Hurt vanity, betrayal, shame, anger, fresh hatred, all roiled together, but pride kept his emotions in check; he had to keep from lowering himself before his companion for whom he had, always, a little contempt. He pulled his knife from a sheath in the sash and twirled it so the blade flashed, showing off his dexterity until calm would come. "Have you told anyone else, Cheno?"

"Why should I? I keep things to myself until I need to use them. What are you going to do about it? Me, I wouldn't want her, not after a *gringo*."

"Nor I." Alvaro swaggered a little as they turned back to town. "I don't need to worry, I can pick from a dozen. I'll see what I'll do after I have thought it over. I'll meet you in the plaza after *siesta* and we'll make some plans. Maybe I'll kill me this Ranger."

Cortina chuckled softly. He knew how hard a time Alvaro was having to appear casual; and he knew, too, that his friend would not pass the *siesta* period in sleep but would lash at his bruised vanity until, meeting him later in the plaza, he would be ripe for anything.

Which suited Juan Cortina. Life had been dull of late in Matamoros, and a little encounter with the *gringos* was a happy prospect.

Chapter 15

Johnny White grudgingly accepted the company of Captain Ross and two of his dragoons, the Irishmen Shane and Kelly, and he rode with them in glum silence. All but two of the Rangers had gone home as their injuries had incapacitated them, and as it happened, these two were the most unruly. They had gone to town in the afternoon, and White had ordered them to be in camp by sundown; which, recognizing the impotence of the command Hays had hastily thrust upon White before leaving, the men had refused to do. Fearing mischief, he had decided to ride after them. The perfect night, faintly silvered by a young moon, was lost upon White, sunk in gloomy reflection.

Hays, McCullough, Walker, and their men were in Mexico scouting out the lay of the land and the position and strength of the Mexican army. They were old Zach Taylor's right and left arms, his eyes, and his ears—and what am I, White asked himself bitterly. Wasting the days watching a group of *rancheros* celebrate their feast days, patrolling the river—and who gave a cuss that one bank was Mexico, the other the United States—looking for the guerrilla Canales, who knew each thorn on the chaparral, each rut and arroyo and stone, and could laugh at the *gringos* trying to flush the Fox. When General Scott came to Brazos de Santiago from New Orleans before Christmas and stopped at Fort Brown on his way to Camargo, the hopes of the Rangers had run high. Scott would need messengers and expert scouts. Scott wanted Taylor's army and someone had to so inform Old Zach. Who could do that as well as a Ranger? Johnny White spurred his chunky sorrel and muttered a curse. Scott, who knew nothing about Mexico or the Mexicans, was going to fight them by technical plan; and anger choked White again as he remembered the scorn of Scott's: "Isn't it the duty of the Rangers to run Indians up and down the hills?"

"By damn," he said to Ross, "it was all I could do not to tell Look-who-I-am Scott that he wasn't sent out here because his super-generalship was needed to take Mexico City, that he was just being moved around on the political chessboard so Old Zach could be smeared over and lose the presidency. Remember when McLane told us Scott was coming, and why? And he can't use the ragged unpaid Rangers, dear me, no. He looked at me like I was something that crawled, the pompous old—"

"Take it easy," Ross interrupted. "No use getting into a lather over it. The army mind is something by itself, and you wouldn't understand. We're all rotting away here and that's part of war too. Someone has to guard the supplies and show the Mexicans who's boss, you know."

From the shadows of a small adobe house came a stone whizzing so close to White's face that he felt the stirred air like a cold finger. He laughed and said, "Major Fortesby's passive policy will never persuade a Mexican, my dear Captain. If you'd been a step ahead instead of a step behind me, you'd have caught that bouquet. That should be sent back in bullet form but no, we have to—"

"Which reminds me, Johnny," Ross cut in sharply, "to remind you there's to be no rough stuff tonight. We don't know whether there's truth in the rumor that Canales was hereabouts, but you know Warrener reported that when he was in town this afternoon the young bucks gathered in the plaza gave him some unusually vindictive looks. By rough stuff I mean shooting; don't let it go any further than a general messing up. Not that I look for anything, but if Canales was here and did some of his fancy talking they might be wanting to show what big bold men they are by throwing a knife at a *gringo*. That rock was an example, we haven't had any for quite a while now, you know."

White retained his thoughts, and the four rode into town in silence, crossed the deserted plaza to the narrow street that held The Skeleton, and tied their horses in the little patio behind it. Only the two Rangers were inside, drinking beer from earthen mugs and singing between draughts, swinging legs from a table edge. Fat Bony leaned against the bar and plucked a guitar in accompaniment. Wailing was the better word, for the song was a sad tale of a maiden deserted and about to die of a broken heart. The Irishmen joined them while White and Ross stood by the fire, White noting with relief that his men were still comparatively sober. Bony put down the guitar and came forward smilingly to take what orders the gentlemen might give.

The door opened and men rushed in. Young men in braid-trimmed suits and high-heeled boots. Dark faces with flashing eyes and unsmiling mouths, faces unfamiliar to this place which they had heretofore scorned to enter. Juan Cortina, Felix Cadena, René de la Ferrière, Carlos del Valle, Alvaro Mendoza y Soría, and half dozen more.

"There's the one." Cortina pointed a finger at White, and Alvaro leaped forward, knife in hand.

"Don't kill them," Ross yelled, backing against the bar and holding his heavy pistol to use it as a club. "They're just kids, Kelly, take 'em and throw 'em out." He recognized them as sons of *rancheros* and orders had been strict to leave them alone. This was just a gang looking for a little excitement. Well, a little fight would do everybody good.

Ross had underestimated the Mexicans, not knowing that they were whipped to a frenzy of revenge. But the Americans had knives, besides the long and heavy Walker Colts that made effective clubs, and were large men, tough as rawhide, strong as oxen, and used to fighting. The young *caballeros* could ride spirited horses and play dangerous games, cast *reatas* expertly, dance with polished perfection. Only Cortina was at least partly a match for the Americans, and a long-armed Ranger tapped his head with a seven-pound pistol, then picked him up and threw him in the street.

In truth, Kelly and Shane had barely gotten warmed up to the fray they loved when the door slammed on the last scurrying Mexican. But knives are lethal no matter how short or uneven the fight. Among the disorder of overturned tables and chairs lay one Mexican, a pale youngster named Alejandro Baca, a happy smile on his still face. Perhaps he smiled because only he had bloodied a knife to the hilt and brought a Ranger low when he had been ordered not to come along because he could not fight. The Ranger lay beside him, breathing in rattling gasps. And behind the bar lay Bony, color draining from his face with the blood that welled slowly from his back onto the floor. Blundering fat Bony, fleeing to the safety of his room, had caught a knife meant for Johnny White.

White examined him, cussing in an unbroken monotone. "Tear up a towel, Shane," he ordered. "We can save him. Kelly, ride out to camp for the doctor, and I mean ride. Is Vorhees dead, captain?"

"Hell no!" The gasping Ranger sat up and asked for a drink. "Dead from a couple of flea bites, that's an insult, cap'n. I wanna drink."

White examined the dead boy, found that he had either fallen or been knocked to the floor just before a table overturned, a corner of which had crushed a temple. He picked up the frail body and carried it across the plaza to the house of the priest.

As Padre Pierre, buttoning a cassock over his nightshirt, pointed at a bench, White told him what had happened.

"I'll swear I don't know why, Father. God knows we've kept the peace as much as it was possible to do. The boys ran them out right pronto, and no one should have even been scratched—Father, they were all worked up about something. The one they call Alvaro accidentally got Bony when he threw a knife at me, but Bony will be all right. I'm sorry this happened, because we don't fight boys."

The priest hurried for the oils to anoint the body; perhaps the soul had not yet entirely fled, and even so Extreme Unction could do no harm. His family could think he received it while still alive and take comfort therefrom. "I will not need you," he told White, himself pulling the boots from the body. "Go quickly, you and your men, before there is war at the very door of the church. Go away, anywhere, until these boys are back at their *ranchos*, you and your Rangers." He turned in a sudden fury, boot in hand. "Haven't you country enough? What are you doing down here in a dry land you do not need nor want? Go chase your Indians, and leave these my people alone. Something to be proud of, indeed—you with your big armies, your fine guns, your devil's own fighting ability—laughing about going to hell when you should be frightened to meet your God—you should be ashamed of your victories. Go capture Santa Anna and with my blessing, for he has done much evil, but leave Matamoros to its laughter and its prayers. I shall attend to Alvaro, and all the rest of them, in the morning. Good night!"

It was not until he was ready for bed hours later that the thought came to Johnny White that Alvaro might be a suitor of Inez and that his own visits to her window might have been discovered. If so—then what? He had believed all Mexicans were dark until he saw Inez. He had considered a man low who married one and begot his children by her. Now, for the first time in many a year, he found fault with himself. "I had no business writing her love letters and going to her window and letting her think she was the one beautiful, the one important thing in my life. I hadn't any right to tell her she was all my life, *querida mía*. It wasn't fair."

There were guests at the Mendoza y Soría home, and Alvaro slipped into the patio and waited for his father. For cold or warm, mist or fair, a time alone with the silence of darkness was a necessity for Don Santiago. Here he brooded, worried, and renewed his will so sleep could not pounce upon it in a weakened condition and have daylight catch him unprepared to have everything his own way. Now Alvaro walked as he waited, pulling off the heads of flowers and scattering the petals; seeing Alejandro Baca's still face, watching his knife sink into Bony's fat back, hearing the rattling gasps of the Ranger. Alvaro's teeth chattered—from the cold, he told himself.

Don Santiago came soon and arm in arm, one as tall as the other, they walked slowly up and down the patio. There was so strong a bond between them, their impulses so overlapping, that it was not difficult for Alvaro to tell his father everything, beginning with his visit to Inez and ending with the precipitous retreat from The Skeleton. "I hid and watched a while and saw the Ranger take Alejandro to the Padre. We had to carry Cheno away, we took him to Rosa. Then I went to Padre Pierre's to see if perhaps the—the thing I was certain of was not true after all. He—he made me come in and look at Alejandro and tell him how it happened and I— he got it all out of me, even about Inez. He said a woman was a weak excuse to commit murder for but that I was neither the first nor the last to let a woman make a fool out of me."

"Yes, *hijo*. An older and wiser head would have done differently but I do not censure you. Women, Alvaro—but let that pass. Baca is dead, and the Ranger also?"

"I do not know about the Ranger, they are hard to kill. Alejandro's father will blame me. Monico de Deza will tell everything, and, if for once he could keep his tongue, someone else will tell."

They walked awhile in silence. From beyond the wall came the urgent clop-clop of a galloping horse, reminding them of the stone-paved trail by the cottonwoods at the *rancho*. Thinned to a thread by distance came the sobbing call of a coyote, free on the plains.

Alvaro grasped his father's hand. "Rancho La Palma. *Papá*, let us all go back there. Tomorrow."

Rancho La Palma. Nostalgia for the peace and loneness of the country was for a moment like a physical blow to Don Santiago. His buckskin suit, the fast Negro taking him over the trails through seas of grass while the wind laughed and ran with them; *El Alabado*, where his voice could roll out over the walls intoning song and prayer, and a hundred voices that were his to command gave answer. He was seeing old Paz swaying her body as she pulled the rope, could hear her calling the names of the Apostles as the deep-throated bell rang its summons. He was smelling the sage and the huisache blooms, feasting his eyes on the lavender verbenas that were rugs carelessly thrown over low hills.

Rancho La Palma, his kingdom. Haven of peace.

Already the (   )[1] the Mexico hills, the hearth flames by hidden camp fires, for Alvaro. "Is it not a point of honor that I go now to Canales, *papá*? Our friends will laugh that the girl to whom the Mendoza y Sorías had offered their name has a *gringo* lover, and that when I went to kill him I— I was thrown out of the place like a child. Won't they bring up Susanita's dancing with an enemy and twist it around to our disgrace? It seems to me my place is avenging Tío Ramón and driving out the invader of our land and—and protecting our girls."

It would have sounded childish to a man who was master of his emotions. But in Don Santiago all the savagery that was twisted into black hatreds for the Americans, all the high-minded pride willed him by two aristocratic families and come to fullest bloom in him, all the vanity of the dictator, poured their blood over his brain and blotted out all thought of Rancho La Palma, all sanity. He dug fingers in his son's arm. "Yes, you shall go, for your honor and for mine. Now indeed it is a duty we cannot—"

"A duty Santiago?" Doña María Petronilla stood before them calm as a Portia in judgment. "I heard you, Alvaro, I was on the portico from the beginning. So you must walk into an American *pulquería*, a place that the pride of which you boast should never have allowed you to go near. Did you hang your pride on a peg outside the door, then, so that you could be on a level with Juan Cortina who incited you? Had this *Americano* taken something from you? I think not. You could have had Inez for your wife last year, you could have asked for her when we came to town. Never having belonged to you, she could not have been taken from you. Protecting our girls, that is big talk, it looks like Inez needed protection from and not by you. Let your friends laugh, it will pass; you have laughed at them in their turn. That you were thrown out is no disgrace—they are big men and they live only to fight, be glad they threw you out like the children you were instead of killing you. Honor, honor, duty! I am weary of the words, weary to death of them."

Often Don Santiago had been irritated to exasperation by his wife's subservience, but now that exigency had given her courage all her words were personal insults to him; the more so because they were true and struck home. However, he said gently, "Your mother heart would keep your children close but that cannot be. We are at war and warred against. Go to your room."

"No." She knew there was no way of reaching to the heart of Alvaro for he had never belonged to her, his loyalties and affection having always been given to his father. She held out a hand to her husband. "There is this, Santiago: we can go to Rancho La Palma at once, where there will be plenty for Alvaro to do; if he wants to fight, there are always the Indians and cattle thieves. There are other girls for him to marry, he and Inez could not have been happy together. With prayer and faith in God and doing what is right, life can be pleasant and the war will not last forever. I cannot believe that the *Americanos* will bother us if we do not show them enmity. That is what can be Santiago. Then there is another way: Alvaro hunting and being hunted, to no end that can be good. If he does not get killed he will never be the same again when he comes back, for the *guerrillero* will stay in his blood and there will always be trouble. Alvaro needs discipline, not lawlessness, to make him a man. It—" her voice broke a little, "—it will make you harder if he goes, Santiago, it will make your life on Rancho La Palma lonely, now when you need again the smile of a little child. Nothing but good can come of Alvaro's staying with you, nothing but evil from his going. Think, Santiago, I beg of you."

His voice whipped at her. "You talk nonsense, Petronilla. Go into the house and leave us alone."

"Very well, I go. But remember this: Your blindness and hatreds will put a curse on the house of Mendoza y Soría and bring it heartbreak. You have the choice."

Don Santiago stood and looked at the aloof stars. The pictures she painted were before him, leaning against the palm tree, he had told himself that he would hate with dignity. Yet he knew, without pondering, what he would say to Alvaro—for he knew himself, and his passions. Lose face, be laughed at, choose womanish passivity? Pah, he had one son who was a woman. And Alvaro need not stay longer than a few months.

"Alvaro," he asked softly, "do you know where Inocente is at this time of night?"

The wind picked up the scandal and sifted it like dust over the vendors and the loafers in the plaza; into the clean-swept tiny yards of the small houses on the edge of town; past grilled doors and into flower-hedged patios and gracious *salas*; through the doorways in the long walls beside the crooked streets where lived the very poor, and the thief, and women like Rosa. It was whispered in the kitchen, whispered among the *mantilla-*

❦

141

decked women going to the Baca home to chant prayers over the body of Alejandro—"Lord grant him the eternal rest, and may perpetual light shine upon him; may he rest in peace. Amen."

Doña Dolores, in her sister-in-law's room, beat a petticoat-cushioned knee as she said: "If you had only listened to me, Petronilla, it would not have happened. You know that only I can put the fear of God into my brother, for I know how his blood flows and why it does so. You might have known that getting some backbone at last would only annoy Santiago, for you did not know how to use your courage. Not a word of Canales, of anything, was I told; if you knew the boys were ready to follow Alvaro, you should certainly have told their mothers, and we women could have banded together and stopped it. Now six of them are gone, not counting that Cortina. Six fine young men and among them René and José Luis, suitors of our girls."

"Be still, Dolores, please, please be still."

"Please, *papá*, oh please don't." Inez was begging. On her knees, tears washing down on her clasped hands. "Not the convent, I would die there, please, not the convent."

Don Eulalio was both the outraged, humiliated father and the stern judge. Nor did Doña Juana intercede for her wayward daughter, in this double bludgeoning of family pride and hopes. The clandestine affair with a despicable Ranger was bad enough, the end of their dreams of an alliance with the Mendoza y Soría house an unforgivable thing. Don Eulalio glared over his folded arms at his daughter and repeated,

"The convent. Only by proper punishment can your mother and I hold up our heads here, as you very well know. It is fortunate that your aunt is assistant to the Mother Superior, and twice fortunate that a boat is here which will take us to New Orleans and from there to Mexico City. By water no one will know where you have gone, though as it is, it would be impossible to take you by land."

"I will jump in the sea and drown rather than spend my life in a convent," sobbed Inez in anguish.

"Not your life. A year or so. Until these infidels are gone and your sin expiated. And pray to God each day you are there that a man will marry you when you return. You know who marries girls who have been disgraced, none of the boys you danced with will look at you. Perhaps a *vaquero* will ask for you, to bake his *tortillas* in a *jacal*."

Inez rose and wiped her eyes. Already life was brightening at the promise of only a year, already her quick mind was leaping ahead. "Must I go—right away, *papá?*"

"Tonight," he said gruffly, "The boat will wait for us. Get your clothes together and pack them neatly."

"Yes, *papá.*" She was very meek. "Might I say good-bye to Chonita? I would like to ask her forgiveness. Is that too much to ask for, *papá?*"

"We can grant her that," Doña Juana answered quickly, struck by the woebegone face of her child. She did not tell her that the duenna had already been discharged and was getting her scanty belongings together. "I will bring her." She hurried out of the *sala* before her husband could give counter command.

When Chonita came, the wrinkles on her face brimming with tears, Inez kissed her and laid her cheek so her lips would come close to the duenna's ear. "Tell Paz to tell Susanita where I will be," she whispered. "Tell Susanita herself if you can. Will you, Chonita?"

Chonita nodded. Inez knew that Susanita was receiving and sending notes to Warrener, though she had steadfastly refused to confide in Inez. Johnny White would know where she was, she was sure Susanita would relay it through Warrener. What good it would do was a question. She remembered suddenly when she had told Susanita that if she were sent to a convent the Ranger would rescue her. "Wouldn't that be romantic? Our children's children would tell about it."

She had laughed about it then, now she was crying. No, she would not cry anymore. "God stay with you, Chonita." She held up her head and smiled.

Chonita smiled an answer. She would wear a hole in the floor before the altar of San Antonio with her knees, imploring him to bring Inez through this ordeal without harm to her. The good saint, she knew, had performed greater miracles than that.

"Nothing of any consequence," Johnny White answered Warrener's question about the affair, over poker in the camp.

"It'll be blown over by tomorrow and everything will be the same again in old Matamoros."

Chapter 16

"At sunrise of the third day of the new year we leave for Rancho La Palma." Don Santiago's eyes flicked over the family gathered at the breakfast table. "Not a word from any of you. This is the last of the year and that gives you three days which should be enough to pack, Petronilla, enough to get the gossip necessary for the summer, Dolores. Angela, you may go to see Sister Gertrudis but you are not staying with the nuns. Luis Gonzaga, tell Juan Bautista to see that the mules, the wagons, and guards are prepared. Dolores, that miserable bird of yours goes back with the servants." He rose abruptly, found his hat, and went out of the house.

"The lord has spoken," murmured Doña Dolores. As she had scathingly told her brother—"Whatever happens to those boys is on your soul; if you had kept Alvaro they would not have gone." They were not on speaking terms. She followed Doña María Petronilla to the *sala*, picked up the infant which was to have been taken from His crib in ceremony on Epiphany. "Even *El Niño Jesus* suffers. I will leave the crib for Angela to pack." She looked around the room. "Petronilla, I think we should take everything of value; I would not trust a Mexican any more than an *Americano* if war brings looting. The servants can sit on top of things. The French chairs, the silver, the tapestries and pictures, the carved chests."

"Yes, Dolores." Doña María Petronilla felt she would be happy if she never had come to this house again.

Susanita hid her panic by feeding the birds. (I must get word to him, I must see him and hear his voice. He must hear me tell him I love him, even if I promised *papá* I would never look at or speak to an *Americano*.)

"Susanita." It was Paz, scolding and complaining. She came close and whispered, "Inez is on the way by boat to the convent of the Immaculate Conception Sisters in Mexico City. She wanted you to know." Old Paz chuckled. "To which I say God have pity on the good nuns."

Susanita felt sweat on her palms. Inez trusted her to get word to the

Ranger. Could it have been less than two months since they had been girls and joked about this which they did not believe could ever happen. Now Clara was betrothed to a widower from Mier and already aloof, happy in the prospect of matronage. (How can I see him, I must risk getting caught. Oh, she had it! A daring, desperate plan—)

"*Señorita*, was there something for me to do?"

It was Manuel's hopeful daily greeting, this time heaven-sent. She sat on a chair and drew him near to her. "Manuelito, could you get a paper to him today, could you?"

He drew himself up importantly. "*Señorita*, all I need to do when I get to the river is yell 'full house two pair' and a soldier comes on a horse and gets me. It is true, *señorita*. They call me 'mascot', but I do not know what that means. I go there often. I eat queer food and it is good, and I learn *inglés* so fast almost they understand me. If I have to wade the river, he will have the paper. For you, and for him, I would not mind the cold water."

She kissed him, told him to wait, hurried to her room and wrote:

Dreadful things have happened, Roberto, and in three days we leave for the *rancho*. I have this plan: Tomorrow at four I will go to the church with my sister and Paz to pray. Angela will go to the nuns and Paz will sleep. I am sure no one else will be there. I will wait for you at the altar of San Antonio in the back of the church; it is a little ways from the wall so a man can hide if there is need. It is a bad sin to meet you in church but Roberto *mío*, I cannot see where Jesus would be angry if he gave us this love. Also you must tell Juan Blanco that Inez—.

With firm finality she folded the paper and took it to Manuel. He disappeared just as Doña Dolores came hurrying. "Susanita, where did that imp go to, I know I heard him. He has to go to Anna's house and tell her the plants and the birds will be sent to her tomorrow. If I don't go crazy— "

"Dear *Tía*, you are the only one who is always sane." Susanita kissed her, wondering if love were ever sane. Surely hers was not, risking so much.

General Scott came back to Fort Brown from Camargo just after Manuel delivered the note to Warrener. Johnny White and his two Rangers immediately offered their services for scout duty once again, and again they were coolly received. Scott was not a man to change preconceived ideas easily. He still did not believe the stories of cleverly thrown *reatas* over coverts of *manzanita* or *chaparral*—*reatas* which the Rangers knew how to avoid. Nor could Scott, newly arrived in an unfamiliar land, estimate the range and influence of the guerrilla and give him due credit for the damage he could do. Falcón, Rebolledo, Canales, bloody names all, meant nothing to the Easterner. He looked down his nose now at the shabby Rangers and told White that his own Lieutenant Richey would leave soon. "And I bid you a good day, *Mister* White."

Warrener caught White before he could voice his thoughts. "Come into my quarters, Johnny, right now. I've been looking for you, it's something important—well, maybe."

Inside little Manuel was standing, quite pleased with himself. He gave salute to White, who gravely returned it, then scuttled away to the kitchen. Warrener sighed as he sat down on a bench and said. "I don't know what it's all about, Johnny, but I have a message for you; from whom it comes doesn't matter. It is that a girl named Inez is being taken to the convent at Mexico City by boat, as a punishment. That's the girl with the red hair, isn't it?" It was the first Warrener knew that White had followed up the attraction for the flirtatious beauty, but he asked no further questions. It was not his to pry into.

Color flooded White's face and drained from it. He dropped into a chair and gripped its sides. His visits to Inez's window had indeed brought on the fracas at The Skeleton, that was plain now—and this aftermath. Honor, so long sleeping as far as women were concerned, stirred and came to life. Or was it honor? Perhaps he had said once too often, "Inez, tell me you love me," and heard the soft *Te amo* in answer, and now could not bear the thought of never hearing it again. Perhaps—but who could say what it was that filled Johnny White now, pulling him to Mexico City. A new adventure? He himself could not have said.

¿Quien sabe? The prospect of getting to Zachary Taylor first and telling him what was coming, and why, filled him with joy. A man forewarned was forearmed. Not that he loved Taylor, who used Rangers only when he had to and also looked down his nose at them, but he liked Scott less and the small revenge would be sweet. Then he would present himself to McCullough, for he was certain the Rangers would get to Mexico City some way, sometime. He had some gold pieces put away, and if he was discharged—well, he could take care of himself. Red McLane had already offered him work.

"Thanks, Bob." He held out a hand to Warrener, lifted a corner of his mouth in a half-smile, and was gone.

Warrener was still sitting on the bench when Red McLane came, filled his pipe, and took the chair. Warrener still did not personally care for

146

McLane, but he respected, and to some extent, admired him. As Red knew of his love for Susanita, he decided to make a confidant of him. After the Ranger left, Warrener had set fragments together and had a picture of the sequence of events. It dimmed the happy prospect of meeting Susanita, for punishment would be swift and sure if they were discovered, and he could not bear the thought.

"You know that I am in love, Red, and with whom. I am serious about wanting to marry her, and knowing how her father hates us and all our works it doesn't need your discerning mind to see I have a problem. They are leaving town in three days and I have to do *something* about it."

Red stroked his beard. "You're sure about the marrying? I mean, your family—they have as peculiar ideas about Mexicans in the East as the Mexicans have of them."

"Oh yes, I've thought of that, but you see I intend to stay in Texas. I have an inheritance from my grandfather and can do as I like. In time I will take Susanita home, when she knows English and has—"

"If you get her. Her father is one of the few men who refused to let me talk to him. Yet he must be vulnerable somewhere, and, if you could get into conversation with him, he might at least open his mind. He sets such store on being a gentleman and that should give you an opening wedge, it being written all over you. I would suggest that you make a call on him, I'll go with you if you want me to. I can out-elegant him in Spanish, I'll bet. Say tomorrow after Mass, when we can assume that he would be in a more tolerant mood. A pity you can't wear that full dress rig. I'll watch his reactions and signal you whether to risk asking for the girl or beg to be allowed to call again. No, I'd better wait outside, I offend his esthetic sense. Unless the girl would marry you first, but I'm sure not. The girls are so trained to obedience and forms of behavior, she would consider it very shocking, love or no love."

After some talk the plan was finally agreed upon, as it seemed the only thing to do. However, Warrener did not tell McLane about the proposed meeting in the church. He knew he would go; it was dark in church, certainly the opening of the outer door could be heard in time for him to slip back of the altar. And if Don Santiago would really look favorably—no, that was wishful thinking, not even a possibility.

McLane and Warrener left their horses back of The Skeleton and walked to the Mendoza y Soría home. Like all the homes of the well-to-do, it faced the plaza, the front door opening immediately upon the street. Set at a corner, it was at a considerable distance from the church which faced the plaza center diagonally from the house, and so enjoyed at least a small measure of privacy before its door; inasmuch as any privacy was possible under the conditions. They came to the plain large door with the carved wooden knocker which McLane lifted. Two gentlemen shaved and brushed and in their best, at their best.

As it happened Doña María Petronilla had fainted in church, and Don Santiago had taken her home and was now sitting in the dining room waiting for the family. He sent Estéban to the door, who opened it cautiously and only a part of the way.

Warrener presented a card, one of the few he had remaining from Virginia. A neat square of expensive paper bearing only his name, in finest engravure. "Ask your master's indulgence to see us, we are here on a matter of importance," McLane told Estéban, in silken-smooth Spanish.

The door closed. In a very short time it opened again just far enough to show the servant, who told them in the toneless voice of one repeating a message with care: "My master has nothing to say to you, *señores*. Not now or at any other time."

McLane deftly caught the door with his foot, moved so he was almost inside, and said in a voice loud enough to be heard, if the man in the dining room was listening at all: "Tell him it is more than a personal matter. Tell him we are his servants, at his feet imploring his favor. Tell him he can order us out, and we will go, but what we have to say will be only of benefit to him, and if he gives us only a few minutes—"

"Estéban," a voice cut from inside, sharp as a knife, "If you have difficulty in throwing out unwelcome guests I will send you help to fully accomplish it."

McLane removed his foot and the door closed. They stood and looked at each other and shrugged. "We have one way open to us, loot'nant, and that is away from here."

With their backs to the street they had not seen the approach of the carriage. A shiny carriage drawn by a pair of black horses resplendent in silver-trimmed harness, colored tassels waving from their heads. It stopped before the men had turned and Luis Gonzaga, elegant in black velveteen and braid and silver opened the door.

Doña Dolores stepped out and, all dignity from the black lace *mantilla* down to the small slippers, secure in the guard of her years and position, stood and detailed the men with round curiosity-bright black eyes. The men, hats off, bowed low to her, and when the girls took places on each side of their aunt they, too, received a bow. Now at last, thought Doña Dolores, I really get to see an *Americano*, I must admit they bow very correctly. This is the Redbeard I have heard so much about, the other the man who danced with Susanita and was in love with her. He is in love with her now—my, what heaven's blue is the color of his eyes! What are they doing here, has Santiago seen them? Can it be possible they asked for Susanita, did they dare? How long the silent tableau lasted no one could later have told. To Susanita and Warrener it was a second and a century of time, as is the way of love. To Angela the excitement of seeing two of the supposedly infidel race at close range was greater than her embarrassment, and she forgot her modesty for a moment in looking at them; dropping the lids over her eyes finally when she became aware of an intentness in the small pale eyes of the amazingly large man. The curiosity of Doña Dolores was so great she had difficulty in refraining from asking a question, so she could hear what their voices sounded like. Her love of fine fabrics recognized the best in McLane's long-coated suit and his meticulousness met with her approval, as his great frame and large square hands both appalled and fascinated her. Oh, if only the proprieties allowed her to talk to him, what a flavor the incident would add to the day!

Luis Gonzaga, guessing what was in Doña Dolores's thoughts, well aware of the stream of love flowing from blue to green eyes, worried about what the big man might do, gave the signal to Juan Bautista to move on. When the sudden commotion startled them all back to reality, Luis Gonzaga knocked on the door and instantly Estéban threw it wide. The Americans bowed again, Doña Dolores condescended them a small but fully gracious nod, swept the two girls before her, and disappeared inside. Luis Gonzaga bowed gravely, followed after the women and closed the door.

None of the family, having their usual eleven o'clock Sunday breakfast with Don Santiago, mentioned the encounter to him. Nor did he ask whether they had seen the Americans, or offer any information regarding their call.

In The Skeleton, McLane turned a wine glass on the table before him with thumb and forefinger, watching the glow of the red liquid. "She had on a dress the color of this wine and the most beautiful white shoulders in the world," he said softly. "I got just a glimpse of her, and no one could tell me who she was. Remember I told you I thought I saw Señora McLane at the *baile* you crashed?"

"What'n the world are you talking about, Red?" Warrener, wanting to laugh at the picture McLane made, was a little hurt that his problem was not being brought up.

"Señora McLane, of course. I've found her. Kind of queer that she should be your Susanita's sister."

Now Warrener did laugh. "Yes you've found her. 'Estéban if you have difficulty in throwing out my unwelcome guests I will send you help.' Or have you forgotten?"

Red took a sip of wine. "There are many ways to get a girl loot'nant. I shall get mine when the time comes."

"Not meaning to be offensive, Red, but I rather imagine María de los Angeles would consider you utterly vile, viewed in the light of a husband. Do you suppose there will ever be a chance to see Don Santiago?"

"I believe one could at his ranch. Do you know, I admire the man. After all, if you're not going to have anything to do with an American, and you are sure your way of life is the right way, the thing to do is keep to it. Providing it means enough to you. Only—God help him, say I."

"And you and me, Red." Warrener touched McLane's glass with his own and drank. "We'll need His help to get the daughters of Don Santiago, my brother."

Padre Pierre had lashed his congregation in his sermon at Mass, throwing caution to the wind. "You fathers must get your sons back from this robber band! Brave soldiers fighting for their country, indeed! *Ladrones*, that is all they are, their leaders teachers of vice, using the war as an excuse for their practices of evil. A fine place for your sons to be, a fine way to teach them to walk in the footsteps of Christ—"

Not knowing, the good *padre*, was smoothing the path of love. It was because of it the Doña María Petronilla fainted and was in bed, and Angela felt that staying with her was a graver issue than the afternoon visit to church. Don Santiago had no time for his family, leaving immediately after *siesta* to a meeting place where the men were gathered to whip up their hatreds anew and now denounce the *padre* as another sympathizer of the invaders. Doña Dolores hurried to make the rounds of her friends' homes, over coffee cups to relate in detail her encounter with the Americans. Luis Gonzaga had left quickly, no one knew where.

"I will go for you, Angela," Susanita said sweetly. "I know that will make you feel good. If Paz will go with me. I would like to walk, the wind is not so strong now."

The wind, which had lulled, summoned a thousand devils when the two were halfway, whirling and dancing and scooping up great handfuls of dust and scattering it again in whistling glee. Clouds scuttered over the sun, driving the last loiterer from the plaza. At the church door a laughing imp lifted Paz's skirt and, in panic, she grabbed at it with both hands. The *rebozo* sailed from her head and spread out like a magic carpet. "*Ay de mí, Jesús Maria,*" she shrieked, "It is the one Dolores gave me and never will I hear the end of it!"

There was a leap, the sweep of a long arm, and the startled old woman was staring into a pair of blue eyes and a strange face that smiled at her, while Susanita tied the shawl over the white hair. "If the *señora* will step back I will pick up her rosary," a voice said gently. Paz could only stare. It was her fixed belief that the Virgin Mary had blue eyes and that people were only given blue eyes by her special favor. "Virgin's eyes," she called them. An *Americano* with them—then they were not entirely evil after all. In truth, this one was a gentleman, he was kind and had saved her *rebozo*. She gave him a small curtsy, a heartfelt "*Gracias, señor,*" a shy smile, and followed her young charge into church.

In a few minutes, in a front pew, she was sound asleep.

Alone with Warrener, Susanita felt strange and shy. San Antonio was looking down at her, surely in disapproval. In the front of church a light flickered in a copper sanctuary lamp with a red shade, telling all who entered that here lived Christ, the Living God, and this was His house. For prayer, not for forbidden rendezvous. It was the first time in Susanita's carefully chaperoned life that she was alone with a man, and guilt pressed upon her. She stood before him with folded hands, her eyes pleading and frightened.

Robert Warrener understood, for he had learned much about these people during his stay in Texas and was well aware of how deeply the proprieties were ingrained in a girl like Susanita, so gently reared and protected. Love might override them later, but not now. He smiled down at her and whispered a commonplace: "I thought you were not coming."

"I should not have come. Roberto, tell me quick it is not wicked being here with you."

"Wicked? Little one, there is nothing wicked in our love. God gives love like ours. Smile for me."

With the smile, restraint lifted, she held out her hand, drawing it back after he kissed it. His voice, she thought, is as nice as his singing, I could listen to it always. "We are going away the day after tomorrow, Roberto."

"So you wrote me. Susanita, do you think your father will ever change? Will he see me sometime, and listen?"

She shook her head. "No, I do not think he ever will. I cannot bear—never seeing you again, what will we do?"

He took her hand, leaned close as he pleaded, "Let us go and talk to Padre Pierre. Now. Would you—if he would consent to marry us, would you, *chiquita?* Say you will. It is our life, Susanita, not your father's. Oh, I love you so, I love you more than anything in the world, I would die for you! Come with me sweet."

"No, no, oh that would be dreadful!" She stepped back from him. "You aren't even Catholic, the *padre* would be—no, I would die of shame, going to him with you now. Do you see? Can you understand that I could love you and still could not—do such a thing?"

"I do understand. Its just that I love you so and cannot bear to have you go away. You don't know what high Episcopal is, it is only a step to the Catholic and a step I will gladly take. There is nothing I would not do for you. Listen then: I will try to get leave in a few months, and I will come out to your *rancho* and ask for you. I will make your father see me. Perhaps he will listen, if he knows how much we love each other."

"Perhaps." The flare of hope died quickly. She knew her father did not consider love important for marriage if other things outweighed it. "I don't know—yes, come to the ranch, but I am afraid for this our love. Now I think it will fade with the years into a beautiful dream."

He held himself from kissing the tears from her eyes; knowing that if he kissed the eyes he would kiss the lips and that, to her, would be shocking enough to have her run from him, would in her code of morals be despoiling her. So he kissed her hand again, just once, and laid it against the other one held at her breast.

They stood there then, wordless. Not needing words, or the touch of a body. As secure in their love as the thick walls of the church were secure against the buffeting of the wind against them. Drawing strength from each other, pouring out love to each other in the silence of their nearness to last them until they should again look into each other's eyes. Building a precious jewel to hold close, and always remember, if they never met again.

It was he who broke the spell. "*Querida*, you must go."

She looked about her, frightened at the deepened gloom.

"Yes, it is already past time." She gripped his hand, overcome for a moment with the pain of parting. "Roberto, *adios*. May God and his angels watch over you, and keep you."

"And you, sweet and dear one. *Adios*, Susanita."

He slipped behind the altar, and she hurried to the front of the church and woke Paz, soundly asleep in a pew. "Paz, I didn't notice it was past time. The wind has worsened too—we'll have to hurry."

"I only slept a minute, *niña*." Paz shook herself, groaned a bit as she bent a knee in genuflection, and sped down the aisle. Outside, she braced herself against the door and asked: "The one who caught my *rebozo*, was that perhaps the *Americano* who danced with you, *niña?*"

"Yes, it is Señor Warrener, a *teniente* of the soldiers at the camp."

"Hmmm. So. Come, the wind will push us home." What then, thought Paz, was all the fuss about? A gentleman was a gentleman in whatever race or language; and this one the ultimate, for he had treated her like a lady though he could see she was a servant, and he had not stared rudely at Susanita. "I will not mention the *Americano* to your father, *niña*. It will be our secret, yes?"

At home Susanita went to her room and lived, yet awhile, with her beloved. Strengthening the hour in her memory so none of it could ever be lost, though she lived to be as old as Paz. For that, she fatalistically believed, was what her love would be—only a memory.

The wind tore in from the wasteland and roared down the narrow streets and whirled around the plaza, and broke limbs from the cottonwoods by the river and the chinaberry trees in the yards, and twisted the orange trees in the patios, and whipped the water of the bay to a froth, and thrashed it into angry waves; and gathered dust and dropped it and gathered it again until it was fine as the finest powder, and made a huge pall of it and flung it over Matamoros.

It was January the first, in the year of our Lord 1847.

Chapter 17

Mother Gertrudis took Angela to a bench in a secluded corner of the garden and let her pour out her woes. Of an order that was not retreatist, Mother Gertrudis and her little band had ministered to the sick and poor, held classes in reading, writing and music during the winter months, journeyed to far missions when their services were needed there. Shrewd and wise, the good Mother had not this winter encouraged Angela to stay with them, partly because she knew that when an arbitrary father was not in full agreement with a daughter's desire for the spiritual life, its tranquillity was likely to be constantly ruffled by censure. Particularly when he had the money and position of a Mendoza y Soría.

"You have told me your father now plans to have you marry, María de los Angeles." She always used the full name when addressing Angela, in loyalty and love to the Virgin under her title of Mary of the Angels. "Is the thought of marriage dreadful to you?"

"How could it, Mother?" Angela wiped her tear-wet face. "It is a sacrament, and Jesus worked his first miracle at a wedding. But with José Luis Carbajal who wants me—any girl at all could be his wife. I fear I cannot make myself clear. I mean I would be just the woman of the house, and there is something inside me which asks for more."

The Mother looked at the girl in astonishment. She had regarded her as somewhat of a nonentity and had some doubts of being able to direct her over-piety into channels of service should she join them. This one, of all of Don Santiago's children, to have his strong purpose! But a purpose, thank heaven, built on a strong foundation of faith. She took Angela's hand and smiled. "Yes, child, I understand, but do not mention it. It would not, I am afraid, find popularity where wife and motherhood of itself is considered complete, and is a complete state surely." A Joan of Arc, this one? Ah, the Maid of Orleans had also been shy, sweet, obedient, and would also have been considered a nonentity. The Mother did not question God's inscrutable ways.

"I would say wait a year, María de los Angeles, if your father will agree. At least do what is possible to ward off an early marriage to José Luis or one like him. Pray, and God will help you. If the path is clear before you, regardless of how it may look to another—mind you, I say if the path is clear, then follow it. Remember, God's ways seem very strange to us at many times, His instruments peculiar. Follow it without looking behind you. Could you do that? Could you?"

"Yes Mother. If I saw the way the following would be easy, though it might be hard. You know what I am saying."

"Then may God point it out to you. Go now, child of Mary, with my blessing."

Padre Pierre intercepted Angela and Paz as they left the garden, asking Angela to tell Luis Gonzaga he wished to see him in the afternoon. "Tell him a friend will be with me, he will know what I mean."

After they had curtsied and hurried away, Mother Gertrudis said softly to the priest, "For once I would like to lift the curtain over the future and take one peek, to see what is in store for María de los Angeles. Something has wakened in her."

"That is your womanish curiosity, sister. And a good thing for all of us that curtain cannot be lifted. Would you, or I, be here, could it have been lifted? I wonder. Poor child, I pity her, more now than before."

When Luis Gonzaga arrived, only a few minutes after Captain Devlin, and Padre Pierre saw the sheer happiness in the young face, he was glad he had brought the two together. "I thought you would come, Luis," he said, and closed the office door against intruders.

"It was kind of you, *Padre*." Luis Gonzaga was shaking Devlin's hand. "I have wanted to see you—my friend. I wanted to thank you again for your kindness and give you a remembrance, *señor*. If you will please excuse me—" Opening his shirt he took a piece of paper about a foot square from against his chest and handed it deferentially first to Padre Pierre. "I drew it from memory and it might be better."

The priest looked at it a long time, then handed it without comment to the American. It was a picture of Padre Pierre. In black and white and done with the utmost care, at first it gave an impression of a cowl over a pair of eyes. A longer look, and a face took shape backed not by a cowl but by a shadow—a face that was a true portrait of eyes and drawn cheeks, yet not the same. It seemed an inner face, the countenance of the soul.

Devlin also looked at the picture a long time. So long that a ball in the boy's throat was ready to burst—he had tried so hard, worked so long—when Devlin put the picture down on a chair and, stepping in front of this boy almost young enough to be his son, bowed gravely to him.

"I pay tribute to genius. *¡Salud, señor!*"

Their hands were locked and tears splashed down Luis Gonzaga's cheeks and onto the hands. They were neither Mexican nor Anglo Saxon but artists.

After the wave of emotion passed, Devlin laughed. "I too have a gift for you, and coincidentally of the same model. Don't laugh too much at me, my friends."

They did laugh, all three together. The sketch was amazingly accurate. "The only thing you left out was the little mole before the ear," chuckled the Padre—and without a trace of expression. The eyes regarded them impersonally from a face without life.

"I should make a good map," Devlin said. "So many feet, so many miles, here a hill, there a valley."

"I shall treasure it always." Luis Gonzaga carefully put the picture inside his shirt. "As I shall treasure the memory of you, *señor*."

"You mean you cannot come with me this summer?"

He turned a grief-stricken face to the priest. "I am already a traitor to my father and my country. If my brother should not—come back, I will be the last Mendoza y Soría. And if he does I—there is a duty—"

"Sometimes one is a traitor only to himself, Luis Gonzaga." The priest laid an arm over the young shoulders. "I do not see that you must take the burden of your brother's and your father's wrong; Alvaro should have stayed here. As for duty, it is a word too often used to cloak selfishness and coercion. God gave you this great gift—watch that you do not throw it away. Watch Luis Gonzaga! Your father will not consider your going?"

"Please, Padre Pierre, I would rather not talk about it." The thought of what could so easily be and was so impossible, the prospect of a lifetime of work on the ranch so contrary to his inclinations, the knowledge that his one understanding friend would soon be gone, was too much for the sensitive boy. He could not bear it here, feared he could not control the unmanly tears.

"I will ride out to your camp and bid you good-bye," he told Devlin. "I think I had better leave now and I—thank you for the picture." To Padre Pierre, "And I thank you for calling me, Father."

The priest walked the floor after Luis was gone. Six steps one way, six steps back, again, the long cassock swinging as he turned his slow voice giving an effect of trailing after him. "Strange, Captain, strange indeed. Don Santiago comes from a family noted for individuality and courage, his wife is far from stupid, yet he expects their offspring to be a flock of sheep that follow a bell he rings. He treasures the portraits of ancestors, and contemptuously calls his artist son a woman, a *marica*. It would be interesting to know what quirk of heredity gave Luis Gonzaga the gift and the temperament so foreign to his environment. I always think of the beatitude 'Blessed are the clean of heart' when I see Luis. You go to church, you have seen his sisters, have you noticed them? I mean as individuals."

Devlin filled a pipe and lit it, taking time to consider whether to tell what he knew; decided that good rather than harm could come of it and answered, "A confidence is held sacred with a priest so I can tell you that the blond one, Susanita, and Lieutenant Warrener are very much in love. The kind of love you read about in idealistic books and the real thing. Or did you know?"

"I rather thought so. Be assured that I hear about everything, Captain. The *alcalde* told me about their meeting at the dance and swore he saw love there; then I hear of an operatic serenade supposedly by the trader's sons, and one day when the lieutenant calls on me I am going over a new *Ave* for my choir to sing. Without success, for I have small talent for song, but he reads it from the notes and sings it with a voice that astounds me. Then I look at him again and I see where the question is not how Susanita could fall in love with him but how she could fail to. Then I notice Susanita, and I see that the happy child is no longer there. And I say to myself, 'Padre, you might know something like this would happen, an American loving the daughter of a man who hates them most. It must be true because it is so inevitable.' Ah well, it was to be expected. If I were a Mexican girl I am sure I would goggle my eyes at these tall, so different strangers too."

"Tell me then, Father, what now?"

The cassock swung against the legs. Six steps, turn, six steps, turn. A piece of wood in the fireplace popped and threw a shower of sparks on the stone hearth. "What now, how can I say? The Mexican mind does not open readily—though neither does the French mind, and many another. The high-class Mexican firmly believes that in him is perfection of race and most of them, like the Mendozas and their wives' families, have married so the blood strain remained pure and in its class. It became a fanaticism with many of them. And it does bring the best—for a time. Up to a certain point. Don Santiago's family has interested me beyond others because I believe that Nature, knowing her own inexorable laws, gives her best before she must give deterioration. Should Susanita or Angela marry one of the boys in their circle their children will be ordinary in looks and intelligence, their tastes and tendencies be downward. The elusive blond strain will not appear at all, for Nature will no longer be laboring to save a rarity; nor will the clear green eyes appear, at least not in such limpidity.

"The same with the boys. Particularly Luis Gonzaga. Luis, to me, typifies the finest the blood has produced, and inevitably lost unless there is new blood, and virile blood. Alvaro has qualities of leadership in marked degree but has been allowed to perfect his natural vices; he would still make a good citizen with the proper direction and discipline. Or perhaps there I am only expressing a hope." He took a chair, gesturing with his hands as he went on. "Love is nothing but an elaborate route to procreation, and Nature works backward from procreation. Where there is a thing that needs preservation Nature really stirs herself and induces love where it will serve her ends. You understand what I mean?"

"In a way. You are taking up a much disputed and complex subject, Father. Would your immediate superior agree?" He smiled, sobered instantly. "If that gave offense, pardon it. Nature has been doing a lot of stirring here then, for I believe every servant girl and—er, dancer, is in love with one of our soldiers. Then she produces the half-breed, that creature of inner strife and vagary—and there goes part of your theory. That is,—but I am in deep waters."

Padre Pierre shook his fingers in impatience. "I am not including sex attraction, *señor*, or license, which is a different thing entirely. I speak of love as God gives it, this love of Susanita and the Virginian. Nature induced it to keep the best of Susanita. Understand, I speak of Nature as if separate from God to make myself clear—but your pardon, I need not involve myself by attempting to explain the great mysteries to an intelligent and devout man. If I could make Susanita's father see that this union would be a great thing; if I could show him that yours is the more virile race now and that Texas will never again be ruled by the Mexicans; that for him and for all like him the *mind* must be made to rule the individual above that of the heart, and the mind must not be retroactive. But he can see his children only as something belonging to him, irrevocably his. He denied Angela the convent and choked a true vocation, but if a consequence comes of that not in line with his desire, he will blame God, not himself. And it might be, for there are depths in Angela."

"The quiet one. I have noticed the bearing of a princess and a perfection of wearing clothes my sister would give much to achieve, and the humility and shyness that go with it so oddly. And so beautifully. I confess my heart sweeps over Luis Gonzaga, Father. A tragedy, to have his genius choked, his sweetness warped, by ranch life under his father's domination. A tragedy for all those children, and I can only hope that a Ranger does not catch the *guerrillero.*"

"He who lives by the sword dies by it. The real tragedy is Don Santiago. When hatred is distilled to its bitterest and dropped into the blood—" The priest held palms up, then spilled them down in poignant gesture. "Ah well, God allows evil that good may spring from it. Who am I to question Him?"

They sat there a long time then, wordless, watching the flames slowly master and coal the log they were licking. "Eighteen forty-six is gone," murmured Devlin, rising to go. "And good riddance, for it had many evil days, Father." And I, thought Padre Pierre, taste the bitter aloes of fruitless endeavor. But he kept the thought to himself. It would have sounded theatrical.

The second day of the year also brought activity to Fort Brown. Red McLane and his shadow, Ike Mullen, left for San Antonio, and Red gripped Warrener's hand hard in farewell. "Remember, loot'nant," he told him, "that if a man makes his plans right and sticks with them till they're carried through, he will get what he wants. Keep after your girl and you'll get her. I expect to have my wife within a year— in fact, I'm starting to build our home as soon as I get to San Antonio, and I'll certainly welcome you into the family. Good luck, loot'nant, and take time off from being noble once in a while. It might pay you."

To General Scott, departing for the quarters he had established at Brazos de Santiago, McLane gave a parting shot. "It'll be kind of funny, General, to have the man you're out here to demote as your commander in chief after the next election," to which Scott gave no reply. When Captain Ross begged again that one of his dragoons be given the message to Taylor as they were best fitted for the task, now that the Rangers were gone, Scott refused the request and accented his refusal by calling Lieutenant John Richey from his escorting troop and ostentatiously making him messenger. Thus putting a black spot on his record, for Lieutenant Richey, entirely unfamiliar with the country, leaving on January third, got only as far as Villa Gran in Mexico. There he was lassoed by the guerrillas, jerked from his horse, and dragged along the ground while spears were thrown at him until finally merciful death came.

There was nothing else to do but bid the general a smiling farewell and express the hope that they would see him again soon, regardless of the resentment they felt toward him. Had Scott but known it, their contempt of him was fully as great as his for them.

When word came at noon that Mexican bandits were driving cattle across the river only a few miles to the west, Ross took his men to see about it. They returned shortly driving a dozen cows and a few horses, and Ross reported laconically: "Somebody had warned them, and the brush was high so they got away. All but six of them. There were eight." Because of the foray, orders were to remain in camp, and while the order did not directly include him, Warrener knew he should comply because of the example. But he was restless and in ill humor and sought out his friend Coley, the violinist, and asked him to go to town with him. "We'll wear old clothes and make ourselves generally inconspicuous, Coley."

Noble. The word rode with him. He could at least have talked to Padre Pierre, perhaps he could have gotten help there. He should have persuaded Susanita, swept her away—but no, he had been too noble. He had even refused himself a kiss. He should have done like Johnny—no. No! Susanita was special. She was sweetness, she was a fragrant white lily. By the time they got to the plaza, Warrener's tenderness for his love was all aglow, and he was glad he had not acted differently at their meeting. If consideration of her was being noble, then noble he would be.

Bony told them that extra watchmen were posted in town against both Americans and possible bandits so no further trouble would come. "Stoop yourself over a little," he advised. "There are two watchmen both named Juan so when they stop you, you laugh and say '*amigos, Juan y Juan, amigos!*' Keep close to the walls, and be very, very, careful." Bony suspected that Warrener wanted a last glimpse of the girl he loved, and fat Bony sighed. Love was so beautiful when it was young, so beautiful.

"*¡Ave María Purísima, las diez han dado y sereno!*" A voice pitched high to carry drifted to them as they came to the Mendoza y Soría home. In the name of the Virgin Mary it was ten o'clock and all was well and quiet—

rather a nice way, thought Warrener, to announce the hours. The house was dark, but as lights and music came from a house farther on, the two, keeping close to the walls, moved to it.

Windows facing the plaza in the del Valle home were flung wide. "I'll tell you what," Coley whispered. "We can be loafers satisfying our curiosity at what the rich do. It's a wonder there aren't a few around doing that, but I guess it's an old story by now. Come on." They stepped to the edge of the light, far enough not to be seen from the inside but at a vantage point to see what went on in the *sala*.

Yes, there she was, talking to a group of young men intent on her favor. So near, so heartbreakingly near. He should be there too; he was as good as the best of them and had been welcome as a guest in homes better than this and filled with more honorable guests. There was Angela, demure in her plain black traveling dress. Señora McLane! What a farfetched, wild dream of Red's. Warrener knew the family well, for little Manuel had told him all about them, and in detail. Luis Gonzaga, gallantly attentive to the homeliest girl there—how dear a brother Luis would be. And *Tía*—oh, he liked Tía Dolores. But he could not isolate the mother in the crowd. A servant in black velveteen trousers and jacket, a red sash tight around his waist, came in with wine in slender thin glasses on a huge silver tray. When all held a glass, a man rose, lifted his, and said, "To our friends who leave us, and may his patron saint James on his white horse ride with him and bring him safely home."

Don Santiago raised his glass to touch that of his host. "I thank you and give you a toast in return. May Saint James destroy the enemy so that when we come again to Matamoros no hateful *gringo* face will offend our eyes. I drink to our boys, fighting for us in Mexico!"

"That wine looks pretty good," Coley whispered, "even if the toast could be improved upon. Isn't he the leader of the agitators here?"

"Be still, Coley." Warrener was shaken. So, in the same circumstances, might his father have offered a toast. They would be friends, if they would ever meet and know each other, the two fathers. As we could be friends, he thought. Why, I could like him, I could easily be a son to him—

He noticed that none of the family raised their glasses, though most of the other women did. He had an overpowering impulse to knock at the door and force his way in and talk to these people. But before he could follow it, the watchmen came, and Coley stepped forward so the light from the lantern they were carrying fell on his face; knowing that his squatty figure, dark complexion and old clothes, plus his speech, passed him easily for a Mexican.

"¡*Amigos, Juan y Juan, amigos!* The poor can always look, *señores,* is it not so? We were about to go, *Juan y Juan.*"

The small wit of the reply pleased the watchmen and they laughed. "Then go with God, *amigos.*"

Back in The Skeleton Warrener ordered an *olla* of Bony's best *tequila* and applied himself to drinking. "If I drink enough," he told Coley, "maybe I'll have the courage to go back there and pull a gun on them and take her away. A man could do it, if he wasn't a rotten coward like I am. If he wasn't so damn noble." Longing, frustration, and reproach were knives twisting in an agony of misery greater than he could bear. "Help yourself, Coley, it's on me."

"¡*Ave María Purísima, las doce han dado y sereno!*" The crier called when they trotted over the cobblestones of the plaza. Twelve o'clock and all was well. "Oh, what sweet delight, thro my bosom thrills," sang Warrener, letting his voice rise and spread wherever it might, spilling the ache of his heart out in the cadenza that sounded like a rippling sob. He didn't care who heard him, just so *she* heard him. When Coley took the bridle and urged his companion on, Warrener sang the "Sweet dreams, my love, sweet dreams," and it followed after them like a cry from a broken heart.

For the first time in his life, Robert Davis Warrener was very drunk.

Had they not been very drunk they would have been warned when their horses leaped aside from the path before they got to the river. Warrener jerked his horse back, spurred him deeply—against a rope stretched across the path. The animal leaped high, screamed, pitched forward, and threw its rider. Threw him high and hard.

Coley's brain cleared itself as instantly as if the *machete* in an upraised hand had slashed the fog away. His Walker Colt, all cylinders loaded, shot flame from its long barrel to where forms and faces were dimly discernible in the darkness. "Run you—" he yelled as bushes crashed, in a fine rendition of all the vilest names his Spanish could furnish, holding in his plunging mount. "Why don't you wait for more, so you can keep these dead ones here company on their way to hell. You stealing, filthy, rotten, underhanded bastard sons of bastards, you—"

It was magnificent. It was, Shane told Kelly, as they kicked unsaddled horses splashing through the river, a gra-a-a-and thing to hear. It was, Kelly told Shane, when they arrived on the silent battlefield, just their r-r-rotten luck to get here too late, and bless his soul, if it wasn't little Coley. "You'll get your mouth washed out with soap for using them nasty words, that you will, Coley."

When Ross and his men came with torches, they found one dead and two dying Mexicans, and blood on the chaparral. A small group, evidently, and clustered together when Coley fired on them, making his shots effective and frightening the rest away. They finally found Warrener, thrown into a clear space in the brush, onto a jagged, sharp-edged rock that had ripped into his head.

"If he dies I'm going to get me fifty Mexicans for it," Coley vowed, tears stinging his eyes. "So help me heaven, they'll pay for this if he dies."

It was as the coach taking the Mendoza y Soría family back to the ranch swung past the camp, at daybreak, that Devlin told the red-eyed Coley, "He'll pull through. He'll be all right by and by. It will take a while, and the old head may be sore a long time, but he'll make it."

And it was Coley's eyes, in proxy, which followed the coach until it was lost to view.

Chapter 18

The wagons—the chairs and bedrolls being moved to the ranch serving as seats for the servants—were ready, the ox carts on the way. And Old Paz, weeping, praying, beating her hands together, walked the patio and refused to get into the wagon. "My Manuelito," she moaned, "we cannot go without him, he is so young, we cannot let a child—"

"A child!" snorted Don Santiago. "That imp of Satan could take care of himself anywhere. Paz, you let him run as he chose, though you knew he was consorting with the *gringo*. I let Juan Bautista go to their camp yesterday evening to look for him, and a soldier ordered him off before he could even ask. He is no longer welcome here." He struck a fist in a palm and glared at them all. "Out—out with everyone in my household who is not an enemy of our enemies! Paz, you brought it on yourself. Get on the wagon, at once."

Doña Dolores swished her skirts and said, "Be assured he is not at the camp until we are well gone. They would send him home. And I do think, Santiago, that we should be allowed to start with tranquility; enough if not too much has already been said about the enemies. After all, Santiago, and you, Paz, it is something to have the courage to follow one's inclinations. It took courage, for Manuelito."

"That is true, *señora*." Paz dried her eyes and dutifully climbed on the wagon. She started to get off again when she thought of San Antonio but the driver cracked the whip and they were on the way. Very early Paz had risen, taken the crudely carved statue of the saint which Victorino had made and given to her and set it on the floor in a corner of the room she shared with Josefa the cook. "You shall stay here all summer," she ordered. "I prayed all night to you to send Manuel to me, and you sit in heaven and won't listen to an old woman." She scolded on for some time, now addressing the saint above, switching back to the wooden reminder of him without confusion of thought or speech. She would miss the precious statue, but the saint had not listened to her prayer and had to be punished; he would stay here alone and not get a single word from her until he sent Manuel to her.

When they crossed the river and rode past the enemy fort, Paz stood up and shrieked "Manuel, Manuelito!"—and sank back sobbing when her voice only mocked her in the hush of daybreak, tears falling on the hard old hands as the road lengthened and no small figure ran after the wagons. Soon she resigned herself. Better so, for Don Santiago might have made him a target for his animosities; and as Dolores said, it took courage to reach for what one wanted. Paz asked for forgiveness of San Antonio. It might be that the good saint knew what he was doing when he did not answer her prayer.

Like a general on Negro came Don Santiago; then the six white mules, tiny bells chiming, bright tassels flying, the shiny black coach swaying and bumping behind them; the outriders and rear guard with Luis Gonzaga on Tabasco completing the imposing entourage. Away, away, from the man-made town and its vices—away to where a man was lord of his world of peace.

It might have been that the pictures of the ranch he loved, in the nostalgia of home life, had been painted overly green and fair. He saw only the spring mornings wet with dew, the drops on the flowering *nopales* like fire opals in the early sun; the carpets of blue and white and yellow blooms in the valleys, the gray *cenizo* spattered with streaks of lavender and pink swelling over the rounded hills. He smelled the musky sweetness of the huisache blooms, velvety yellow pompoms on the trees beside the big gate.

His spells of longing had run ahead of the season. He knew it was too early for the pictures his homesickness had conjured, for the winter was barely passing, but still the pastures seemed overly dry, nothing as it should have been. Tomás was right when he said, "There has been little rain and the weather cooler than it should have been, the winds too strong and drying," but Don Santiago chose to look at the explanation as an excuse for negligence. The master and his *caporal*, chin straps tight against the puffs of wind that tugged at the large hats, were riding over grass that should have been higher and greener, that looked much too seared. Someone, thought Tomás, will pay for this. He cannot take it out on *El Señor Dios* who makes the weather, so it will be one of us.

Taller than most was Tomás, high-hooked nose like an eagle's dominating the long face crisped brown by the subtropic sun of many summers, hardened by the never-ending winds of the plains, lined by the sharp-edged chisel of loneliness. For Tomás rode from one camp to another, from spring-fed water hole to earth-banked reservoir. Eating beef with the *vaqueros* one evening and sleeping with them on a hilltop, the next night counting the stars through the canopy of a cottonwood with the smell of sheep rank as carrion in his nostrils. No wife had Tomás, since his bride of a month died—how many years ago? It no longer mattered, after her face had dimmed until it was, one day, no more with him. "He is married to the cows and goats," shrugged the mothers of daughters. "He has forgotten how to laugh, let him be." A good overseer, Tomás, and loyal.

"Yet it seems to me that the sheep were left too long on one spot and grazed it to the ground," Don Santiago insisted. "Tell me of this Indian raid and tell all of it, Tomás. All, I said!"

"There is not much to tell." Now from whom had the master heard it? True he was home a week and had seen everyone, but only the *vaqueros* knew of the raid, and they would not tell when he ordered otherwise. He had so ordered when he had seen that his master returned with less tolerance than he had taken with him. "One day the Indians were there, and when we fought them in the valley, others drove off the cattle behind the hills where we could not see them. When we went to follow we saw there were too many against us, and we had to let the cattle go." Tomás leaned forward and smoothed a tangle in he mane of the sorrel he was riding. "The cattle got away from the Indians somehow and came back again, and the Indians went away, and we have not seen them since. There has been no further trouble with them."

"I said to tell *all* of it, Tomás." The words were like sharp pieces of ice, dropped one on the other.

Tomás suppressed a sigh. A nice thing to tell with Don Santiago in this ugly mood, but as he already knew there was nothing that could be done about it. "After our fight some Rangers came looking for the Indians, and I told them of the cattle, and they followed the tracks and killed most of the Indians. They had many guns and I am sure it was a good fight. They brought the cattle back. Otherwise they would have been lost to Rancho La Palma forever."

Don Santiago gave Tomás a look of pure contempt. "And when they asked for a steer you gave them the best one in the herd."

"But, *señor*, it is a small reward to give one steer for saving fifty. Besides, they could have kept them. Also the Indians would have bothered us again.

They were most courteous besides doing us great good." Tomás was careful not to mention that the Rangers had stayed a few days to rest the few who were slightly wounded and had fraternized agreeably with the *vaqueros*, lifting the endless monotony of their existence. As far as Tomás's experience with the enemy was concerned, it had been all to the good.

"I do not believe you," Don Santiago said flatly. "That is the story I was told, but it lacks even the shadow of truth. Rangers do not act so. I could not believe that they would bring back cattle and then ask—ask!—for one. I do not believe that they could be courteous. If your story were true, they would be fools, and the *Americanos* are not fools, Tomás. If they were in your camp, why did you let them go? You know my orders were to kill those who came on my land. I think there were no Indians at all. These Rangers frightened you and stole what is mine and you acted like old women instead of men. You lie very poorly." His jaw muscles tightened. "I will take the matter up again. For the time, Tomás, understand that I am more than displeased with you."

He does not quite dare, thought Tomás, to use the whip tied to his saddle on me, but oh, how he would like to. Fortunately, they had come to their objective, the headquarters of the sheep and goats. Here were stout corrals and shelters built around a spring and connected with a *jacal* in which José the *vaciero*—provisioner for the herds—lived with his young wife Tecla. It was three miles from the *hacienda*, built there by Don Santiago's grandfather, not only for the spring but because he could not abide the smell and bleat of the animals and did not want them within sight and sound of the home of his dreams. The *jacal*, built of upright posts of ebony to form the wattle-and-daub walls topped by a roof of straw, was more pretentious than most of its kind and boasted two good-sized rooms. A provision room for seed and grain was connected to the *jacal* by a roofed runway, making a cool porch on which hung wet *ollas*, bird cages, trailing vines in swinging pots.

Tecla had been maid to the women at the *hacienda* before her marriage to José and a great favorite because of her smiling, willing, and efficient service, and the bed with the white cover instead of the usual pallet of the *peon*, a table, chairs, and a few china dishes, were gifts of appreciation from the *hacienda*. The stockade of posts that formed the corrals and enclosed the spring swung around the high strong wall with a stout gate, and against the wall flowers bloomed and vines rioted—planted and cared for by Tecla. Slabs of sandstone formed a floor outside the door and more slabs made benches in the yard. Altogether it was a delightful spot and did credit to those in charge of it. Added to the stout stockade, José had dug a cellar and contrived an ingeniously concealed trapdoor in the event of direst need in an attack, though so far the few Indian attacks had been desultory.

Plowed ground stretched away from the walls and, as the two men rode up, a young woman dressed in a bright blue full skirt and a bleached sack waist rose from a kneeling position in the rows of a neat green garden and made obeisance. A woman serene of face, quite pretty for all her dark skin, and heavy with child. Usually Don Santiago had some pleasantry for Tecla, but today he stopped only to sweep a hand over the emerald beauty of a field of maize and ask why it was patchy, why it was not higher. Tecla went back to her weeding, glad she was here in the field. She knew, too well, that look on Don Santiago's face boded evil for someone in his path. "Let it not be José," she breathed and crossed herself.

It was true that the gate needed repairing, as did one roof corner. True that the log troughs needed cleaning from the green water slime, that too many turkeys were standing around instead of hunting bugs. Don Santiago pointed them out as though they were major crimes instead of occurrences to be more or less expected. José, a small man who managed to give a dapper air to his *peon* attire, gestured volubly as he explained, "The gate hinges broke only yesterday, *señor*, and I am about to fix it. The roof I will mend when the sheep that are sick do not take all my time, and the turkeys have rheumatism. The turkeys always get the rheumatism at this time of year and always they get over it. As for the troughs, they are cleaned out on Ash Wednesday. It is not yet Ash Wednesday."

At which logic the master only scowled and asked Tomás where Victorino was. "He was to be here, why isn't he?"

Luis Gonzaga rode into the upper corral and reined his horse beside Tomás just as the old goat herd came through the lower gateway, walked carefully through the press of goats there and finally stood before the horsemen. Because he had been forcibly pouring an herb concoction down the throats of the sick sheep he was dirty and rumpled from the white hair down to the bare feet, the dilapidated hat hanging on the back of his head.

"May the good God give you a happy day, Santiago, and to you also Tomás," he greeted.

"The same to you, Tío Victorino," answered Tomás, the words running over Don Santiago's gruff, "*Oye*, Victorino, how are the flocks?"

"Well enough, Santiago. The herds in the north pasture have increased, those in the south remain the same, but—"

"But what, but what?" Don Santiago interrupted in a rage. "Must there be a but to everything? What happened?"

"The Indians have carried off a number from the west pasture, and there were a pair of coyotes that were like six devils in their cunning and—"

"Why not add a pair of lions also while you are at it, Victorino? I suppose you also gave a sheep to the Rangers. I suppose they killed the coyotes for you and were most courteous, and drove off the Indians for you too." It was a lash at Tomás, who took it without change of expression.

The old man drew himself up with dignity. "Tomás can tell you that the Indians were very bad until the Rangers came and chased them away and killed many. It is the first time I have seen an *Americano*. They came riding up to me in the pasture and said, '*Tío*, we have something for you,' though how they knew I am called *tío* I do not know. Yes, they had shot the coyotes and they had for me the bodies which later I skinned. Most graciously they asked for a sheep for their evening meal, and I gave them one with a crippled leg. How did you know, *señor*?"

"Victorino, you lie! Why do I hear nothing but lies?"

The goatherd, his cheeks ashen, took a step forward and held his head high. "Santiago, I have grown old in the services of the house which I have loved next to God alone." His voice was firm and clear. "But when you doubt my words and cannot greet me with anything but a scowl, when you interrupt me at work I am doing for you, then, with the privilege that years of servitude give me, I say that I am ashamed for the house of Mendoza y Soría."

Don Santiago, in prime from the good food on every festive table in town, his active nature spilling over with the release of pent-up energy, had found the customary slow movements of the workers and the dozens of small jobs always waiting to be done a thorn in his flesh. The grass with its bleached curl of sear was a burning iron on his nerves, and the loss of livestock, though no more than the usual winter toll of coyote and thief and sickness, magnified to impoverishing numbers. Resentment that the Rangers—those vilest of marauders—had eaten meat from his ranch was sickening as the taste of bile in the mouth. All these things and more, to which the absence of Alvaro was not the least, capped now by Tío Victorino's words, gathered together into a whole that swelled and swelled, like a bladder pumped with air; and, like a bladder when the skin is stretched beyond its strength—burst.

Don Santiago leaped from his saddle, the uncoiled rawhide whip in his hand, and raised his arm and brought the lash around the goatherd's shoulders. Again and again, as the very action reddened his rage the more.

Luis Gonzaga, the first to recover from the horror of this shocking deed, rushed to the shrinking old man and shielded him with his strong young body, taking the biting strokes until realization was a cold douche quenching his father's anger. When the realization came, Don Santiago, lips tight and twisted, swung into his saddle and galloped away. Tomás, after a moment of indecision, followed after.

Victorino, shocked to coma by the unbelievable outrage, lay inert in the arms of Luis Gonzaga. Not realizing in the excitement that the better way was to leave him at the *jacal* with José, frightened by the still, colorless face, Luis with the help of José lifted him in front of the saddle and, riding slowly, took him to the *peon*'s quarters at the hacienda and hurried to the patio.

Doña Dolores, now that the household was in smooth running order, was assailed with boredom. More than anyone knew, she loved clothes of rich material and missed the necessity of change of dresses the social life in town had given her. This morning, with the excuse that it had seemed uneven at the hem, she put on the new purple and black striped dress and was moving slowly, like a model, up and down the portico.

"It does touch the floor when you stand," Susanita said. "You might too easily step on it when you walk." As the petticoats and the stiff material pushed the skirt well away from the small feet, Susanita might have wondered how this could be accomplished. María de los Angeles saw a small dip in the front, "No, more on the side, *Tía*, I believe." Yes, on the side—no, the back, Paz thought.

Doña Dolores took a chair and let the skirt spread about her, enjoying its richness. "I shall leave it as it is. I might as well lay it away anyhow. Parties will be few with our men chasing here and there to talk each other into further tempers, already a messenger has been here to whisper to Santiago. Men and their tem—why Luis, you look as if the sky had fallen. What is it, Luis, why are you coming through the servant's gate?"

"*Tía*, please, I have brought Tío Victorino. If you would please come, perhaps he would open his eyes—"

Forgetful of her finery she hurried out with Luis Gonzaga, an animated magnificence that brought every pair of eyes, young and old, to marvel and admire. The old goatherd had revived by the time she arrived, and she stayed only long enough to get the story, then rushed back to relay it. Alas, many hands had been laid on the cloth to feel its fineness, and there were black smudges on the purple satin, white dough on the black wool stripes. Then the skirt had dragged over the fine dust the dry weather had put over the hard-packed earth, and now a pale film bordered the hem.

While the women were viewing this tragedy Don Santiago dismounted at the gate, poured himself a drink from the *olla* hanging from the roof of the covered gangway, then strode into the patio and defiantly faced his sister.

She wasted no time, turned and blazed at him. "So it has come to this, that you lay the whip on an old man. Had it been an evil thieving old man there might have been an excuse but one with the soul of a saint who has given us a lifetime of loyalty and brings cheer to everyone—it is with shame that I call you brother, Santiago. With shame!"

Susanita and Angela started sniffing into handkerchiefs, Doña María Petronilla sat still but gave him eyes heavy with reproach, old Paz stretched ears from behind the grapevine. He glared at them, hands on hips. "It is none of your business what I do and that is why I came here, to tell you so. My goatherd, be he young or old, is responsible for the animals lost. When he lies to me and dares to give meat to the despicable Rangers, punishment is due him. Since when has that right been taken from me?"

"But, *papá*," Angela said quickly, "Christ told us we must do good to our enemies, also we must feed the hungry and a few goats when we have so many—"

"Be still!" He raised a hand, dropped it again. Flares of anger moved up his cheeks and into his hair. Angela's platitudinous sermons had always goaded him to anger,—a thing which she had never discovered. "Those preachings are for women. Go love the *Americanos* then, if it gives you so much pleasure. I am surprised that it has not already been done by both you and Susanita. Even that should not have been spared me."

He noted the sudden pallor in Susanita's face, the flush in Angela's, the twisting of his wife's fingers, the quick blankness of expression Doña Dolores assumed—and thought it was shock at this thought, never dreaming the reason why. For the mother had always known, Angela had seen the ring, Doña Dolores remembered the meeting at the house door on New Year's Day, when eyes met and clung.

"Why should it be spared you?" Doña Dolores demanded. "Because of you hard-headed men there will soon be nothing left for our girls to marry

men and *Americanos,* and every girl has a right to marriage, my
The servants and *peons* are shocked and angry, and I need not tell
it is wise to keep them happy and docile."

last one of them needs a lashing too! Should I run my affairs by
the feelings of a creature like a *peon*? A thing with the body of a man and
without his soul. You women—pah!" He swung on his heels, and the tap
of them, sharp and hard, proclaimed his indignation as he strode to his
horse.

Paz came with coffee on a silver tray and Doña Dolores, lest the ghosts
moving here became too real and stay too long, laughed a little as she
said, "I suppose it is my tragedy that I fail to feel inferior to men. Certainly it is a peculiar fate that thrust me into my brother's household to
eternally quarrel with him."

"You are here because we need you," Susanita said, kissing her lovingly,
and Angela added, "I may need you very badly some day, *Tía.* You are so
strong."

Candles burned softly behind Doña Maria Petronilla's eyes as she smiled
and said, "I have so often wanted to tell you that my life has been easier
because of you, Dolores. Yes indeed, we need you."

Doña Dolores smiled happily, and they fell into small talk, taking up
crochet hooks, needles and yarn, pretending that Don Santiago had not
been there at all; each one trying to move the cloud his outburst and harshness had left so it would not touch the other.

The master of Rancho La Palma stood beside the high stone cross which
centered the bluff that was like the fragment of a huge stone wall. It was
the first visit to his rendezvous since his return, and he had galloped to it
in a need to justify the morning. His kingdom stretched as fair as ever, but
the magic of it refused to come and fill his soul. He had rationalized his
deed to himself, but the gnaw of regret had not lessened; Tío Victorino's
grief-stricken eyes refused to leave. There was a flatness in his mouth, as
if he had drunk water long stagnant.

And then a man with his own face came and stood beside him and looked
at him with quiet eyes, pointed an arm and said, "Listen to me, Santiago.
Those dark spots in the distance, there, and there, are your steers and cows;
those moving white spots are your sheep; those galloping horses being
driven to a corral, the oxen and mules and fowls you do not see but you
know are safe at home. Those are yours to do with as you choose. The
gardens and fields and orchards are yours, and all the pasture that stretches

far beyond your vision. But those that take care of them—they too are made in the likeness of the Creator; they have feelings and a right to kindness. A master who is truly a great master, Santiago, is loving and gentle and understanding, and gives a man his due when he acts as he deems best. Tomás did well when you were in town, yet you would have liked to put the whip upon him, and you withheld even the smallest word of praise. You did not even try to believe what was told you about the Indians because you did not want to believe anything good about the Rangers. The lash fell on your own son, forever to your shame, because he was kinder than you, his father. Your family has loved you and given you obedience, but, Santiago, your heel on their necks—your heel on their necks? Will you in the end know happiness if you refuse it to them? Are you, deep inside of you, happy that Alvaro is a *guerrillero?* A master, Santiago—have you forgotten that the master must be servant also? Who is master, the one who lashes, or the one who stays his hand? Learn first to master that most rebellious of servants—yourself."

The man pointed to the great white *hacienda*, its wall faintly tinged with gold and mauve and rose. "Much happiness has lived in the patio there, Santiago, and it can become greater than before. Do you hear—listen, it is plain—the songs and laughter and prattle of little children; do you see the guests, glad to come because they find joy and serenity in your home; do you hear the *peons* singing because you are good to them?"

The man held out a hand and smiled. He had a warming, a sweet smile. "Your choice is now. You can be the man you are, or the one I am. You know me. I am the part given you by your splendid mother and I once lived in you."

Don Santiago scooped up earth and looked at it, and as he looked, possession took him in the grip of its pride, and he gave himself to it as a shameless woman to a lover. He struck out with empty hand at the man with the quiet eyes, and struck again and again. He walked to the edge of the bluff, and saw the *hacienda* gleaming like an opal in a setting of gold. "Mine," he whispered. "Mine!" Ecstasy filled him, lifted him, and held him suspended.

He opened his palm and looked at the earth he held, and doubled his fingers over it again.

He walked to his horse, turned, and went back again. "This I promise," he said aloud, "that I will not lift the whip again to anyone, be it *peon* or child of mine." To the man with the quiet eyes? To God? To himself? He could not have said. It was an urge which pulled at him and which he obeyed. But he said it righteously, not in the humility of the servant to the Master.

New life flowed as he rode home for *El Alabado*. He felt as though fires had purged him and waters washed him, and he was all that he should be.

Chapter 19

José, ill at ease in the office of Don Santiago, inched the brim of his straw hat around and around in nervous fingers, his eyes on the magic of the covered sheets at which the master was at work. José had never heard that the pen was mightier than the sword, but the point of the long feather, black with ink, was potent with mystery and he regarded it with awe. That a man could have a piece of furniture made only to hold writings was another thing that put people in two classes; the *hidalgo* and the *peon*; and only the *hidalgo* and his family could have the privilege of the written word. Not that José thought of it as a privilege, his simple mind recoiling at the very thought of penetrating its mysteries.

"Come, come José," Don Santiago tapped the desk impatiently with a fingertip. "Out with it, what brings you here?"

The hat revolved with greater speed, José swallowed the lump fear had put into his throat with effort, and said haltingly, "Don Santiago, a stranger comes. A man with much writing on papers and great red seals, from the *palacio* of the *gobierno*. He has hands three times the size of mine and a laugh which is good to hear—I mean it would be good to hear if—it—"

"If he were not an *Americano*, is that it, José?"

"*Sí, señor.* He comes on a matter of great importance, he says." José swallowed again, then decided to say no more. Don Santiago's kindly mood was no indication that his temper was not sleeping very lightly behind it. "If I may go, I have need to see Doña Dolores and may I see her? I have a message from Tecla. This Señor McLane (José pronounced it *McLann*) comes soon. There is another *señor* with him who is, I suppose, a servant, though he does not act like one."

"Doña Dolores is, I think in the *sala*." Don Santiago waved José away, to clear the doorway for a better sight of the two strangers riding into the outer patio. They dismounted. *Por Dios*, what fine horses, thought Don Santiago—and the one took the reins while the other stepped forward.

Estéban blocked the way, waving hands and imploring in an anguished voice, "Come no further, *señor*, I beg of you—"

"Tell Estéban," Don Santiago told José, "to bring the man here to me. I will see him."

José delivered the message and, with a prayer for strength in his heart, sought Doña Dolores.

"So it is a boy, "Doña Dolores beamed, seating herself on a stool in the middle of the *sala*. "Was Dominga there on time? How then is little Anselmo? Born on the feast of San Blas, that is a good omen for the child. Blas Anselmo, that is a good name too."

José put the dusty left foot on the right one, reversed the procedure, worked toes against the cold tiles of the floor. Painfully he brought forth; "That is what I wished to tell you, *señora*, about the `Anselmo.' It will have to come fourth and not after the saint's name as you ordered. He—the name the *padre* will write in the book will be Blas Alfredo Pablo Anselmo, and he will be called Alfredo.

"Alfredo?" Amazement overrode displeasure. "There are no Alfredo's in our family; it is not a name used on Rancho La Palma. And Pablo, why the Pablo before Anselmo also?"

"It is because of the shot from the *pistola*." José concentrated on the umbrella of skirt and found the going easier. "I hear the horses, and I look out and see these two *Americanos*, and I behold that they are very big and strong, and one has a red beard like wine, and the other one of yellow with curls. It is a beautiful beard, *señora*. It made me think of Cortez and how people thought he was a god—"

"Never mind what you thought. The beard of Cortez was bright red, not wine or yellow. What has that to do with naming the baby, I should like to know. You go about it in a most roundabout manner indeed."

José cringed a little. "You will see, *señora*. As I have said, I see them and I am afraid. I have never seen an American, and Don Santiago says they murder people, and we may not talk to them, so when I see them coming I close the gate quickly, though I notice that the horse of the red one is lame and needs attention. I close the gate and run in the house where Tecla is groaning. She has groaned a long time, and I send one of the herders to get Dominga. The men are at the gate and calling to be let in, but I do not stir. It is most frightening, Doña Dolores."

"A rabbit frightens easily, José."

José ignored the slur, there being no alternative, and took a fresh breath.

"The *señores* talk together, and the yellow one points a *pistola* at the *jacal* and shoots. It is a most huge *pistola*. He shoots high into the sky, but the noise is like thunder, and I rush out and unfasten the gate and swing it wide. The reason I do that is because when the shot comes Tecla is groaning in a new way, and I rush out and say, '*Señores*, honorable *señores*, wait with the shooting till my wife has had the baby, I beg of you!'"

"'Baby, what do you mean baby?' asks the red one, and I say my wife is having a baby. And as I am saying it, Tecla screams loud and calls for help and I run inside and—I do not know why, *señora*, but I am so scared when I see her face all puffed up that I—I hide in the corner. It is the devil pushed me there and took away my strength—"

"Yes, blame it on *el diablo*," Doña Dolores put in crisply. "Then what happened?"

"Why, the *Americanos* come inside, and the red one goes to Tecla, and the men talk in their language, and the yellow one says there should be hot water for washing—"

"José, do you mean to tell me that strange men were in the room with your wife?" In her shocked indignation Doña Dolores rose and José retreated a few steps. "A woman having a child and men there?"

"But *señora*, what could I do?" José was close to tears. "They were there and what could I, a small man, do against them? And that the red one helped bring the baby—Estéban told me not to be surprised at anything the Americans do; he said God and the *gringo* can do anything. So I am not surprised. The baby is born, Tecla is even smiling a little, and the red one is talking in Spanish. It is strange to me how they talk their language and then our own, like you use first the right and then the left hand. It is a most fine boy, the red one is saying, and he shall have my name. He will be little Alfredo. When the yellow one hears this he laughs and laughs until tears run in his beard like rain in bunch grass. Red, he says—they talk right on in our language, *señora*, it is amazing—your name is Alfredo; that is the funniest thing I have heard in all my sainted life. Though confidentially, I do not think it has been very sainted, *señora*. Neither one has a saintly look to me, even if personally I never saw a saint. He slapped his knee and laughed some more while this red one, this Alfredo, bathed the *niño*, and oiled it, and wrapped it in a cloth, and put it in the basket Tecla had ready. Yes indeed, *señora*. It is most strange to see, and he says he is the oldest of twelve and three times twins, and he knows all about babies, not only from at home but because wherever he goes it seems there is a baby coming and his help needed. Twelve, and three times twins, that ceases to be God's blessing, *señora*, do you not think so?"

Doña Dolores' eyes were wide with interest. The man could be no other than the one who was at the door of the town house on New Year's Day. Yes, it was quite possible that José was telling the exact truth, the man had left an impression of great capability upon her. "I would not presume to say José, not having seen them. What happened next?"

"Next? They kept on talking while the red one put a wet cloth on Tecla's forehead and fixed the bedclothes like a woman would. What is the matter with 'Alfredo,' he wishes to know; it is a good Christian name. Alfredo was a great king if you did not know it, my heathen friend. Heathen indeed, the yellow one answers. Where could you find a more Christian name than Pablo, which is his name—only first he calls it Paul, *señora*, which I suppose is what it is called in their language. He says did not God himself go out of His way to strike him down and talk to him, with special lightening, yes, indeed.

"He could do some striking down on you, Alfredo says, and then he laughs and says, 'Little Pauly, that is good.' He asks is he lying, and the yellow one says no it is written so in the Bible at home. The *niño*, he says, should have the name Pablo because it is a better name."

So then they stand and look at each other, and I see where perhaps a quarrel is coming, and I stand between them, and I bow first to one then the other, and I say I wish the baby to have both names of the worthy *señores*. It would be a privilege, I said, and two fine Christian names—see, *señora*, one must use good judgment at all times. A little flattery in the right place—"

"Most diplomatic," Doña Dolores agreed, smiling a little. "I find it quite an imposing name for a child born in a *jacal*. I suppose that 'Alfredo' is so important that even the good San Blas will appear only on the *padre*'s baptismal book. It will not even be Blas Alfredo."

José wished for the comfort of the hat he had left outside, pulled his fingers instead. "Surely the good saint understands, else how could he be a saint? And I am sure it is true that Alfredo was the name of a great and kind king in a country of the *inglés*. It is a fine story as the red one tells it, he even plays the harp like Susanita, this king, and think of that! The little one will be a fine man, said the red one, and the yellow one said yes, finer than any, and I see that something is expected of me, and I bring out the little *olla* of *mezcal* and a cup. It is a big cup because I have no small one, and I think my eyes must fall from my head when I see them pour it full and drink down the *mezcal* like water. It was something to see, *señora*. Then Alfredo hands the cup to Tecla and says she must anyhow wet her lips because it is for the *niño* and she laughs. She is feeling fine, and these two strangers make everything so happy we forget even our decorum. I must drink too, they tell me, and I do and I think if my little Alfredo Pablo grows as strong as these and can take strong drink like—"

"I do not doubt it, José, if he has the example." Doña Dolores sat again but was far from relaxing. "Then what? Where are they, and what do they want?"

"They have most important business with Don Santiago. We get the stone from the horse's hoof, and they say they will come again to see their godchild, and they give Tecla a christening gift—oh, only a few *centavos*," he added hastily, thinking he might have made a mistake in mentioning the gift. Most certainly it would not do to say that the coin was gold. Gold! José's eyes widened at the memory. "This Alfredo is with Don Santiago now, and Pablo stands at the gate. I came to tell you about the little *niño* and if I may go now, *señora*—"

"Tell Tecla we will come to see her. It is too late today but perhaps tomorrow. Go with God, José."

"May he remain with you, *señora*," answered José, leaving the room with backward steps; giving silent thanks that the ordeal, though not as trying as he pictured it, was over. He was a little proud of his presentation.

Courtesy and the obligations of a host, part of Don Santiago's bone and blood, had allowed Red McLane a seat on the rawhide chair in the office. Red, having long learned the value of matching manners to manners, was entirely at ease, though he knew full well that his unwilling host had both hatred and contempt for him. Red shrewdly guessed that curiosity, the key to many a locked door, was responsible for his reception, though his proud face behind the desk remained impassive. With a polite "*con permiso*," McLane laid papers on the table: references and orders for safe conduct in both English and Spanish, and impressive with flourish of script and colored seals. He talked while Don Santiago glanced at them, in the compelling yet modulant voice of the man who, needing it at its best to gain his ends, had cultivated it well. It was tuned perfectly now to fit the small space of the office, sliding from phrase to phrase in Spanish as good as his hearer's own—and Don Santiago prided himself on the quality of his speech. It did not belong to the coarse largeness of the men any more than did the clothes conspicuous only for their fine fabric. One looked for some loudness of voice, manners less restrained, a flashy ring on a finger, and found the contrary a bit disconcerting.

McLane put a finger on a paper. "As you will notice, Señor Mendoza y Soría, I have authority from the governor, and I may say that I represent, in spirit at least, all of the thinking, the wiser, men of Texas. Putting it bluntly, you Mexicans are a conquered race, but what you are not as yet aware of is that the conquering boot of the *Americano* has no heel. We will take our families into the land of the Indian and fight him, we fight in battle, but we are soft nevertheless. As a nation we do not confiscate, do you understand? Even Texas, which is ours by conquest, will be paid for in money. What I am trying to tell you, *señor*, is that you are no longer a colony of Mexico, and adjustment will have to be made to make you a part of the new Texas. I have come to offer you a pleasant, remunerative way to make that adjustment."

Don Santiago, his emotions banked for the time, leaned back in his chair. "The Nueces River is the boundary and that leaves me in Mexico. I refuse to believe otherwise."

"Unfortunately, *señor*, refusal of belief changes nothing. I give you credit for more reasoning power than that. As I just told you, Mexico will be paid, she is figuring right now how much to demand for Texas, New Mexico, and California—and she has officially accepted the Río Grande as a border. I know this is true, *señor*. And she is selling all of you right along with it and without a tear. If you must be loyal, put your loyalty where it will do some good."

"Interesting. Do you *Americanos* consider loyalty a thing to be picked up like a basket and moved about? You amuse me, Señor McLane. You were about to suggest—?"

"A cooperation. Reason will tell you that when two races like the Anglo Saxon and the Latin meet they meet as strangers. When it's the particular mixture that is the American and the mixture that is the Mexican—not being personal, *señor*, as I know your Spanish blood has been kept pure— why, you couldn't avoid trouble if you had the angel Gabriel with you. But a lot of it can be avoided with the right way of thinking and a place to bring troubles and straighten them out. To get down to business, it is this."

McLane took another paper from the pouch lying flat against his side inside his coat and put it before his host. "It makes you a sort of judge, you will notice. Gives you favor at the capitol so that there will always be an ear there to listen to you. You will be the spokesman for your friends, these *rancheros* whom you know. You will bring us their grievances, and we will see that you get justice. The main thing is that when you begin to understand about us and the way we run things you can explain to your friends, see? Have them comprehend that it's to their benefit to be good citizens. We will give you the title of '*magistrado*', and it will not be long before you are somebody, Don Santiago."

The thin lips curled as a single finger moved the paper aside. "I have no reason to believe that I am not—somebody—now, Señor McLane."

McLane leaned a little closer. "Would I be here otherwise? It wouldn't do either me or Texas any good to offer a position to a nobody. But one can always be more than he already is. I know you are not the richest man, and the fifty or so sections you own isn't much, according to standard. But you have personality and influence. Men look up to you and they will listen to you."

"Listen to me betray myself and them into the hands of you who are our enemies?" Tiny flames were showing in the black eyes, though Don Santiago did not move. "To put it very plainly I should go about praising those who are in power and for reward I shall receive the mockery of a *magistrado*'s cloak. Do you believe it would hide the treachery beneath it?"

"No, no, no!" McLane was on his feet, consternation in his voice. "Can't you see, won't you see, what it means to you people? You can't get together in small groups and fight us like you are doing now; it can only bring you ruin and misery." He put his hands on the desk, real concern in his face. "You've got to record your land and get boundaries fixed; surely a man of your intelligence can foresee the land-hungry Easterners who will come here and grab what they can. It is already being done. Good men will come to Texas, but there will be many, far too many, who are the chaff winnowed out of their home places; thieves and murderers and men generally bad. You can say, 'This is my land,' but if you can't prove it where are you? Get yourself set right now in the beginning and you'll stay set. That's good business, *señor*. With you Mexican *rancheros* it is self-preservation. I want to be your friend, Don Santiago. You will find that I can be not only a powerful but also a true friend to you. You Mexicans will need friends, here in the state capitol and Washington. You will have one in Washington when Zachary Taylor is president—wait a minute, I know that you are going to say that Taylor is fighting you now. You should know that he has always been bitterly opposed to the unwarranted killing of a single Mexican, had used the Rangers when he had to, and gotten rid of them as quickly because they were ruthless in the killing of Mexicans. There had to be a ruthless element in the Rangers; most of them are fine if given the chance to be, and more of a friend to you ranchers here than you realize. Far more, *señor*. You should remember that Taylor gave an armistice of six weeks when your Lieutenant Colonel Nájera was killed at Monterrey, and grieved at his death. Why, if it was anyone but that lying, treacherous piece of vanity, Santa Anna, whom the Mexican government persists in backing, this war would have ended long ago. You yourselves have no use for Santa Anna, why pretend loyalty to him and the government upholding him?"

"Taylor will be back, and he will be the president of this United States, and he'll be your friend if you let him. Bell will be our governor, and he'll be you friend too if he sees he ought to. His mind is not closed."

McLane slapped a hand on the desk as his excitement mastered him, and his pale eyes were intent on the dark ones opposite. "Organize now, Don Santiago. Get your friends to come in with me, *señor!* You have everything to gain and nothing to lose, neither your pride nor honor nor anything else. We like family and tradition also and cling to it. You know Mexico is rotten and is through with you; where else put your loyalty than with us, to the country where your home and land is? Being a good *Americano* now can't do anything but uphold your pride."

"You who know nothing about pride and have never possessed any should be able to tell me about it." Infinite contempt lay in the voice. "You do not even know when you offer a man an insult. Why are you here? What is beneath all this—this solicitude for myself and my friends?"

McLane stood straight and summoned dignity. He wore dignity well and without the pomposity which attaches itself so readily to the large man. If Red McLane was self-made, he had done a good job of it. Had Don Santiago shrewder perception, he might have taken his visitor for an example of these *Americanos* swarming into Texas, and profited thereby; and seen the impotence of a handful of people who measured greatness by old traditions and old bloods, and the camouflage of pomp and ceremony and dress which only money can obtain.

McLane bowed, not without grace. "I am, Don Santiago de Mendoza y Soría, a representative of my state's government which is now also yours. Let us say that I am an emissary of good will working for the good of all. This is your commission, already signed." He put a small role on the desk, opened it, and set an odd-shaped stone Don Santiago used for paperweight in the middle of the sheet. He said, with proper deference, "May I ask permission to come again, after you have had time to study this and think over what I have said?"

"This is my answer to you and yours." Don Santiago took up the paper, folded it once, tore it in two, and dropped it on the desk; then gave each piece a flick with a thumb and forefinger towards McLane. A small, but most aggressive, gesture. "Estéban!" he called sharply, and at the servant's appearance he said to him: "If the *señor* and his friend are hungry or wish to spend the night here, show them a place in the quarters of the *peons*. They are to be treated well. He took up his pen and started writing on the half filled sheet before him, the task which the coming of José had interrupted.

McLane hesitated a moment, told Estéban that they were riding on, bowed to his host and, without attempt at the formality of farewell, went out. Then hearing women's voices in the patio, he asked Estéban for a drink of water, please, for himself and his friend.

As it happened, Doña María Petronilla with Paz and the girls were on the portico opposite the *sala*, hidden from view by a screen of vines, and heard everything José told Doña Dolores. When she came to them she found the girls giggling, their mother smiling, and Paz beating her hands together.

It was Paz who spoke first. "I must go there at once! Early this morning the *niño* is born and almost a day is past, and it sounds to me as if not even a prayer was said over the little one. I never heard of such heathenish goings-on in all my life, Dolores!"

"I should have closed the door and you would not have heard and could sleep in peace. It's too late today, Paz." Doña Dolores moved a stool so she could see through an opening in the vines, and watched McLane and Estéban come out of the office and stop at the *olla* for a drink. Not knowing that McLane's hearing was acute and the asking for a drink only an excuse for delay so he could hear what was being said, she went on, "I imagine the little one will manage for this night."

"Then I must go early in the morning." Paz was firm. "If there is no one to go with me and no cart to take me. I will walk. You know the *niño* must be warmed over a fire of rosemary sprigs to keep the evil spirits away, as the devil cannot stand rosemary. This *niño* certainly needs it, brought into the world by a man, of all shameful things, and an infidel *Americano* besides. Also I must baptize it—what will become of that child with such a beginning?"

Doña María Petronilla said soothingly, "Angela can go with you, and Estéban will drive you in the cart. Susanita and Dolores can go the next day; I am sure Tecla will enjoy two visits more. Would you like to go with Paz, Angela?"

"Oh, I'd love to!" Angela said eagerly. "And I'd like going early. I am anxious to take Tecla the pretty christening robe I made and some delicacies too, if Nicolasa can make them. And of course it is true that we should hurry to baptize the child and say some prayers."

Just as Doña Dolores was ready to report that the *Americanos* were leaving, a man rode past them into the patio. "Gabriel! Gabriel is here, Petronilla," she said instead, rising from the stool. "I must run to the kitchen and see about the custard he likes, and the chicken *mole*— Petronilla, shall we have chicken *mole?*" Her face pink with excitement, Doña Dolores forgot the strangers as she hurried to the kitchen.

Chapter 20

The two Americans rode slowly down the trail, Ike grinning as he said, "I told you could save yourself a lot of trouble by not coming. So we were welcome to the *peon* quarters and we were to be treated well. The old *don* couldn't quite get over his law of hospitality and kick us out, but the *hacienda* is not for common creatures like us. Do we go on to where the Rangers are camped? We'd have to kill our horses to make it, and yours is still a bit lame besides."

Red McLane smiled happily. "We got a solemn duty now, Ike; we got a godchild. Did you notice the *caballero* who passed us? His name is del Lago and he's a close friend of theirs, leastwise I saw him often with Don Santiago in Matamoros. That means the *don* will be at home with his guest in the morning, and José won't get in bad if he keeps us because the boss won't be riding hard on his slaves. I like José."

"Uh-huh. I'll live to see lots of things, Ike, and so will you."

Ike did see things, and soon. He heard his friend ask José for scissors and a razor and, by the last light of day, removed the red beard. "Mighty poor cutting tools," Red told José. The next time I come to see little Alfredo Pablo I'll bring Tecla a pair of scissors and you a decent razor. Shaving with this is martyrdom."

"*Sí, señor,*" José agreed, wondering how luck had so suddenly come to notice him. He crossed himself quickly then to ward off any evil connected with it.

The morning was bright and warm. Ike followed José to the corral, but Red's duties were in the *jacal* where Tecla was already out of bed and at her household tasks. When Paz and Angela came to the door, Red was sitting on a bench, weaving his body as he crooned a Presbyterian hymn to the angry, complaining infant in his arms.

The woman stood and stared in amazement. They had only half believed the story José told Doña Dolores, but had they believed it all, they still could not have visualized the way of this large man with the tiny child. The baby suddenly stopped crying, waved a tiny fist, and closed his eyes, and Red rose and bowed as well as his cradling arms would allow.

"*Señora*," first to Paz in deference to her age, then to Angela: "I had the pleasure of seeing you, *señorita*, on New Year's Day as you came home from church. Your charm and beauty laid a spell on me which your appearance brightens the more."

Angela felt blood warm her cheeks and recede again. What should she do? Involuntarily her feminine heart thrilled at the compliment, though she was a little shocked at its forwardness, yet her raising and the stern commands of her father forbade any friendliness with the stranger. Little Alfredo saved the situation by screaming anew, and Red's concerned "ssshhh, ssshhh" as he rocked the child was so comical that Angela burst into laughter. Tecla came and Paz, to be heard above the laughter and the squalling, screeched a high: "Tecla, get some clean water at once for the baptism; the little heathen will scream himself to death if we don't hurry. I know good and well he isn't baptized—what a temper, Tecla, what a shameful temper he has!"

Too concerned with the more important spiritual duty, Paz gave no attention to the proprieties, though Angela was still laughing. Paz grabbed the infant and plumped him into Angela's arms, took a spoon of water from the cup Tecla was holding, and poured it on the tiny red forehead. To the accompaniment of outraged protest she murmured, "I baptize thee in the name of the Father, and of the Son, and of the Holy Ghost."

"Amen," finished Red McLane solemnly. When Paz pressed her lips together and glared at him, he said, "My father did that many a time. He was a minister. Like your priest only somewhat different."

"I do not understand," Angela said, forgetting that she was being very forward in speaking to this stranger. "Your father? How then had he children if he was a priest? Or is it some sort of heathenish church?"

Angela for whom the world was classified into Catholics, Unbelievers, Heathens. Priests of her church, priests of the pagans. Angela, who knew so little of the world—.

Opportunity had never needed to beg for attention with Red McLane. Very deftly he set a chair for Angela out of Paz's way, switched the now whimpering Alfredo to his mother as he kept Angela's interest by telling her of his father and his church. When he asked, "Will you tell me of your faith now?" she did not even think of the impropriety of talking to him, or notice that he was seated opposite her. No one ever listened to Angela when she expounded the beliefs which were so much a part of and so dear to her, and Red's rapt attention gave her a happiness that swept all else aside. Angela was a missionary, glowing with zeal. While Red adroitly asked questions and Angela answered them at length, Paz burned the rosemary she had brought on the hearthstone; cleansing small garments in the fragrant fumes, whispering prayers for added potency as she held the baby over the ashes to get their purifying warmth. The Holy Infant had loved rosemary, so she firmly believed, and not a child was born in Rancho La Palma but Paz thus drove away the devil. Once, looking up, she felt uneasiness at her poor chaperonage but shoved it aside with the argument that Angela, who was so pious, would surely be a good influence on this man and could not possibly suffer from the contact. The man could not be bad and be so gentle with a child even if he was an *Americano;* also, they were talking about holy things. It would not be right to interrupt them.

Red McLane sat and listened. Not that the precepts of any church were of interest to him, but he had trained himself to always listen and carefully stow away in his memory the things he had heard; there was always a time when he had use for them. As he listened, he admired the sweet animated face, warm brown eyes, and neat black hair, the graceful way she held and moved her head.

Not as a man in love. As a man who, wanting something to fill a specification, is shopping for it.

Paz had to remind Angela that the christening robe—to be used when the Padre came to the ranch in summer—had not yet been shown to Tecla. Paz swept the room and remade the already smooth bed, got the baby to sleep in his basket. "So young and already a will of his own, Tecla," she sighed. "I fear his guardian angel will have plenty to do." It was when she heard Red's hearty laugh mingling with the light ripple of Angela's that Paz decided it was time to go. Past time, her conscience told her.

Red McLane gallantly kissed Angela's hand. "I would like to hear more," he told her. "Of course I must come again to see my namesake. Would I dare hope you might be seeing him also at the time?"

That was intrigue. Wickedness. Even the zeal of her faith could not surmount it and she shook her head. "Unless it be in the plan of things, *señor,* I could not—come here if I knew you were here."

"Then I shall hope that you will be here, not knowing. You did a very good deed this morning, *señorita,* telling me many things about your church I have always wanted to know."

Angela smiled. "Of that I am glad. Go with God, *señor.*"

"And may His angels watch over you, *señorita.*"

"So," said Ike, when they were riding again.

"So," answered Red McLane. And having spoken volumes, rode on in silence.

In the *jacal* Tecla was shaking her head. "Don Santiago would kill us both, surely he would drive us away, if he knew what happened here and that we gave the *Americanos* hospitality. And Angela—yes, he would kill us."

José pressed a gold piece in his palm. He had taken it with real reluctance when it was offered for his hospitality. Two pieces of gold, one for him and one for the *niño,* here in this *jacal.* It did not seem possible. "He will not find out, Tecla; only Estéban knows and he will never tell. Estéban tells me many things, he says the *Americanos* pay their servants money for the work they do. Money to spend, Tecla, just think of it!"

Tecla rubbed the coin and held it to the light. "That I do not believe, it is only talk. Yet—how well they treated us, how nice it was to have them. I do not know things, but I look for trouble, José. Much trouble."

Paz also thought so, when both she and Angela, careful of their words, left out all mention of the red-haired one when they told of their visit upon arriving home. Trouble would come of it, she was certain.

Only Angela felt no foreboding. Angela had planted the seed of faith in what she believed was fertile soil, and the day was good. Very good indeed. Her conscience was clear. If she had disobeyed her father—this was something belonging to God, and God's things came first. She had done no wrong and had been properly chaperoned all of the time.

While his daughter was laughing with Red McLane in the *jacal* three miles away, Don Santiago sat in a shady corner of the patio with his friend Gabriel, drinking coffee and dipping *polvorones* as they talked. Don Gabriel del Lago brought news, somewhat vague but comforting to Don Santiago.

The *guerrilleros* were very active in Mexico, harassing the invader and lassoing their scouts and in general doing a great deal of damage. Santa Anna was drawing new troops together to meet Taylor once again and this time he was certain of victory. It was said that General Scott was preparing to leave and had dreams of marching on Mexico City. There had been some trouble in Matamoros, and an officer had been killed or injured. "Which will make no difference," Don Gabriel sighed. "Where one

Americano is killed there are ten more to take his place. I do not look for any victory in Mexico, Santiago. What little trouble we can make for them will, I fear, turn around and come back to us. Sometimes I think it would be better if we resigned ourselves and became American citizens, hateful though it would be. We are that already by their law, and it might be better for us if we recognized it."

"I am ashamed of you, Gabriel." Don Santiago put a hand on his friend's knee. "Or would be, did I not know that you are not yourself today. You are *triste*, that comes to all of us now and then. I have something to show you, excuse me a moment." He went to his office, soon returned and handed the torn paper to Don Gabriel.

After his guest had perused them, Don Santiago explained, giving the substance of McLane's talk and proposition. "He was already in the patio when I saw him, and I had to extend him the courtesy of a host. Most unwillingly, I assure you. I endured him, but the insult was none the less strong. I—I, Santiago de Mendoza y Soría, son of a father who rightfully hated them, brother of Ramón who was killed by them, to be a *magistrado* for the *Americanos!* I to coax my friends—"

"Wait, wait a moment, *amigo*." Don Gabriel knew too well what his host's indignation was building to and he was in no mood for high angers. Today he felt depressed and tired, was indeed *triste*. "Do not blame the man, *amigo*. I do not doubt that he was an emissary for his governor; he did not impress me, in Matamoros, as a loud-mouthed boaster, but as a man very certain of his ground before he put his foot upon it." He was silent awhile, and the light wind beat the stiff palm leaves together as if in applause. Don Santiago rolled two corn husk cigarettes, his hands shaking with the effort to control himself, and called Estéban to bring a lighter. When the servant came with a bit of flaming tallow on a stick and lit the cigarettes for the *señores*, Don Santiago took deep draughts of the black tobacco into his lungs; allowing his friend to talk until his own anger should be cooled.

Don Gabriel tapped the paper with a finger. "It is amazing, Santiago, how their minds leap ahead. It is a quality we lack, for we live in the past and the present and see the future with our emotions only. We believe a thing must be so, or so, and then we wait for it to be so. These *Americanos* say, 'This should be so, I will make it be'. And in that—mark my words—in that is where we are already beaten. Do you see what this McLane has in mind?"

189

"Perhaps I have been too angry to see."

"It is plain enough, they select their officials by vote, a vote of the people. If we are citizens we can vote, but what do we know of the candidate? Nothing at all. So one man who has influence over his friends, and that includes the servants of these friends, making a goodly number of individuals—that one man is given some sort of position, favors, and honor. You, in this case. McLane then tells you what candidate to vote for, and I do not doubt but that he will make him appear in the most favorable light to you; you tell us whom you represent as *magistrado*, and we and our servants all vote for the man McLane wants in office, doubtless to further his own ends. It is most clever, and I give the man credit for great vision. Even the *peons* are citizens under their law. It will be, after a time, that whoever controls the Mexican vote will get the office. As I said, their minds work quickly and far into the future. However, it might be that there are some of them who see what our plight will be and, in genuine sympathy, wish to help us. Did you tell the red-beard of the bandits who stole out Gáspar and by force of numbers drove him from his ranch? It could have been a test. You might have said: 'See that justice is done to Gáspar de la Guerra and I may believe you.'"

Don Santiago's eyes were wide with incredulity. He was so shocked that he spoke slowly, as if he were taking the words one by one from his mouth and laying them in a row. "You mean that you would have considered this abominable thing, you a del Lago?"

"Today, yes. Perhaps not tomorrow. Today it seems to me that we are like men who stand on a shore and watch a tidal wave coming towards us because we are afraid to run to the mountains. Today I regret that we did not show Canales the door at our last meeting, and that I did not urge you to keep Alvaro and the others who went with him out of Mexico. Though I have regretted that before today, I have lain awake many nights thinking, have ridden many miles to clear my mind so I could convince myself that we are right—and I have not succeeded. The more I ponder on what Padre Pierre told us at our first meeting, the more logical it seems; for I have asked myself, who was the better man to guide us, Padre Pierre or Canales the *guerrillero*, and the answer was plain. I am wondering, Santiago, whether we do not after all owe some allegiance to the new government. Now that I see this paper, I wonder whether it might not be wise to at least think it over. It is time that we, too, look to the future."

Don Santiago's answer was that of the man who, having locked his mind, has thrown away the key. He said shortly, sternly, "There is only one course, Gabriel. In my eyes I best serve my God and His people by doing my utmost to uphold our traditions and our beliefs. I shall become more strict in their observance, in the future."

To which Don Gabriel gave silence for an answer. There was nothing to say. And he would not again, he knew, bring up the subject.

The distant chunk-chunk of the ox cart became louder, finally stopped at the gate, and Paz and Angela came into the patio. They curtsied to the master and the guest and went inside.

Don Santiago welcomed the diversion as a means to again show good humor, a part of the tradition he was upholding. A host was ever gracious. "Tecla's firstborn is a bit of an occasion to the women," he explained with a laugh. "It is just another *peon* and of small consequence."

And had there been someone to tell him that Destiny might use so lowly a thing as the birth of a *peon* to shape her ends, Don Santiago's laugh would have been loud and long. The birth of a *hidalgo*, yes, but never a *peon*.

Chapter 21

The huisache burst into golden bloom and flung its heady perfume into the patio, withering to a memory in all too short a time. There was the sheep shearing, soon the *alleluia* of Easter. And suddenly it was summer, a summer that came early, and would be long and hot and somnolent.

Early one morning Tomás came to the *hacienda*, concern deepening the lines spearing from his mouth. There were *gringos* in the hay valley beyond the ridge of malpais. "There are two men and a woman. They stopped their wagon by the hill of the flat rocks and are building a house of stones, and they dug out the seep spring there and have water. We were keeping the stock in the valley this spring to thicken the grass, and their horses and a few cows and goats are feeding there. I had only Simón with me when I saw them, and I thought it best to first come and tell you. What should I do?"

It was the action the master of Rancho La Palma needed. The women had irritated him when they tried to please him in every way, now they irritated him more because they no longer tried to please him. Gabriel del Lago's defection was still a wound. He was lonesome for Alvaro and worried about him. Luis Gonzaga was a constant thorn, the servants and *peons*—something had happened to them also; only yesterday Crispín, the stable boy, had given him a sullen answer. Tomás's news promised a break of monotony, a diversion from thought.

"Is Simón with you?" he asked, careful that his voice should not carry beyond the terrace. "Pedro is at the *jacal*. Get fresh horses, see that your *escopeta* is loaded, and Luis Gonzaga and I will meet you at the *jacal*. At once, Tomás."

"*Sí, señor.*" Tomás bowed respectfully and hurried away.

In a screened corner of the patio Susanita was sitting for her portrait. Luis, unfamiliar with the use of oils, mourned over the result. "Your eyes look like grass, I cannot get that touch of gray in them. Your hair looks like metal, your nose is a *polvorón* stuck to your face. If you really looked like this I would never acknowledge you as my sister. Oh, Estéban, I did not see you—what is it?"

"Your father wishes you to ride with him at once." Estéban picked up the buckskin jacket lying on the grass and held it for the young master, careful to say no more and betray that he had been listening.

Susanita kissed her brother. "I will put your things away. You haven't been yourself at all the last few days, Luis, I hope you and *papá*—don't anger him, today."

He held her a moment, holding back the impulse to confide in her, turned quickly away to join his father who was already mounted on Negro. Perhaps today something will happen, he thought, so I can tell him. It was the third day since the young Mexican, pretending to have lost his way, had whispered, "The doctor goes in a week." And Luis had not as yet found the courage to brave his father's scowl.

Don Santiago was glum and remained so after Tomás and the two *vaqueros* joined them, so the journey was a silent one. It was past noon when they came to a ridge of jagged black rocks, circled it, and came noiselessly on an apron of sand about a hundred feet from the squatters, where Don Santiago signaled a halt at the base of a large rock.

A woman with a scanty skirt pinned up halfway to her knee was wielding a shovel in a shallow hole, evidently mixing adobe for mortar. A tall woman, thin, angular, drab, even from a distance anything but prepossessing. A short, red-faced man was laying bricks on a short shoulder high wall, and another man closely resembling the woman was cementing the rocks with adobe he carried from the table in a gourd dipper. Brother, sister, and husband, Don Santiago deduced, and gave the signal to ride forward.

The red-faced man dropped a stone as he saw the riders, took up a shotgun leaning against the wall, and walked to a spot about six feet in front of Don Santiago. "What do you want?" he demanded truculently in English, then repeated the question in halting, barely understandable Spanish.

"*Esta tierra es mía,*" Don Santiago answered, speaking slowly, waving an arm to make the man fully comprehend that this was his land. Then he pointed to the wagon and the grazing horses, to the distant horizon, and flipped his hand as he ordered sharply,

"*¡Sálganse! ¡Váyanse! ¡Pronto!*"

To the right of Don Santiago was Tomás with the *escopeta* in his hands, next to him Pedro; on the left was Simón and Luis Gonzaga. Even to one ignorant of Spanish the meaning of the words must have been unmistakable, but the man did not answer or move. Don Santiago pointed again and repeated, "*¡Pronto! ¡Váyanse!*"

For answer the man raised the gun and aimed at Don Santiago. With its explosion came the roar of the old *escopeta*, powder smoke a curtain of acrid stench. When it drifted away and the horses were quieted, Don Santiago's hat was on the ground some distance behind him. And before him the red-faced man lay on his back, very still.

The tall man came forward and stooped over the body, shaking his head when he saw that life was gone. As he straightened and looked at them, Luis Gonzaga heard his father mutter: "What are you waiting for, Simón?"—and saw the *pistola* in Simón's hand.

The man also saw the *pistola*, threw his arms high and screamed: "No no, in God's name don't shoot me too!"

It all happened so quickly that Luis was scarcely aware of jerking the gun from Simón until he held it in his hand. He looked at it, looked at the ashen face of the trembling American and, blood hot in his cheeks, urged Tabasco close to the man. He spoke to him, slowly and carefully, telling him that he must go at once, that this land was part of Rancho La Palma and no trespassers were allowed.

The man dropped his arms and knotted his forehead in the attempt to find the meaning of the words in a language he knew so little of. Finally comprehending, he took his turn making Luis understand that they had seen no markers anywhere and had thought the land belonged to the first who took it. He illustrated by piling up a few rocks to which Luis shook his head. "It is not necessary to have markers, all the land here has belonged to us for a hundred years. You will have to go farther west"—he pointed to the sun, then made motions of scalping the man—"and there are many Indians, it is not safe."

The woman came from behind the wall and put a hand on her brother's arm, pointing a dirty bare foot at the dead man. She said in English: "I knew he'd get hisself kilted some day, and I wisht I could say I was sorry. You lettin' them run us off, George, ain't that what they want?"

"It's their land, Katie." The man looked apologetically at Luis Gonzaga, at the four sitting on their restive horses like spectators. Pedro had brought Don Santiago's hat and the shot holes in the high rolled brim were plainly visible. The woman pointed a finger at him and screamed, "That's what they say, and even if it's theirs they're only Mexicans. We be white folks and this is the United States, ain't it? We got the right of it. They kilted an American, you goin' to let that get by? You allus was afraid of—"

"Shut up! Henry drawed the gun and it weren't the first time, and he got what was comin' to him. Shut up and go away." To Luis Gonzaga he said that they would go. "*Vamos, sí, pronto.*"

The contempt in Don Santiago's face was as plain as the venom in the woman's, the gist of her words easily guessed by him. The dilapidated wagon with the dirty, torn cover, the scrawny cows and swaybacked horses, the ragged clothes and gaunt frames of the brother and sister, and the re-pulsiveness of the dead man, all made a pitiful picture. If this, he thought with some amusement, was what the land-seeking invaders were like, they scarcely constituted a menace. He summed them up in one epithet: "*Puercos.*" And gave the signal to leave. Looking back before they rounded the ridge, he saw the woman removing the clothes from the body, her brother digging the mud hole deeper for the grave.

It was a scene that was to be repeated in variation for many years to come, until an empire of state would rise on land that had scarcely a square yard of it that had not been wet with blood. The fugitive, like the man Tomás had shot; the land-greedy who justified their rapaciousness with the word "pioneer" and used it as a blanket to cover their evils—sullying the good word and the constructive men entitled to it; the trash, the "*puerco,*" like George and his sister, squeezed out of a community that re-fused to support them any longer; the wanderer, fleeing from nothing but himself; the adventurer, his conscience and his scruples long dead. All these, and more, came to Texas like buzzards to a feast.

"Remember the Alamo!" they shouted and visited the sins of Santa Anna upon all his countrymen, and considered themselves justified in stealing the lands of the Mexicans. Some built themselves a house of righteous-ness like a snail builds his shell and carries it with him. "The Mexicans are Papists, Catholics who worship idols and pray to a woman they call the Blessed Virgin." They pillaged and stole, and insulted, and called them-selves a sword of the avenging God, and shouted their hymns to drown their consciences.

They came on and on, and killed, and were killed. And the earth took their bodies, dust to dust returning, and sent up its flowers in the spring, and its gift of grass. And smiled in the sun, and lifted its face to the rain.

Don Santiago rode ahead, conflicting emotions warring in him. One moment angry that Luis Gonzaga took the *pistola* from Simón, feeling that it would have been better to have killed the other two humans and their miserable stock; the next moment glad there was no further bloodshed. It was easy to say one would kill every *gringo* who stepped on one's land, but in actuality it too closely approached murder. There was war, they were invaders, yet he had let them live. Nor had he sent Tomás after McLane and his man, to kill them in the night. Hostship, though given unwillingly, had left McLane's person inviolate. And for those in the valley, his pride had not allowed him to stoop further when Luis Gonzaga stopped Simón. Besides, life was less kind than death, for such as they. Still it angered him, and the unpleasantness of the episode was like something sticky on his hands. He wished he had let Tomás attend to it.

"Luis Gonzaga," he called, and when the boy came and rode beside him he said harshly, "You interfered in what was my affair. Have you forgotten that I am still master of my *rancho?* It would appear so."

Luis wondered whether the question was merely to use him as a vent for emotions or whether it was a preliminary to a more vital issue. Luis's heart was a wound, bruised with the beating of wings these three days and a hammering the harder since his impotence with oils—for he knew he could paint if he had training. Resentment burned that he had been dragged along on this mission which belonged to the *vaqueros,* and he felt that his father knew it would be distasteful to him. Perhaps now was the time to say what must be said. He summoned courage, kept his eyes on Tabasco's ears, and said, "I know I am great disappointment to you, *papá,* but if I do not like killings and cruelties, it is that I was made that way and I cannot change." Now, now, say it quickly! "I do not like—anything here any more. With all my trying I cannot become a *ranchero.* I know I never will."

"I have meant to bring up the subject before this; now is a good a time as any to tell you my patience is at an end, Luis." Don Santiago looked at him, and a sudden wave of longing for Alvaro washed over him; so poignant that it filled his throat and he had to ride on awhile without further speech. Frustration wrenched him to agony that he, a Mendoza, the family that fathered *men,* had a son who painted pictures—a thing for the nuns in the convents to do. He looked at the land about him as he rode down draws white with short-stemmed daisies, past hollows rich with the velvet of winecups, between low hills purple with verbenas. Ah, *Cristo,* but it was beautiful, beautiful! That anyone could say he did not like it was as great a crime as blaspheming the Creator. He had meant to temper his command to his son, but now all his restlessness and dissatisfaction came to culmination and he struck out sternly. He told Luis: "I, your father, command you to learn the things you must. I command you to be a *ranchero* as I am, as was your grandfather and his father before him. Your task begins today. As soon as you get home you will destroy those childlike things with which you amuse yourself, you will burn all your paints and crayons. This is my final command."

Luis Gonzaga drew rein on Tabasco and put a restraining hand on his father's arm, forcing himself to look without flinching into the coldly hostile black eyes. Now was the time. Padre Pierre was to the right of him, telling him "God gave you this great gift, watch that you do not throw it away. Watch, Luis." Devlin had hold of his hand, and the clasp was strong and warm. "I will not say good-bye, Luis." And strength came like cool water, and courage calmed his leaping heart. His voice was steady and sure as he said, "*Papá*, I wish to study art. I want to go to the *Americano* towns of Baltimore and New York, I have—I will—"

If lightning had come down from the serene turquoise sky and struck his son dead, Don Santiago would not have been more surprised. It was a full minute before he could stammer, "New York? You want to go to an infidel town—you have a friend there—how can you have? What are you talking about?"

"It is the lame doctor who is Catholic. He paints pictures and I met him at Padre Pierre's. He asked me to go with him and it will be arranged that I study art. He is—my friend." Luis stretched a hand to his father, palm up, imploring. "*Papá*, please try to understand that it is the only kind of living I care about, that it is something inside which tears at me as the *rancho* tears at you when you are in town—*papá*, I beg of you, let me go."

Don Santiago raised a hand to strike and drew it as quickly back again, slapped instead with a loud "No! I say no! Despicable as your consorting with a *gringo* has made you in my eyes, hard as it will be to stand the sight of you, I forbid you to leave Rancho La Palma!"

Luis Gonzaga instinctively cringed a little when rage twisted his father's face to fearsomeness. Only a little, for the wings had broken their prison and were already soaring free. He saw, clearly, that the real issue was not his consorting with an American, or even his leaving; the issue was a test of the mastership of his father over his family. However, Luis made one more appeal, so that later he should have no regret of omissions.

"*Papá*, I wish you had known him and could have heard what he had to tell. It is not as we think; this town of Baltimore was named after a great *hidalgo* who was Catholic, and his state was named after Our Lady; it is called Maryland. Others live there also who are not Catholic and they live in peace—*papá*, it has seemed to me that is as it should be. Please, *papá*, you could ride with me to Matamoros and talk to him and you would see—"

"Lies! I do not listen to their lies. Nor will I listen to you, Luis Gonzaga. I said you are not leaving here!"

"Yes I am, *papá*." Devlin was holding hard to his hand; Padre Pierre's eyes were deep and compelling. "I know that I am doing right and I am going. If you will not give me your blessing then I will leave—without it."

Don Santiago looked at the set face of the son he had considered a weakling, and he saw a determination there to match his own. And he knew he was beaten, knew that no punishment would make him master of the boy. Don Santiago looked again and told himself that the boy was gone. Ironic, that he had tried so long to make a man of him and at last succeeded in this strange manner. Now he had the man, and wanted the boy instead.

"I give you permission." If he could not dominate he must keep a pretense of it. "Not only that, I order you to leave, and in the morning, you will leave Rancho La Palma, Luis Gonzaga, and never again set foot upon it. You have already ceased to be my son."

He spurred Negro to join Tomás and the *vaqueros* ahead, and Tabasco followed.

The moon dropped its enchantment, softly, into the patio. For the moon loved Texas, and it went a little mad when it came over the big white *hacienda* and saw the flowered courtyard, the women's wide skirts spreading around their chairs like huge inverted blooms. It smiled on the young man standing straight and tall behind the chairs, on the man walking back and forth before them, gesticulating with his hands. It beamed and threw a special radiance into the great room roofed by the sky.

But the moon could only see, not hear. "I need not sleep first, Dolores," said Don Santiago. All the first heat, when he had brought them all out here and told them, had tempered to a hardness more formidable than the hot rage. "Luis Gonzaga knew my law about speaking to the *Americanos*. His traditions, his superiority of class, should instinctively have held only contempt for them all. No, Luis, I do not wish to hear again that some of them have breeding and refinement. I not only do not believe it, I do not choose to; as I do not choose to believe that they have fine cities and culture. He has asked to go with this—this one of our enemies and he shall have his wish."

"I have also asked for your blessing," Luis answered, holding tight to his mother's hand as he leaned over her. "For *mamá*'s sake I ask that you still call me 'son.'"

"Son!" Don Santiago spat the word. "The name of Mendoza will be dragged in the dirt, a blot forever, is it not enough that I do not forbid you to keep it?" He stopped in front of his sister. "This is your fault, Dolores. I did not want to go to town, I had a foreboding of evil. But no, I was scolded and cried over until against my will—"

"Nonsense, Santiago." Doña Dolores waved a fan widely and its shadow leaped at her, leaped away from her. "If you have forgotten, I will refresh your memory as to why we went, my brother. We gave in to you with good enough grace, and then one day you got a letter saying that hatred was getting together and wanted you to help hatch more trouble. Then, then, how we were ordered to rush around and get ready! It is from this distortion of yours, this obsession that nothing good comes from the *Americanos,* that our miseries come into being and thrive. And yours, Santiago."

"I must then lose both my sons," Doña María Petronilla's voice held the calm slowness of defeat. "I am glad for Luis to go but to go with bitterness—Luis is still a boy and it is hard to go in a strange land among strange people so far away from home. He needs our love, Santiago."

Angela could not refrain from saying, "*Papá*, if Luis met this man at Padre Pierre's house, then God arranged it."

Then round and round again went the same arguments, the same pleadings and appeals. Only Susanita was quiet, pressing the heavy seal of the ring into her palm; the ring she could wear only when no one would see it. A hand had reached to her heart, and its hard fingers were squeezing out its blood. Agonizingly, drop by drop. She must tell Luis to tell Roberto not to come now, perhaps not ever. Her eyes filled with tears. They were all hurting *papá* so, and she would hurt him most of all when he found out about Roberto. Now the last hope was being killed when the cold voice said, "You have not forgotten, Dolores, how our brother Ramón came home to us here and the father he loved, already dying from the wound given him by his enemies. He used his last breath to praise them and say he wished he had been one of them, there at the Alamo. Do you remember, Dolores? He said, 'So could a man die in glory, his soul forever free. So could he die and leave a name never dead.' They had something wonderful, these *Americanos,* he told us. I see him now, his life-blood running out on the tiles. The lesson was there then, telling me plainly to keep my children away from their devil's charm and contamination. I did not heed it, but I will heed my father's behest and hate them, and I can pluck those out of my heart who consort with my enemies. Yes, and die without seeing them. I make no compromise. A woman thinks she can compromise with honor, but a man knows he cannot.

"But this I will do. I will forgive Luis Gonzaga if he burns his paints, works hard with Tomás, and learns to be the *ranchero* I wish him to be. His is the choice."

He turned away from them and walked out to the patio and the tap-tap of his heels on the stone-hard earth told a story of inner turmoil; faint as an echo when he came to the row of yuccas that made a fence, sharp as hammer strokes when he passed the patio gate. He would walk there, the women knew, through most of the night. With his devils and with his ghosts.

"Come Susanita, Angela." The girls rose and kissed their mother, looking like animated moon flowers as they moved ahead of Doña Dolores. Poor young ones, Dolores thought, and poor Petronilla, what she will still have to endure. She did not think 'poor Santiago'; indeed she sniffed as she stepped on to the portico. Compromise. What else was a woman's life but compromise, and who made it so?

In the patio Luis brought a child's chair and set it at his mother's feet, resting his head against her knee as he had done years before. They did not speak of what had gone before; instead Luis told her everything he had been told of the land where he was going, of the place art and music and learning had among the people whom Devlin knew; of Devlin himself, their friendship, how the man regarded Luis's gift, what should be done with it. "He said he had neither son nor younger brother, *mamá*, and had always felt the need for both."

The mother felt at peace. Better for Luis to be with strangers who cared about him than having to suffer daily from his father's disapproval and contempt. Better for her to have him close to her like this, wrapped in a love beautiful as the silver night, and lose sight of him, than see him daily and never have him. Now if Santiago would come and sit with them awhile—she willed him to come, whispered a prayer as he came near the gate. But his head did not turn to look at them, the tap-tap of the boot heels did not miss a beat of their steady rhythm.

Luis said: "You and this night will paint itself on my heart and never be lost."

She kissed his forehead. "Whenever the moon is full, Luis, I will sit in the patio and have you with me again."

"And I will sit with you awhile, when the moon is full. When I know how to paint I will make a picture of it, *mamá*, and your face will be very beautiful because my memory will always see it so."

Luis Gonzaga, knight-errant; his sword, honesty; his shield, cleanness of heart; his armor, gentle kindness; his battle cry, joyous laughter.

Doña Dolores had insisted on cheerfulness, so when Luis came to breakfast smiles greeted him. The girls wore bright dresses and flowers in their hair, Doña María Petronilla had a lace collar fastened with a jeweled pin on a plain black dress, Doña Dolores wore her treasured large jet comb back of a high twist of hair. "Even if it is for evening, Luis knows I wear it on special occasions, and he will know it is for him," she explained. His father was gone, leaving no message other than a heavy money belt at his son's place; and at the gate, two armed *vaqueros* waiting beside the saddled Tabasco to ride with him to Matamoros. Luis picked up the belt and asked why his father had given it to him but none of them knew. It was there when they came into the room.

"Tell *papá* I thank him," he told Doña Dolores, handing her the belt, "but money without a father's blessing I will not take. I will not need it."

Doña Dolores left the room and in a short time returned with a worn belt of dark leather packed tightly with coins. "It was your Tío Anselmo's belt and the money is mine. I do not need it and I give it to you gladly. It cannot be said that a Mendoza is even temporarily beholden to another, Luis."

He thanked her and put it under his buckskin suit, bending his head to hide his tears. Then they were all gay, pretending they did not know this would be the last collation they would have together again. Only old Paz, bringing the chocolate, let the tears run unhindered from one wrinkle to another until Luis held her, called her a baby, wiped her face, and kissed a cheek. Whereas she slapped him and they all laughed, as if it was very funny, and Paz dropped back into role by scolding at the lumpy way his clothes were packed, took them from the sack, and refolded them.

Too soon it was time to go, for there was now no turning back. They went into the *sala* to kneel before the crucifix on the wall and Angela prayed ten *Aves*, to which they responded in chorus. While the mother pleaded silently, "You had a Son too, Mary, and sent Him out into the world. You who know the agony of parting; keep watch over mine and beg thy Son to keep him from harm."

Last embraces, a wild sob from Susanita as she flung herself upon her beloved brother. The scent of gardenia that was his mother; "I will write Padre Pierre, *mamá*, and he will send you the letter." Heliotrope, which was Doña Dolores: "Dear *Tía*, watch over *mamá* for me." The violet loved by Angela; the rose fragrance so suited to Susanita; the pungency of the tiny sacs of dried herbs Paz hid in her skirts, each one a charm against evil.

"*Adios, adios.*" So many things to say, forever left unsaid, unuttered because the tears were too close.

Quickly, quickly, lest the sight of the wide portico with its potted plants and bird cages, the patio with its palm tree, become too dear. Lest there be too long a waiting for one who would not appear. Lest all the servants gather close and leave a wailing in the ears. Oh, quickly, before the bright road ahead becomes black with shadows and beckons no more.

"*Ay*, Tabasco, *vámonos*!"

Nowhere was there sight or sound of Don Santiago. Luis Gonzaga shielded his eyes with his hands to look at the high bluff, but it was empty. Only the stone cross stood there, all golden in the morning sun.

Chapter 22

Summer's heat, this year, had a special malice, as if the sun must assist in the withering of hope. The defeat of Santa Anna at Buena Vista by Zachary Taylor was a heavy blow to the *ranchero* patriots north of the Río Grande, for in spite of his former defeats there remained a faith in him. Even a treacherous, vain leader was better than no leader at all. The position of the *rancheros* was tragic. Mexico had cast them aside, they knew Santa Anna too well and despised him; the glowing words of Canales in the role of liberator had paled and showed the sorry seams of boastings. The Americans were so utterly alien in their lack of courtesy and religion, their unwarranted arrogance, there seeming indifference to dress, that there was but one desire—to keep themselves apart from them. There seemed nothing to do but cling more closely together, be more stern, and hope, and hope.

Then before hope could strengthen, General Scott was in Vera Cruz—Vera Cruz, where innocent blood ran in streams. Vera Cruz, the slaughterhouse. Vera Cruz, where the victor's wreath was a sorry, a wilted thing.

From there Scott moved to Mexico City, and for the second time in history a conquering army traveled that mountainous way.

"It is terrible, it is the end," reported a soldier who had deserted Santa Anna and fled north, finding a few days shelter at Rancho La Palma.

"The *guerrilleros*, what of them?" Don Santiago asked. "What of Canales, are his men being killed?"

The man's eyes lighted. "Ah, our *guerrilleros*, they make it miserable for this new general. Canales is still The Fox, and I hear his men do not often get caught or killed."

"You do not know any of them, then?"

"No, *señor*. When I ran from war, I ran from all of it."

If Don Santiago was regretting the patriotic zeal that sent Alvaro away, he refused to admit it even to himself and always mentioned him with pride. Luis Gonzaga he never mentioned and pretended not to hear when anyone else did so. He rode much and was gone days at a time, but that had always been his habit. Less laughter, higher rages, moodier silences were the only changes in him.

Susanita pretended she was the same happy girl she had always been. There was nothing to do but wait, and hope, and dream. As long as nothing adverse was happening, worry could be postponed, and thanks be to God that René de la Ferrière and Carlos del Valle were in Mexico and could not press their suit. María de los Angeles wore her nun's garb for a day and folded it away. Angela too dreamed and waited and hoped, praying that the nebulous thing would take form; supreme in her faith that the way would be shown to her by the Great Giver. Doña María Petronilla cultivated serenity and strengthened her will so she could defend her children's happiness. Susanita, she thought, was getting over the officer after all. Worry could wait awhile. Doña Dolores took up her girlhood occupation of spinning, and the cheery whir helped calm nerves and did much to keep a balance of peace.

Trying, all of them, to ignore the cloud over the *hacienda*, to stifle the fears that would not die.

One evening when rain had washed the world clean and Don Santiago's voice held a small note of happiness as he sang *El Alabado*, a messenger came from Matamoros. A swarthy Mexican who exuded importance and bowed low to Doña María Petronilla as if he were a courtier. Padre Pierre, he told them, would be at Rancho La Palma on the feast of Don Santiago's patron saint, July the twenty-fifth. "If it be God's will that no Indians kill him on the way," he added unctuously and unnecessarily. An oily little man, this Hernando, and Don Santiago thanked him curtly, gave him a coin, and sent him to the servant's quarters out of his sight.

Hernando sought Paz and handed her a sealed paper with instructions to give it to Señorita Susanita, as he said he had been charged to do. "There is something in it for you," he said, "from one called Manuel."

Paz rushed to find Susanita, who was fortunately in her room. The old woman was so excited she saw only the sheet Susanita handed her when the seal was broken and did not notice more were quickly shoved under a pillow on a chair. Paz opened the door for light, excitedly asking, "What does it say, what is it, who is it from? Tell me quick, *niña*."

"Look, Paz, Manuel wrote it himself." Susanita moved a finger under the letters which, some huge and some cramped, wandered over the page, and read, "*Abuelita, estoy bien y muy contento; te quiero mucho.*" (Grandmama, I love you and I am well and happy.) The "Manuel" was carefully done in even letters, the period after it very black and round. Susanita laughed softly. "Just think, he is learning to write; isn't it wonderful? Be careful, Paz, that *papá* does—"

"I know, I know." Tears stood in the old eyes as she rushed away, clasping this miracle against her breast, she knew. Writing was not for a *peon*, it would only inflame Don Santiago anew if he saw it. She would keep her pride and happiness to herself. It was not until she was in bed that Paz remembered how incensed she had been when Estéban had repeated what the *Americano* with the yellow beard had told him, that all men were born free and had the right to learn to read and write if they cared to. One was born to be master, another to serve that master in humility, without aspiration. Yet it seemed right that Manuel should be more than an unlettered peon. But if it was right for Manuel it was right for another, and that was not right at all. Round and round went Paz, reasoning until finally exhaustion brought sleep.

Susanita's joy at the letter from Warrener was short-lived for at dinner Don Santiago announced: "There will be a *fiesta* when the *padre* comes, and you will arrange it, Petronilla. There have been fewer Indians, and it will be safe for our *ranchero* friends to be merry with us. God knows it may be the last time for many days that we will have the old happy times together in our patio, with these accursed *gringos* overrunning the land like locusts."

Cold was the paper inside the waist of Susanita's blue dress. (I will get leave soon and ride to the *rancho* and ask for you, *mi* Susanita. I will present my credentials and plead my love and make him listen to me.) *Papá* would look at no credentials, or listen. *Papá* might even punish her as Inez had been—no, only Manuel knew of the notes and he was with Roberto. (Manuel is my companion, mentor, pupil, teacher. He tells me about your dear ways and the little things you do, and I string them like pearls on a golden chain and wear them round my heart.)

Susanita decided to give the messenger a note to Padre Pierre asking him to tell Roberto not to come now. But in the morning when she asked for Hernando, he was gone. "Back to his *gringos*," Nicolasa told Paz, "where I hope he stays. He and his money and his words from the infidel language and his talk of being free. It bodes no good, Paz. A *peon* is a *peon* and this talk is not for us."

"Our godson," said Ike Mullins, guiding his horse into a furrow of a field sloping to the *jacal*, "has a will of his own. Listen to that yell, sounds like cussin', Red."

Red McLane chuckled. "It does at that, Ike. And the sun hardly out of bed. Pure temper, that yell."

Blas Alfredo Pablo Anselmo was still complaining about being left alone on the floor with only gourds to amuse him when McLane, having left Ike and the horses at the corral, greeted Tecla at the oven beside the *jacal* where she was baking bread. They went inside together and Red picked up the child, held up a shiny gold coin, but passed it on to Tecla. "He'll swallow it; this is better for you, little rat; here, bite it." From his pouch he brought a silver mug with a big, ornate handle, put it and the now cooing Alfredo on the floor.

Having paved the way, McLane got down to business. He wanted to see María de los Angeles and could Tecla in some way bring her here? He was, Tecla noticed, clean-shaven, and even her eyes could see that the dust-colored suit had quality for all its plainness, that the shirt was linen and the black Mexican-style sash of the finest silk. She would, she told him, bring José.

They discussed it as they walked up from the corrals. "I am shocked that he should dare to want Angela," Tecla said.

José shrugged. "Why not? What have other suitors to offer far above what he has? I believe she likes him. Haven't you been wanting to talk to her about a gift for Don Santiago for his feast day? Couldn't you have her come here?"

"Yes, the embroidered initials in his handkerchiefs. None can do as fine work as I, and he is so particular. You think it would be right, José? I could say a pain in the stomach presses me, José? He would drive us away if he knew about this man being our good friend. Then Angela—don't you think she would be very angry to find him here?"

"She will be happy if she can talk religion, you know that. Don Santiago has gone to the far camp with Tomás; even Victorino is gone, and there is no one who need know. I will myself ride to the *hacienda*. Remember, Tecla, he is our friend."

Don Santiago had come to breakfast with a temper and left the household in a state of nerves by the time he rode away. When José came in with his message, Angela was eager to go, and Doña Dolores put down her sewing. "In truth I am weary of this house today," she said. "The *jacal* will be a welcome change and Tecla makes better coffee than all our kitchen help put together. I will go with Angela, Petronilla—child, tell José to put the mules to the light wagon, will you please? Susanita, get the handkerchiefs and thread, and my *mantilla* like a good girl."

"Yes, do go," Doña María Petronilla urged. "I will try to teach Susanita how to spin; we have let her go too long in learning something useful."

When Tecla, hearing the chuk-chuk of the axles in the loose hubs, looked up the road and saw wide black skirts spread around a stool in the wagon bed, a striped sunshade held over a black *mantilla*, she grabbed the *olla* and fled to the spring for water. She was not going to explain the man playing with little Alfredo in the *jacal*—not to Doña Dolores! She stayed at the spring until José brought the wagon to the corral, then took time in setting the *olla* on her head and walked very slowly up the path.

Red McLane set the baby on the floor and bowed low to the startled Doña Dolores filling the doorway. "Ah, *señora*, I thought for a moment you were your beautiful niece."

Taken off guard and immediately flattered she found herself answering, "My niece—surely not at my age, *señor!*"

"May I offer you a seat?" He picked up the baby and deftly set a chair forward. "Your age, *señora*—but you are far indeed from years when one speaks of age." He bowed to Angela, set a chair for her before she could do anything about her astonishment, set the child in her lap, and kept on talking to Doña Dolores. "Your niece here who resembles you so markedly is beautiful, certainly, but the richness of beauty and the perfection of it will not come until she has your years, *señora*. Too young wine has no flavor, as you know, *señora*."

"That is true, yes." Doña Dolores actually simpered, coy as a sixteen-year old. Had not her first love, the poet, made many verses telling of her loveliness? Though none since extolled her physical charms, not even Anselmo, he had always believed it a certain blindness on their part, hugging the delusion of good looks as only a homely woman can. Now she slipped her *mantilla* back to show the glossiness of her black hair, carefully arranged into an intricate loop on her head. She was justly proud of her heavy hair, and kept it in perfect coiffure always. She had heard—it was over coffee in the de Baca home in Matamoros—that the *Americanos* were very discerning in feminine pulchritude, more so than the Mexicans.

"You are the child's godfather?" she asked, to get back to dignity. "José has told us of you."

❧

"A thousand pardons!" McLane clasped his hands apologetically. "The unexpected pleasure of seeing two such charming ladies made me forget my manners. I am Señor McLane. We met in Matamoros but I do not flatter myself that you remember. You left an unforgettable picture in my mind, with a beautiful niece on each side to enhance you."

Doña Dolores blushed with pleasure. Quite a personable man. Really. The attire of a gentleman, the courtesy of one, alien or no. Don Santiago should realize that there were exceptions to everything, and quite possible that there were a few good *Americanos.* "I remember you, *señor,*" adding hastily, "the color of your beard was so unusual. We of Spanish descent have much redness of hair but not that—ah—"

"Purple effect," he finished, drawing a stool so that he faced them in a triangle. While talking to Doña Dolores, he was nevertheless aware that Angela's chirping to the baby was a pretense that she was not listening. But he knew it was important to make a friend of the dignified aunt; Angela could wait. And he liked Doña Dolores. Just then the child got a hand in Angela's hair and she called, "Alfredo, *niñito,* no, no!" and he grasped opportunity and said, "The name, *señora*—when I asked that he be named after me, I did not know there was a promise that he be named after your honored husband. When the *padre* writes it in the book it shall be Blas Anselmo, nothing more."

"No indeed." Doña Dolores lifted both hands. "We are so accustomed to calling him Alfredo that by now it seems a fitting name; though a trifle imposing for a *peon.*"

McLane threw out a hand, spread fingers held upward, light in his pale eyes. "*Señora,* when he is grown he will have a word to say about the way he is to be governed."

"How utterly foolish! This child is a *peon, señor.*"

"If it is his will, not otherwise. A servant, perhaps, but not bound as now. Ah, *señora,* if I could only show you people how powerful can be your voice in government, with the proper leader—for the poor have a voice under our law as well as the rich. If I could get you to see that working *with* us will be to your benefit and can change—why, it can change history. A subjugated man who keeps his resentments will not benefit Texas. As it is now each side thinks the other has nothing good and that will be multiplied with the years if not corrected. Had Don Santiago seen eye to eye with me—did he tell you, *señora?*"

Doña Dolores restrained her eagerness to know, at last, what had transpired that day in the office, for Don Santiago had kept complete silence about it. She asked sedately, "Should I know of it, Señor McLane?"

Better and better, thought McLane. He repeated what he had told Don Santiago, leaning heavily on the "*magistrado*" when he saw the pleased look on her face; noting that his namesake was asleep and Angela was listening, he added, "There will be great opportunities for doing good, for the aftermath of war is always worse than war itself. I see a great field for doing good, for women perhaps more even than men. To the good Samaritan then the binding of wounds both of spirit and body. I had hoped to enlist the aid of so representative a man as your brother, *señora*; it means so much to us all of us." Then seeing Tecla in the doorway, he added quickly to exonerate her from duplicity, "Indeed, I had just arrived here a few moments before you came, on my way to see him again. Most opportunely, for it is seldom I have the pleasure of talking to a lady who has the intelligence to not only listen but understand."

Doña Dolores drank this in a single gulp and enjoyed the warm glow of it. Intelligence—odd, that it took this stranger and foreigner to see that she had it. A most discerning man! Though this time McLane was sincere and the compliment warranted, for she plainly saw the picture he drew. And she loved what she added to it: People coming and going at the *hacienda*; a stimulant to living, in the *Americano* guests; the women reflecting in the glory of the deference to Don Santiago's position as *magistrado*; long fine dinners once again, with silver and linen; a chance to wear good clothes and jewels. The wart on her cheek glowed red in the pleased excitement of what could be.

"*Señor!*" She made a slight movement with her hand, and McLane had a distinct impression of being coyly tapped on the wrist with a fan, as plainly as if she were carrying one. "Now I know you are all flattery, shame on you. But—do not come today. My brother is not at home, and I fear his mood this evening will not be receptive. Perhaps you had best not come until I have spoken to him, though I fear it will do no good." She sighed, and for a moment her face was old with weariness at the prospect of the empty years ahead. "I feel I should warn you that he wants no *Americano* on his land, if he knew you were here—"

"I know *señora*. I will come again, surely it would be too much to expect more to be added to this pleasant encounter. I trust that God will be good and I will meet you again."

Doña Dolores blushed like a girl. "That will be as it may be *señor. ¿Quien sabe?*"

Angela spoke for the first time, a little shyly. "Do the Protestant people pray to God, *señor?* I have wondered."

When Doña Dolores turned her back to give Tecla the handkerchiefs and discuss the initialing, McLane took a square sealed paper from his pouch and put it in Angela's hand, whispering, "Read it when you are alone, *señorita;* it is of gravest importance." Then quickly answered her question that indeed they prayed, both long and loud.

"I used to wonder when I was a child, listening to my father, whether God was deaf. I believed He was."

Laughing, at ease with each other, they exchanged peculiarities of people who prayed. Tecla asked if she might serve them coffee, and McLane gave his attention to Doña Dolores. She asked him about San Antonio, about his own country. What kind of dresses did the women wear, how did they do their hair, were they pretty, did they use powder, was it true that they had a voice in how the household should be run and their husbands pampered them, were there *bailes,* music? McLane answered each question as if it was of utmost importance, his fine voice and flair for description putting a certain drama into even the small things. When the coffee came he told them about food and how it was served, "Silver?" Doña Dolores was astounded. "Silver on the table and glasses and thin china, and servants in special clothes to serve? I can scarcely believe it."

It was time to go, and long past time. Though what, Doña Dolores asked herself, was life but endless time, one dull day piled on top of another. José brought the wagon, McLane gallantly kissed the ladies' hands and helped them over the wheel.

"*Adios, señora, adios señorita; vayan con Dios.*"

"*Si Dios es servido.*"

Angela, refusing to listen to a conscience accusing her of guilty secrecy, sought a shady corner screened by hibiscus, and broke the seal of the letter. It read:

Most *estimable señorita.*

After much deliberation I am entrusting my message to you on paper so that no word of it be lost, and being thus able to refer to it from time to time, you will the better be able to direct your thoughts. If I too often intrude myself, I ask your indulgence and forgiveness.

The world is in an upheaval which we cannot ignore and which touches your people, the Mexicans, most deeply. They will suffer both materially and spiritually with few to minister to them, they will be maligned and misunderstood. From this cataclysm strong souls will be born to be the guide of the bewildered, to scatter light and happiness like the sun. Padre Pierre told me you wished to enter the convent. María de los Angeles, your gift should not shine like a feeble candle in a room. I consider first your gracious manner and your winsome charm, already setting you apart even before there has been opportunity for their proper development. Think of it in a home that will be wide in its entertainings, that will have seated at its table men who hold power and position. That will be my home, being built now in San Antonio. Think of yourself in such a home, so lovely a hostess that none can forget you. Then remember that many will come to kiss your hand who are ignorant of the beauties of your Church and faith and in their ignorance think badly of it. Will they not think less harshly after knowing you are one of its devout members? For your charm will grow with the years and the fame of it will spread. I felt this when I first talked with you, and I would have said, "If she were pagan, then I would like to be a pagan also." You wear your clothes with an air, and there will be clothes, many of them, with the jewels that will match but cannot dim your loveliness.

Consider, then, the good you can do your people. Many will be homeless and will need comfort. The good *padres* at the church will need money and encouragement in this their task, and it will be you who can organize groups to help them. You can go to the humble homes of the poor, there will be the sick to visit and comfort. We will see that there is a school, you and me, to teach those who wish to learn. The *padres* will have true friends in us when they need friends.

I have money and will always have money, though this is a subject I am certain you do not understand. However, you will soon learn that it means much to have it, and you will never need beg me for it. Then last I offer my regard which is both deep and sincere, and I will ever hold you in its tenderness. I will communicate with you in whatever way will be most feasible, sometime in the future when you will have had time to weigh your course. In the meantime, I ask that God's blessing remain with you.

Alfred McLane

A stilted epistle indeed. One that had cost much sweat and many hours of endeavor, written as it was in an acquired language. After Angela had carefully read it for the third time, she hurried to the room she shared with Susanita, lit a candle, and drew two chairs to a table while she urged her sister to shorten her *siesta* and get out of bed. "We will have to hurry before Paz or someone comes."

First pledging her to secrecy, Angela told Susanita everything that had happened. "He looks better without the beard." Regarding the letter: "I thought it was some questions on religion, so it seemed my duty to take it. I have brought it to you because I do not understand it, and I could not show it to anyone else, certainly not to *papá*. I—I am greatly disturbed, Susanita."

"Your conscience is too tender, Angela." Susanita was more disturbed herself than she cared to show at this almost unbelievable happening. "And Tía Dolores actually talked to him and liked him—oh, that's why she looked so young and happy when you came home. Do you know, Angela, I often wonder if there isn't a part of us that is completely ours given to us at birth which cannot possibly belong to anyone else. How can we completely belong to *papá*, if we have separate souls? *Tía* is so strongly herself is the reason why she—oh, I don't know how to say it."

"I know. I have wondered too whether obedience to *papá* in everything comes first. I feel that it was my right to be a nun. But read the letter, sister, and hurry."

Susanita pulled Angela's head down and kissed her flushing cheeks after she finished reading, laughing as she said, "Oh, Angela, you are so innocent, you are stupid—why, the man is proposing to you! Look, he tells you what a hostess you would make in his home. Winsome manner and gracious charm—my, I thought you were merely sweet and pretty. See, Angela, you are the wife of an important person—how is he important, I wonder—and your graciousness leaves an imprint on all who come to your house. Clothes and jewels. Yes, you wear them with such sweet modesty, you're not vain like me. Hmm, Señor McLane and his lovely wife. The charming Señora McLane. The gracious wife of our host—oh, Angela, Angela!" She buried her face in her sister's lap, shaking with laughter.

"I do not think it something to laugh at, Susanita."

"I'm sorry." Susanita turned to seriousness. "It was the crude way he put it. Imagine you married to an *Americano*—" Not both of us, came panicky thought, not both of us! It is different with me, we love each other. "You couldn't, Angela. He isn't even a gentleman, a gentleman would never mention his money and say he would buy you clothes and jewels. And sending for you to come to a *jacal*—don't be stupid, he bribed José to come here and sat there waiting for you, I am surprised *Tía* didn't see through that as she knows Tecla likes to come here. The first time might have been accidental but this meeting was not. Not twice, Angela. He gets around Tecla and José—but how silly of me even to talk." She kissed her sister. "How crude, bribing you with nonsense like helping your people. His coarse bigness can't be anything but repulsive to you."

Angela bridled. "The Creator made him so. He is—is alive. To me piddling things like Carlos del Valle are the repulsive ones." Hearing Paz's footsteps, she said loudly, "Tune your harp awhile, sister; I'll come in a minute to practice our songs for *papá*'s *fiesta*."

But solitude brought only confusion. The walls of her small world fell away, and she saw life stretching out wide and full to brimming. For her the corporeal and spiritual works of mercy, sweeter by far than prayer. Feeding the hungry, visiting the sick, comforting the afflicted—. Not for a moment did she doubt McLane's honesty, regardless of what Susanita said. But marriage? The very idea was preposterous. And yet—was this perhaps the way? If it was, more would be shown to her to make it clear. She put the letter under her clothes in a chest and joined Susanita.

"Was that by chance a billy-doo you had for the little lady, Red, offering your heart and hand? Listen, Red, is it fair?"

The two were stretched out for the night in the safety of a small grassy spot in the center of a mesquite thicket. The bushes were high, there was grass and mesquite beans for the horses, the hard earth was nothing new to their bodies. McLane was taking no chances of riding near a camp of *vaqueros*, Indians, bandits, or even Rangers; in this land only a fool failed to protect himself. "Why not?" he asked in answer. "What's unfair about it?"

"Everything. You want to marry a Mexican girl from the higher class because it'll be to your advantage to get the Mexicans on your side. This girl has a vulnerable spot and you work on it. She believes she is converting you to her church and that's a joke that isn't funny, Red."

Red grunted. "I ain't got anything against it. I got religion yelled at me and beat into me when I was a kid to last for a lifetime. It don't make no difference to me who ties the bonds around us, minister or *padre*."

"But why pick on the daughter of the man who hates us the most, why so hell-bent to have this Angel girl? There's lots of girls. Don't tell me you're in love, Red. Don't, please, I couldn't stand it."

Love? It was not in his plans. Not aware of Angela's piousness and so not seeing her through its obscuring veil as did those that knew her, he had instantly recognized the potentialities of modest graciousness which he wanted in a wife, as he had seen a prettiness easily built into beauty. When by judicious inquiry he had found out about her religious zeal, it had fitted his plans neatly, for it could mount hurdles otherwise deemed too high. A Lady Bountiful without charity's condescension would be a great help in bringing the Mexicans into a voting organization controlled by him, far better and costing no more than outright buying. Men laughed at him, but he knew his vision to be sure, that the man who could promise a large Mexican vote would control the elections. Don Santiago's refusal to work with him closed the door to a courtship of Angela, so she herself would have to choose. The end, he was certain, justified the means, therefore it was entirely fair.

Love? He did not need it. He could be kind and tender to a wife like Mary of the Angels, and a "thank you" for all the miseries that went with love.

"Go to sleep, Ike," he answered. "We got to be getting to San Antonio and finish my house."

Chapter 23

❧

La fiesta del Día de Santiago was in full swing and the patio, illuminated by
lanterns hanging along the portico edge, held a merry crowd—if one judged
by the babble of voices, peals of laughter, the music and dancing. Occasionally firecrackers brought faces into sharp focus to the cries of *"Viva
Santiago on his white horse"* and *"Viva* Don Santiago, our host." With
full intent of putting the war and the encroaching invaders behind them,
the *rancheros* had come to Rancho La Palma to wish its owner happiness
on his feast day, and seemingly had succeeded.

Starting days in advance, those farthest away traveled to the nearest
neighbor and gathered a cavalcade as they moved, so that they might travel
in the safety of numbers; converging upon the *hacienda* before nightfall,
there to take over the guest rooms, confess their sins to Padre Pierre and
rest for the next day and night. Early in the morning there was Mass in
the *sala* on the long table converted into an altar and covered with the
linens made especially for the *padre's* visits. The guests filling the *sala* and
portico, *peons* and servants on their knees in the patio. After Mass there
was baptism of the *peon* children born since the *padre's* last visit, marriages
were performed and betrothals blessed.

After dinner and *siesta* there were races and contests by the men with
the women as spectators. All this was just a preliminary for the evening,
when the children were put to bed and the night that the Mexican felt
necessary for real merriment was a soft benediction over them. For this
the men brought their good suits and the women their party dresses, to
compliment their host. Don Santiago, resplendent in his black velveteen
suit trimmed with silver braid and polished silver buttons, was the courtly
host, his natural arrogance perfecting him in the role he loved. He gave
adroit flattery to the fat *mamás* sitting like blackbirds along the portico,
leaving a little envy of his wife with them; suffusing the cheeks of the girls
with a well-placed compliment, gallantly bowing before the homeliest ones

and asking the favor of a dance as if it really were a favor. Doña María Petronilla was a shadow, unobtrusively seeing that the trays of food were not spaced too far apart, the wine neither niggardly nor too abundant, the old folks comfortable and not neglected. The rustle of Doña Dolores's skirt was everywhere, putting the elegance and gracious hostess-ship to Doña María Petronilla's unobtrusive efficiency.

"I feel," Doña Dolores told her sister-in-law, meeting her in a momentary rest in her room, "very much like a spoon that keeps the broth stirred so the grease cannot rise to the top, and, not being wooden like the spoon, I am tired out. We cannot keep them from talking about what is in their minds and eager on their tongues. If Señor Carbajal had any sense in his square head or had regard for us he would have stayed home and kept José Luis and his news there too. It was most inconsiderate. Santiago and I have done our best to ignore things and keep our guests happy, but now that the time is shortening and they go home in the morning we might as well let the talk go as it will. Poor Paz can't stand beside that gossipy Anita Morales all night, Paz is nearly dead from weariness. What do you think, Petronilla?"

"Think?" Doña María Petronilla let the smiling mask slip from her sad face. "It is not a *fiesta* with both my sons gone and everybody wondering about Luis Gonzaga. If Padre Pierre had stayed—ah well, Dolores, we have given our best, let them talk. I am glad Susanita is gay. Go and dance, I must rest awhile. I am sure no one will miss me."

The Carbajal family had not arrived until the middle of the night when everyone was sleeping, and what with the religious services immediately upon arising, the guests had had no chance to do more that look at the follower of Canales, José Luis. Then when they swarmed about him, remarking his emaciation and racking cough, José Luis took the stage and without regard for his host gave out the news that René de la Ferrière had been killed and was buried somewhere in the hills of Mexico. Padre Pierre had quickly intervened, led a prayer for the departed soul and announced that here was not the time for grief. "I personally have fasted long enough, and I know all of you are anxious to get to the dining room." He then took José Luis aside and warned him sharply to say nothing further either about himself or the war, except to Don Santiago in the privacy of his office. "This is not the place for it."

So José Luis kept silent except once to say that he had been heartily sick of it all and was forever through with war. To Don Santiago he gave the news that Alvaro was well, enjoyed the life of the *guerrillero*, and by his daring had won the distinction of a name, "*El Lobo*." José Luis gave Don Santiago a cross which René de la Ferrière had entrusted to him when he was dying: for Susanita, and to tell her that he loved her and regretted having left her. "It was not as we thought it would be, *señor*."

Don Santiago put both the cross and the message away for the day. There must be only joy, without clouds, for today.

Ah yes, joy, when war is a boil that no lilting music, dancing feet, or star-studded roof, can keep from heading. In a secluded corner by the grape arbor the older men gathered, and Gabriel del Lago quickly took the lead by saying, "Even though my host does not agree with me I feel I must speak what is on my mind, for it may be a long time until we again get together. We are a beaten, a conquered people, and we *rancheros* are a group apart and but a handful. It is all very high-sounding, this dying for a cause, but death is death, our families are left without protection when we are gone, our land will be for anyone to take."

"So you kiss the *gringo*'s foot, Gabriel? Is that the way you avenge René?" asked Señor Mora, laughing derisively.

"I speak of saving our land." Don Gabriel was unmoved. "We have titles, and I am told they are recognized but must be recorded with the new government, which seems sensible to me and should seem so to you. The war has not touched us here, and there is no blood on our hands. There are many who bear us no ill will, and if we go with courtesy and dignity, it is my belief that we will be treated so in return. Now before it is too late, before the greedy ones come in hordes and finding the land unregistered take it by force, because they know there can be no dispute about it."

Señor del Valle spoke up. "Let me tell you what happened to Don Juan Antonio, who did what you are suggesting that we do. Three leagues of his land were taken from him and given to the state. What do you say to that, Gabriel del Lago?"

"But he has fifteen leagues left and that is his; no one can touch it. Three leagues is not much to preserve fifteen, it seems to me. One pays for war, *señores*."

Someone laughed derisively. "Some *gringo* will settle on those three leagues and it will be but one place to plant his feet firmly—for reaching. Once let them in and we are lost. Look what happened in East Texas twenty years ago when the Mexican government gave them land, they wanted more and more and in their insolence considered it their right to have it all. Their own leader Stefano Austin could not hold them back. If he could not hold a few then, can he hold the many now? Can anyone hold them back?"

But Don Gabriel kept his stand. "Even then things could have been adjusted and there would have been no need of war. Many things can be adjusted now; there are just men among them who will listen to us. If we continue to make trouble and refuse to cooperate now, then later it will be difficult; later no one will listen."

"I suppose they would have listened to old Gáspar de la Guerra," sneered Señor Montoya. "If one licks their boots one gets a kick from it—and has it coming to him, say I."

"Perhaps they would have listened" Don Gabriel persisted. "They bring their own bad men to justice. He might have tried at least. Where is he now?"

"Living with a cousin in San Patricio," answered Don Santiago. "I hear that the cousin and his friends are planning a raid on the *gringos* on Gáspar's *rancho*, and I hope it is true and they kill them all."

"That will not help anyone, it is things like that which come back to us, though we are innocent of them, Santiago. I do not see where Gáspar's pride would have been lowered had he sought the authorities and put his case before them." Noting growing displeasure in most of the faces before him, Don Gabriel said, "But I came here to wish my friend well and to enjoy myself by dancing. I will select the prettiest girl and for a time forget my age." He walked to where Susanita was holding court, forced her admirers aside and asked for her favor.

Doña Anita, the gossip, leaned to her neighbor. "Did you hear that? She said 'Oh, I'd love to, Don Gabriel,' just as sugar sweet. She is a heartless flirt, laughing and dancing on, you might say, poor René's grave. What do you suppose has happened to Angela; she seems to have lost her fear of men. I notice José Luis follows her every move, can it be that she is in love with him? I don't envy the man who gets either one of those girls; Susanita as useless as a pretty doll, Angela with her piety. I often wonder what will become of the Mendoza y Soría family."

Her neighbor shrugged, "Whatever the master of it wills, you know that. I married the man my father selected for me, and I have no complaint to make but in my day there were no *Americanos*. That one Susanita danced with in town—my husband had to punish our Carlita the next day, the child said she could easily fall in love with the tall *Americano*. I think all the girls envied Susanita. Look at the scandal of Inez—"

The gossip laughed. "That was one time Alvaro did not get what he wanted—my, how it must have hurt him to have a *gringo* shove him aside! I would like to know what happened to Luis Gonzaga; all we can find out is that he went away with an *Americano* and broke his father's heart."

On and on, whisperings and speculations, behind screens of waving fans. The men would break up their groups to dance, for they were drawn together by the magnet of a need to discuss this menace at their *hacienda* gates. A menace worse than war, for it was creeping silently on their children. The report that Luis Gonzaga had willfully turned his back on his people to take up life with the *Americanos* was, they all noted, neither affirmed nor denied by his family. True, Luis had been a misfit, but the thing could happen to their own as well.

Doña Dolores closed her ears and danced gaily, sniffing silently at Don Gabriel's application to the young girls. As if he were twenty and not forty-three, she'd like to tell him how silly he looked; Angela, pitying José Luis, brewed him a cup of herb tea for his cough, starting gossip anew and bringing a satisfied smile to his mother's face; a little too pious, Angela, yet that meant amenability too. Don Santiago, seemingly as fresh as the morning, stopped teasingly to scold Susanita; then went to the compound outside the wall where the *peons* were celebrating with the servants who had come with the *hacienda* guests.

In the center of the adobe floor of the square a buxom girl, maid of Doña Profilia, the wife of Valentino de Olivares, was dancing a *fandango* with Estéban; full breasts bulging in the tight red cotton blouse, stumpy legs showing when the blue skirt whirled to the provocation of old Blas's fiddle and the clap and chant of the group around him. The two dancers had kicked off their sandals and in bare feet displayed a footwork amazing in its speed and intricacy. Don Santiago kept in the shadow of the wall and watched them sighing a little for the freedom of those who were almost slaves, never bound with the restrictions of those who kept them such. As he watched, the couple put back to back and whirled like a top as the fiddle screamed at them, leaping in the air at the last high note, laughing as they ran to their applauding friends.

Blas put down the fiddle and wiped a hand across a forehead, laughing as he said, "Anyhow, a man can sweat when he is a *peon*."

Estéban echoed the laugh. "Sweat? Yes, we sweat, old man, and for nothing but the meanest existence. Just wait, Blas, one of these days we will know the jingle of silver in our pockets."

"Silver, did you say?" Ema, the buxom dancer, shrilled the words as she stepped again into the square. "Who is going to give it to me, your master or the *gringo*? Or an angel come down from heaven, Estéban?" She clapped her hands and chanted liltingly, "Silver to buy me a dress of silk, and slippers with heels and a comb for my hair. Ho, ho, ho, ho, ho—" She stepped into the figure of the sedate *contradanza*, mimicking the high-class lady so well that the dress of silk and slippers with heels were almost real.

Estéban stepped into the square and lifted an arm. "My friends, I heard many things when I was in Matamoros. The *gringos* hire Mexicans, pay them well, and they can do what they please with the money. Not like our masters who charge us for rags of clothes and tobacco at so high a price that we are always in debt to them and are never paid a wage. Not all the *gringos* hate us, and soon their law says we can vote and our vote as good as the masters. Doesn't that sound good to the ears?" And to the girl: "How would you like to be maid to an *Americano* woman, Ema, and be given the silk dresses she no longer wants instead of letting them rot in the chests like your mistress does, because only the *doña* and her daughters may wear silk?"

Ema clapped her hands over her head. "Ho, ho, then I would have to find a mistress as fat as I am Estéban." She broke into song, twisting her body before a dark-faced *vaquero*. Old Blas started a waltz, hissing at those close to dance, and soon Estéban was pushed out of the square by the circling dancers. Old Blas did not like talk like that.

A half dozen *hombres* edged back close to where Don Santiago was standing and muttered the rebellion that had been stirring in their hearts for many months. One, the coachman of the de Baca family, corroborated what Estéban had said. Another jerked a thumb at Ema, dancing again with the second *caporal*. "You see how loose she is, but you need not wonder why. Her master used her when she was little more than a child, and she is still at his command and that of his sons also. Now no man will marry her because she will be too seldom in her husband's bed, for being in that of the master. She took it the easy way since two children were stillborn to her and she no longer conceives, and you know the end. She is already anyone's woman, though her mistress does not know that. The poor thing was an orphan, but even if she had not been, it would have been the same, for she was a very pretty child; the *peon* belongs to the master and none dare say no to him, though he take their daughters and their wives. I for one will watch my chance to work for an *Americano*. Our souls are not our own now."

"Souls, did you say souls, *amigo?*" A third one chuckled. "Our masters believe we have no souls any more than a mule or a sheep, as you well know. They have us pray and baptize us and have the *padre* marry us because that gives them God and His wrath to hold over us, and they can pat their fat stomachs to praise themselves for giving us something they also have. The joke of that is that we have souls after all, which should surprise them when they meet us on the other side. I often think about meeting my master when we are both dead and tell him to look, *señor*, see what a nice soul I have, much nicer than your own."

Moved more by shame than guilt at his spying, Don Santiago went back to the patio, walking softly in the black shadows so he would not be seen. He noted with relief, when his sister hailed him to ask whether he wanted coffee served, that a number of guests had retired, among them José Luis. Don Gabriel was cavorting with Susanita in a quadrille, looking like a boy parading in his father's best suit. Acting like a boy, thought Don Santiago, smiling as he watched. Angela was also dancing, and her father was surprised to see how graceful and poised she was, how charmingly she responded to her partner, the paunchy Señor Carbajal—who, doubtless, was already seeing her as his daughter-in-law. Well, perhaps, perhaps. It would not be a bad alliance as far as family and wealth was concerned but José Luis—contempt puckered Don Santiago's mouth as he recalled the talk he had had with the young man in his office after *siesta*.

The hardships of the *guerrilleros* were uppermost in the mind of José Luis. Yes, they had killed some soldiers belonging to General Scott, but the gringos would be in Mexico City anyhow as there was no stopping them. Yes, they killed a few Rangers and Alvaro particularly shone there, but immediately the Rangers took revenge and killed many more Mexicans, so it would have been better to have left them alone in the first place. They were devils, and one could not fight the devil and hope to win. Often the food was scarce, and it was cold in the mountains, and riding through thorn brush with ragged *chaparejos* was torturous, and the ground was often wet, and no wonder he had this cough, sleeping so often in the mud. So when René was killed, he had ridden away, hiding from Mexican as well as *Americano*, and starving, and—Don Santiago slapped at the air with an impatient hand. Pah, what a weakling! But the milksop kind of husband Angela would like, and certainly better than the convent for her.

"Santiago, I ask you for the third time, do you want coffee served?" Doña Dolores's acerbity struck through his dreaming. "It is time that they go to bed, but it seems the young folks—and the fools among the old ones who should know better—cannot get enough of dancing; the *mamás* cannot get enough of gossiping, and the men must keep telling each other how important they are and how hateful everybody else but themselves. But it is your *fiesta*, and if you want it to last till dawn, we will have the coffee. Petronilla and I, not to mention the servants, are dead from weariness which of course makes no difference whatever to—"

"Now, now, Dolores, what ails you?" He laid an arm affectionately across her shoulders. "You are always the one who hates to see the dawn come to a *fiesta*. Something is worrying you. Come, we will leave it to our guests." They walked forward and as the quadrille came to an end he shouted, "My friends, I would like to greet the dawn with you, what do you say? There will be coffee to keep you awake and wine to make you merry."

"Thank you, not I." Señor de Baca took the middle of the dancing-square. "With your permission I will seek my bed for the long journey ahead. Some wine first, for a toast."

"A toast, a toast." Voices were eager, hands reached for the mugs passed around on trays. A *fiesta* without a windup of toasts was a sad festival indeed. Señor de Baca raised his mug high and sang out, "To Don Santiago de Mendoza y Soría, may he live long and happily, and may his patron saint bring blessings to him and his family."

From all throats came assent. "*¡Salud!*"—*Viva* Don Santiago!" —"*¡Salud!*"—

Don Santiago motioned to the servants to refill the mugs. "Thank you, and may I give another? To the things that are Mexican. To my son!"

There was a moment of silence while they looked at each other, a little stunned at the method their host used to tell them that their surmise of Luis Gonzaga was true. To my son. He now had but one. Halfheartedly someone shouted "*¡Viva Mexico!*" and there were a few echoes. But none said, "To Alvaro," or "*Viva* Canales." With their love of family this struck deeply, particularly as the other son was leading a life of danger. They did not quite know what to say or do.

Doña Dolores rushed to the fiddler and guitarist and ordered them to play a waltz quickly, then rushed to Don Gabriel and whispered, "Gabriel, do something! There must be no more agitation—oh, don't stand there so stupid! Get a partner and dance, quickly now!"

He stepped forward and said lightly, "We have years in which to give *vivas* to Mexico and only this one more dance in which to forget her for awhile. Everybody dance, say I." He led off with Doña Dolores, Don Santiago followed with his reluctant, weary wife, and all the married men whose wives still danced sought them out. The young folks gave way to them, content to watch and inwardly snicker a little at the puffing of most of the women who were shapeless from childbearing, overburdened with petticoats, and stiff-legged from much sitting.

The music stopped in abrupt fortissimo and, suddenly weary, all left the patio for their rooms. All but Don Gabriel, who sat and talked awhile with his host before bidding him goodnight. A servant came with candles and stood inquiringly before the master, but Don Santiago told him to put out the stubs still flickering like imprisoned spirits in the copper lanterns.

Soon there was only the darkness and a silence that, intensified by the preceding merriment, seemed to roll in from the vast plains over the wall and pile itself layer upon layer in the patio. It seemed to Don Santiago as if there were no one in all the world but he, and he put a hand on the black pillar beside him to see if it really was the palm tree. No one but he—and the specter that never left him and now pawed at him with hungry hands. The specter that sat daily at table in the chairs of his sons, and jeered at him, and mounted a horse to ride with him. He had learned that a man can say, "You are no longer my son" and not be able to throw him out of his life—and he knew now that in toasting to but one son he had shouted the name of the other. Today he had heard the gay laughter of Luis Gonzaga lilting high above that of the guests, and sickened awhile because it had been an illusion. And Alvaro—his first elation over the news that Alvaro was well and happy and doing damage to their enemies was now a weight of fear that dragged at him. José Luis's pessimism and wan appearance, the death of René, brought Alvaro's dangers close.

Things had gone wrong. Even if José Luis had not come he knew he would have been cool to Padre Pierre, giving him the courtesy due a guest and the respect due his cloth, and nothing more; for he had furthered the friendship of Luis Gonzaga and the *Americano*. Gabriel's deplorable weakness was a blight on the day, particularly as later some of the men were inclined to agree with him. Worst of all was the scene outside of the wall among the servants. Loyalty was a prerogative of the master, the lack of it in the *peon* sufficient cause for death. Don Santiago remembered vividly when his father had himself put the heavy lash to a *peon* who voiced disloyalty until the rawhide was wet and red, and shrugged a shoulder later when word was brought that the man was dead. That was what Estéban deserved, and all Don Santiago's heritage of right, by might if need be, drew at his blood urgingly right now. No, he had made a promise after his temper had caused him to strike the most faithful of underlings, Tío Victorino, that never again would a whip be a scourge in his hand. So that was why Estéban had been so cocky this summer, at times almost presumptuous. The *gringo* was even striking at a man's *peons*, jingling silver, enticing those who were not completely animal and had some intelligence, like the second *caporal*. He wondered now whether it might not be wise to address the *peons* at *El Alabado*, call on their loyalty and make each a present of some silver. "This house which is mine is also yours, and we can keep and protect it only when we are united in a common love and a common and just hatred." He stooped to pick up a handkerchief of white lost by some girl, sniffed the heliotrope fragrance, and stuffed it in his sash, the question already answered. When a master had to preach what should be in a *peon*, like marrow in a bone, and even buy it, it was not worth the having. It would, in effect, be giving in to the *Americano*. He would deal with Estéban later, when the time came.

He was right, right. And he had to champion the right, though loss eat out his vitals. "God cannot desert His people," he whispered to the palm tree, striking it vehemently with a fist. "He may punish them but He will never desert them. La Palma de Cristo—so will I stand and weather the winds, and be a stronger pillar for my own. And if a limb be cut from me, yet will I stand strong, and dig my roots the deeper."

When old Paz, obeying a pagan instinct from her Mexican-Indian forebears, came out to greet the rising sun, she found the master relaxed in a chair, a smile on his sleeping face.

Chapter 24

On the fourteenth day of that blood-smeared September of 1847 when General Winfield Scott entered Mexico City, Lieutenant Robert Warrener and his small escort of soldiers came to a hedge of *uña de gato* banking a grassy hollow about a mile below the *jacal* of José and Rancho La Palma and made temporary camp. It was *siesta* time, his horse was tired, he himself feeling the effects of the long ride, but Warrener rode on; slowly, letting the animal stop to nibble grass now and then, never urging him beyond a walk. All living things were asleep, it seemed, for the rolling plain and low rock-rimmed mesa shivered off heat waves in unbroken somnolence. He should have taken a *siesta* himself on the grass at camp, Warrener thought, but somehow he had never been able to take up what he recognized as a sensible custom in this subtropic land. He laughed softly at the idea of sleep, when Susanita was so near.

Sleep? Nerves, jerked tight by both the anticipation of seeing his beloved and the difficult interview with her father set his heart to thumping painfully against his ribs. The ache in his head started again in protest at the mental repetition of: "If it is family you want, Don Santiago, without boasting I can offer you—" "A love like this is God-given, *señor*, and can work only for good in its destiny—" "My father is also a landed man as you are, and I have money of my own; Susanita would never know poverty and deprivation." Over and over again he had held that interview this past week, until a man not already past the bounds of sanity must have gone mad. For is a man in love sane, and is not the lack of it salvation for him? Imagine a sane man riding off his path to look closer at short-stemmed marigolds spread like a ragged shawl on a hillside, proudly bright in this second blooming, and smile tenderly at them because they were the color of the hair on a certain head; imagine a sane man swinging down from a saddle to pick up a glassy pebble green as sea water because it was like her eyes.

Horse and rider dawdled on. The animal contentedly, the rider leashing his impatience by telling himself, half aloud: "Take it easy, Bob, you'll get there before they're awake as it is, and you need a little time to get hold of yourself; you're running a temperature and you need cool, calm dignity." When the turn of the trail at the clump of cottonwoods flung the huge square of white wall with its watchtower at him, his heart turned completely over and dropped into the polished boots. He shriveled smaller and smaller until he was a bug perched on the saddle. Who was he to ride to a man's castle and demand his daughter—he a member of an enemy army, part of which was even now despoiling the capital of what had been this man's country? Sweat broke out on his forehead, and he wiped it off with a handkerchief no longer clean, which he stuffed hastily back into his trousers. He wanted to whirl his horse and spur him away as fast as he would go.

Then he was riding past a gaping *peon* and was off his horse and in the patio with its cool shade and greenery, fragrant oasis of rest and peace. He thought of his home with its wide veranda fronting a lawn thickly green under wide old elms and was suddenly at peace. He was the son of a gentleman, citizen of a country that, with all its faults, built with the bricks of courage and democracy. He was a man after his mate, and he meant to have her.

As he was wondering what to do, a girl tripped down the portico steps heading for the shady side of the patio. He recognized Angela, took off his hat, and moved forward to speak to her when Doña María Petronilla came in sight carrying a basket of sewing. It was the first time Warrener had really seen her and, recognizing her only by that unmistakable manner which sets the lady apart from the servant, felt dismay that this plain little woman with the nondescript black dress and gray-threaded black hair could be the mother of beautiful, golden Susanita and pretty, graceful Angela. After a startled glance at him, Angela delegated the role of hostess to her mother and hurried away to the grape arbor.

He bowed low and said, "*Buenas tardes, señora*, and may I present my humble self, Robert Warrener."

Doña María Petronilla nodded gravely, while her eyes skipped over the uniform and fastened on the face that just missed being handsome, the mouth with its quirked up ends, the eyes of deep heaven's blue with their backdrop of merriment; a young face that belied its contour by the stamping of strength in the rounded chin, wide forehead, and narrow high nose.

She thought: "He is here to ask for Susanita. It is not past then, as I had made myself believe." She smiled a very small smile, politely.

"It is like heaven," he was saying, covering their mutual embarrassment as best he could, "coming from the heat of the plains into this delightful patio."

"Yes, isn't it?" She nodded agreement, adding, "I have heard that among your people the houses are not built with a patio. How then have you comfort and a friendly place to meet your visitors?" (What sort of home would you take my baby to, if you took her away from here? Love is not enough when the family is alien and living is ugly; she is not accustomed to common things, she was not intended for them. She cannot live in a barn, or without birds and flowers.)

They moved by unspoken agreement to the shade, Warrener tripping at times in his Spanish as he answered, "My father's home, as are all the large houses, is high, *señora*, with bedrooms and the ladies' *salas* on the second floor. A wide and open stairway leads to them from the *sala* downstairs, so that"—and laughter danced in his eyes—"the ladies can look like beautiful queens as they come down the steps." (None has ever come down who looked half as lovely as Susanita, neither my mother nor my sister nor any of their friends. I can see her on it now moving slowly step by step, with the green velvet dress with the emeralds on her neck and ears and lovely arms—do you remember the night I danced with her, do you remember?) "Our houses have many windows of glass, *señora*, and not dark inside as yours are, for we have many days without sun and winter is too cold to sit outdoors."

"You have no portico, you live inside all of the time?" (Days without sun, and cold. I do not like that, not at all.)

"But yes! In the *inglés* we call them verandas, and they are wide open porticos with high pillars painted white; and there is grass thick as a carpet, and it is watered to keep it green if there is not enough rain. The trees are much larger than your cottonwoods, and they have wide branches that throw heavy shade over both lawn and house. When you drive up to such a house you drive under these great branches and there are flowers also and shrubs and vines that bloom, and ahead of you is this big white house with green grass like a rug all around it; and on the veranda are girls like bright flowers, and they twist the men who are their slaves around their pretty white fingers." (Do I make it clear, mother of Susanita? Do you see that we have gentle ways of living also, and that she will be a queen in the setting I will build specially for her, whether it be here in your land or in my own—do you see?)

"Do you have servants, then, and *peons*, who do the work?" (My Susanita has not worked, *señor*. A little, to play at it. She is in the kitchen now with Paz being shown how to make a dessert because the time was heavy on her hands and it was her fancy. You need not crane your neck and stare so, the kitchen is not close and she cannot hear your voice, nor will I tell you where she is.)

"There are negroes who do the work. I do not think you have ever seen any for I have seen none in Matamoros. They are slaves very much like your *peons* but in a different way. On the whole our way of living is not so different from your own, *señora*, unless it be that we give greater deference to women, and frequently the rule of the house is shared between man and wife." (I want you to know that Susanita would never be treated as I see you have been. I want to ask you where she is, and I do not dare. I want to see her so badly it is a huge pain inside me.)

"I see, Señor Warrener." (I see also what you have been trying to tell me, and I believe you have told the truth. I see that you love her very much and I am afraid, so afraid for both of you.) She set down the basket. "You wish to see my husband?" she asked, gripping her courage.

"If I may. I wish to—yes, if I may see him, please."

"Come, I will take you to his office and call him."

He followed her to the office near the gate. She opened the door and waved him inside, unable to bring herself to do what her mother heart bade her—put a hand on his arm and beg him to go again; in the name of the Holy Virgin to go quickly, and forget Susanita, *señor*, and forget us all. Her courage crumpled before she came to Don Santiago's room and instead she ran to that of Doña Dolores.

"Petronilla, you look like death!" Doña Dolores ran to her and put an arm around her. "What is it, what has happened, are you ill?"

"Who would not be ill, Dolores?" She sank onto the chest at the foot of the bed, holding onto her sister-in-law's hand. "The *Americano*, the young officer—he is in Santiago's office to ask him for her, and God help us all! If it had been before the *fiesta* but now that he knows René—"

"It is his fault that René is dead, not the *Americano*'s," Doña Dolores interrupted, seating herself on the chest. "Why did you not send the officer away? It would have been opportune with Santiago still asleep. There will be trouble enough, you shouldn't have taken him to the office."

"He would have come again and again, I could tell that. If it cannot be, he might as well know it at once. I—Dolores, I liked him. I myself would give him Susanita. Besides, there is a deep love there, the kind that does not come to many women. I thought if you told Santiago he was in the office—"

Doña Dolores sighed as she rose. "Had you shown him a little independence years ago, you wouldn't be shaking like a leaf when you feel you have to disagree with him. Don't be afraid, I'll remind him of his duties as a host and as a father, and I'll also remind him that the present choice of husbands for his daughters is deploringly poor."

Righteousness and indignation almost lifted her to her brother's room, but all she said when she stood before him was: "The *Americano* officer is in the office waiting to see you, where Petronilla directed him. I hope you will not forget you are a gentleman, Santiago, and I also hope you will let your brains and not your temper rule you." She could not forbear to add, maliciously, "Not like the time you turned away the honor of being a *magistrado*, and making life less a burden for all of us if you had used your brains."

Before he could ask her how on earth she knew about this and show her where her place was, she had rustled away.

Had Red McLane seen Don Santiago seated behind his desk he would have noted that in manner at least the Don filled the chair of *magistrado* very well indeed. He sat in chilly dignity like an impersonal judge listening to a culprit plead his case, all emotion controlled. Only his eyes glowed like hot carbon under the ledged shelves of brow, and Warrener forced himself to look at him—and bravely, faltering only when he searched for a suitable word in Spanish, he offered his qualifications as son-in-law. He pleaded their love: "We met face to face by sheerest accident, *señor*, and love was there. Had we never met again that love would have stayed with us; it will stay with us now until we die." He told of his family and traced it back to England to the time when a Warrener was knighted. "The first Warreners came to Virginia in 1620, *señor*, and it is an honored name in Virginia to this day. I mention this because I know you consider it important, though personally I believe that a man's worth should be measured by what he himself is regardless of his forebears." He offered his fortune, "which I am now glad I have so that Susanita shall not lack the things that money can buy—. That I am an officer in an army fighting your people is to be deplored, but can it not be overlooked, *señor*, and treated for what it is, a twist of circumstances?" He mentioned his religion and saw no objection to taking the step back again to the Old Faith if that was asked of him; though he was careful not to add that if hers were pagan, he would willingly be pagan also.

When there was nothing more to say he waited, clenching his hands so that the nails were pinpricks on his palm, to keep from moving his feet, biting his lips or otherwise betray the torment within. His head was aching almost unendurably, to which was added the agony that he had forgotten something important, something very important. Sweat felt cold across his upper lip and ran in tiny rivulets from his armpits down his sides. He wanted to scream: "Say something, why don't you say something?" Then suddenly the hysteria left him, like water washing clean; and holding his pride high, knowing he had done the right and the honorable thing, he waited for what would come.

Don Santiago rose, cold rage so mastering him that even the stern codes of traditional custom forbidding the host to harm the guest under his roof were the thinnest of restraining threads. With Red McLane his antagonism had been somewhat diluted by curiosity and amusement at the veneer of polish still so thin in spots over the natural uncouthness. Also he had recognized that McLane's mission had a certain value, and there was the added flattery that Don Santiago was the only man really suited for the proposed position of *magistrado*. True, he had been angry at the man and in contempt offered him the shelter of the *peon* quarters, but that was for his nationality rather than a further personal feeling. But this one with his pretensions of breeding; this upstart of a family of upstarts; this traitor to the uniform he wore; this weakling too spineless to hate an enemy; this presumer, daring to look at a girl so far above him; this braggart boasting of his money; this spawner of bastards hiding his lechery behind noble talk of love; this infidel who would defile the Faith by his lying embrace of it; this thief, murderer, barbarian—*Sangre de Cristo*, asking for the daughter of Santiago de Mendoza y Soría!

His mouth twisted until the lips were bloodless and ugly and the long fingers of the left hand flattened on the desk crept inward until the knuckles were high bleached scars. And then, in the tidal wave of an added rage that this intruder wore the invisible cloak of a gentleman with such careless ease of perfection, Don Santiago was swept away from his moorings of courtesy, the anchor of hostship jerked loose and was flung wide.

Hanging on the wall behind and a little to the right of the desk was a carved cane with a sculpted goat horn for handle, gift from old Tío Victorino and patient result of many days of labor. On the opposite wall back of the officer hung an old heavy sword with a rust-spotted blade— and while the devil in Don Santiago cried out for this sword the rush of his anger put his hand to what was nearest him. Even then his shocked mind cried "Stop, stop!"—but it was too late to halt the swing of the arm. To his horror he saw the head of the cane, the curved sharp goat horn, come down on the brown hair. Once, and again. The second time the stick, where gouging of the wood to create a winged angel had been too deep, broke in two and bounced the handle to the floor.

If the room had not whirled like a crazy top, Warrener would have seen Don Santiago trembling, his face white as a sheet. If he could have taken instant thought, he might have known that, for a few moments, the feelings of his host were numbed by the pain of regret. And had he been more conversant with the Mexican temperament, he would have given his most deferential bow and a murmured, "*Señor*"—and departed. Instead, when the room righted itself again, Warrener crouched to pick up the broken cane, and when he put it on the desk Don Santiago had regained an outward composure.

"The casualty, *señor*," Warrener added lightly, "seems to be an angel. I had believed they lived eternally." In the effort to ignore the episode, a certain insouciance controlled the added: "May I ask, Don Santiago, that you be—ah, specific in your objections to me as a son-in-law? I might be able to correct the deficiencies if I knew them."

That Don Santiago's rage was turned upon himself for his exhibition so unworthy of a gentleman, and by him who so stressed the word, made it none the less violent. The young man's ignoring of this crime and his light laugh were construed as a mocking taunt, and the Don's voice was thick with a new anger as he made reply.

"You forced your way here, *Americano*, you took advantage of a weak and frightened woman to be put under my roof. You have one deficiency and that is complete and entire—yourself. I would not give you Eugenia, the half-wit daughter of one of my sheepherders. Now go! And quickly before I call my *vaqueros* who are not handicapped by rules of politeness which unfortunately forbid me to put a knife to your filthy army coat. Go!"

Warrener's wish was to bow low and leave the office slowly, clattering heels noisily along the portico so Susanita would hear; or even go so far as to raise his voice in the song she knew as theirs before mounting and riding away. But the injury to his head in Matamoros had been deep, and the horn handle had come down on the spot longest in healing and still sensitive. Balls of black fuzz were moving before his eyes, something was hammering at the base of his skull in relentless, agonizing repetition, as if a wedge were being driven into bone and splitting it apart.

The hate-filled eyes of Don Santiago came near, had a black veil thrown over them before they could spring from their sockets, appeared again from a distance, vanished back into it. Out! urges Warrener's saner self. Get out and away before you show yourself a weakling who can't take a tap on the head with a thin cane—you, a soldier. Get out before you do something you'll regret, or tell this man what a fool you think he is—as if you could judge; as if you wouldn't do what he had done, and more. Get out and away—.

Angela slipped away to the kitchen while her mother was talking to the stranger, to tell Susanita that the man whose ring she wore hidden against her heart was in the patio, talking to *mamá*. But when she came to the kitchen where Susanita and Paz were mixing and measuring, one pupil and the other teacher, scruples held her tongue. It would be like her impulsive sister to forget herself in her joy and do something she should not. If *papá* were not at home—no, only tragedy would result from telling her sister. So Angela stood and looked on silently, in her worry and excitement even forgetting to pray as she was wont to do. Martina was shelling beans into a wooden bowl, Nicolasa kneading dough on a table, the other two engrossed in their mixing, and none of them paid any attention to Angela or asked her what she wanted.

And then, the unexpected happened. Luciana, eyes bulging, mouth open with the magnitude of her news, hands grasping at the air, burst into the kitchen and exploded with: "An *Americano* has been here! One tall as a tree and with eyes—close enough I was to see them, crossing the patio from putting the master's shirts away—eyes like the Virgin's mantle, so blue! From the office he came, fast, and blood was running down a cheek, and when he got on his horse by the gate Estéban had to help him! *Por La Virgen Santa*, what is happening? What does an *Americano* want here? Is this—," she broke off, eyes popping still further as they stared after Susanita running out of the room, bowl and flour and sugar spilling from her lap onto the stone floor; with Angela following and old Paz a-muttering but far from slow third.

Down the portico steps in a single leap, across the patio and out of the gate like a skimming white bird went Susanita. No plan, no thought of her action, obeying only the cry in her heart to see him, the beloved one. Forgetting that she was a lady and grabbing the arm of Estéban, her voice choking as she asked: "The *Americano*—where is he, is he gone?"

The trail at which the brown finger pointed lay like an old white scar long healed, across the green slope. Empty. There it turned at the cottonwoods a drift of dust hung a moment as she looked, then dissolved like mist in sun.

Angela's arms were turning her sister back to the patio, as she whispered to her to stop crying, to remember *papá* was near. "God's will will be done, Susanita, stop crying, do—see, *papá* is signaling to us to come to where he and *mamá* are, and you must make the best of it." Angela took a handkerchief and wiped the wet cheek. "Don't say much, *papá* looks terribly angry. Don't tell him about the ring or the letters, it will be better not to."

There was no rage, this time, to spray over them. Don Santiago stood with arms hanging and hands opened and his voice was flat with defeat as he said, "You broke your promise to me, Susanita. You, whom I trusted most. Look at me and tell me why."

Her eyes found his, strange without their usual flames, sunken deeper in the caves of sockets. She freed herself from Angela's arm and took a step away from her, dimly aware that Doña Dolores had risen from her chair, that her mother had lifted hands from her lap and given an involuntary cry of alarm. She seemed apart from them all, even her misery her own and not to be shared. She kept thinking: "I waited so long, I waited all spring and summer to see his face once more. Some of you knew he was here and you didn't tell me—" Promise? What was *papá* talking about? Oh yes, that she could not see Roberto again. She had been a child then, afraid to acknowledge a love still so new and shining. She was not afraid now. Lifting her tear-stained face while she said, in a low but assertive voice, "I already loved him when I made—when you made me give you that promise, *papá*. I could not have stopped loving him, nor he me, and I will love him until I die. I am sorry if I hurt you, *papá*."

Don Santiago paled as though a lash had crossed his face. A flash coaled his eyes and left them again like weathered char. All expected the worst storm ever to strike the patio, and Paz, hidden behind a vine, crossed herself and called upon heaven to avert it. Doña María Petronilla's labored breathing was a weeping thing, and Angela, in near-terror, moaned scatterings of prayer half aloud.

But Don Santiago asked very quietly, even gently, "You are telling me the truth, Susanita? You love this—this *Americano* and feel no shame when you admit it?"

And she answered calmly, bringing her folded hands up to her breast where hung the ring, "Yes, I love him with all my heart and soul and I am not ashamed. I am glad."

He turned and walked away without a word and went to his room.

Doña María Petronilla opened her arms and Susanita, forgetting she was a woman and no longer a child, ran to them and yielded to their sweet comfort.

Angela put a hand on her aunt's arm and asked, "What will happen now, Tía Dolores?"

"The good Lord alone knows, I have never seen him like this before." Doña Dolores shook her head. "Be assured it will not be anything good, Angela. Listen, what is that?"

From the house came a dry, hoarse sob, and was so like a heart retching and throwing out the bitter bile of faith betrayed.

Doña Dolores ran and closed the door of her brother's room, against the agonized sound of his weeping.

Chapter 25

Lieutenant Warrener twisted his fingers in the mane of his horse and let him go, knowing he would find his way to the impromptu camp where his fellows were. A devilish mess, and his head all over the place. The bushes rising up to his face, settling back and dwindling to nothing; the earth flattening and running ahead of him. Getting dark all at once—no, must have been a cloud. Couldn't take a tap on the head with a thin little cane. Couldn't—

"Loot'nant, what the devil?"

Couldn't be Red McLane's voice. Going crazy all over, hearing things. Somebody shoving him—"Let go my arm. Let me alone, I tell you, or I'll—"

"Now, now, Bob, it's Red. What're you doing humped over the saddle like that? Here, I'll help you get off and we'll stop in the shade of this here tree. Come on now—hell, you know how to get off a hoss, don't you?"

Stretched on the ground, the earth righted itself again, and Red's words were understandable. "I went down to Fort Brown to see you and got it from little Manuel where you'd gone. You should have let me know; fool thing to travel in that uniform and that handful of soldiers makes it even worse. It's different with me, I can ride most anywhere with my fancy seal papers and they know me because I make 'em laugh. I lit right out after you, did you have any trouble?"

"We met some *vaqueros* driving cattle," Warrener answered. "Longest-horned creatures I ever saw. I mean the cattle were. A vaquero rode up and shoved a rusty old *pistola* at me and told me to *vamos* or he'd finish me. I gave him some money, gave 'em all some money, poor devils never have money. He said 'Go with God, *señor*; we have not seen you; we passed here an hour ago and so could not have seen you'"

"Ummm." Red rolled two corn husk cigarettes, took a copper tinderbox from the pouch against his side, struck spark to the charred end of the cloth worm flattened into a metal tube, lit the cigarettes, and pinched out the smoldering cloth. "Your luck that you didn't have a skirmish. Not enough of them or like as not they were plain curious to see what the infidel invader looked like. Here, take this smoke and tell me about the boss of the *hacienda*. He lay you out like this? You were ready to fall off when I came, I wasn't a minute too soon."

"It was mostly the old trouble and then the heat, you know." Warrener smoked gratefully, enjoying the blessed relief of lying still. Of his visit he merely said that he had asked for Susanita and been refused, and of the blood which still oozed in tiny trickles he gave no explanation or even mention. Nor did Red press him, he could guess that the Don had gotten a little madder than he wanted to and had done something about it.

"I have to go back again if he kills me, Red. You wouldn't understand that I have to see Susanita even if she doesn't see me. I have to—to *look* at her."

"Well, sleep awhile and let me cogitate." Red wondered whether it would be safe to take Warrener to the *jacal*, less than half a mile away; he could plainly hear the high-pitched "*Arre, arre*," of the herders as the vicinal flocks were driven to the safety of the corral for the night. He would have to send word to the soldiers to make out until morning and keep hidden. The thing was getting his friends at the *jacal* in bad if Don Santiago found it out. He had managed it twice now, but a third time was too much to ask of luck. What to do? The question needed a lot of cogitation, he decided.

The strike of hoofs on hard ground and against the stone interrupted his thoughts. First faintly heard, it soon came closer until there was the unmistakable creak of leather and the sharply indrawn breath of the horse. Red knew the trail swerved before it came to them, and he rose and leaned against the tree to look. The rider was Don Santiago, and in a braid-trimmed cloth suit instead of the usual range buckskin. Red watched horse and rider trot toward the *jacal*, turn onto another trail without halting, and go on until they dwindled to a dot, then were absorbed by the rose-flushed, golden plain. Red nodded. That suit meant a call on a neighbor, and the nearest one was thirty or forty miles away. Doubtless more, as he knew that most of the ranches ran to fifty or sixty sections. The *jacal* would be safe for the night and morning, and a tentative plan he had might go through. He wakened Warrener, helped him mount, and rode beside him up the slope, calling as he came close to the stockade:

"*Ave María, José, amigo*, it is the Red One!"

José and Tecla insisted that the half-conscious officer be laid on the high glistening white bed which was Tecla's pride, but Red shook his head. "One of the rawhide frames beside the storeroom, José. I shall stay with him and after all, we are men, no? Tecla, water to wash his head, please. There is danger in travel these days." They did as he asked without further comment, leaving their wonder and speculation until such time as they should be alone. José swaggered with importance meanwhile, inquiring about Pablo, and how warm the day, *señor*, like July. It was not until Warrener drank some milk and slept again, and Tecla served a savory stew for evening repast, that Red took José aside and told him carefully what he wished him to do.

Only Doña Dolores and Doña María Petronilla were enjoying the delightful coolness of the patio, a place of shadowed mystery under the star-spangled sky. Susanita had cried herself to sleep, and Angela sat beside the bed holding her sister's hand. From the quarters of the *peons* came the faint scrape of a fiddle and nasal song, terminating in a burst of laughter that soon fluttered into silence.

Doña Dolores stirred and sighed. "Poor Santiago, truly I feel sorry for my brother, Petronilla. Here now he leaves before *El Alabado* and rides in the night like a lost soul—"

"Save your pity for my children, Dolores." Strangely, it was the timid woman who took the aggressive role usually played by Doña Dolores. "I cannot imagine my husband ever riding like a lost soul. He rides around to justify himself, though why he put on his good suit and what is in his mind I cannot imagine. Be assured it bodes us no good, Dolores."

"You talked to him before he changed his clothes, Petronilla, when I tried to he would not listen. Did you—surely you did not speak for the *Americano*. Do you really feel kindly to them?"

The darkness hid a smile. Dear Dolores, so poorly hiding her curiosity. "I never had the strength of character not to feel kindly toward everyone. Should I feel unkindly to the only man who ever interested himself in Luis Gonzaga, and loved him, simply because he is of a different race and fate throws him into an enemy army? Dolores, I have wished often that my children were like, say the de Dezas."

Doña Dolores nodded. "Many of them, one homelier than the next, born stupid, and nothing learned to it. I can see the advantage of being their mother, and no *Americano* will disturb their household asking for a daughter. Would you really give him Susanita?"

"Give, Dolores? The true gentleman cannot hide his heritage and he is that. He looks—*good*. So many of our young men are anything but good. I do not know, but it seems at times though it is not right that my husband should dictate our lives. What will become of my beautiful sweet baby? What of Angela? She would have been happy in the convent but now—have you noticed the change in her, Dolores?"

"She is human if that is what you mean, a thing I would not have thought possible. I have always resented, Petronilla, a man ruling me as if I were a bought slave, but here in this house there is nothing that can be done about it." She sighed so long and deeply that in the still darkness it sounded like the sob of a disembodied spirit. The sigh of woman the vassal, its echo centuries old.

Doña María Petronilla echoed it softly, reliving the short scene with her lord and master; before, in the semidark *sala* she had begged him to look at this change of conditions, to lay aside his prejudices long enough to at least consider this man, alien though he was. "You might have married her to René, yet what was he but a spoiled, selfish young man dependent on his father, and not even loving Susanita enough to stay at home and court her and watch her so he would not lose her. Running with the *guerrilleros* because he thought it would be fun and a girl should be happy to wait his pleasure. Yes, I know I speak of the dead, and I pray God may rest his soul, but the truth is the truth, Santiago. It might even, in these troublous times, be to our advantage to have an *Americano* in the family; at least things would not happen to us as did to Gáspar. Think, Santiago, think!"

Words. Like the handful of pebbles a child throws on the hard ground. He had let her talk and answered not a word. Had leaned against the mantel until she was through, and left the room without as much as looking at her. A little later he had emerged from his room dressed in the cloth suit, marched past her in silence, swung into the saddle of his favorite mount, Negro, and ridden away. Where to? For how long? That was his privilege, to account to no one if he chose not to. Theirs but to bow in acceptance.

Doña María Petronilla longed now for the courage to take Susanita to Matamoros and prevail upon Padre Pierre to marry her and Warrener. She sighed again, knowing herself to be incapable of it as it was to reach out and pluck the stars from the heavens and sew them around the hem of a dress. She rose, murmured that she would be back again, and went inside.

Which was exactly what José, hidden in the shadows, had been hoping for, and with a guarded "Doña Dolores" he moved forward and stood before her. "I have word from the Señor McLane, *señora*. He said I was to talk only to you because you had brains, understanding, and good judgment. I tell it to you as he told it to me, in those words. He said you were a woman a man could talk to without getting either impatient or resigned."

With the night hiding the wave of pleasure warm in her cheeks, a lifetime of being a lady controlling her eagerness, she asked what the message was in a tone disappointingly casual to José. He leaned low to whisper: "They are both at the *jacal*, Señor McLane and the *Americano* officer. Señor McLane thinks you could make a very good reason to come to the *jacal* early in the morning before he takes the other one away. He is, says the *señor*, a sick man but not too greatly so. He also says he will kill me dead if I as much as mention Señorita Susanita's name and I should tell you that also. Though, Doña Dolores, we are the servants of the master, we know what goes on, for we have eyes and ears, and we have known of this officer for a long time, from those who were in Matamoros, and indeed he seems a fine *caballero*. Señor McLane said to finish my words by telling you that he sent me to you because you had understanding as well as feeling and that, thanks to *El Señor Dios*, you were still young yourself and so could doubly understand."

Had McLane seen her then he would have been certain of some truth in his flattery, for the smile on Doña Dolores's face was not the careful one of middle age, showing no more than a measured amount of teeth. José got the flash, for a moment of all of them, and could have sworn that the sound he heard was a suppressed giggle. Though that, he assured himself, was not possible. He was imagining things.

"My greetings to the Señor McLane," she answered finally. "Tell him that I will take the matter under advisement. Do you understand, José? *Juicio. En tela de juicio.* Can you remember that?"

"Of a certainty, *señora*." José prided himself on being at least a step above the ordinary stupid *peon* and he let injury lace his words. "I must return, if I may." He bowed smoothing his shirt as he added, "We have loyalty, Doña Dolores, Tecla and Victorino and me."

"Who questions it? Go on home, José, where you belong."

Doña Dolores had never heard the doctrine of mind over matter nor the theory that youth and beauty were anyone's prerogative if belief of it were sufficiently deep, yet for a little while she was proof of them both.

꩜

239

Tilting her head to the stars, for a time she felt her blood flow with the sweet swiftness of youth and knew of its optimism and illusions.

When her sister-in-law came again and sank into a chair, Doña Dolores came to reality. Fool. A vain old fool of forty who was, had always been, would always be a homely woman. But that still left intelligence, "a woman a man could talk to." She smiled and preened herself. Well, she could name more than one who would not have understood that message which to her was plain as day: That she was to bring Susanita to see the man she loved before he went on, if she considered it discreet; that surely she understood they were entitled to a short time together, whether it would be the beginning or the end of things for them. "Do I look my years, Petronilla?" she asked abruptly.

"What do years matter when one is no longer young? I had not thought about it, but I might say you look well, Dolores. Not a gray hair, not a line. If you did not have your fine dignity you might be taken for a little younger than you are. Why do you ask?"

"An idle question, sometimes one thinks of peculiar things. I believe I will go to see Tecla in the morning, for an excuse to take Susanita away. The baby will distract her, heaven knows the poor child needs distraction."

"Do, Dolores. She is awake, go and tell her now. I would like to sit here alone. It was a night like this—no, there was a moon but that does not matter. I will sit with—Luis Gonzaga awhile, Dolores."

Poor Petronilla. Doña Dolores wiped an eye as she stole away. Poor, poor Petronilla.

Estéban drove them down in the light wagon through a world delightfully cool. Birds were migrating from the north countries and a flock of swallows, the sun catching and reflecting their blue backs in enameled beauty, darted and swirled about the wagon all the way to the *jacal*. *Doña* waved a hand. "See, Susanita, the swallows are omens of happiness and they are staying with us. Paz will tell you that they are the smiles of the angels brought to life to cheer us."

Susanita smiled dutifully. "Yes, *Tía*, it is nice."

They winged away when the wagon stopped and, as if life were determined to be bright this morning, crimson cardinals whirled from a clump of *manzanita* and perched on the stockade. José helped the women from the wagon and Doña Dolores whispered to him to keep Estéban out of sight and sound. She did not like or trust the second *caporal*, and she felt guilt in not confiding in Petronilla. Still, she told herself hastily, at least Petronilla could assert innocence if Don Santiago found out about this meeting—. She was in the *jacal*, McLane was bending over her hand, and she was presenting Susanita to him. Warrener, romantically pale, came from the other room as McLane was saying, "Señor Warrener has been most anxious to meet you, *señora*."

It was so smoothly and swiftly done that, to her astonishment, Doña Dolores found herself seated on a bench outside the *jacal* opposite McLane; out of earshot of the two inside but so she could see them with a slight turn of the head. Very neat, she thought. Very efficient, this redhaired man with the flattering tongue. He was telling her about the house being built for him in San Antonio, drawing the plan on the ground with a stick and telling her about such wondrous things as windows, and lamps, and a musical instrument he called a piano. It was all so engrossing that she could, in fact, pay small attention to anything else.

"You are strange, Susanita *mía*. Tell me why." Warrener reached for the hands folded in the lap of the pale green cotton dress and warmed them in his. There were so many things he wanted to say, so many eager words her stillness was holding back. "I know you love me or you would not have come. Why are you sad, *querida*?

"Because you must not come again, Roberto, and I will never see you again. Not—not ever."

"Not ever? That is a long time." He smiled, coaxing her to a happier mood, telling her she was a yellow rose with pale leaves. "Without the thorns. You are the perfect rose, sweet one." The words came, tumbling fast against the reach of time; words that warmed her and brought color to the creamy cheeks and a light to the lovely green eyes. He pleaded with her to come with him now. "I am sure Padre Pierre will marry us. There is a little house near the fort which will do us until this mad war and my service are over, and then we will live wherever you will be happiest. I will teach you English and take you home so my family there can see what a beautiful wife I have—." Painting bright pictures for her, walking with her in a dream future that would be heaven because they were together, wherever it would be. Caressing her with his voice, with his eyes, holding her hands. Pouring love over her like perfume, weaving a sheltering cloak out of their need of each other. "Ride with me now, dearest, will you? Right away." He moved and took her arm to lift her. "Come beloved. You and I, together always."

She burst into such wild sobbing that Doña Dolores got to her feet. "Leave them be, *señora*," McLane said, restraining her. "He told me he was going to plead with her to go with him this morning, and I imagine she is crying because she cannot bring herself to go. One must love with a certain madness to run away, do you not think so, *señora?*" He knew Doña Dolores, did Red McLane, so he added, "As I believe you would be great enough, mad enough, to do, were you that golden-haired niece of yours."

"Ah, this love," Doña Dolores sighed. "You are right, *señor*, it takes either a madness or a great strength, and my poor Susanita has neither." She was glad Susanita could not do so shocking a thing, yet she was sorry too. She took a look inside, noting the tightly clasped hands. "Poor children—Tell me more about the windows, *señor*—do you mean that your house will have light and sun in the rooms as if one were outside? But that is wonderful!"

"It is *papá*," Susanita finally managed to explain, blinking back the tears that wanted to run forever. "If you could have seen *papá* you would understand. I broke his heart and he loved me so and was so proud of me and spoiled me. He used to take my hair and wrap it around his finger—oh, Roberto, I cannot tell you! If *papá* had called me names and stormed at me—I love him, too, and when I heard him—no, I cannot go with you. I am not brave like I know Angela could be, or daring like Inez. I am sorry to—fail you and you must think I do not love you but I—"

"I do understand, beloved. That is why I love you because you are as you are, gentle and sweet and good." He kissed her fingers one by one, kissed the palm, and closed the fingers. "Something will happen to bring you to me, I know it will." Essaying lightness because their hearts were so heavy, he added teasingly, "When you are in distress and in the grip of a villain, I will come on my charger and will carry you swooning away. Will you promise to swoon for me, sweet?"

He was thinking that she looked like a rain-washed rose, and he would die if he could not have her. She was thinking he was so brave to laugh, so wonderful not to plead further, so understanding, and she could no longer live now that she knew she could never be his wife. Plumbing despair, clinging to hope, covering their sick hearts as best as they could.

When Tecla came from the garden with young Alfredo on her hip, the four were inside the *jacal*, laughing with McLane—who had the gift of imparting that precious gift and knew to give, or when to withhold it. Doña Dolores held out her arms for the child and asked Tecla to notify Estéban that they were ready to go. When her aunt was occupied with the child, Susanita remembered the paper folded in her belt and handed it to McLane; wordlessly, but wanting to tell him how Angela had sat up hours with a candle and had written and rewritten her message. She also would have liked to tell him that she changed her estimate of him and now thought him to be everything nice, but managed only a whispered "Thank you." He would know what for.

Doña Dolores thought it best for the men to stay inside because of Estéban. "When a servant becomes insolent his loyalty is weak and it is best not to test it." She was suddenly the proper gentlewoman, taking the parting bows and murmured compliments of the men with an exact measure of dignity, putting her charge before her and moving without further ado out into the sunlight and to the wagon.

Susanita looked back just once as the mules leaped into harness, shoving back her *mantilla* so Roberto could see the sun on her hair. His last whisper to her had been, "I shall remember the sun on your hair, *querida mía.*"

Vaya con Dios. Go with God. Go with ashes in your heart where once had lived such shining dreams. Go to the *hacienda* and be a loving daughter because you were too much the coward to be a wife. Go one way while he goes another, never again to meet.

"See, *niñita*, the swallows again, going home with us—that means your dearest wish will come true. Look at them, I do believe they think you are a flower!"

"Yes, *Tía.*" (A yellow rose with pale green leaves.)

The birds whirled once above the wagon and flew away. Then there was only the chuck-chuck of the loose fitting axle, in a world without sun or flowers or birds or joy.

When Warrener was stretched on a blanket at the encampment, a short distance from the soldiers playing poker, McLane squatted beside him and opened the letter. Angela's education had been rudimentary and her spelling and orthography far from what it might have been, so he read slowly, going back over the lines. He smiled indulgently at the crooked lines which told him:

To the Señor Alfredo McLane.
Your letter has been given careful thought and you compliment me by attributing graces and virtues to me which I fear I do not possess.

The future you hold before me fills me with an inner joy which I cannot deny, in its capacity for filling my life with the doing of good. I am not certain that it is what God wished for me so my answer to you is neither yes nor no. My father would not only forbid it but would refuse to ever see me again and perhaps it is my mission to soften his heart toward the people he calls his enemies. I believe, *señor*, that God will show me the way clearly and when I see it nothing will hold me from following it. Until I see the way may I beg of you not to come here for things have happened which do not dispose my father kindly to the *Americanos*, which I can only pray will change though I fear that would not be soon.

Be assured, Señor McLane, that I include you in my prayers and that my meeting you has not been without pleasure.

María de los Angeles de Mendoza y Soría.

"Now there's style to that name," Red murmured. "Nice and fancy, that's what I like. Well, I wouldn't say she exactly poured out her love for me, but she's too modest for that anyhow. Look at it another way, she wouldn't have had to put in that last line, but she wanted me to know she likes me. That's what she meant, all right."

"Who likes who?" Warrener opened an eye. "Not that I care."

McLane put the letter carefully away in an inner pocket. He was too accustomed to voicing many of his thoughts to Ike that he had for the moment forgotten that Ike had been left behind on this trip. He straightened the blanket under Warrener. "Of course you care, loot'nant, we being, you might say, brothers now. You'll get her yet, just like I'll get Mary Angel."

Warrener's answer was a grunt. Brothers, he and McLane!

Red put a plug of tobacco in his mouth. When he was married, he wouldn't chew. Anyhow, not too often. Until then—well, it helped a man to think and sort of gave him company too. He smiled happily, moving jaws slowly. Know what you want, be sure you want it, figure whether its use to you was at least as equal to the wanting, then study about getting it, and get it. As simple as that. Prayer was all right, but prayer was too often only wishing, and if you didn't put action after the wishing, what good was it. So Mary of the Angels was waiting for God to show her the way, was she? Maybe God would, who was he to deny it; the thing that counted now was that Mary Angel was in a receptive mood, you might say; any little thing at the right time would be God's pointing to her because she wanted it and would be looking for it. Made a fine team, she would do the praying and he the acting. Prayer was all right. He'd have his sons pray— here Red actually blushed—but he'd teach them to hustle also. Whether you prayed a Catholic rosary or bowed your head while a minister made up a prayer and hurled it at the Lord—you got busy as soon as the "Amen" sounded. He'd pound that into his boys and into his girls too. Just didn't sound reasonable that the Lord would go around handing out things when you sat and folded your hands. "There ain't no prayers going to make Don Santiago stop hating the *gringo*," he said half aloud. "I can't blame him. If I had a daughter like Mary Angel I wouldn't want an ornery infidel like me to have her either. And I don't know as I'd give sweet Susie to the loot'nant either."

After which cogitation Red McLane called to the soldiers to wake them in an hour and be ready to go, and stretched himself beside the sleeping Warrener.

Chapter 26

Night was fluid, running ahead of Don Santiago. (Night was a woman, laughing tenderly as she wrapped her soft veils about him. Night was a siren kissing him, warm hands on his heart—.) Always he had loved it and often ridden in it till dawn. He knew the silver glory of the plains when the moon was full, the enchantment of the hills, the mystery of the valleys. He knew, when the moon tilted, that a valley of yucca-palm in bloom was a chorus of angels with bells in their hair, waiting for a baton to swing them into music. He knew that the scrub-oaks clinging to a rocky point, stunted, and gnarled, and twisted by a thousand storms, turned into old women who whispered and plotted evil. He knew the "whoo whoo" of the nightbirds, the call of the coyote for a mate, and the killer howl of them in a pack. He knew the high death cry of the rabbit, the terrifying scream of the bobcat. He knew the way the owl glided on spread wings, the dipping beat of the whip-poor-will. He knew that the smell of wild mint, when a hoof crushed it, was fire running down the nostrils, and that of sage a hand clawing at the throat.

He knew, tonight, with the air a caress like a tempered lake on a naked body, and the stars swinging lanterns to light the traceries of the trails, that in all the world no nights were like those over the land that was his. As he knew, giving himself to the star-silvered darkness and its healing fingers, that the mission of this ride was right. The day was gone, and with it the inglorious deeds which defiled it. There was only tomorrow, no yesterdays. Mile after mile ran into eternity behind them, and it was as if he and Negro were one—a centaur rushing through a world created only for him, breaking through one snare of enchantment but to become entangled in another.

A tree that arched a branch like a huge curved arm over the trail brought him to earth and told him that he was close to the del Lago *hacienda* and daylight still some hours away. That was good. He dismounted, dropped the reins, and stretched himself on the grass for the short rest that would bring him to the house refreshed. Good old Gabriel. He could still see the pink face turn crimson when the candle in a nearby lantern flared high, in the patio after the *fiesta* when the other guests had retired. Embarrassed as a boy, Gabriel had finally brought out his astonishing proposal.

"I know I am not young, Santiago, I realize I am not handsome, but I have wealth, an honorable name, and a heart which beats for her. Give Susanita to me for my wife, and I will cherish her above all things and love her better than life."

He had needed self-control to keep from laughing in his friend's face at this preposterous idea. His beautiful baby married to fat Gabriel del Lago, almost as old as her father! A little anger had risen that Gabriel could dare ask, but he had gracefully done the proper thing: Gabriel would have an answer in due time—. And then the *Americano* came with his presumptions and boastings. How had he dared think himself the equal of a family like hers, the blood strain carefully kept from contamination through the generations by planned marriages. Memory of the dance came sharply— what a fool he had been not to see then, what a fool to believe that an imaginative, romance blinded girl could put it behind her. Well, there would be a stop to all that foolishness now, he would not risk a recurrence. Gabriel had asked for Susanita's hand. Good! And Susanita could consider herself fortunate to have so good a husband. He loved her, and that was more than many a wife had, more than her own mother had. What if she did not love him? Esteem, if not love, would come later. What if he was forty and she eighteen? The proverb said: Gray hair in a husband brings honor to a young wife.

Then the plain was fresh-bedewed and translucent, heralds in scarlet raiment drew aside the purple curtain of night and raised their trumpets to call: Hear ye, hear ye! Make way for the new day! Here comes the sun, O earth, and ye that walk upon earth. Make way, make way! Then into the hush came a rush of wings—white wings—swirling and dipping and soaring, myriad fold—. Again Don Santiago felt this rushing surge lifting him, and he threw up his arms, dropped to his knees for a short prayer, let himself be lifted, and stood there, face and arms held high to the Creator. He felt as if bathed in fire, and made new.

He was smiling as he rode into the patio, and now took a certain pleasure in the weeds and high grass that overran it. Susanita would not have time to mourn her lost love, she would be so busy correcting the servants' negligence. The planting of flowers and vines would immediately give her a feeling of possession and quickly make it home to her.

"*Ave María Purísima*," came Gabriel's answer as he hurried from the house. "Santiago, what has brought you here so early? You must have ridden all night—is it Alvaro?"

Don Santiago laughed as he dismounted and put an arm around his friend's shoulder. "I have not come on a sad errand, Gabriel." As they entered the house Don Santiago again noted the need of a woman to superintend it, for dust lay thickly everywhere, pictures hung askew, and even the pride of the del Lago family, the coat of arms graven on steel, lay on its side on the mantel. Yes, Susanita would have plenty to do, plenty of work to drive the officer from her mind.

"Juana," Gabriel called, "set another plate and be sure the coffee is hot. You must be tired, Santiago. Breakfast first, then a nap, after that the cause of your errand."

"You must think me odd, *amigo*. As if I could not rest on Mother Earth after a ride and be completely revived by hot coffee. You and I are still young, Gabriel."

It was not until they were almost through eating that Don Gabriel's somewhat slow mind put meaning to the cloth suit, his guest's good cheer, and the remark about being young. He asked hesitantly, "It can't be that Susanita—"

"Yes, Gabriel—my son."

"Son?" Gabriel gulped, dropping his cup and spreading a brown stain on the soiled white cloth. "Will . . . will . . . "

"She marry you? Why not, aren't you our friend? What more fitting than closer ties binding us? You have always been like one of the family, Gabriel."

Don Gabriel excitedly led his guest to the *sala*, where, his face beaming like a pink moon, he walked round and round a table shoved carelessly out into the room. "Santiago, you cannot dream how happy you have made me. I can tell you now that I thought you looked down your nose at me when I asked for her—I cannot believe Susanita could love me."

"She will marry you, Gabriel; is not that sufficient?" Don Santiago dropped to a chair and waved a deprecating hand. "You know, we as a people talk much of love but do not find it important to a successful marriage. Love makes fools of men."

"I understand." Gabriel sighed and the light of joy went out of his face. He put a hand on his friend's shoulder. "It was asking too much."

❧❧❧

"You really need a wife, Gabriel." Don Santiago looked around the room and let its dust and disorder speak for him. "A young girl like Susanita whom I know, will take to housekeeping like her mother. María Petronilla is a splendid housekeeper."

"Do you think she will like it here? We could live in Matamoros all the year if she found it too lonely here."

"Not Matamoros, of all places!" For a moment Don Santiago doubted the wisdom of this marriage. For just a moment he saw again the love on Warrener's face and heard Susanita's brave declaration of her own. But he drowned it quickly in the resentment of everything *Americano*, and shoved aside the whisper that he should be honest with Gabriel and tell him why his suit was finding favor. "Keep her on the ranch," he said sharply. "She is used to ranch life."

"But she is so young and loves dancing and pretty clothes. It would not be right to hide her beauty here. I want to give her everything I can, everything she wants."

"A spoiled wife is not worth—that, Gabriel." Don Santiago snapped his fingers. "Keep a wife in her own chair or she will soon be sitting in yours. However I will leave that to you. The important thing is to discuss the marriage."

"A most pleasant discussion for me." Don Gabriel laughed so that his round body shook. Susanita would love him eventually, he would be so good to her she would have to love him. "I want to have the biggest and most talked of wedding, and she must have the most elegant of wedding gowns, the best that can be bought. I will go all the way to New Orleans. And the house must be remodeled and done over to suit her. I'll bring masons and carpenters from Matamoros and send for the rarest flowers and—"

"Not so fast, Gabriel. All that can be done later. Both Petronilla and I (God forgive me the lie for she knows nothing of this) think the wedding should be as soon as possible. With conditions as they are, life is less secure than ever and I do not want to wait. Susanita has been indulged beyond the age of marriage as it is. Let us say right after All Souls Day, when Padre Pierre can take a few days and come to the ranch to marry you. The wedding will be at the ranch."

"But—but the wedding dress, the dresses for the trousseau, what of them?" Don Gabriel asked in concern.

"I am sure something can be done for her, and she has plenty of dresses now, far more than she can wear."

"But what does she say about this—this hurry? I am sure she could not like it, not in her heart."

"She is a dutiful daughter and will obey my command."

"But please, Santiago, I would not be happy if she did not want this hurried marriage and would rather wait until everything is prepared as is the custom. I would not be happy."

"Gabriel, Gabriel!" Don Santiago walked the length of the room in his exasperation at this deplorable softness. "I have told you she will obey my wishes. If I want the wedding the week after All Souls, it shall be then."

"I want to be sure of her happiness, Santiago."

"Happiness? Since the *gringos* came happiness has fled for all of us. It is now a question of what is best for us as a people, not whether we are happy. Come, show me the new colt. You have always loved fine horses, Gabriel; is that why you haven't loved women and stayed a bachelor?"

They left the house, Don Gabriel talking as they moved. "An Arabian from the stables at Parras and a neat little sum he cost me too; the breed was brought by the Marquis de Aguayo nearly three hundred years ago and has been kept pure. As for my marrying, I really do not know why and have often asked myself why." He filled his chest with the fresh morning air. "I still cannot believe my good fortune. Christmas will not find me a lonely man this year, and by next year perhaps—" His face colored and he hurried on to hide his confusion. "Come, I see Antonio beckoning to us."

Don Santiago's thoughts were not on the colt, for his conscience was very much alive. He was seeing Susanita's repugnance at marrying this man; he had witnessed his friend's simple joy and desire to make his young bride happy. In his heart he realized the unfairness of the marriage, not only to his daughter but also to his friend. What right had he to make two people unhappy—for loveless and unhappy this marriage would be, with Susanita's heart forever with another, Gabriel tearing his heart out to bring joy to her. Then a voice whispered again urging him to look closer at this Warrener, to consider that what he considered best might not always be best after all—. He pulled at his lower lip. Pah, he was becoming a weakling also. The children would bind the marriage. His grandchildren, without alien blood.

Gabriel's babbling became clear. "—have him trained for her, even my best horse is not too good for her." He was caressing the face of the Arabian as if it were the girl and not a horse. "She will love my Moro here."

"But our married women do not ride! My girls are the only ones allowed to ride at all and after marriage that would be a scandal, Gabriel."

It seemed, now, a foolish custom to Don Gabriel, and one he would defiantly thumb a nose at, he told himself. "Ah well, Santiago, she will always be a child to me. Look the sky is turning gray and the wind coming from the north." He turned to the *caporal*. "Be sure to walk the colt, Antonio, and tell Pancho to build a fire in the *sala* and then get a chicken for the cook to make a stew for lunch."

Before the blaze in the *sala* they smoked corn husk *cigarillos* cured with cognac, and Don Santiago took deep draughts to ease his restlessness and cover his impatience at this maudlin exhibition of his future son-in-law. "I insist on telling you of the *donas* Susanita will get from me," Don Gabriel was saying, opening a carved box shaped like a tiny chest. "My mother's jewels, this was my father's wedding present to her and Susanita shall wear it." He swung a chair and the diamond pendant broke into rainbows. He lifted a rosary of matched pearls, dreams of loveliness flushing delicately in the light of the fire. "My mother's First Communion present from her uncle, the bishop of San Luis, and I want to see it in my bride's hands. This is my mother."

Don Santiago studied the miniature politely. "A sweet looking woman. Wasn't she a beauty?"

"Yes, but I inherited from the del Lagos in looks. She was French, my father met her on one of his trips to Mexico. She died young; my old nurse told me she died of loneliness. She never got used to this solitude; every evening she would put on one of her fine dresses and sit in the *sala* as if waiting for company. My father had promised to move to Mexico after the birth of the child, but she died soon after I was born. That is why I suggested taking Susanita to Matamoros for I do not want her to suffer as my mother did."

Every word was a hammer stroke upon Don Santiago. He knew he should tell Gabriel about Warrener but that would end the marriage. As it was, only guileless old Gabriel would not dream of suspecting anything behind this sudden acceptance of his proposal and the hasty marriage. One married hastily only in gravest emergency. But all Gabriel knew was his silly love, and it was all he could talk about. There were sapphires. Two thousand pesos in gold. "My mother was so small or I would ask that Susanita wear her wedding dress, all of the finest hand embroidery. A comb set with opals to flash in her hair; earrings of filigree, shawls from China. . . ."

It was torture to listen. All the more torture because Gabriel's round body had a habit of fading away and a tall slim one coming to take its place. "When I see those sapphires, Santiago, I almost wish her eyes were blue so she would look lovelier when she wears them." Eyes of blue—oh, curse the man! If he could only tell him to be still, for the love of God, be still!

Early the next morning Don Santiago said farewell to his host and left for Rancho La Palma. Wearied of Gabriel's lovesickness, wearied of himself. Already seeing the anguish in Susanita's eyes, steeling himself to meet it.

It had to be done. It was the only thing that could be done.

Chapter 27

The storm was of even greater intensity than Don Santiago had expected. Susanita's heartbroken cry—"No, *papá*, no, not Gabriel, not an old man—*papá*, what are you saying?"—was not given a chance to echo in the *sala*, drowned out by Doña María Petronilla's distressed protest,

"Have you gone completely mad, Santiago? You cannot marry her to Gabriel—why that is dreadful, dreadful!"

Doña Dolores swished her skirts back and forth before him—he was standing before the fire—spitting her words at him like an angry cat. "Gabriel! You went to him without saying a word to any of us and he—why the old goat—don't go lifting your hand, Santiago, or telling me to keep still because I'm not going to. Goat, that's what I said! I suppose he was so pleased he swelled up like a. . . a . . . oh, I can just see the conceited little—so the two of you sat there drinking and bought and sold Susanita as if she didn't have a heart and soul—that sweet child for that blatting, mangy—I shall tell him what I think of him just as I am telling you what an unnatural, cruel father you are!"

In her pause for breath her brother cut in icily, "You have quite shown yourself, Dolores, as lacking the attributes of the lady your birth and raising should have made you. You have nothing whatever to say in this, and I will hear nothing further from you, certainly not such shocking language. Your position in this my household does not warrant the eternal poking of yourself into its affairs which I have so patiently endured these twenty years. Sit down and put on the appearance of a lady, at least." Don Santiago speared each face with eyes hard as obsidian. The outburst of his sister was what he needed to drive out the misgivings he had felt when he first gave the news, and he was again master of himself. And master of them. The patriarch whose word was not gain-said nor his decisions disputed.

"Petronilla, you should be at my side fighting the encroachment of the barbarian *Americanos*. A girl's head is full of nonsense and easily turned, and it is our duty to protect her future, the least you could do is give an understanding of my duty, even though it does not seem possible to give the accord I have a right to expect. If the safety of our daughters can only be bought by immediate marriages, we cannot hesitate." He looked at her and waited for her obedient "Yes, Santiago," but she held enough spirit not to agree with him.

He turned to the weeping Susanita. "One might think you were being married to a *vaquero* instead of to a man of fine family who asks but to be a doormat for you to wipe your little feet on. The house is to be remodeled not as he, but you, like it, new and rare flowers for the patio for you, dresses, jewels, horses, not a woman in the country will be so indulged, and you are most fortunate. You do not think of Tía Dolores as old and he is her age, still a young man. Do you consider me old, then?"

"I cannot bear the thought of his touching me," she whimpered. "I don't want his jewels and—and things—I—oh, I wish I were dead, dead, dead."

"Nonsense!" His indignation was mounting at all of them, now that Angela put an arm around her sister and kissed her. Even Angela. It came to him that Angela had been acting somewhat peculiar lately, with independence. Well, he would nip that in the bud. José Luis Carbajal was getting stronger, and a proposal from him was certain. An acceptance was certain also, whether Angela liked it or not. "Susanita, to be a good wife and mother living in virtue and obedience is the destiny given to women by God; it is better that your life be not further complicated by emotions that are unseemly. I do not want to hear the word love mentioned again. The marriage will be the week after All Souls Day. Gabriel is bringing money for the *donas*, and he wished to buy materials and have a large wedding, but I told him you women would arrange a trousseau for the time being and the rest could be attended to when Susanita was mistress of Rancho Olmos. Petronilla and you, Dolores, get together what you can." He walked to the door, turned to add, "Further words are unnecessary. Gabriel will be here in a few days to make the formal call, and I want no long faces. Petronilla, make what arrangements must be made."

They were alone. A group of four living at a time when, indeed, their only destiny was to serve man and bow to the master of the house. And so, after tears were drained out and protests wore themselves thin against the wall of futilities, they accepted this new decree of their lord.

"I will pray," Angela said. "I will storm heaven with my prayers. Don't cry any more, Susanita, there is still time for something to happen."

"It is his right," Doña María Petronilla told them, "and in the end may be wisest after all. There will be nothing else to do. You will be happy after a time, Susanita."

"Yes, *mamá*." (If happiness is a lifetime of faithlessness, for I will belong always to a man not my husband. You don't know, *mamá*, you never loved as I do.)

When Don Gabriel came with his gifts a few days later, Susanita managed a surface cheerfulness, giving an impression of maidenly shyness whenever she excused herself and went to her room. Only Doña Dolores showed her displeasure, wearing her stiffest dress to form a complement to an unsmiling dignity, with difficulty keeping back the excoriating tirade she longed to pour over him. Don Gabriel cut his call as short as the proprieties allowed, the change of relationship in the household putting a certain restraint upon him which Doña Dolores's attitude did nothing to change.

It was decided that Susanita wear her mother's wedding dress. Don Gabriel had brought his mother's dress, and Doña Dolores felt a deep pleasure when she could not get it on Susanita. "I'm glad it's so small we can't do anything with it," she sniffed. "He won't get the satisfaction of seeing it worn and that pleases me." She laughed as she told them the secret she had kept all these years, that the candle which had fallen on her wedding dress and veil and destroyed it had been deliberately dropped on it by herself. "For which thank the Lord because I wouldn't have Susanita wear it, not to marry Gabriel del Lago."

She and Doña María Petronilla went over the list of things required of the daughter of a *don*, a ruling rigid as law. Six linen sheets with pillow cases to match, embroidered and hemstitched, and a similar set of cheaper cotton material. One wool blanket with the wool carded, spun into thread, and woven by the bride herself; six pillows to match the blanket, brown with a colored border, these to be set on the floor of various rooms. At least three tablecloths with napkins. "I still have all my linen sets, as you know, Petronilla," Doña Dolores said, "and well I remember embroidering my eyes out on them. Let me give them to her." Of the cotton things the house chest was full, many of them new, and Doña Dolores offered her tablecloths. "What good are they to me? I am tired of having them around."

Over the blankets the mother was really distressed, for when Susanita had shown small aptitude and no enthusiasm for carding and weaving, she had been let go. "I suppose I had a vague notion that knowledge would come automatically with betrothal, when she had to do it." The two were in Doña Dolores's room, the big chests open and linens spread on the bed. Doña María Petronilla wrung her hands. "How can she teach her daughters, I am sure Gabriel won't even allow her to use her useless little hands. But this is awful, Dolores, awful."

Doña Dolores snorted. "Why should she work? The Lord gave her beauty and sweetness, and I'd like to know why she should weave a blanket for Gabriel del Lago. I wove one this summer, as you will remember, to keep my sanity, and I'll weave the pillows later if Paz doesn't. Who will know the difference? Let us not worry the poor child, Petronilla."

"If there was time I would make her do it just the same, Dolores. Oh, the sash, what about the sash?"

Doña Dolores took a package from the chest and rolled a sash over the white bed cover; cream-colored wool with a border of red, green and purple stripes on the ends. "Many a tear I wove into this sash for Anselmo," she sighed. "I even dyed the colors myself. If Gabriel recognizes it so much the better, though he won't; man demands that we slave for him and never looks at the finished work. He can have the shirt I made for Anselmo also, and when he finds it too tight, the silly fool will feel complimented that Susanita thought him thinner than he is. It should still be white as I wrapped it in bluing cloth."

Doña María Petronilla was shocked. What in the world was the matter with Dolores? She fingered the sash as she said hesitantly, "It looks as though we will have to use it, and it is beautifully done but not the shirt, that I could not allow. It does not seem right." The girls came into the room just then and she added hopefully, "Perhaps Susanita could make the shirt if Angela helped her."

"I can see it finished for his burial if they have the tucking of it to do," Doña Dolores laughed, then dropped the subject to talk about the clothes a bride had to have, bringing out some of her own that had gotten too small before she could wear them and had been laid away.

The requirements besides the wedding dress (and they were all paid for by the groom) were all new linen underwear of petticoats and chemises and ruffled drawers, finely hand-sewn and preferably embroidered; two bright silk dresses for summer wear afternoons and two of calico for the mornings, all French goods; for winter wear one velvet dress and one of cashmere or merino; pieces of heavy black and white satin to be made into shoes later as needed; a black and white *mantilla*.

Doña Dolores held up a petticoat eight yards around the bottom with eyelet and satin embroidery all over it, gathered onto a yoke so as not to conflict with the gathers of the dress at the belt. "Everything I had was embroidered but then I had magic fingers. I could not learn to play the harp, but put a needle in my fingers and I made music. Besides all that I made for my trousseau, I crocheted an entire surplice for the *padre* who married us, do you remember, Petronilla? When I think of it!"

The mother was troubled. This haste was not right. All the linens should have the spread fan which was Susanita's mark, a letter on each of the eight slats to form her name. The first Susana had used the emblem so on her linens, and it had been Don Santiago's fancy that it be put on Susanita's handkerchiefs. "It is a disgrace," she complained, "I cannot see the need of this haste where nothing can be done as it should be." (I know why the haste. He wants to get her safely away from the *Americano*. Oh my poor, poor baby.)

"It does not matter, *mamá*. I cannot see that it matters." Susanita smiled and kissed her mother. Roberto would not care if she came to him in rags, and it would not matter if they had a single sheet and no tablecloth at all. And if she could not bring things to him who would not have demanded them, how could she be anything but indifferent to what she brought another? "I am sure Don Gabriel will not count my sheets and my petticoats." She decided she would do her crying at night and cover her misery and despair before her mother. If she needed to weep against a breast, there was dear Tía Dolores, who understood so well. She would do as Padre Pierre once preached, take each day for itself, and remember that the things tomorrow brought could not happen until tomorrow came.

October passed, and All Saints Day came. Angela and Susanita gathered wild larkspur and oleander blooms and banked them on the table in the *sala*, and set statues and pictures of the saints in a row before silver candlesticks, halfheartedly, for they knew the table would remain and be redecorated for the wedding. When Angela asked her aunt whether the altar looked all right, Doña Dolores answered snappishly that she supposed the saints would be pleased, adding somewhat blasphemously, "There's enough of them in heaven that they could do a little something for us women, it seems to me. I suppose it's the same there as it is here— everything for the men!"

Don Santiago led the rosary and the litany of the saints while the family knelt and bowed heads as they answered. Of all of them only the mother had a heart filled with devotion, spilling it in supplication for her children. Angela's petitions were such a mixture that, she thought disconsolately, even God could make nothing of it. Doña Dolores found that she was not praying at all for the resentment controlling her, answering in words without meaning; almost laughing aloud when her brother intoned "San Gabriel" in the litany and Angela alone answered, "Pray for us." (Yes, pray for the silly old fool, your namesake, San Gabriel, it's time you looked after him and gave him some sense.) Susanita, after one desolate silent soul-cry of "Holy Virgin Mary, don't let me have to marry Gabriel!" knelt still as if carved from wax, moving her lips without sound.

"A mighty poor service," Don Santiago said sternly. "I am weary of these sad faces. Susanita, at least try to look as though you were soon to be a happy bride."

"Yes, *papá*, I am happy." (So happy I cry the night long.)

All Souls Day and its dolors and prayers. "Lord, grant the poor souls the eternal rest, and let perpetual light shine upon them; may they rest in peace, amen." Doña María Petronilla wept all through the prayers, fearing that Alvaro was one of those souls. And Don Santiago, the same fear in his heart that his son was dead, rode like mad all the day, his face white and set—.

November the third, and Susanita stood for hours while her mother's wedding dress was let out here and there, and basted and sewed, and fitted again and again. "Even the dress," grumbled old Paz to Doña Dolores, "is against this wedding, the way it refuses to fit no matter what we do. It is like a shroud on my poor baby, and I'd like to tell Santiago so."

"Tell Gabriel, Paz." Doña Dolores bent her head over the ripped hem. "He could have refused. I believe he would refuse now if he knew how miserable the child is—that is, if any man can believe a woman would be miserable at the prospect of marrying him. However, he will make her a good husband, if there is such a thing as a good husband, which I very much doubt."

Paz scolded: "Women are put here to serve men. You would be happier if you accepted that, as I have told you a hundred times, Dolores."

Susanita heard them and turned back to her room. Not Roberto. She would not be forever ordered about like *mamá*, forever obeying. Perhaps Gabriel would not either, but if he would be kind that would only make things worse. She beat fists together in futile despair. In a week. Only a week from today and the arms of a man she did not love—old arms would close around her. God, oh God, no . . . God, why didn't you give me the courage to go with Roberto—.

November fourth. A day nearer. Angela, convinced that heaven wanted to be stormed, spent every hour she could in their room on her knees, praying with a fervor she had never felt before. Susanita took the dress to a sunny place in the patio to sew up the hem. It had touched the floor when her mother wore it, but it was too short for Susanita, and a streak showed above the edge of the let-down hem. When her father came by and lifted her face she smiled at him sweetly and asked where he was going.

"Let me ride with you awhile, *papá*."

"Not today, *hijita*. I am going to the little valley where you once found the bluebells, remember? Tomás is branding calves, and you do not want to see that, and it will be very dusty besides. Then I may ride on to see Gabriel, to tell him you will be happy to see him when he comes for you."

"Gabriel is nice, *papá*. I have always liked Gabriel."

Something seemed lost between them. As if, in his stern dictature, he had hurt his old love for her and left but a semblance of it; as if she, in the mockery of pretense of happiness, had retreated into an inner house and closed the door. She kissed him dutifully, and when the jingle of his spurs was lost in the distance, the tears came again in a flood and dropped upon the dress. (*Mamá*, what are those spots on your old wedding dress? Here, all along the hem. They look like tear stains, *mamá* . . . They were tears, daughter. That is why you have never seen me cry, I shed all my tears before I married your father . . . Then why did you marry *papá*, why didn't you run away? . . . Because I was not brave, daughter. All I could do was sit in the patio and sew on this dress, and cry, and cry. . . .)

The shadow of the palm tree was a long spar that lay over the wall, and Angela was laying a scarf over her mother's shoulders against the chill when the little man stumbled into the patio and dropped to the ground at Doña María Petronilla's feet. Dust powdered the gray-streaked beard, the lined brown face, the old felt hat that drooped over the bloodshot eyes. Dirt was a crust on the stubby hands and bare feet, on the ragged homespun clothes.

"Pablo!" Doña María Petronilla recognized him as the man who had a fruit stand in the plaza at Matamoros, year after year. She had befriended him a number of times and taken food to his wife during one winter's illness. "Pablo, what brings you here in this condition? Angela, get him a drink of water, Susanita—"

"*Señora*, they have Alvaro!" The voice was high and quivery with the fatigue that trembled his body as he rose. "They came last night to Matamoros, the Rangers, thousands and thousands of them, and they are killing and robbing today, and they have Alvaro and two others, and they are going to hang them in the plaza in the morning." He spilled the words one on top of the other as fast as he could, as if fearing he could not finish and dropped to the ground. Soon he raised his head and hurried on with his message: "I took the horse from my brother's farm, and I rode until he would go no further—he was old, *señora*, as I am old, and then I ran and ran—and I missed the trail and thought I was lost until all at once I saw the *hacienda*. They are killing everybody—it is so terrible I—they have Alvaro, I saw him, so I know, and in the morning they hang him—it is the end, *señora*, the end."

"I will see that he is taken care of." Paz helped the man to his feet and led him away to the servant's quarters.

"I know where *papá* is." Susanita took command while the others were still paralyzed with shock. "Angela, you see that a good horse is saddled for me, and I will ride to José's, and he will go with me to find *papá*. Estéban—oh, he is sick, I had forgotten. I can ride to José's alone—hurry, Angela!"

"No, Susanita." Doña María Petronilla's lips were white as her face as she gripped Susanita's arm. "A man can go. Juan Bautista can ride that far."

"There is not time to waste and I know where he is, *mamá*, he told me before he left, and I can ride faster than anyone here. It is not far to José's and nothing will happen to me. See, I have on this dress with the fullest skirt, and it is black and won't show me up so easily; I can ride astride and it will cover me. I'll get *papá*." She kissed her mother and ran after Angela, the white satin dress spilling from her arms and spreading on the floor very much like the shroud it had seemed to be.

Chapter 28

❧

The *vaqueros* were still in the bluebell valley when Susanita and José galloped into it and jerked their horses to a stop to ask Tomás for Don Santiago, leaving him gawking as they wheeled and galloped off again when he told them the *hacendado* had stayed only a short time and then gone on to Rancho Olmos. "Many hours ago, *señorita*."

"What is this?" asked one of the *vaqueros*, pulling at a long mustache, "When the *señorita* rides astride like a man and alone with a *peon*, the world is falling to pieces."

The world was indeed falling to pieces, for Susanita. Back in the *jacal* she was beating hands together and pleading with José to ride to Matamoros and save Alvaro. "*Papá* is only living for the day when Alvaro comes back—José, he must come home, don't you see that he must come home?"

"What can I do there, *señorita*," José threw out his hands. "I, a poor *peon*! Do you think the Rangers would listen to me? I would not even get near them for they would kill me. I have heard that they say 'Kill a Mexican first, then ask him what he wants.' It is a pity you cannot go, with the army officer so in love with you. Forgive me the familiarity, *señorita*, I would go gladly if I could do something."

Roberto! How strange that she had not once thought of him. If it could be done, Roberto would save Alvaro, for her. He might not, now, even know that the Rangers had Alvaro, if as Pablo said they swooped down on the town in a raid of their own. "Let me think, José." She went outside and leaned against the *jacal*. She and Tía Dolores riding down with the coach and the mules, could they make it? But the wheels were off the coach, Juan Bautista had removed them only that morning to straighten them and had them in a block vise, and the mules were in the pasture. In the morning, Pablo said, and that might be very early. She would have to go herself, and at once; she could not even go back to the *hacienda*. It would

mean riding all night with a *peon*, unattended by a woman; going to a soldier camp and pleading with strange men— things a lady would die before
doing, almost impossible for one like her who had always been sheltered
and protected. She would not, she thought, do it for Alvaro who had
brought it upon himself, who so often had been mean to her and was always selfish and exacting. But for *mamá*, to keep her heart from breaking.
For *papá*, longing for his son. And surely *papá* would love her again, he
might even postpone the wedding in gratitude to her, and in time break it
off. Why, there was no question of what to do, for there was only one thing
to do. She went inside the *jacal* and told José, "The sun is already setting
José, but fortunately there is a moon bright enough to show the trail. You
will go with me, and if God is good we will get to the soldier camp in time.
My horse is not the best one, nor is yours, but they will hold out; feed
them corn while Tecla fixes something for us to eat. Hurry, José."

Tecla came between them, a hand clutching the blue blouse between
her full breasts and twisting the cloth. "Señorita Susanita, you cannot do
that; what will people say. Even if you saved Alvaro, the disgrace of your
going unchaperoned could never be forgiven. No one would ever forgive
you—I mean your *papá* and Alvaro and their friends, it is too shocking a
thing to do. You cannot go alone with José."

Susanita put an arm around Tecla. "There is no one to ride so far, and
besides there isn't time to go back to the *hacienda*. This is different, Tecla;
I am going to save my brother from being hanged. Come, fix us something to eat, José is already feeding the horses."

When the eggs were fried and set before them, Tecla quieted down,
accepting the fact that she would be widowed and Susanita dead, or if not
that, disgrace for them all. Alvaro was scarcely worth it in her opinion,
and it was hard not to say so aloud. "I will tell Victorino to tell your *mamá*
after you are gone; he would not let you go if he knew it now. He would
tell you that not even hanging is as bad as a girl's public disgrace."

Tecla was weeping bitterly when they mounted the horses, watching
them from the doorway with small Alfredo held tightly against her.

Dusk was beaten back by a lopsided early moon, and the trail, [like a
mark drawn by a huge finger across the dark of grass and brush][1] lay whitely
before them. As the horses stepped outside the stockade, terrors of the
trail rose before Susanita. It would be beset by those who toiled only to
take away from another what he had: *gringo* bandits, Mexican robbers,
Indian marauders, and at the end of the trail, the hate-filled Rangers in-

flamed by their killings and plundering. It might so easily be death for them, and she suddenly saw José as more than a *peon* born to serve; he was a man with wife and child, loving life. "José," burst from her kind heart, "it may mean death for you. Pío could go with me, he is at the corrals, isn't he?"

There was not a moment's hesitation in José's answer. "Death to save the young master would be an honored one; as it is an honor that I do my best to keep you from harm."

Susanita wrapped the *rebozo* borrowed from Tecla about her head, set herself comfortably in the saddle, took the reins in the grip her father had taught her, loosely, ready to tighten in an instant. "We waste time, José." He spurred his tough little mustang ahead of her long-legged bay, and the horses dropped into the steady trot which is the gait of the plains.

It seemed to Susanita as mile after mile of moon-brushed plain met them and slipped behind that she was a different person entirely. As if the love-struck, weeping, frightened girl was still in the patio spilling tears on a wedding dress, and a woman who looked like her was riding in a world that, also, was a new and different one. She had known the night only within the sheltering walls of the patio or the confines of the coach in town. Wings were on her shoulders and she soared in a world that was free. She was alone in it and free, free—so soaringly, blissfully free—.

"Señorita, I hear something." José brought her to reality as he looped a rope around the horses' noses so they could not whinny and led them to the shelter of tall brush. The clatter of hoofs on hard ground came near, saddle leather creaked. They were close, were gone. Friend or foe? They would never know. But it was as if the night riders had touched Susanita in their passing, and left fear to hang on her stirrup.

So long the night, so endless the trail; so hard the saddle, so pounding the trot. "José," she protested, "I am young, why should I be so tired? Are you tired?"

He made her stretch out on the ground awhile. "It is long past midnight, do you see where the moon is? We are not *vaqueros* used to riding hour upon hours. And sixty miles of riding will tire a *vaquero*, we have gone further than that. It will kill our horses."

"José, you are good. *Papá* will reward you well, I know."

José had a different opinion but he made no comment. What would Don Santiago say? He knew what Alvaro would say. Alvaro would not believe that even a *peon* like he could ride through the night with Susanita and treat her with respect. For a moment José hoped they would not arrive in time to save Alvaro, who judged all men by himself.

After a time weariness and fear hardened to that unfeeling state which is labeled "endurance," when nerves are hypnotized and muscles sleep. The moon, having risen early, retired early and left the world to darkness and the bone-shivering chill which presages dawn. The horses stumbled often, hung heads, stayed on the trail only by instinct. Night creatures leaped from bushes and sped away. A coyote chorus set up lamentations in weird, frightening yowls and barks. It is the time, or say the old ones, when sick bodies cease to struggle and release the soul, which wanders about lost and frightened, until the last of night is fled and dawn lifts them away to the spirit world. (So say the old ones, and Paz claimed to have seen these ghostly souls of people who died before the dawn.) It is they that bring the chill when their hands touch the living, they who set teeth to rattling and bodies to shaking—José crossed himself repeatedly, and begged the saints to protect them.

Susanita dozed a little and dreamed she saw Alvaro hanging from a tree. "José, José, will we get there?" she cried out in terror. "We'll be too late, José too late!"

"If our horses last, *señorita*. It is in God's hands."

Lieutenant Warrener was in full uniform long before daylight and seeing a flicker of light in Major Fortesby's adobe house he knocked upon the door. "Warrener, sir," he called, and went inside at the impatient "Come in, come in," and took the stool pointed at by his commander.

"Dammit, Lieutenant, this is a mess." The little man's fingers picked up small objects scattered on the table before him, put them down again, moved them. "A blot on the history of the Rangers I call it—and could you discover, lieutenant, why they come to Matamoros from Mexico to raise hell? Why didn't they stay down there?"

Warrener felt sorry for his commander, too much the scholar for his border post. Still, what else could he do but send a protest to the Ranger Captain Hays and keep his own men in camp and froth and fume all of that murderous yesterday when the Rangers marched into town, shooting, plundering, running wild like devils released from the confines of hell. Warrener rose. "I haven't been able to find out, sir, unless it is that they got word somehow of the prisoners held in the Matamoros and came up to release them."

"The worst robbers and cutthroats in the country!" Fortesby banged the table, his small pointed gray beard trembling with anger. "Didn't they suppose that if good citizens had been locked up by the Mexicans, we'd have gotten them out again? My God, we work to establish a comparative peace and now the Rangers disrupt it, let the cutthroats loose upon the country once more, and kill half a hundred Mexicans guilty of nothing but defending their homes. I shall formally protest this. I shall write out a full report of the unwarranted invasion and—arrumpg, what I want to know is how we can get them out of Matamoros again? I understand they are planning some sort of celebration this morning, do you know anything about it?"

"Some public execution of guerrillas they caught, to edify Matamoros and put the fear of God in the Mexicans. Sort of looks like the said fear should be reversed, I might say. What are your orders, sir? I am up early because I couldn't seem to stay in bed. As you say, this is a mess."

They talked awhile, and when reveille sounded Warrener left the office. As he was returning to his quarters, Captain Ross intercepted him and held out a glass to him. "What do we do with what is coming down the road, Bob? Much as I can make out it's a girl on a horse dead on its feet and a Mexican hanging on the stirrup and trotting alongside. They look all in, but golly, Bob, it's suicide for them to go to Matamoros. She looks young and pretty."

Warrener focused the glass, gasped, almost dropped it. "It's Susanita," he said, his voice shaking. "Get horses quick, for us and for them—and, for the love of heaven, hurry!" They ran after Ross so not a second would be lost.

José stopped the bay and leaned against the trembling body. "Soldiers come, *señorita*, to kill us. It is the end." And he buried his face under his saddle skirts so his tears could not be seen. A man did not cry and what was death after all, but he was so tired; so terribly tired, and the thought of Tecla and the *niño* were a sickening pain. It was all right, he told himself, he was but a *peon* and without the bravery of a *caballero*. He closed his eyes and waited, too tired to even remember he was her protector. There would be a shot, and the end.

Susanita let her weary head droop. It had been a mad errand. "The soldiers will not hurt us, José," she told him, weakly. Perhaps they would call Roberto for her—.

"Susanita! Susanita *mía*, you are half dead!"

❦

265

Strong arms lifted her and held her against hard button and wool cloth that smelled of tobacco. For awhile she rested there, like a bird finding shelter after a storm.

The word "Alvaro" in José's voluble explanation of their errand and their plight since his horse had broken down some miles back—all detailed in the hysteria of his relief—jerked Susanita awake. She asked to be helped onto the horse brought for her, made sidesaddle shift as well as she could, and told Warrener why she was there. José and Captain Ross discreetly rode ahead, eyes and ears open only for danger.

"I will be honest, Roberto," she finally managed to say, "If you can free my brother for me, all I can say is thank you. Unless perhaps—oh, I cannot even talk."

He stopped the horses, cupped her chin in his hand and shook her face. "Lift those eyelids and look at me, or I'll kiss them open." And when she looked at him he told her, tenderness breaking through the words, "I would walk over fire for you, die or live for you, and ask only what you could or would give me. If you could give me nothing, it would still be much, could I but do something for you. Do you understand, my darling?" He did not tell her that he did not intend leaving her go. She was too tired and worried for that now.

"Yes, I understand. I never doubted that, Roberto."

"Then let us go. I will take you to my commanding officer, see that you have food and can wash the dust from your face, and we will see what can de done. Your hair needs combing, *señorita*.

It was dear of him, to save her with his matter-of-factness. For an instant she thought: "I will not go back at all if we can free Alvaro. He in my place, and that should be fair. I will stay."

Your hair needs combing, *señorita*. She looked at him, and all heaven was in her smile.

Chapter 29

Captain Jack Hays turned his Rangers loose on a town that had despised them and let them know it. Too many of the Rangers were adventurers to whom killing was a lust [sweet in savor;][1] far too many had built a racial prejudice into a hatred that justified all crime against anything Mexican. It was war, and they were not yet glutted with war. Hays had managed to stop them from demolishing the entire town, but this morning doorways gaped wide, streets were strewn with household goods, the plaza held pilfered wagons piled high with loot from stores and homes. Only the church, The Skeleton, and the houses of the women of the night like Rosa were left intact; the church, because all of them had a ragtail of religion in them, and Padre Pierre, still shaking from a siege of fever, had crept out of bed and clothed in cassock and biretta had huddled before the door of the house of God. They had walked past the barred gate of the convent grounds, walked past the church, not quite daring.

Aftermath, this morning. Hays and his officers sat around a table in the hall they had made their quarters, waiting breakfast. Major Fortesby's tongue-lashing was a wound that smarted, for this morning they saw it was in great measure justified. More than one of the released prisoners had had to be shot, most of them would do no credit to the Ranger force which took them in. The sack of Matamoros, on November fourth, 1847, was nothing more than a Roman holiday and Hays knew it now.[2]

Which was one of the reasons why he gave careful attention to the young lieutenant from Fort Brown, pleading for the life of one of the guerrillas locked in the *calabozo* and to be hanged in an hour. The other reason was the lovely girl sitting beside Captain Ross, so intriguing with her boldness, so obviously an aristocrat; holding to her calm with an effort in an atmosphere surely shocking to her. Warrener, apologizing to Susanita for the necessary use of English to plead her cause, found it easy to dramatize the ride of the night, calling attention to the dark circles around her eyes which he knew intensified the limpid beauty of them. He skillfully stressed the fact that a brother was in the East and a protégé of Captain Devlin, allowing the impression that if the *don* their father was not for the Americans neither was he against them, letting Hays think that Alvaro had been restricted at home and his youthful sense of adventure played upon by Canales until he ran away with the guerrilla leader. "It cannot matter to you, sir," he finished, "whether one Mexican more lives. It matters a great deal to a family of law-abiding ranchers—a father who is without a son, a mother broken with grief and worry over her firstborn, a sister who sacrificed all things a girl like her holds dear. You know what she has suffered, is suffering right now because of the unconventionality her bravery has forced upon her. I will see that her brother goes home, and I am certain he will stay there, harming no one, profiting by his lesson."

"You missed your profession, lieutenant, you should be a lawyer." Hays's upper lip lifted in a half smile, a curved line of red in a stubble of beard. All of them were bearded and dusty, looking wild and disreputable beside the meticulous finish of Warrener and Ross. Hays drummed fingers on the table, the half dozen men around him whispered together. Hays went on, talking smoothly and swiftly. "As you doubtless know, it is not our custom to take guerrilla prisoners, least of all to carry them with us. This one was a prize, in a way, because his depredations were so—ah, manifold, if I may use the word, his evasion of our traps so clever that he achieved that high ambition of the desperado, a name. He is known as *El Lobo* and a wolf he is, too. He's a bad *hombre*, lieutenant, and I agree with the men that a public execution in a town where he is known would be very beneficial. The other two with him are harmless enough, I believe, and have evidently had their fill of war. Unfortunately a fourth one of this gang whom we particularly wanted, one Cortina, got away. *El Lobo* should be hanged—and high."

"According to the tenets of war, yes." Warrener put fingers on the table and leaned to Hays. "As to his depredations, what would you have done, sir, had you been a young Mexican fighting an enemy who invaded your country? Given a tea party for the Rangers?"

There was argument and counterargument. While Susanita, sitting beside Captain Ross, hands folded in the lap of her black dress, the spun-gold hair combed smooth and lifted above the pretty ears in a flat knot that came to the forehead, now and then raised the fringed eyelashes to give troubled gaze to the uncouth Americans at the table. She did not know that they watched to see those eyes of clear, beautiful green. She thought they must see her in an unfavorable light, sitting here among men and unattended by a woman. Warrener had not told her why he insisted on her coming with him and she was too innocent, too unversed in the ways of the world, too ignorant of the ways of the American men, to even dream of the certainty in his mind—that if Alvaro would be freed it would be because of that most powerful of arguments: the sight of a beautiful girl in distress.

She thought it was Warrener's eloquence which caused Hays to lay his hands on the table with the palms up and give an order which Warrener, taking the stool beside her, told her was that prisoners were to be brought to the hall. "He says if I can get them out of town and to their ranches, all three of them, I can have them," he said.

Breakfast came and Hays shoved it aside, ostensibly to talk to Warrener but in reality to watch the happiness glow in Susanita's face and fill himself with the sweet loveliness of her. The lieutenant's girl by the looks of it, and for a moment the Ranger captain knew envy. He took a gulp of coffee and set the cup impatiently aside. He had small impatient gestures, perhaps because his stature of five feet and eight inches made him seem a boy beside his tall companions. His voice was impatient now also, for he was angry at himself because of his weakness in giving in. "It's your luck, lieutenant, that Matamoros was well stocked with—ah—alcoholics,[3] and my men still in what might be called a passive mood on this, the morning after. You said you had soldiers with you?"

"Twenty-four, sir, outside the door."

"My men are in the plaza and I will give orders that they stay there, and I'll keep the jailers with me here. You should get your prisoners to the fort easily enough and after that it's your problem. Your promise to get them home to their ranches is not questioned." Hays took a swallow of coffee. "I can only hope that neither of us rues this, lieutenant. As I said, two of them are harmless and quite likely to let gratitude at their release turn them into fair citizens, but this girl's brother—I would say in him is the culmination of all the arrogance and dominating importance of the Mexican male to the exclusion of all else. I release him to you against my better judgment."

Susanita's heart leaped high and raced madly when she saw the three prisoners. Carlos del Valle, Monico de Deza—they too! Now indeed she was glad she had come to save these two who had often serenaded her last winter and fought for dances with her. They looked at her in surprise, raised manacled hands to wipe at the dirty unshaven faces, bowed to her across the dozen feet of space separating them, and stood with downcast eyes.

But not so Alvaro. Susanita gave an involuntary gasp at sight of him. Somehow he had managed to shave, his trousers were brushed and his shirt at least half clean. He now wore a long mustache with twirled outstanding ends, sideburns ran down to his ears and his black hair lay back smooth and shiny. His black eyes traveled insolently over the Rangers, passed Warrener as if he were not there, and flung contempt at his sister so plainly that blood diffused her cheeks. What Hays had said about Alvaro fitted him exactly, and Warrener mentally agreed that no good could come of this.

A Ranger told the men in Spanish that they owed their freedom to Susanita and would be paroled to Warrener, to be returned to their homes on the *rancho*. "You understand? You are to stay at home and be good *rancheros* and good citizens."

That Carlos and Monico regarded this as an opening of the gates of Paradise was evident in their faces and a voluble and sincere gratitude tumbled from their lips. Alvaro merely bowed, and Hays had to look again at Susanita to keep from rescinding his order; and when Alvaro asked if he might speak to his sister alone, Hays granted it with bad grace, nodded to Warrener and jerked a thumb at a far corner. He drew the cold breakfast to him and ate, calling himself a fool. Seven kinds of a fool.

Alvaro grasped Susanita's wrists when she stretched hands to him. "No, don't kiss me," he snapped. "When I saw you, *you*, sitting alone in a room of men—how did you come here? When?"

She told him what had happened from the time Pancho came to the *hacienda*, hurt to tears at his manner to her. She had scarcely finished when he flung further indictment at her. "Riding all night alone with a *peon*, you a Mendoza y Soría! Going to a soldier camp, riding with them, consorting with them, alone! Couldn't you let me die instead? It would have been an honor to our name, dying for my people and my country, now you have dishonored us forever."

"Alvaro, no, no!" If he had beaten her with a whip, the pain would not have been as bad. "I had to save you for *papá* who is so lonely for you. Alvaro, when I heard they were going to hang you I—"

"Saw a fine excuse to come to your lover, isn't that it? You needn't lie to me, Susanita. A woman of pride would have been glad to have her brother die, if his living meant her disgrace. You with a lover and a *gringo* lover at that, I could have died of shame before Carlos and Monico."

"That is not true." Anger beat back the tears and she took a step away from him. "It seems to me a poor kind of pride for a woman to let her brother get hanged and not try to prevent it. I was afraid of the night, and I am not used to riding far, and I got so tired I could only bear it by thinking of you, and it was not easy for me to be among men unattended—do you think I did not feel shame, sitting there? Yet I did it gladly, it was all nothing, if I could save you from so dreadful a death. I am so tired now I can scarcely stand and you—you insult me. It is a nice way to say thanks, my brother." She turned from him walked to where Warrener was waiting and asked him to take her away. "Wait, first I must thank the kind *señores*."

Winsomely, charmingly, she thanked Jack Hays, giving him her hand; which he gallantly, and a bit lingeringly, kissed. The rest of the men got quickly to their feet and bowed and she smiled shyly at them. "*Gracias, señores*, and may God keep you and reward you."

The soldiers surrounded the prisoners, Captain Ross took charge, and they clattered down the deserted street to Fort Brown. Warrener helped Susanita onto the horse she had ridden to town, mounted his own, and took the reins from her and lopped them over an arm. He asked her to keep her head down, draw the shawl well forward, and close her eyes. He did not want her to see the houses with the doors closed tightly so they looked like frightened women with arms over their faces, nor those with broken doors showing the emptiness inside. Shouts and scraps of songs came to them and he circled the plaza, coming to a small house facing it from the way of a side street. He rode his horse to a door and knocking on it, calling, "Lieutenant Warrener, *amigos*."

Susanita opened her eyes when arms were around her, a dear voice calling her name over and over. Before she could make sure she wasn't dreaming she was inside lying on a sofa and kind fingers were loosening her bodice and removing her shoes. Inez! "I can't believe it—oh, you look like at least three beautiful angels, Inez. I am so sleepy, and I am afraid to sleep because you won't be here when I waken; will you really be here—are you really here now?"

She was already asleep when Inez answered her.

Later, over hot coffee in the patio, served by Chonita the old duenna of

Inez, the story was told. The laughing girl Susanita knew was still there but womanliness and dignity balanced the old audacity. They recalled that it was a year ago when Inez had jestingly remarked how romantic it would be to be sent to a convent and have Johnny White rescue her. "Only it wasn't a prison to be rescued from, the nuns were so good to me and made things as nice as they could for me," Inez related. "Even the praying on my knees wasn't a punishment because I kept praying for Yon-nay to come. He likes for me to call him Yon-nay because I say it so funny, he says."

When Johnny White found Hays in Mexico, he had received a hard dressing down. Later he was wounded in the left arm and when it stiffened he asked to be discharged. With a companion he managed somehow, in that dangerous area, to get to the convent at Mexico City. The role of knight-errant still pleased him, and he felt a certain duty as she was there by fault of his. White had pictures of chains and dungeons and starvation and his great worry was that he would not get there in time to save her from slow death. The ordered, happy community into which the gate tender ushered him was a surprise to him, as was the courteous reception by the far from stern Mother Superior. And he lied. He said Inez was his wife and he wanted her. Up to then he had not intended marrying her, had only a vague idea of what he would do with her, yet now it seemed the decent and the only thing to do. He would marry Inez and be good to her, he told himself sternly, robing himself with martyred righteousness.

Then when they brought her, the robe dropped away. The more he looked at her the easier it became to call her wife.

"When the Mother took me to him and asked me if I was his wife," Inez told them, "I told them yes before I could even think that it was a lie. In my heart I had been that for so long, you see."

They were married in Mexico City and came to Matamoros by boat. "We came here because I wanted to ask *papá* and *mamá* for forgiveness. They weren't here in the house; none of the *rancheros* are in town this winter, and we were in time to save the house from being broken into by those terrible Rangers. Some of the houses on the plaza were, though Yon-nay did what he could to hold them back; I do not know whether your *papá*'s house was broken into or anything stolen. We looked up Chonita and she was glad to come and look after me. So here we are in *papá*'s house and we have sent a letter to the *rancho*. You know *papá* is not hard inside, and they have no one but me. We are very happy, Yon-nay and me."

With rare tact Inez refrained from asking Susanita personal questions until she should volunteer information herself. Warrener had sent a note to Johnny White while Susanita was preparing her toilet in a hastily pre-pared tent at the fort, sketching the situation and telling him Susanita would be brought to Inez after they had seen Hays. While Susanita slept, White told Inez what had occurred in the hall as he had heard it from Warrener, adding, "Bob says that *El Lobo*—how I'd like to punch his nose!—evidently said some nasty things to his sister and she is upset more than she shows"— so prattled on about herself and finally had her reward in a relaxation of Susanita's still wan face, with now and then even a bit of laughter.[4]

"He says I must learn English, and already I can say 'geeve me a kees.' We are going to San Antonio, Señor McLane is going to make a paper with news and Yon-nay is going to work for him. He says we will be poor, but we will have enough to eat, and I tell him then that I would rather have only half enough to eat and be with him than have everything with someone else. Chonita is so shocked when he pulls my hair down or sets me on the mantel. She says that is American crudeness and not the con-duct of a gentleman." Inez rose. "Come, you need more rest and I will take a little *siesta*. He is the man for me because we are both a little wild; you are a lady and sweet and you will be happiest with one who is always a gentleman. Come, sleep now."

Susanita did not sleep. The world outside, noisy with the exodus of the Rangers back to Mexico, was shut away by the thick walls of the house, and there was only silence to background her thoughts. Already the events of the night and the morning were receding and the future stood before her, looking at her with grave eyes. She saw Alvaro and the line of cruelty on his contemptuous lips; only the shadow of it had been there before he left to go to Canales. Sensuousness mastered the handsome face, and she shivered now as she remembered the repulsion she had felt when she put her arms out to him. Was it possible that her departure from convention could outweigh its results? Surely her father could not think so; her father could not think evil of her as Alvaro had. But she would have to tell him everything from the beginning, how else would he know. Yes, she would have to go home, she saw that plainly. She would not have to marry Gabriel now, and perhaps when she told *papá* how Roberto had pleaded—it could be. He might accept Roberto, then. He would love her again, and they would all be so happy again.

Warrener came, and Johnny White, while there was still sun in the pa-tio. All of Inez's clothes had been left in the town house, and Susanita felt

273

much better in the blue-flowered ruffled dress Inez gave her. She blushed when White kissed her hand and gave her his devil-may-care smile, and blushed again when she looked at Warrener's blue coat and remembered how her head had lain against it. Then quickly Inez and her husband were out of sight, and it was just as she had known it would be: her hands held tightly, the dear face close, the warm voice telling her how much he loved her and begging her to go with him to Padre Pierre. "I have talked with him often, and he will marry us even if your father does not consent. Dearest, the only person you owe anything to now is yourself—" Over and over, the old pleadings a man uses to gain the woman he loves.

Perhaps if Alvaro had not said that she used his plight as an excuse to go to her lover she might have surrendered to the haven of his arms. But that had to be disproved. If she stayed she would put truth to the words and that she could not bear. "I feel that I must see *papá*, Roberto. And *mamá* and dear Tía Dolores and Angela, and Paz too, must be told how it was. Then I must tell them how fine José was, *papá* must know that. I was raised to think that *peons* do not matter, but I see differently now. I—I guess I grew into a woman on that ride, Roberto. I am not the same. If I were that same girl, I would be too frightened to leave you—and then I would cry for a long time and not always be the happy wife you should have. Do you see?" She told him about Gabriel and the wedding dress, talking fast, she would not voice the insistent plea: "Keep me here, don't let me go. *Mamá* and tía will understand and *papá*—it is you now, not *papá*. Keep me, hold me." She finished by saying, "If *papá* should insist that I marry Gabriel, if it is possible that he could, I will get very sick. Angela would help me pretend, I think *Tía* would too."

"And then? What then [sweet?],[5]" Warrener smiled to hearten her. He knew how the high-class Mexican families raised their daughters, beset with inhibitions and all independence snuffed out before it could grow. Duenna-ed and chaperoned, until aloneness left them both bewildered and oppressed with guilt. The few that braved the iron-bound conventions brought swift punishment and even death upon themselves unless a twist of circumstance saved them. Particularly was this true on a tightly knit group like the *rancheros*, who made a fetish of the old ways. He could guess what Alvaro said to her, and he was terribly afraid that Don Santiago would take the same view. But he knew that if she did not go back, she would never be wholly content or free from the feeling that she should have done differently. If she stayed, certainly her father would refuse to have anything to do with her; she would always think that, had she gone home, love and forgiveness, even reward, would have awaited her. He could let her go safely enough, as José had promised to get word to him if there was distress, and he felt certain that the managerial, homely, and altogether grand Aunt Dolores would protect her niece.

"Then?" Her face was troubled. "I do not know, *querido*. You will help me to get home? You won't, please, ask me to stay any more. It only makes it harder."

He kissed a palm and doubled the fingers over it. "There will be a carriage for you, early in the morning. Now I have a surprise for you."

He called "Come on, good-for-nothing." There were running feet, a cry, and a small cyclone hit Susanita.

"Manuelito!" She pushed him away to look at him and the urchin swelled with importance, drew himself erect, and saluted smartly. Manuel in a fitted uniform brave with shiny buttons, boots on his feet, so clean it was beyond belief. Then he had to show off his accomplishments and carried on a conversation with his lieutenant in English. "I can write it too, *niña*, and read. What do you think of that, Manuel reading *inglés*. Not much yet but I learn fast."

"I think you are lying to me," she smiled, "for you are much, much too thick in the head. Your grandmama was glad to get your letter, Manuel; it made her very happy."

At mention of Paz tears ran down the dark cheeks, but Manuel stood his ground and forced his lips into a smile. He was not going to throw himself upon Susanita and cry out his homesick love for grandmama Paz, for he was a man and a soldier. He stepped back a little more to put temptation further away. "Tell her not to worry, but tell her I love her and— hope I see her—sometime. You will, *niña?*"

Here too, she was thinking, is one who had courage to take what he wanted, and he still a child. And then she thought,—but it is taking more courage to go back than to stay. "I will tell her how proud I am of you and she will be proud too, Manuelito. I will tell her how fine you look, and had boots on, and were so clean I could eat you like candy."

Warrener had to be in camp before dark and he had first to see about a carriage, so he and his "bodyguard," as he called Manuel, prepared soon to leave. Alvaro, he told Susanita, had been sent home in the morning, but he did not tell her that Alvaro, from a gold case he had managed to secrete from the Rangers, threw a coin in the dust to pay for the old nag they gave him, though the animal was in exchange for the mustang of José's, still too lame to be ridden. Warrener had taken a chance on Alvaro's insolent: "You have the word of a Mendoza y Soría that I ride immediately to my father's *rancho*." It is not the word as much as the certainty that Alvaro, as well as the other two, were most anxious to show themselves to their families.

So parting once more, somewhat formally. Warrener was aware that with the Mexicans kissing before marriage was considered immoral, but he would have broken down that barrier—if he could have trusted himself to let her go, when once his lips touched hers. She had begged him not to go to the ranch with her as his presence would compromise her, so in the morning all he could do was look at the carriage as it went past the fort. Conventions, suspicions, restrictions, and nothing to be done about it. Soldiers to flank her conveyance, José beside the driver, and he who loved her—he bit his lip to keep back the words which would have shamed him before her. He would have all night to excoriate fate.

"I trust I will see you soon, Susanita. *Adios.*"

"God keep you and thank you for your kindness."

(I should be making her stay, I'm a fool to let her go.)

(I wish he would not listen to me, and would hold me so I could never, never get away.)

"*Adios . . . Adios.*"

Chapter 30

The *sala* was a judgment hall. Besides the light from the fire, candles flickered in the sconces on the walls and in the silver sticks on the mantel, converging their illumination on the high-backed ancestral chair where sat Don Santiago like a king upon his throne. As if, Doña Dolores thought impatiently, a person had not even the right to the shadows to decently cover their emotions. She sat on her favorite stool which she had moved to directly face the master, in a vague notion that so she could take the brunt of what should come from him; playing her crochet hook with a certain nonchalance, moving her lips silently to count the stitches swelling the lace that snaked whitely over the black lap. Beside her on a low chair sat Susanita, hands in her lap, drawing composure from her aunt and holding her head high, keeping her face immobile. Doña María Petronilla and Angela occupied a bench by the fire, Angela with an arm around her mother. Alvaro, as was his right, stood behind the chair which he as heir would occupy some day, only his roving black eyes betraying his impatience.

And outside the closed door, ear pressed close, crouched old Paz.

The silence, accentuated rather than broken by the crackling fire, hung in the room like a presage of doom.

Finally Don Santiago stirred, and in a flat, hard voice said, "So your lover the *gringo* would not marry you after all, isn't that true?"

"No, *papá*, none of the things you think are true." Susanita kept her composure, though blood welled hot in her cheeks. Angela had told her what had been said after Alvaro came home so she was not too unprepared. "The Señor Warrener loves me but he is not—my lover. He pleaded with me to stay and marry him, and when I told him I had to come here, he wanted to come with me. He is—is honorable." This was not right, this was not at all as she had pictured it. She had believed that she would be asked first to tell the full story, and it would be interspersed with their love and praise. But this judgment, this accusation, thrown at her before she could speak—how could he be so unjust?

"I know about the *gringos* and their honor," Alvaro sneered. He was dressed in his most elaborately braided and silver-trimmed suit, the mustache shiny black on the clean-shaven face. "A remarkable behavior, yours. You ride all night with one who, though he be *peon*, is still a man. Then you perform a toilet at a soldier camp, ride into town not with one but two of their officers, then sit in a hall where more men, and the worst of them, the Rangers, can look at you. Doubtless you remembered the hall, scene of your first disgrace, when you danced with a *gringo*."

(O yes, she had remembered. She had closed her eyes and heard the music and the singing of the birds, had seen herself in the green velvet gown and the emeralds, had felt again the thrill of Roberto's fingers for the first time.)

"Then he puts you where it best pleases him to have you, and he comes to the camp alone so he can send me and Carlos and Monico away. You stay the day and the night in town, I suppose, no one knows where, and come home alone in a carriage with a soldier escort. Exactly like a mistress."

Anger struggled with tears, and won. She took a small pleasure in telling him, "I stayed at the Sánchez home, with Inez. I was so tired I could have died."

"Inez!" said Alvaro as Don Santiago echoed, "Inez—how comes Inez in Matamoros in her father's home?"

Perversely, she told them only, "She is married. He went to the convent after her. She is very, very happy."

Alvaro bit a lip. Injured pride was born again, all the stronger because Inez was the better off for refusing him, and he struck at his sister to heal his pride. "This Warrener, then, came to see you in the house of a woman—like Inez." The inference in his words was plain, his sneer ugly.

Tortured over the shame piled upon her, Susanita said, "Señor Warrener is not like you think."

"Between a male saint and a female saint build a stone wall," Don Santiago quoted a Spanish proverb.

"Why are you this way?" Susanita rose and held out her hands to her father, tears running down her cheeks. "*Papá*, why do you sit there and call me names and let Alvaro insult me when I endured humiliation to save him? I did it for you, and for *mamá*, not for myself. It was so very hard for me. Now when I saved him and Carlos and Monico too, you treat me as if I had committed a crime. I come home and only Paz comes to greet me, *mamá* and *Tía* and Angela are afraid to talk to me, I am scarcely allowed any rest before you call me here to—to say dirty, mean, horrid things to me."

"Sit down. Wipe your face and stop crying." Don Santiago's eyes passed from one to the other of his womenfolk, and sadness was heavy in his voice. "A true lady, Susanita, knows that her honor must be kept unsoiled above all else, because it belongs also to her family, is part of a proud name and the first obligation to the master of the house. Death is nothing, be it for herself or for another, if she but save her honor. Alvaro's death, regardless of its manner, would have been a glory to our name as against the shame you have put upon it by dragging it in the dust."

Doña Dolores could stand it no longer and flung out an acidulous: "It is easy for Alvaro to prattle of preferring death when he is very much alive and safe; and enjoying it too, I notice, by wearing his finest clothes and acting important. Easy for you, Santiago, when he is here with you. You men are always so noble when it costs you nothing."

Don Santiago struck a fist on the chair arm and shouted, "Will you keep quiet; I see where she gets her waywardness, Dolores, from you! Another word and out of the house you go. I have endured you for too many years." He spilled the overflow of his anger on Susanita. "I cannot believe otherwise than you took the opportunity to see this lover of yours a last time before you married Gabriel, trusting that the freeing of your brother would cover your shame. Not only I, but all our friends, will believe that when the *gringo* saw your public shamelessness, he refused to marry you. Else why did you come? I am amazed that you should be so lacking in sensibility as to show your face to us again."

Susanita looked at Doña Dolores, drawing comfort from the love and faith reflected there. "I thought it was the right thing to do," she answered steadily. "I did not think of what you call my honor, *papá*, because I knew there was no need to. The *Americanos* thought I was very brave, and they gave me a respect and courtesy Alvaro would not understand. There are men, *papá*, against whom a girl need not be chaperoned. I am sorry you only know the—the other kind. And it would have hurt Don Gabriel too badly if he did not know how it all was, and there was nobody but me to tell of it."

"You have already hurt him beyond repair. Even if he still would marry you, I would forbid it, I would not give my best friend a girl put up to mockery the rest of her life; a wife always to be sneered at, the parentage of her firstborn doubted. Your honor, Susanita, was also mine, and that of the man to whom you were promised. You took what was not only yours and mine, but his also."

Susanita could see, they all could see the picture; women whispering, secure in their guarded virtue; men shrugging, smiling knowingly. Looking for evil, wanting to see and believe it, finding it even when they knew it did not exist, building it from the rottenness in their hearts.

That inexorably, was the thing that long custom had made law. Ironically, the Mexican *caballero* gave stern codes of honor to his women—waiting but the chance to dishonor them. He made an inflexible law of chaperonage, to protect them from himself. No woman exposed herself alone to the public, that was the law, and when she did expose herself she announced to the world that she belonged to men. Not Don Santiago himself, not one of the men he knew, had they been in Warrener's place, would have given Susanita respect, regardless of the circumstances. It was inconceivable to him that she could have put that in the background, deep as her concern might have been. Carlos and Monico would thank her, but they would not marry her. A man might do what he pleases and hold his head high among his fellows. Let the bound and hedged thing he put on his women and called not only theirs but his honor; let him see a blemish there, though it existed but in his imagining, and she must suffer.

In Susanita's case it was unthinkable that men of an inferior race, as the Americans were viewed, could treat a girl with greater courtesy and gentleness than a Mexican *caballero*. Her staying with Inez clinched the last doubt. Inez was bad, and that the accursed Ranger married her only angered him the more, for it was not what his son would have done; no wife for Alvaro touched with the breath of scandal, though it had been of his own making. It was true that Don Santiago would have preferred his son to be hanged rather than have his daughter do what Susanita had done, even though her motive was completely unselfish—which he did not, and could not, believe. And, added shame, a *gringo*. A low *gringo*.

Honor! It was a fetishism. It was a weapon in the hand of the master, to keep his woman enslaved, and his fingers had twisted upon it so tightly he could not let go.

It was Doña Dolores who answered. She kept on crocheting, very slowly, a contemplative, half-smiling look on her face, her voice softly soothing.

"Do you remember, Santiago, how everyone was ready to criticize and ridicule you the morning after Susanita danced with the *Americano?* You made them think she had done the right thing by standing your ground. You could do that again. You have the power and position, are looked upon as a leader. Santiago, you could say: 'Susanita did a brave thing, more than most girls would do. Travel is so unsafe that brave men keep off the trails, but she rode even in the night with only a weak *peon* for protection. She never once thought of herself; she thought only of her brother and humiliated herself in public because she loved her father and wanted to give him his son. The rules and laws we have made did not count when she could save her loved ones from death and sorrow. Nor do they count for me. I am proud of her. I have the finest, bravest daughter a man ever had.' Then, Santiago, you could go further and reward her by letting her marry the man she loves and tell your friends that you consider the happiness of your children of greatest importance. You could accept him and, in time, find good in him, at least enough to take joy in your grandchildren.

"At first much would be said against you, but it would not be for long. As I said, you have the power and position and they would follow you; the few who did not would not matter. Gabriel would understand. I think he would feel proud of her. And I am sure in his heart Gabriel is uneasy now because he knows Susanita does not want him, and if he was told she loves another, he would step back. Before you do anything hasty, Santiago, consider what I have said."

Yes. Yes, he could do that. The weights on his heart snapped off and it lifted, pulsing warmly again. He looked at Susanita and saw the child he loved, who loved him in return. If he remained firm, all stigmas would be removed from her and fade away, for he was looked to for guidance. What he did, what he said, would be accepted. He would not need to see Warrener often, would need to condone him only in part. "It is not my will, *señores*, I recognized a Higher Force and bowed to it." Yes, he could do that. He was the leader and they would follow him.

They would follow him.

It was like a great voice thundering. It was lightning striking the house Doña Dolores had built, driving it into bits of kindling. Another would excuse his daughter or sister for a lesser reason than the saving of a brother; and then another, until the law was broken. The law had stood during the years because it was a good, a right law. Susanita's remission began when she danced with the enemy and he had not punished her. He was certain now that she had seen Warrener again; perhaps there had been notes. Sanctioning this marriage would be sanctioning indecorum. If he pleaded his daughter's love, it would break a father's control over his daughter's marriage—where would the proud Mendoza line be if love had been considered? Susanita's very beauty came from a grandmother who had loved one less worthy than the Mendoza she had been ordered to marry. It was like a house. No matter how strongly built the house, one could not tear out a corner of it and expect the house to stand. One by one, then, the old things, the good things, would begin to go, and it was to preserve them that there had been the trek to this Indian-infested wilderness a hundred years before. Rancho La Palma was built on them, the *hacienda* mortared with them.

They would follow him.

He was the bulwark against the encroachments of alien ways. He had to give example, unbending, though his heart might break—ah, *Cristo*, the pain in it now! Pain spread in him until it seemed his body had been emptied of its organs to make room for it. *Cristo*, Thy crown of thorns; Thy heavy cross; Thy five wounds—Thy agony—.

You are women, he thought, when his wife's anguished sobs filled the silence, and he saw the tears running down his sister's cheeks. You can have the relief of showing your misery. Even that is denied me, I must be the stern patriarch, unfeeling, as if I had no father's heart. You are weak women, and do not know how blessed it is to be weak. Then, soon, the patriarch administered the anesthetic of righteousness. The fact that Susanita alone was not weeping but was sitting upright, gripping her hands to brace herself for what might come, showed her guilt; were she innocent she would be the picture of abjection, would even be on her knees pleading with him. Guilt was brazen. There was the law, he the judge, she the culprit. He had a duty which must be followed. Now.

He said slowly, evenly. "You have forfeited your rights as a daughter, Susanita, but I am not cruel. You may stay here in the *hacienda* if you wish, but you will be given a room away from the family, and you may not eat at the table with them or sit with them or show yourself to a guest. If a servant brings you food, that may be, but if none does, you must go to the kitchen and get it. If your mother and Dolores and Angela speak to you when I am gone, it will be against my wishes, and I myself will never see you or speak to you again. Or you may leave the *hacienda* and go where you will, but the doors are forever closed to you. Did you hear and understand?"

Susanita did not allow silence to tear at them. She rose and stepped into the pool of light before the large chair, head high, arms hanging straight against the plain dark dress. All of the childlike happiness, the laughter and sweetness, had dropped from her as if it had been a shawl held together with a hand. In its place was a new dignity that made her a woman, all through with childish things. Nor was there a tremor in her voice when she told her father:

"Tía Dolores has already told you what I wished to say. There are many more things I would like to say, but even though you no longer see me as a daughter, I still see you as a father; I will not say them. Only one—that Roberto would have made you a better son than the one who stands beside you. You have wronged and insulted me and for what? To keep it hard for other girls. It is hard, to be watched and watched every minute and never have anything to say about what one likes or wants. It looks right to you, but it is not always right. Your door is closed against me, you say. But mine, *papá*, will always be open to you."

She turned and walked out of the sala. Click-click, the narrow heels played a tune on the tile floor. Unfalteringly she walked, and the door magically opened for her and closed behind her with a sharp snap. Heels that had danced so happily on the tiles, had run so lightly across them to the high chair so their wearer could kiss the man sitting on it, and tell him how much she loved him.

Click-click, tapped the heels, gouging into the heart of Don Santiago. But he sat still, only his fingers curling tight around the chair arm. A single tear, round and sparkling, ran from an eye and spread its bitter salt over tight lips.

Doña María Petronilla stole out like a footless ghost, Angela, a shadow behind her. There was the scolding friction of Doña Dolores's skirts, the tramp of Alvaro's boots.

Don Santiago de Mendoza y Soría sat alone in the high-backed chair, like a king upon his throne. Until the fire coaled, and grayed to ash. Until the candles on the mantle and in the wall sconces burned low, and sputtered, and threw up a last high flame; one by one until the last one died, and left the *sala* to darkness.

Paz had Susanita by an arm and whisked her to a black corner of the patio where she whispered: "*Niña*, I heard everything. I knew what was coming, I suffered under your grandfather, and I knew what your father would say, I knew it so well that I already arranged everything, when José came and you were in your room resting. I will tell you about José. He came to tell your father he was sorry, but his great concern for Alvaro had driven out all thought of wrong; he had a stupid mind and so could think of only one thing at a time. He would take whatever was his due, even if it was banishment from Rancho La Palma. There was a cart ready to fall to pieces and a team of oxen so old their service was long past; if his master would give them to him, he and Tecla would go if it was their master's will that he should not be a bad example." Paz sniffed audibly. "I listened, I heard him. He made it sound as if it would kill him to go, and your father agreed that an example had to be made before the servants. *Ay, ay*, I could have laughed when he said, 'Yes, José, go away. I will give you the cart and the oxen, and I hope things will not be too hard for you.' José and Tecla have been wanting to go to the red *Americano*, Alfredo's godfather. He wants José to look after his horses and drive his coach for him. It was a good excuse for José."

"What has that to do with me?" Susanita asked impatiently.

"Everything. After what you told me about Manuel when you got out of the carriage, my heart tore itself from me and flew down there to him, and my old body must go after it. Estéban also wishes to go away now that Alvaro is home, so I had him tell Victorino to have a wagon at the cotton-woods at first cockcrow; I know Victorino will if he knows it is my wish. You and I will be there waiting for it, to go to the *jacal* where we leave with José and Tecla. For Matamoros, if God gives us a safe journey."

"Oh Paz, yes!" Susanita kissed the old nurse impulsively. "It will be safe because there are no Indians now, and we will look too poor for anyone to bother us. But my dresses—Paz, I would feel naked, going to a man with only what I had on my back." Partings, misery, humiliations were already receding before the prospect of, at last, going to the beloved one who was watching and waiting for her.

"A *maleta* is already in your room. I told you I arranged everything. Go now, fill the sack with your clothes, say good-bye and meet me here. That will already be midnight, the first cockcrow, Don't cry, *niña*, it is better this way."

"I am through with crying, Paz. I will be here."

All the women were in Susanita's room when she came there, and Angela bolted the door. Susanita ran to her mother's open arms, holding her close. María Petronilla stroked the golden hair and murmured, "We think you were very brave and fine, little one. We know your Roberto, and your father does not. Do not judge your father, he has only done what he saw as his duty. You had better go, though my soul weeps as I tell you to. Only I shall insist that he sends you down in the coach and—"

"No, *mamá*." She drew away, kissed Doña Dolores and Angela, pulled the sack from under the bed and told them what Paz had done. "You know *papá* would object to Juan Bautista driving me away in the coach, and there would only be more trouble. It is better that I am simply gone. Nothing will happen and Roberto will be waiting for me."

The mother smiled, lifting her anguish with the knowledge that Susanita would be happy. Luis Gonzaga was gone—and stayed with her. Susanita would go—and always be here. "We will be happy now, *hija*." she said. "Angela, help your sister fold her dresses. Dolores, come with me."

They left the room and Susanita took clothes from the chest and laid them on the bed. The *maleta*, a sack made of canvas with an opening in the middle so an equal portion would hang on each side of a saddle, was put over a chair. "You can have my trousseau," Susanita said lightly as they folded and stuffed clothes into the sack. "Will it be José Luis or the redhaired *señor*? Oh, Angela, not both of us with *Americanos* for husbands, surely! But he is nice."

Angela grasped her sister's hand and whispered: "You will see the Señor McLane sometime. Tell him I have decided, but I must wait yet awhile until God shows me just what to do. He will, I know. Why not both of us married to *Americanos?* They are for us the best men. *Papá* refused me the convent, so he will have to take what comes."

Susanita nodded. She had often said that Angela had the stronger will, and now her words and the firmness of the rounded chin proved it. She took that chin in her hand now. "Angela, do you love him? There must be love to be really happy. Do you?"

"Love?" Angela's eyes were wide. "He has not asked for it. I like and respect him, as he does me. I do not think we will need what you call love to make a successful marriage. We are different, the Señor McLane and I."

"I will tell him. Yes, I can see where you do not need the things I do, but you do need others I do not—listen to how mixed up I am! I hope it will not be too hard for you with—with *papá*." She kissed Angela and they held each other, for the first time in their lives feeling a truly sisterly love binding them.

The women returned and Doña María Petronilla put a cloth-wrapped bundle in Susanita's arms. "It would please me if you would wear my wedding dress after all, and my veil. I will be able to picture you as a bride, then."

Doña Dolores pressed a box into her niece's hand. "From me the emeralds, *chiquita*. You know they belong to the women of the family and are mine. I got them from your father to give to you as a wedding present, and I must say I give them with greater pleasure now that there is a different bridegroom. I never wore them, for emeralds do not suit me, I had the feeling they did not like me."

"I could not take them now, *Tía*." Susanita did cry after all and let a tear splash on Doña Dolores's hand. "It may not be safe, keep them for awhile. I—I—what can I say to thank you? And, *mamá*, this time I will put the dress on—so happily. Thank you, *mamá*."

Soon Paz came, scolding and grumbling to cover her emotions. It was time to go. She put the huge sausages of sack on her shoulders so none could embrace her, scolding so nothing more could be said. In truth the old woman was torn to shreds at leaving this her home where she had served so long and been nurse to its children. The old roots, she told herself determinedly, would grow in a new soil. Her baby here needed her to get to her mate; little Manuel was motherless. Old Paz saw the path pointed out to her by what she believed was a Divine finger and unhesitatingly, without a glance backward, set her foot upon it.

Old Paz, the likes of whom the angel records in a book of gold, thought Doña Dolores. But she said, as the door closed, "Stubborn old fool!"

They knew what she meant. And sat on the chest, the three of them, to weep for the two the night was swallowing. To weep for themselves, in the lonely days that were to come.

Chapter 31

It was noon when the old cart, clumping up and down on the spindle that served for axle in the hole of the solid wood wheel worn large by count- less miles of friction, creaking and complaining, oxen plodding stolidly forward on trembling old legs, crawled past Fort Brown. Dust was a veil over the three women crouched on the sacks in the cart, dust covered the ragged *peons* lifting bare feet in the shuffle of weariness. Not for worlds would Susanita have had Warrener see her as she was, and pulled the *rebozo* over her face as soldiers poked at the sacks. They were allowed to go on, and while the oxen drank deeply of the river, José and Estéban stood and dug toes in the wet sand, grinning like small boys. Watching closely as they went on and water lapped the cart bed for it would, they fatalistically agreed, be just like the oxen to give out and the cart fall to pieces in the middle of the stream. But they came out safely, wound through the chap- arral, crept past forlorn *jacals* of thatch, past small adobe houses where women eyed them curiously from doorways, naked children clinging to their skirts. Finally the narrow street, ankle deep in dust, joined the plaza, and the cart clumped past the homes of the de Bacas, the Carbajals, the Mendoza y Sorías—to arrive at last, all praise be to God and His saints, at the end of the journey.

They had met with a party of six Americans who asked them where they were going, and José proudly showed the paper Red McLane had given him, embellished with a seal and stating that here passed a faithful servant who was not to be molested. The man read and passed on. Estéban had cunningly forestalled a band of Mexican renegades by running toward them and asking for help. "A cruel master has driven us away, and we have nei- ther food nor money, nothing but straw in sacks, so my sick daughter and crippled old mother can know little comfort. We are in a sad plight, *amigos*, and crave your help." It worked well, for the renegades rode on, Susanita setting up a pitiful moaning to give full color to the story. Estéban had suggested that they dress as raggedly as possible and they did, indeed, present too poverty-stricken and pitiful a picture to incite covetousness.

Now the years of days, the endless plains, were behind them at last. Paz went to the door, lifted the knocker and banged it hard.

Chonita opened the door and screamed for Inez. The woman went inside, and the cart with the two men crawled to the corral in the rear.

Lieutenant Warrener was dismounting from his horse when Johnny White, late of the Rangers, rode into the compound and beckoned to him. Johnny's face was all smiles as he said, "I brighten what's left of your day, Bob. Susanita is at the house, waiting for you. It's for good, this time."

The joy on Warrener's face quickly changed to apprehension. "You're not just having fun, Johnny? I've watched the road—are you telling me the truth? Is she all right? What happened? Did her father throw her out? I was afraid he would, I shouldn't have let her go." He swung back into the saddle. "Wait till I report to Major Fortesby before—"

"Wait a minute now. Listen—" White told him of Inez's fear that something would happen again to keep the lovers apart. While Susanita drank hot chocolate, she told Inez everything that had happened, down to the parting with her mother and the wedding dress given to her. When Susanita had bathed and was asleep, Inez spread out her dresses, and when the white satin and the veil shimmered on the bed, Inez could wait no longer. She called her husband and told him:

"Those two will sit and sigh and hold hands and let days go by because it's decorous to wait to get married, or some other reason just as foolish. You go and see Padre Pierre, Yon-nay, tell him everything, and arrange the wedding for this evening. I think right before sunset will be nice, don't you? I'll get everything ready and wake her in time to get her dressed to get married, and bring Manuel too, of course. I'm sure you won't have to drag him."

Sheer joy glorified Warrener's face as White finished. He wanted to shout, to dance, to do a dozen silly things, but all he did was clasp his friend's hand and say, somewhat huskily, "Thanks, Johnny. Tell Captain Ross to get the carriage set up, will you? You know I had to buy it to send Susanita home, and it's here, and coming in very nicely. Send me Coley and get Manuel shined up, if I'm not asking too much of you. And—and thanks again, Johnny."

Padre Pierre and Warrener had become fast friends, the Virginian filling the gap which Devlin had left, the priest in turn a solace to Warrener in his pointless existence. It is not the easiest part of war to pass endless days at an unimportant post like this one of Fort Brown. Padre Pierre favored this marriage because he was certain of the belief he had expounded to Devlin—that the house of Mendoza y Soría had reached its ultimate in the present generation, and must inevitably go downward unless new and vigorous blood were united with it. There would be no beauties, artists, women with the spiritual strength of Angela, men with leadership and intelligence—nothing but the ordinary and perhaps even less, if they married in their correspondingly weakened group of acquaintances. To the good *padre*, God had sent this fine young man here and put Susanita in his path, and given them a great love because it filled a plan of betterment. When Johnny White came to him, he agreed without hesitation that the marriage be performed at once. He would, he said, have everything ready at sundown.

Susanita, bewildered, finally gave herself over to the ministering hands. Paz twisted strands of the shiny clean hair around hot pokers, "You know your *mamá* loves curls, so you must have them, and be sure to tell her when you write." Chonita heated the ponderous irons and pressed the dress and petticoats and veil. Inez rubbed oil on the hands and face, drawn with the dust and wind and neglect of the long trip. It seemed so unreal, so like the fringe of a nightmarish dream. She would waken any minute and find herself dressed in wedding finery—to marry Gabriel. Then forebodings came: Perhaps what *papá* said was true, and Roberto did not want her now; Padre Pierre would scorn to marry them; Roberto was sick or had been moved: Roberto would not get here, someone would kill him; Yon-nay had been killed on the way—.

The last curl was in place, the veil ruched and pinned, the white satin flowing in shirrings and soft folds to the floor. It was beautiful and right—everything would always be right, now that Roberto was here. She touched his hand to see if he were real, and when he smiled down at her she blushed. "Did you look for me, Roberto? Suppose I had not come?"

"I would have come after you. Come now, beloved."

Paz refused to ride in the carriage and hurried ahead with Chonita. Warrener sat beside Susanita, Inez and her husband facing them, Coley on the driver seat; Captain Ross rode the left and, bursting with pride, Manuel the right flank, shaking his boots so the shiny new spurs on them could jingle, to the delight of the dozen soldiers bringing up the rear. Padre Pierre was standing at the church, greeted them warmly, and to Susanita's great delight opened the church door, where candle flames waved a welcome from the gloom of the altar.

She clapped her hands. "Oh, *padre*, you will marry me in the church, really?"

"Why not? It is your church, and that is where marriages should be performed. You certainly look like a bride, my child." He smiled at them all, shook a finger at Manuel, stopped to whisper to Paz that God would reward her for her unselfishness, and led the way into the church.

Paz, her face of wrinkled leather screwed up comically with excitement, smoothed out the dress which she had smoothed for María Petronilla, so long ago; grumbling under her breath at the poor fit and the streak where the hem had been let down; bringing the veil a little further forward, deploring the plain white rosary in the bride's hands. Warrener so tall in his fitted uniform, stepped beside his bride, and they walked after the priest who was garbed in black cassock and white surplice, a biretta on his graying hair. Behind them, the Whites, Inez in a dress of dull blue and a white *mantilla* over her hair. Paz and Chonita. Captain Ross, Coley, Manuel. A poor wedding party for a daughter of the house of Mendoza—if one did not count the abundance of love. Doorways facing the church emptied, loafers converged, and a goodly crowd emanated by curiosity filed into the church, gaping and whispering.

Susanita heard her voice repeating words after Padre Pierre, heard Roberto echo them. Padre Pierre raised his voice and said, "I pronounce thee man and wife."

He blessed them, and it was over. She was Señora Warrener, until death should part them.

In the rectory where they signed the record book, Padre Pierre told Susanita: "This has been a happy task for me. While it is regrettable that your father does not approve, do not let that be a cloud over you, child. Saint Paul says, 'Leave thy father and mother and cleave to thy wife', and that is the way of life, Susanita. Your duty lies with this man, and you must give him laughter and not tears; you must not weep for what has gone, not ever."

"Yes, father, I understand. Thank you."

Not tears, any more. She had been washed clean of the pangs of separation and homesickness by tears on the slow journey by ox cart, by the valiant example of old Paz. New life was flowing in her, the future spreading richer, fuller, before her. No, not tears. Not any more.

Susanita was writing home, sitting at a table on the porch at the rear of the little house. She had been married a week: "—there are times where I really feel quite sedate," she had written. Now she looked at the misty blue of the distant hills. She could not tell them at home that the house was small with a hastily tacked on room for Paz, scantily furnished with what the town afforded, and too close to the camp to have much privacy. "We are very comfortable in a nice house, and we are very happy; I am busy hemming linens. Paz grumbles more than ever so you know she is not unhappy. Roberto has the coach for her whenever she wants to go to Mass, but she feels very uncomfortable when she rides alone, even when Manuel is with her. Manuel studies very hard and we are all proud of him. I went to Mass on Sunday and prayed for all of you." She put down the pen and looked at the hills again. It would not do to add that several of the *rancheros* were in town and the Señora de Olivares had looked right through her, and Lolita Viscaya had walked very primly past her. *Papá* would approve, but in his heart he would be very angry at them. "Inez's *papá* and *mamá* forgave her and are in town now, and they are all going to the *rancho* awhile before the Señor White goes to his work in San Antonio." It was better to say no more, *papá* would not like to hear that they were all very happy and had been very nice to the Warreners too; *papá* would feel too hard against Inez's father, Don Eulalio. There were so many things she wanted to write. She wanted to say: "Señor McLane is here and is talking with Roberto, I can hear their voices. I am beginning to like him very much, and I can see that he is a great man." It would not do at all to write that. She laid down the pen and listened awhile; she was learning English, and it pleased her fancy to try to catch a few familiar words. She knew they would tell her what they were saying if she asked them, so felt no guilt in listening.

"You like it here," Red McLane was saying. "You like the country and you like the Mexican people when they give you a chance to. You don't want to take Susanita too far away from her people and that's a good idea, for even if she doesn't see them, it's kind of being with them because it's familiar around here. The war won't last long now, and you say you can get out of the army when it's over. You have money, buy up land around here. It is inevitable that a town will be built on this side of the river. Fort Brown will be kept up—don't ask me how I know, loot'nant; it's my business to know—and there'll be a need of houses, army men aren't going to leave their families at the other end of the country. A lot of the houses of the Mexicans in Matamoros are in bad shape and the younger *rancheros* will build their winter homes on this side of the *río*, and a good store will make money too. You might as well get in on the ground floor and be one of the new town's founders. Buy up the land so you can sell it again at a profit, get help to lay out a town, and start building your house. You'll have to, in a way; you can't keep Susanita living here any longer than you have to, and you certainly aren't going to build in Mexico. Matamoros is never going to get anywhere, and that old circle of diehards will snub Susanita to the last; besides, you're American. There's a future here for you. Grab it, is my advice."[1]

"There's a lot in what you say," came Roberto's voice, "I want to take Susanita to Virginia later when she knows English and can enjoy talking to the people there; my folks must see her and she them. I'll talk it over with her."

Susanita wrote: "The Americanos are very peculiar in many ways, but they are nice and show me much courtesy. Their food still tastes queer to me, but I am getting to like it, though Paz cooks for herself because she says her tongue is too old to take on new tastes."

Red Mclane came and stood across the table, smiling down at her with the diffidence not in character with him. Susanita was so patrician and delicately lovely that she seemed in a world miles above him, and he felt like a big blundering oaf before her. She knew he wanted to ask her about María de los Angeles so she told him at once, to relieve his embarrassment, that she had a message for him from her sister, and carefully repeated what Angela had said.

"She means that too, and I know it would be best not to try to see her because it would only make trouble. I know Angela, *señor*. She will wait patiently until whatever she takes for a sign from God comes to her, and nothing will move her before that. Then she will let you know. We are sending a man with letters to Rancho La Palma tomorrow; if you wanted to write one to Angela, I would wrap it inside one from me, and no one would know. A short one, if you would, please."

"Thank you." He did not know whether to call her "*señora*" or "Susanita," and "Mistress Warrener" sounded queer too, so he left it hanging in the air, as it were, for the time being. "Whatever you would like to tell me about her I'd appreciate hearing and thank you for."

"Sit down, *señor*. I would like to talk about my sister."

Soon Roberto came and they talked about little things, laughing together. She thought: "I will have to get accustomed to being treated as if I were a queen and not inferior and to a world that is not all women—."

Padre Pierre had received a letter from Luis Gonzaga, and Susanita read it over again when she was alone before folding it with her own. While Luis had written directly to his mother, it was an open letter to all of them and Padre Pierre had told her to read it before sending it on. He told of the life of those among whom he lived, the cities and the churches, the big house of Devlin's and the housekeeper who scolded them just as Paz did, of his progress in the study of art. He was even earning his way. "It is strange that the sketches where I make a little fun of the people is what they ask for. Señor Devlin lets me do only a few of them and then he puts a price on them which is shockingly high. That makes them of value and to be desired, he says, and it seems he is right. I am learning about painting with oils, and the doctor has a wish to go to Spain next year and he will take me with him. Think of it, *mamá*, to go to Spain! You will write and tell me where you want me to go when I am there. I speak English fairly well and the people are very nice to me. There are many beautiful girls, and some day I will marry one though so far none has touched my heart. It is still too full of you, dear *mamá*—"

Susanita finished her letter, trying to visualize the reception of the package at the *hacienda*. Would *mamá* read them to *papá*, would he listen if she did? Would he want to hear? She had a moment's nostalgia but she shook it off. Whatever happened, her life was bound with the husband she had chosen. They were happy, they would make happiness. Always. She was glad she had gone home; it had been the right thing to do after all. She knew now that she could, and would, keep her face turned forward toward the future, without lingering glances for what was past and gone.

Chapter 32

At Rancho La Palma the forms of living went on as before, inasmuch as they could be kept so by Don Santiago's restlessness and Alvaro's petulance and superciliousness. They were away a great part of the time, riding down horses, displaying to each other their mastery in the saddle; Alvaro, when they came to a camp of the *vaqueros*, showing off new feats of daring he had learned in Mexico. Doña María Petronilla watched them apprehensively when they took the reins from Silvestre at the patio gate. Don Santiago inciting his horse to rear and then leaping in the saddle—a thing he had not done for many years now and which she knew he should not do. After him, Alvaro, always finding the saddle in some spectacular way. Doña Dolores stood beside her in the patio one morning and said, when the whirling dust cloud was settled and the galloping hoofs out of sound, "How different things would be, Petronilla, if Santiago had made Alvaro marry and stay at home. There were plenty of girls besides Inez for him to marry, any of the girls would have been only too glad to have him. Perhaps there would be a child, and his wild nature would have been put in the background instead of ruling him as it does now. In time he would have acquired the dignity of a *don* and been a good enough husband and father and *patrón*. He needs a lashing every morning instead of his father's approval. What will be the end, Petronilla? They cannot go on this way."

Doña María Petronilla shook her head sadly. "We can but wait for it, Dolores. That is the lot of the Mexican woman, to first wait on a man's will and then wait for what comes of it. I am glad Susanita is married to an American." She said it defiantly, looking up at the sky as if it must fall that she could give voice to such heresy. "As for Alvaro—" She did not finish, nor did Doña Dolores finish for her.

Alvaro strutted and boasted and domineered. *He* was the man who most worried the *gringo* army, and he could have gotten General Scott himself if Canales and his lieutenants had not been jealous and restrained him. *He* had the prettiest of the camp women, and it was only because a woman could not bear to lose him when he put her aside for another that he was caught; she had betrayed him to the Rangers, preferring him dead if she could not have his favor. The real reason the Rangers had let him go in Matamoros was because the Rangers were still afraid of him, afraid of reprisals if they hanged him—. Pedro, the *vaquero*, poked the camp fire and remarked to his friend Alban: "*El Lobo* howls, but he does not know that it sounds like the yip of a half-grown coyote. *¿Un hombre muy grande, no?*" Alban kept on braiding the rawhide for a new reata. "No. But we need not worry, Pedro, he will go away again: this *rancho* is too small for one so big."

Alvaro filled a need for violence in Don Santiago, born from his frustrations. There was a need of something to cover the breach in the wall where a son and a daughter, and old nurse and valuable servants, had gone through. Leaving the house early in the morning after Susanita's departure and not returning until the women retired, he did not know Paz was gone until the afternoon of the second day. At *merienda* the coffee did not suit him and he asked that Paz be called to make him some fit to drink.

Doña Dolores allowed a little malice in her remark of: "Paz? Why, Paz went with Susanita, of course. The girl had to have a chaperon. For reasons of my own I did not take on that duty though you so kindly told me, Santiago, that you are weary of me here. Paz is gone from Rancho La Palma."

Only a muscle twitched in Don Santiago's cheek as he kept his eyes on the cup before him. Dolores could guess that in a way the going of old Paz was a greater blow than that of Susanita, for the faithful old nurse was part of the house, had been a part of their lives from the moment they were born. Death leaves a bright angel in place of what it takes, but the living leave only vacancy when they walk away and close the door behind them. Paz's grumbling and fussing—it must have struck deeply into Don Santiago's heart that both were gone, knowing that from him had come the edict that sent them. If it had struck, there was no betrayal. He drained his cup, set it carefully down, and went to his office. There he wrote to his friend Gabriel and told him what had happened, certain that Gabriel would approve of his action. He called Alvaro and told him to deliver the note in the morning. Then he rode to the bluff on which stood the cross of stones, there to gather to him what he saw and weave it into a garment to wrap around his soul.

He strode firmly to his place on the terrace when the bell rang for *El*

Alabado, and when those who belonged to him were gathered before him, his voice rolled in an organ peal over the wall to the winds. What was gone was chaff, winnowed out by their love for things un-Mexican—depraved and perverted and better away.

Trouble came several weeks later when Don Santiago put a hand on his son's shoulder, one evening, and said, "Lead the Angelus, son, this evening. Stand beside me."

More than one servant scowled as Alvaro intoned: "The angel of the Lord declared unto Mary"; more than one gave the answer "And she was conceived by the Holy Ghost" in sullen muttering. Domitila, buxom and pretty and smiling, still burned with anger and shame of the morning when, spreading clothes on dew-washed bushes, Alvaro leaned from his horse, ripped her blouse and laid his hands on her full breasts; Eusabio, who had not polished the silver trim on the young man's saddle to suit him, and felt a stinging quirt curl round his neck; lame old Lino, who had fallen to the ground and struck his head, in leaping out of the path of the horse Alvaro was spurring; Leocadia bowing her head when Jorge the hostler looked at her, because she could not bring him virginity when she married him—because of Alvaro. Silvestre, betrothed to the flower-like Juanita. Gregorio and Anna, grandparents of Juanita. All these, and many others, answered the prayers with their lips but not their hearts—resenting the son of their master.

Gregorio came to see the master the next morning and found him in his office. Taller than any of the *peons*, Gregorio seemed to have taken something from the trees he tended and grafted so expertly and the garden he helped supervise, for he stood with a dignity and freeness where another would have bowed and cringed. In all the land none had his skill and knowledge of orchardry and gardening, and Gregorio was well aware of it. It was his privilege to drop the title of *don* when addressing the master, and, after a short pull at his stubby gray beard, he dropped his arms and said, "Santiago, in the lifetime I have worked for you I have asked no favors. The fruit you have had in abundance came to you because of me and I worked for that gladly, asking little in return. But I ask a favor of you now. Alvaro has been looking overly long and often at my grandchild Juanita. Her father, as you should remember, was killed by the Indians and her mother died from snakebite, so Juanita is both daughter and granddaughter to us. We have been proud of her delicate beauty and are glad that she loves Silvestre because he is kind and good and will never be harsh to her. She was too young when the *padre* was here last, but we planned marriage at his next visit. Santiago, order Alvaro to keep his hands from her!"

Don Santiago looked at the clean long patrician hand on his desk and drummed the fingers of it idly. He did not need to look at Gregorio to know that his was wide and short-fingered and grimy, and hard as horn. He shrugged, raised an eyebrow, and answered, "The servant belongs to the master, Gregorio, as does everything he has. God made the one to serve the other and that is the law. You know the saying: 'Tie up your little hen, for my rooster has a world to roam.'"

Gregorio stood still, looking down at the man whom he had served so faithfully. He opened his mouth to speak, closed it again, turned and left the room. Silently, for his feet were bare.

To his wife Anna, squat and broad and sturdy as he, now setting new onion plants in the garden, Gregorio relayed the master's words, his lips twisting in anger as he added, "I slapped Estéban in the mouth when he said our lives did not belong to the master, and we had rights of our own as the *Americano* said. My mother was one of the women who had to go to Santiago's father, Don Francisco, when it was his fancy to have her, and my father only bowed his head and said nothing. He never knew whether he was my father or whether I was one of Don Francisco's bastards. We loved Santiago because he at least left our women alone, though that was only a certain pride forbidding him, but now he is proud that his son— Anna, I do not see that we need to endure it." He crumbled brown earth in his hand and flung it away. "I swear that if Alvaro forced himself on Juanita I will kill him with my bare hands!"

Anna set down her basket. "What can we do? We cannot watch the child every minute, and you know how small she is. That is foolish talk about killing, what would it gain?"

"I have made my plans." He waited until the women setting plants on either side of them were out of earshot, then waved his hand at the orderly row of fruit trees below. "Those trees are like my children, yet I can harden myself against them. Anna, we have it as truth that Señor Fierro has sold his rancho to an *Americano* and is going to Mexico to his place at Mier. The Fierro rancho has a large orchard in sad condition, for, after all, there are not many Gregorios in this world hereabouts who know the language a fruit tree speaks. You know Silvestre has a way with horses above others, they speak to him and understand him. Anna, you will get the food;

297

tell Nicolasa if you must but keep it secret from the others. Make a bundle of our clothes, it will not be a large one I am sure. I will take them to the orchard at *siesta* time, and this evening when it darkens none will see us go. We are strong and Juanita has sturdy legs and youth. With San Rafael and the Holy Virgin to protect us, we will get to the Fierro rancho. If our going is brought to Santiago and Alvaro rides out, he will go east, thinking we follow José and Estéban. The nights are not too dark, and I know the way well enough; we can hide and sleep days. If we die—then let us die with honor, Anna."

Anna nodded and rose immediately. She had given this her man thirty-four years of obedience and drawn happiness from it. She said: "Call Juanita and take her with you to the orchard, she is at the end of this row with the girls there. I will go now and see about food and gather our few clothes." Nor did she, when she left, stop to look at the fields she had loved, or turn to look at the plain stretching to danger and strangeness and, perhaps, death. Not now would she mourn, for things become dear by long association, lest the young folks sense her mood. It was the old oak against which the sapling leaned.

Don Santiago stroked his nose when an enraged Alvaro brought the news the next afternoon, shouting that he would track them down; he would beat both Gregorio and Silvestre to death; he would drive Anna home ahead of his horse, he—

"No. Let them go, *hijo*." They were in the dining room waiting for coffee. Spending the night at a *vaquero* camp, Alvaro had let his hunger for Juanita fill him and looked for her at once upon his return, only to be told by Juan Bautista that the four had gone, no one knew when or where. Alvaro's temper, flaming high when he found the little dove flown from him, flung sparks in the dining room as he tramped its length now. Don Santiago waved him to a chair and said quietly, "They will starve or the Indians will find them, wherever they may be. A Mendoza y Soría, Alvaro, does not ride after a *peon* who has turned against his master. It elevates his mastership but lowers his pride, my son." He knew that it was he who had driven them away, but he justified himself that he had only followed the old law and not forbidden his son his rights, and he salved his conscience now by a refusal to allow search for them.

In truth he was hard hit at what was a new loss. The couple at the *jacal* were sloppy and careless where Tecla and José had been clean and vigilant, Estéban had kept the servants and *peons* in good order, and the carelessness now that he was gone was already noticeable. The orchard and garden were the pride of Rancho La Palma; too late Don Santiago appreciated Gregorio's worth. His jaw set tightly. He remembered Padre Pierre's preachings, that the old order must change to meet new conditions. Not here at his *rancho*, he vowed anew. What rights were left to a master, when a *peon* was allowed to make an issue of his daughter's virtue? Let them go. He did not want them. Surely he—*he*—could not ride to find them and beg them to come back.

Alvaro flung his heavy braid-trimmed hat on the table and scowled at it. "I don't see why you don't do something, *papá*. If I had been in your place, I would have ridden to Don Gabriel and told him what I thought of him—the old fool! 'He wanted only Susanita's happiness, if she loved the *gringo* he was glad she was married to him, she was a brave, fine woman'— oh, it sickens me whenever I think of it. Well, I will do something. I'll ride to Matamoros and kill this Warrener and also the Ranger to whom Inez says she is married. I can—"

"No! No, I forbid even the thought of it, Alvaro. This—this Warrener—" Don Santiago brought out the name grudgingly, running a thumb inside his sash nervously, "does not exist, understand? And you gave your promise that you would not leave the confines of Rancho La Palma."

Alvaro laughed. "My promise? A promise to a Ranger!"

"Yes, your promise." Don Santiago slapped the table with a palm. "We are not of the same cloth as Santa Anna. You remain here on the *rancho* until I give you permission to leave. As for Inez, she would have had you two years ago when we wished you to marry, you have no one to blame but yourself there. And remember, there will be no further talk of killing anyone in Matamoros. The women are late for *merienda*, go and call them."

It was the first time Don Santiago had spoken harshly to his son and Alvaro respected it. If he was surprised that his father wished no harm to come to Susanita's husband, he kept it to himself. The monotony of the ranch was already pressing down upon him but he could endure it yet awhile. His good friend Cheno Cortina might ride this way, and he could slip across the *río* with him; they might form a band of their own; they had often discussed it when they were with Canales. A wife and children and such things as leading a family in prayer—some day, doubtless, but it seemed a dull enough fate now. That was for boys like Carlos and Monico and José, who had wept with joy to be home again. Pah, like soft women! *He* was a man.

Came Christmas, but no *posada* this year. Now that most of the Rangers were in Mexico City, the Indians were active again, and more and more bands of both Mexican and American brigands were roaming the country, so that it was wise to remain at home. Don Gabriel, this time taking a guard, rode over to Rancho La Palma, and was in high good humor for one so recently deprived of a young and lovely bride. No one mentioned the happy *posadas* of last year, careful to speak of things without consequence. The grass, the cattle, the Indians. Don Gabriel shrewdly guessed that all was well with Susanita, for Doña María Petronilla bore a certain repose which would have been impossible with her had her baby been unhappy. He was careful not to ask about her, they as careful not to mention her. María de los Angeles moved in quiet serenity, and Doña Dolores, resplendent in the purple and black striped dress (to which she had added six rows of black ruchings across the skirt bottom), actually sparkled. The day was misty and cold and the men sat before the fire in the *sala* when the women took up other duties.

Three gentlemen in velveteen and silver and braid, finely booted, smoking *cigarillos* before a roaring fire. The older men's sashes black, Alvaro's a rich crimson—all dressed in their best for this the Good Day. Don Gabriel contemplated a boot tip, leaned against his chair back, and said in a casual tone of voice, "I suppose you have heard that Señor Fierro has sold to an *Americano*."

"So I heard. I can scarcely believe that a *gringo* would *buy* what he wanted, Gabriel."

"It is true nevertheless, Santiago. I myself saw it." Noting the clouds forming on his hosts face he quickly explained: "I went to see Don Pío, that is— I had not exactly remembered when he was leaving—and found the *Americano* there instead. He was courteous enough and he told me, in most execrable Spanish, to take immediate steps to record my boundaries or another not as honest as he would take it from me. He bought, he said, because he wished to give his family a home without discomfort, and he did not wish to violate the commandment 'Thou shalt not steal.' He is a huge man with yellow hair and a voice which I am sure can be heard all over the *rancho*. I met his *señora*, a woman as big as he but with a quick laugh. I have never seen so big a woman, and I felt most peculiar, Santiago, I can tell you. Of course, I would not have gone had I known they were already there." Which was far from the truth for an overwhelming curiosity had egged him to go to see these new neighbors, he had known full well that the Fierros had already gone.

There his horse had been taken by a young man who looked familiar, and he finally recognized Silvestre, but when the servant pretended not to know him, Don Gabriel gave no sign. Later, riding home past the orchard, he recognized Gregorio of Rancho La Palma, pruning the rank growth of the orchard and singing happily as he worked. Don Gabriel had not stopped to ask Gregorio the why of this, and he deemed it wisest now not to mention having seen them. It was, he decided, not any affair of his.

Don Santiago did not rebuke his friend. It would not have been in keeping with his position as host particularly on Christmas Day when all animosity was supposed to be suspended. He smoked awhile in silence and finally said, "Many of our friends are preparing to go to Mexico as I suppose you know, Gabriel. I stay, though trouble has come and will be here a long time. Already it is not the *Americanos*, but we, who are the alien people."

The old year gave way to the new, and there were rumors and more rumors. The January wind carried them, twisted them, scattered them. Homeless Mexicans frightened from the cities eked out an existence by partly riding, partly leading, old broken-down horses from one *hacienda* to another, bringing news for the temporary food and shelter granted them. News they had heard, or guessed at, or imagined, knowing that the worst their fancy conjured was happening or would happen somewhere. The rangers in Mexico City were killing Mexicans by the hundreds—no, by the thousands, *señor*. They were devils from hell itself, and they were rightly called "*los Diablos Tejanos.*" Where are we to go, *señor*, if we are to be driven from Texas only to be killed in Mexico? Has *El Señor Dios* turned His face from His people?

Americans roamed over the land in groups, looked for the places where the grass was the greenest, where the land showed fertility, where the plain breathed like a smiling woman laving her body in the sun. Coveting. Visioning homes. Building dreams of empire. Not caring—too many of them not caring that homes had stood here for a hundred years. Now and then one offered to buy at a fair price, laying down gold as did Leeds to Señor Fierro, neighbor of Don Gabriel. A righteous man who walked in the way of the Lord, Caleb Leeds said of himself, and it was true. Mexicans formed wagon trains and fled this land dominated by the invading peoples they considered inferior to themselves, and utterly contemptible. They carried white flags and asked that they be allowed to go their way unmolested, in a search for a place where there would be peace. In a world where there was no peace.

To Señor del Valle, whose ranch was rich in grass and had besides a long strip of subirrigated land, came two that looked as though they had been chopped from brown wood. They also wished to buy and laid down gold—but only a little, not enough to even pay for the *hacienda*. When the señor asked them if they thought him a crazy fool, they shrugged and put their hands—such huge, hairy hands—on the big pistols that hung from their hips. Señor del Valle could take what they offered, or he could take nothing at all. They would, they said, give him the right to consider. Señor del Valle, the cousin who acted as a *caporal* for him, one Jeremías, and half a dozen *vaqueros*, followed the *gringos*, set upon them when they made camp, killed them, and threw their bodies in an *arroyo*. Then the *señor* tore the plaster from the *sala* wall and took out sacks of gold and silver stored there and prepared to join the wagon train to Mexico, leaving the ranch in charge of the *caporal*. "If you can keep it, Jeremías. One can kill two of them, but not dozens."

Families moved from San Antonio and points north, and at Matamoros the French merchant de la Ferrière and his Mexican wife joined them. His establishment had been looted by Mexicans and Americans alike when the Rangers struck the town, and he did not restock because the ghost of René haunted the store. Besides he wished to get away from the border, he said. There would be only trouble and sorrow there for many years, regardless of which side of the río one lived.

News of all these things was brought to Rancho La Palma, and if they worried and grieved Don Santiago, they also strengthened him. He would stay where he was and fight for the things that were his and the ways he believed to be right. Even if in the end it might mean death—then let it be death.

Chapter 33

When Don Santiago, Alvaro, and Tomás rode through the limpid beauty of an early morning in February, they could not know that, on this day, the treaty of Guadalupe would be signed by which Mexico ceded the land north of the stream known as the Río Bravo, or Río Grande, to the United States, and putting all the land east of the line that had been drawn as New Mexico's boundary into the sovereign state of Texas. It would be many months before that news came, but the shadow of its certainty had lain darkly below the Nueces all summer. Until Alvaro on his return had dispelled it completely, Don Santiago had clung to the hope of the Nueces for a border. With that hope gone, more and more he had allowed a vague dream of getting land for himself in Mexico possess him until, this morning, it ripened into a kind of desperation. Something was driving him, a madness hammering at him seeking an outlet. They would ride to the river this day, he told the two, giving no reason because, in truth, he had none to give other than that the long ride was a necessity. Some of this was caused by Alvaro's restlessness which of late had made him a thorn even in the side of the father purblind to his faults and overindulgent to his whims. Then he wished to get away from the *hacienda* and the thirty miles to the river exactly suited for distance. A rider, he had noticed, had come the evening before and gone again, and Doña María Petronilla had been overly happy at dinner. That meant a letter from Susanita, and there was in him again that battle of the heart that clamored to read it, and the unswerving code of paternal discipline that denied her existence, with the heart, ever the loser, still shedding its painful tears.

So they rode this morning. Alvaro on a tough buckskin named Pancho, the sun picking glints in the silver band of the rolled hat, on the conchas of his bridle, on the *chaparejos*, on the roweled spurs. Alvaro sang ribald songs, but Don Santiago was strangely grim and silent, impatient with the gray pony he had had to take because Negro was lame. Tomás stayed a little behind, with the stoical indifference to what might happen that was characteristic of him, carrying his favorite bell-mouthed *escopeta* unreliable though it was, believing faithfully that shot need the funnel guidance after it left the muzzle of the gun. Alvaro had a long-barreled *pistola* which he pulled out occasionally as he rode along, aimed it at an imaginary enemy, and put it back in the fancy scabbard against his hip. It would not be long now, he was thinking, before he would gather a band of his own, be *El Lobo* in truth this time, and harass the Rangers and the *gringos* all up and down the border—and what could his father do about it? A promise to a Ranger might be binding to some but not to him, not to The Wolf.

None of them saw the early white poppies and buttercups, smiling like groups of little children in newly starched dresses, or that the sky trailed scarves of white chiffon over a gown of blue, like an artful girl proud of her beauty; or that the birds were trilling mating songs, and the breeze whispered of things exciting and strange. Spring shouted her alleluias from a newly washed earth but none of them heard, not this morning.

For more than a mile on this side of the river the land was brushless, rising in a broken low ridge above the mud banks that held the shrunken chocolate stream. Don Santiago sat his horse on the highest piece of ridge, staring at the river that was so mighty it cleft a nation in two. Over there Mexico, where the invader would be driven out and life would go on in the sweet groves of custom. Where sons subverted their ambitions to the father, and daughters—daughters—. Red fog covered his eyes until the world was clear again. Land in Mexico. This was his land on the north side of the stream, on which rested the lifework of his father and his father before him. Yet if he had a bit of Rancho La Palma not in this country so suddenly alien—he looked back of him at the swell of grassland, jewel-green and fair in the sun, and the madness that had rolled inside seeking outlet boiled over and spilled like hot water on flesh.

About thirty feet upstream the river narrowed to brook size, part of its water diverted to a narrow draw that made a pond before it lost itself in sandy soil. The draw made a large U around the twenty acres or so of upland, wandering east a ways before it flattened out to bottomland. Don Santiago stood in his stirrups to look at it, pointed at the river neck, and shouted to Alvaro and Tomás below him.

"There! Where the river backs, do you see? Tomás, tomorrow you bring *peons* and dam the river so it flows way around—you see the draw? There are rocks here on the bluff and there is plenty of brush—"

Alvaro rode up, looked at the land and shook his head. "But, *papá*, that cannot be done. There would have to be a dam as high as a house and stronger than one to make the river take an elbow. It is lower now than we have ever seen it, but when the spring floods come—" Was his father mad? What was the matter with him?

"Yes, the floods, Don Santiago." Tomás also shook his head. "It is not called the Río Bravo for nothing. You and I have seen it so wide that it seemed a sea, and wild as a thousand charging bulls." He looked at Don Santiago in wide-eyed amazement, wondering whether the master had gone insane. "It is against the law of God to change what He has made," Tomás piously crossed himself, "and besides, it cannot be done."

Yes, of course. How childish his little dam. But the madness still pounded his nerves and jerked at his body in a demand for action. Under other circumstances he would have spurred his horse, forced him to leap over bushes, ridden him until both of them were half dead with fatigue and the flames in him burned to ashes. Now he dismounted, ran to the bluff at the river neck, and tore at a boulder half exposed on its face. Sanity pleaded, reason urged, but in defiance he pulled the harder, pounding at earth as if it were the faces of the *Americanos* who had broken his ordered life and taken what was his away from him.

Tomás and Alvaro sat on their horses, not knowing what to do. The boulder loosened, pulling Don Santiago with it as it dropped onto the hard mud flat. It scratched his face and a drop of blood lay readily on his hand. What a fool, he thought, what a crazy fool. And he burst into laughter that was terrible in its mocking bitterness.

Laughing at himself, for the south boundary of his land ended "where the Río Bravo flows."

He looked at the boulder, his earth-smeared clothes, his hands. In a last gesture that was partly defiance, partly mockery of himself—or perhaps it was a clearing away of the last shred of his madness—he lifted the large heavy stone and flung it into the water.

The green jaras on the opposite bank waved, parted, and riders were on the shore before the water in the neck accepted the stone and formed a smooth flow around it. A voice called: "*¿Qué va aquí?*"

Rangers, six of them, bushy of beard, each carrying two huge pistols, a rifle, rawhide *reatas*. Ragged, brown as Indians, they loomed tall and grim; and repulsive, to the eyes of the three turning to face them. One of them, as young as Alvaro, rode into the water and stretched a pointing hand,

and the sun caught a ring on his finger and turned the opal in the filigree setting into iridescent flames.

Alvaro spurred his horse over the bluff and splashed into the shallow water, his face livid and eyes blazing. "Where did you get that ring?" he shouted. "That ring, you stole it from a woman!"

The Ranger laughed and turned the hand to watch the fires move in the opal. Later Don Santiago, standing with spattered hands hanging; Tomás, carved of wood, sitting his horse on the bluff; the Ranger captain and the four strung along behind him on the mud flat—later they all wondered why, in those few minutes, they held the role of passive spectator. Silently listening to the Ranger's boasting, watching Alvaro's face turn white with rage.

The Ranger laughed and rolled his eyes as he smirked, "Oh, not stole, señor. She gave it to me, and a right pretty lady she was too. Made me a present of it."

That ring, Alvaro's father had once given it to him when he left home to follow Canales. Pictures shuttled across his memory at the sight of it. Dark, wicked-eyed Cruz dancing between the campfires, twisting her body and offering it for the highest bribe; Cruz in his arms, the ring on her finger; Cruz his woman; Cruz in love with him, demanding, restricting; Cruz throwing a knife at him when Carmen came and offered redder lips and a body less riddled with the lusts of men; Cruz wild with jealousy, spitting venom and vowing vengeance, disappearing. The ambush, when *El Lobo* and his confederates took their usual foray for food; the humiliation of being prisoner of the Rangers; the *calaboza* in Matamoros; the noose waiting in the plaza. Susanita with Warrener, before Hays—. Quick as thought itself ran the pictures, as Alvaro looked at the beautiful ring he had given Cruz, and which she had bestowed on an enemy to whom she had betrayed him.

And quick as thought the *pistola* was in Alavaro's hand, an explosion shook the still world, powder smoke was an acrid cloud covering the smiling face of the Ranger. When the cloud lifted they saw the body sway on the plunging horse and splash into water.

Another explosion, and a third, and Alvaro's buckskin pony reared and flung him from the saddle and raced away over the plains.

"Stop, stop shooting!" The Ranger captain shouted in English, jerking his horse to shield Don Santiago who was standing in a daze in the mud. "Stop the fool up there with the *escopeta* but don't shoot! This is Warrener's father-in-law—you Andrews, put up that gun! Take them out of the water—God almighty, stop!!"

Swinging his horse aside he dismounted, stepped before Don Santiago, and said, in poor but understandable Spanish, "I regret this more than I can say, *señor.* Be assured it would not have happened had I foreseen it. Had I recognized your son sooner—" He stopped, embarrassed, for the words were a blatancy before the still tragedy graying Don Santiago's face as he saw the men lift his son's body from the shallow river.

(The uncaring river, washing blood from both bodies and blending it into a ribbon of red and carrying it away. Bloods was not a new thing to the Río Bravo.)

"You may keep your regrets," came cold answer. "Will you go, and leave me with—what is mine?" Don Santiago walked slowly, as if pain were dragging at his heels, to where the body of Alvaro lay on the mud flat. A Ranger retrieved the fancy hat from the river, dropped it beside the body and rode across the stream to assist his comrades in tying their dead over the saddle. Not that he or any of his comrades had regret or sorrow for the braggart who had called himself *The Wolf*, but the dignity and silent anguish of his father was a lash hurrying them away. The captain, noting that the runaway buckskin was circling back to his fellows and Tomás riding out to catch him, gave orders to leave. The jaras waved their green tops again, then closed together.

Don Santiago was alone with the body of the heir to Rancho La Palma. And if he did not strike his breast and cry: "*Mea culpa, mea culpa, mea maxima culpa,*" it was only because movement was denied him. But his heart repeated it, over and over—my fault, my most grievous fault. He stood there so long looking down at the young face with its awful smile of triumph that Tomás became frightened and walked up to him and touched him.

"Don Santiago, night will catch us on the way if we do not start soon. I have the horses. I thought I would put—him on my horse, he does not shy, and ride Pancho."

"That is right. Tomás. I will hold the horse while—"

"*Sí, señor.* Here are the reins."

Tomás noticed, when his master climbed into the saddle, that his movements were those of a very old man. He remembered how Don Santiago had lifted the large stone and flung it into the river, and he asked solicitously whether there was anything wrong, was he hurt somewhere?

307

"No, Tomás." Don Santiago gave the *caporal* a small smile. "I am all right, everything is all right. It is the will of God, Tomás, and I bow to the Holy Will."

Tomás crossed himself, and they turned the horses heads towards home, Tomás leading the one with the body tied to the saddle. Home, Don Santiago thought dismally, to María Petronilla.

When a woman wakes each morning to a fear of what the day will bring and feels a presage of doom for her son, the shock of its final coming has had a buffer. So it was with Doña María Petronilla when the violent death of Alvaro became a reality she had both dreaded and expected. She looked at the face that had been that of a stranger ever since his return from Mexico, smoothed back the hair, and kissed the forehead, accepted her husband's terse "There was a quarrel at the river," and went to her room. For so many years she had gone to Him who refreshed the weary and the heavy laden, and she knew He would not fail her now.

Doña Dolores took up the duty left to her, ordering the weeping Angela to her room. In all truth, Doña Dolores felt small grief for her nephew, and what tears she shed were for the brother whose eyes were dull stones in a face riven by grief. She wanted to fling at him: "You and your hatreds and your misguided patriotism did this." She wanted to point to the rafter in the *sala* on which was carved the motto *"Dios es Señor de esta casa,"* and read it aloud and tell him: "It says the Lord is master of this house, Santiago. This is what happens when you forget that and think only *you* are." But that would be a cruel thing to do, and now there was no place for anything but kindness. And she knew she did not need to tell him, sensing that much of his anguish was self-recrimination. It was she who called Juan Bautista on the terrace, to order that David the carpenter make a coffin of the boards stored in an unused room these many years for that purpose. She dug into chests and found a skirt of black velveteen discarded long ago, enough of it good so it could be used to cover the outside of the coffin; also a piece of white cambric to line the inside. She gently reminded Don Santiago that a man must ride to Don Gabriel, a *peon* ordered to dig a grave. Then she, herself, so the servants should not see the two dreadful wounds in the chest, cut off Alvaro's clothes and burned them in the fireplace in the *sala*, and laid him out in the braided cloth of the *caballero*.

Servants gathered in the *sala* to pray the rosary for the repose of the young master's soul, later to gather in their compound outside the patio and whisper and wonder. If it was anyone but Tomás who had been with them they would know what happened, but that frozen-tongued *caporal*—. What vengeance was God visiting upon Rancho La Palma, that now it had no heir? Don Santiago had cast off Luis Gonzaga and even if he had not, Luis was in a faraway world and lost to his home. Luis Gonzaga was a *gringo* now. Truly, evil days were upon them, the saints had turned away their faces and closed their ears. *Ay de mi*, not even the funeral as it should be, with men of his class dressed in their best to carry the coffin to the burying ground outside the wall; travel was so unsafe that only Don Gabriel could come, and with a guard. *Vaqueros* would have to set the coffin on their shoulders—*vaqueros*, Diego, think of it! No messenger had been sent to Susanita—had you noticed, Francisco? Has Doña María Petronilla asked for Paz, Nicolasa? And what if she had, Rosa? What good would it do her to ask?

Dios de Dios, but the *don* looked like death itself. What would happen next? Something will, Servando, something will. The whip is in the hand of the Lord now—.

Chapter 34

Don Santiago was having coffee in the patio with the women, something he had not done in such a long time it almost seemed as that a stranger sat with them. It was a still day and the afternoon sun warm enough to induce a certain languor, so the silence between them fitted into the mood of the day and did not seem constrained. Angela rose and was about to ask to be excused when a rider dismounted at the gate and came inside, fumbled a minute with his shirt, and drew out a small square packet with a red seal. With this in hand he walked forward and announced that he had a letter for Señorita María de los Angeles, looking inquiringly at them all.

As Angela reached for it, Don Santiago took it out of the man's hand, motioned him away to the servant's quarters, and said to Angela: "Since when does a daughter of mine reach for a letter without my permission, and be sent letters without my knowing of it? What does that mean?"

Angela pressed her hands together, not knowing for the moment what to say. The messenger was a new man and either had not received or had forgotten instructions to watch his chance and present the letter to Angela unseen. As her father broke the seal and unfolded the sheet it came to her that here was a sign. Else why had he sat with them this afternoon contrary to his custom, and been there at the time the letter came? Even the blundering messenger was meant to be, she was certain. She drew a deep breath, sent a silent prayer for strength, and stood unmoving as he read aloud:

To the Señorita María de los Angeles.

I have heard of the death of your brother and hereby send my sympathy and condolence. I wish also to inform you that the house is ready in each last detail, with a special room for the homeless. This was to be a surprise to you, but I am telling you now in the hope that it will hasten your decision to be my wife and the mistress of my home. I anxiously await the return of my messenger, trusting he brings me a favorable reply from you. I remain, humbly at your service,

Alfredo McLane.

Don Santiago followed up the reading with a repetition of his former question, "What does this mean?" A bit flatly, still too surprised for anger.

Yes, now was the time. It could not have been arranged better. Ignoring the astonishment on the three faces turned to her, she said quickly, "If you will allow me, *papá*, I will get the other letters that I have and explain everything to you from the very beginning so you will understand." Without waiting for his permission she went to her room and returned immediately with the letters in her hand. She stood before her father and, without perturbation, told him about Red McLane; omitting only that the second time she had met him in the *jacal*, Doña Dolores, and not Paz, had been with her.

"I did not, *papá*, think of him as anything but a soul and a chance for me to implant the beauties of our Faith, or at least to dispel what prejudice or ignorance of it he might have had. When I read the letter he gave me—here it is—I did not at first even see that he was offering me marriage. If you will please read it, *papá*, I will finish what I have to say. When I answered the letter, which I thought it only polite to do, I told him I would wait for God's guidance, and I asked him please not to try to see me. I did not show you the letter then or tell you I had met him because I was sure you would not understand."

There was something so sincere and compelling about this new Angela that Don Santiago opened the letter and read it, asking his wife at its end whether she had read it. "No, *papá*," Angela said quickly, "I kept it all to myself because I knew it was a thing alone for me to decide, and *mamá* would have considered it her duty to forbid me to think further of or write to the *señor*."

Contempt lifted Don Santiago's face in a half smile as he said, "Then I will read it aloud so she and Dolores can hear. No gentleman could have been guilty of anything like it, and I marvel that you, my daughter, endured its impudence." He read it aloud, nor spared it. Angela's cheeks turned red, but she did not lower her head. When he finished she took up her story, telling of the conflict within herself which she had undergone.

"When he wrote at Christmas of how the people, our people, were suffering here in Texas and no one to encourage or hearten them or bring them comfort or protect them, I saw plainly where my duty lay. You yourself heard news bearers tell of the same thing, so I knew he was telling the truth. I would have accepted him then, but—well, the reason does not matter." She could not tell them that it was Alvaro and his sneerings and avocations of violence, at Christmas time. "I prayed and waited. This letter is as if it came from God in answer to me. Here my life is wasted, there it will be filled. I am the kind of person who needs a life—filled."

Don Santiago perused the letters and handed them to his wife, laughing as he told Angela: "So it was God who sent a *gringo!* A huge, big-handed coarse creature who never knew the finer things in life until he came here and was clever enough to play on a girl's weakness to get her." He pressed his memory for what it had retained of McLane's visit to him. Votes. He had wanted to enlist Don Santiago's help in consolidating the Mexicans for their future votes, dangling the title of *magistrado* before him. "Had you thought, Angela, that all this concern over the misery his countrymen are visiting upon the poor Mexicans is to further his personal ambitions? You are to be a lady of mercy so that he will have their allegiance for his schemes, that is plain to anyone. Had you thought of it?"

"No. But it would not matter now, my mind is made up. They will need to give allegiance to someone, will they not? He is a kind and good man, and I have not been as uneasy in his company as I have been with those we have always known. That his hands are large and he is a little awkward is as the Creator made him and of no account whatever, *papá.*"

"He is far more a gentleman than many another," Doña Dolores put it, calmly. "Angela wished to spare me by not mentioning that I was with her in José's *jacal,* but I do not see that it is anything to be ashamed of. He is a most pleasant gentleman indeed, and I must say a most discerning one. He was courtesy itself to me."

Now the flames that had not been in the eyes for many a day came into them, so that they looked like shining black coals about to redden with the heat pressure against them; as they always looked when the banner of his pride was torn and trampled by one he had taught to respect it. Not the rages anymore—not since the retreating heels of Susanita had gouged his heart and left wounds which would not heal. Yet his feeling was now pure anger, that even Angela had dared to disobey him and go so far as to commit herself to a promise of marriage without consulting her elders. A shameful thing for a girl to do, an immodest, degrading thing. On a level with the cheap *Americanos.*

"What are you waiting for then, María de los Angeles? Go to your *gringo*, get out of my sight and my house and stay out! And you can go with her, Dolores, and good riddance to both of you! I'll even order Juan Bautista and a guard to take you in the coach so no time will be lost. Go now!"

Angela did not flinch at his harshness, nor even step back when he put his hands on the chair arms and half-lifted himself forward as if he were going to spring at her. No human angers could frighten Angela now. Hers was the rod of steel, for she had seen a vision and was obeying its voice. Lights and shadows flitted over the dark braids wrapped around her head as she shook it slowly and answered softly, "No, *papá*, you cannot do that to me. In the convent I would have been safe all my life, perhaps I would never have even seen an *Americano*, and I would have been happy and certainly no discredit to you. By your refusal you brought this other destiny to me, and you have no right to drive me out as you did Susanita. I will be married here so *mamá* can be with me, and I leave the house with honor and cannot be pointed at. I shall pray that you look more kindly upon the Señor McLane and give me your blessing." She stretched out a hand in a pleading gesture, smiling a little.

He leaned back and away from her, staring ahead beyond the gate, unseeing. What she had said struck so deeply that he could not deny it. In his disregard for her wishes he had overlooked the factor of that deep religious zeal which uproots kingdoms and rewrites the pages of history. Through his anger and the desolation creeping into it ran a thread of admiration, even a feeling of kinship that she could take a stand and give no compromise. Sacrificing herself to a man like McLane for principle—for he would not have understood that her matrimony was a holy state also, a sacrament instituted by Christ; nor would he have believed that she did not find McLane repulsive. Believing the contrary, her sacrifice was all the greater, her strength the more admirable. But Angela, to have his strength of will, to be as principled—Angela! The meek one he had thought so weak, and always a little despised.

He was beaten by her logic and a sense of justice made him agree with her. "Very well, Angela. Make your plans and do as you wish. But I refuse to see you married to an enemy, and I will give my house grudgingly." He rose and looked at María Petronilla, keeping to her role of bystander—which indeed she was—and at his sister Dolores, the wart on her cheek a crimson signal that her emotions were stirred. "This my house, where the blood of my brother Ramón left a stain on the floor of the *sala*, from a wound given him by an *Americano* invading the land which Ramón was defending. This my house, where only last week I brought the body of the only son left to me, killed by a despicable Ranger. I wonder that my father does not rise from his grave, that the house which was his is to be desecrated by such a marriage, where my last child is lost to me. Have you nothing to say, either of you?"

Had he spoken in grief Doña Dolores would not have answered, but his anger was too much for her and she flung back at him: "You seem to forget, brother, that Ramón's last words were that he wished he had been one of the men inside the Alamo, and die so nobly. For that our father struck him, and it was this blow of hatred—a hatred which you accepted and nourished, Santiago,—which spilled Ramón's blood on the floor and denied him a decent death in bed. Of your oldest son I remind you that 'he who lives by the sword shall die by the sword.' You have another son, two daughters, and sons-in-law of whom you could, if you put aside your prejudices, be proud. What should Petronilla say? It is you who brought her to where she accepts whatever comes in silence. As for *your* house, it was our father's and therefore mine also, and I refuse to be driven from it. If I go at any time, I shall return whenever it pleases me."

He looked at the women in turn. Frustration—at sight of his wife dropping back to her old obedient passivity, resentment at the sister who too often spoke the truth, amazement at the weak daughter who defied him—had its thorny way with him. He walked away from them and went into the house.

Angela kissed her mother, asked forgiveness for her secrecy, and drew them into making plans; lifting them into the future to quickly cover what hurt her father might have given them. "I would like to send the return message that we will be ready for him quite soon. What day shall I tell him? You understand, don't you, *mamá*. And you, *Tía Dolores?*"

Doña María Petronilla wondered why she felt neither pain nor sorrow at this latest development following so quickly after the tragedy of Alvaro's death. It was as if pain had become an anesthesia, leaving her a body that merely went through the motions of living. "Yes, I understand." She smiled at Angela. "I am glad for you, I truly am, *hijita*. Have Dolores help you, I know she will be glad to. Do these *Americanos* follow our custom of furnishing the trousseau and giving *donas*? What about your dress?

Angela blushed. "He wrote at Christmas—I did not give *papá* that letter—that he already had everything and a wedding dress of lace. He—he likes beautiful things."

When Alfred Isaiah McLane, imposing in his fine suit and broad black hat, was presented to Doña María Petronilla, the tight bands holding her broke, and warmth flowed again in her heart. Because he said, bowing over her hand with his most disarming smile:

"Your daughter Susanita has long made me familiar with your motherly goodness. I can only hope that you will look upon me with kindness, *señora*."

"Susanita, you have seen her lately?" Joy gave her youth, for a moment, and brought faint coloring into an almost lifeless face. "If you will tell me of her, your hope is a reality, *señor*."

Doña Dolores came, regal dignity a cloak to cover her eagerness, losing it when he told her: "I have looked forward to meeting you again almost as much as I have to María de los Angeles. It is my wish, if I may expect a double blessing, that you will return with us and stay awhile until my wife will no longer be embarrassed with her duties. I have no companion for her, and I thought she would like having you as everything will be strange for her. A room is ready for you."

"That is indeed a kindness, *señor*." Angela came shyly forward and offered her hand. "I thank you for your thoughtfulness with all my heart."

"Do go," Doña María Petronilla said quickly. "I really would not mind being alone for awhile, Dolores, as I am sure you can understand."

While Dolores was protesting halfheartedly at leaving her sister-in-law, McLane brought the *padre* forward; a lay priest from the church in San Antonio, who stiffly acknowledged the introductions and immediately retired to the room assigned to him. A silent, somewhat sour Spaniard who viewed changes, and marriages like this one, with foreboding. A Catholic in form only, this McLane, by virtue of a baptism undergone because the Mexican law required it, and the *padre* did not like it. But there was no excuse for a refusal, and besides the *Americano* gave generously to the church—which God knew, needed it. When he was told that the master of the house, not approving the marriage, had absented himself at a neighbor's, the *padre* felt a secret accord with him. He would do the same, were he the father of the girl. *Diablo*, what was the world coming to, when child went against parent—.

As it was already night it was decided to have the marriage in the morning. McLane, with his magic ability and tact, asked whether the priest might preside at dinner, thus eliminating the empty chair at the head of the table that might have loomed too poignantly during the meal. With his hearty laugh he covered the curious peerings of the servants so that soon they ceased to be noticed. Telling of the first time he ate turkey *mole* when coming to Texas, when he was the guest of an *alcalde* in an East Texas town. Not knowing it was generously seasoned with hot red chile he had put a goodly portion in his mouth. "The will power displayed at the table was wonderful to see. Now I can eat the hot dishes as well as anyone but then they were new to me and my mouth was very sensitive to chile. I ate the *mole* with a fine unconcern of its fire and the tears kept pouring out of my eyes and I am sure out of my ears also. I ate every shred of it on my plate too. My host kept back the laughter bursting in him just as heroically, wiping his mustache continually to cover his smiles. We kept the formalities to the end of the meal." McLane told the story so well it could have been happening right there, and even the *padre* shook with laughter.

Red McLane did love beautiful things, as much for themselves as for what they represented. His father had, from necessity, made poverty into a virtue, but to his oldest son it had been a thing to hate and run from; and, in his own case, remedy as soon as possible. Yet he had an eye for quality and a shrewdness in spending and was not above asking advice when he needed it. He had asked Susanita to make a list of what a trousseau should have and this, along with a dress and a shoe of hers for fit (the sisters were the same size) he took to a French dressmaker in San Antonio. So certain was he that his plans to marry Angela could not fail that, months before, he had ordered a trader to come to him with his finest stock of materials. He had brought only a small portion of the wardrobe that had been prepared for his bride with him, and that only to show her mother that her daughter had not been shamed by niggardliness.

After dinner Doña María Petronilla claimed him, to tell her about Susanita, and Doña Dolores and Angela brought candles to the bedroom where the boxes were piled. On the top was a note: "If I have overstepped any propriety or breached etiquette I ask that my desire to have the best for my bride may pardon me." Doña Dolores smiled as she said, "He must have been very sure of you. Look, Angela—*María Santísima*, but one could forgive anything for these!" Doña Dolores, who so loved fine fabrics and exquisite workmanship, reveled in the lingerie of cambric and linen and embroidery and silk and lace, fit for a princess, and even Angela fingered them lovingly. When Doña Dolores held out the wedding dress of Brussels lace that looked like bits of all lovely dreams woven together, Angela caught her breath. "*Tía*, don't you suppose God will understand and forgive me when I wear this; don't you think He will allow me to be very vain, for just once?"

Angela wore the wreath of wax flowers holding her net veil as if it were a crown and the lace gown as though it were a regal robe, happiness lighting a lamp in the soft dark eyes and transforming the pretty face into beauty—and looking very small and delicate beside the large man she had chosen to marry. A strange couple, and the very pictures on the *sala* walls stared at them, thought Doña Dolores. A strange ceremony, where a daughter of *dons* married an alien stranger.

"I do," Angela answered the *padre*. Without regret or panic, for she was seeing the bright land where both the corporal and the spiritual works of mercy reared their glistening white spires.

"I do," answered Alfred McLane. In a joy that filled him like heady wine, that this ambition of his was fulfilled.

How different, this pronouncement of man and wife. Susanita's feeling had been an ecstasy of purest love for the man beside her. Angela's was an ecstasy of the soul, for God. Warrener's marriage, to him, was love that was an end in itself, all things bearing upon it and bending to it. McLane's was a link in power, a staff of respectability, a means to an end—.

They stood on the portico so the servants could see them and bring them best wishes. And, as far as Doña Dolores was concerned, to see the lace gown and the diamond that hung in a pendant on the bride's breast, and the long train looped over an arm. All of our friends will hear of it, she vowed mentally, and I shall describe it in minutest detail. They will say it is the *Americano*'s vulgar display of money, but they will be envious just the same. Santiago will say that also, but he will mean it, but, of course, he is not a woman. All the women will chew bitter bread when I tell them.

The breakfast was over all too soon, Angela was in the new traveling dress of black merino trimmed with loops of silk braid, Doña Dolores was ready, the boxes were tied on the coach. It was time to go. Doña María Petronilla kissed Angela and whispered: "Come back, perhaps next Christmas. It may be that by then your father—oh pray, Angela *mía*, that his heart may soften!" To Doña Dolores, reluctant to leave her: "It will be best to be alone awhile with Santiago, this may accomplish what I have been so hoping for. You need to go, life has been so dull for you, Dolores. Enjoy yourself when you can." To her new son-in-law: "I need not tell you to be good to her for I know you will be. Thank you for the beautiful picture of her you leave with me. I trust we will meet again soon—Alfredo."

To herself, when the dust had settled and the creak of wood and leather and the sound of hooves was lost in the distance: "I must bear the loneliness. I must be gentle with Santiago and give him what happiness I can and never let him know that memories, and now and then a letter, do not fill one's empty arms."

Slowly she walked to the inviting group of chairs in the sunny patio, beside the bed of crimson lilies of Our Lady of Dolores, and sat in one of them and folded her hands.

There seemed, just then, nothing else to do.

Chapter 35

❧

It seemed to Doña María Petronilla, when the master returned, that he took his steps with a certain care, but the lithe body was erect, the swing of it imperious, as it had ever been. When he went immediately to the dining room, she went to the kitchen for coffee and herself brought it to him. Fearful, dreading as much the ashes of wrath as its fire in the eyes that mirrored his mood. When he lifted them to her finally, they held a peculiar glow which she could not diagnose—and was to see daily there, unchanged. He said, simply, "I am tired, I will rest till dinnertime."

They had not had dinner alone together since—with a shock Doña María Petronilla, flipping through the pages of the years, discovered that she and her husband had never had dinner alone. First there had been his father and brother, later Doña Dolores, the children, guests. When Santiago came she would smile and take his hand and tell him that. She would ask him—he came in while she was musing and walked to his high-backed chair at the head of the table, waited until she took her place at his right, asked a blessing, and started to eat his soup. A need of saying something, a desperation to reach a vulnerable spot in him, a horror of the silence in the large room, drove her to speech when the soup was eaten and the *guisado* started. Brightly, smiling a little, as if amused at what she was telling him; trying to say it without giving offense; picking those happenings she thought he would like to hear.

"The *padre* sat in your chair at dinner. They arrived at dark and the *padre*, Spanish and so fat, Santiago, was cross as an old woman. He said such a long prayer that the soup got cold, but he had to laugh when the Señor McLane told a story. He has a great laugh and he makes others laugh, the Señor McLane."

No answer. It was as if Don Santiago had not heard.

Bravely she went on, wanting him to know what she had to tell. "He had seen Susanita a short time ago. She is very happy. The Señor Warrener has bought much land around the fort, and he will build a house and start a town across the river from Matamoros, and he has already written to the bishop to ask for a priest, and a church will be built. Paz gets homesick often, but when the *señor* offers to send her home, she will not go because she says then she will be homesick for Manuel and Susanita and the church and her new friends, and besides who will see that the house is kept in order if she goes. The de Dezas were in town and Doña Juliana thanked Susanita for saving Carlos, when she met her at the church door, and she allowed Susanita's husband to kiss her hand and that of her daughter Hilaria. Though I imagine a bit stiffly, Santiago."

He might have been alone, for all the attention he paid her. He sat rigid and severe, eating slowly.

He wanted to hear, she thought, or he would tell her to keep still. She picked at the food, keeping her voice steady as she hurried on. "Señor McLane brought a little of the trousseau to show me; I have never seen anything so exquisite. Even Angela was a little vain, and I do believe a saint would have been, and Dolores was enraptured, as you can imagine. I wish you could have seen the wedding dress, all lace such as has never been seen in this house or in Matamoros, with a train and a veil that was like mist, and a diamond on a chain on her breast."

A bitter laugh, as he helped himself to more coffee.

She hesitated, summoned courage to say, "It was a good marriage for Angela. He will direct her piety so she will have her fill of it, and he will give her the worldliness she needs. Any other man would have had an overly religious wife on his hands and that is not good for the peace of the house-hold. I even believe she cares for him a little, and you know she could not seem to care for any of our young men. Santiago, it is—it is good to care."

(My husband, oh please! Smile an answer to me now when we go to the *sala* tell me you are not displeased with Angela. Be glad that we are alone for awhile and tell me so.)

Only the slap of Eulalia's sandals as she served took up the silence. There was the ting of a cup in a saucer. Abruptly, when he rose, he asked whether Dolores was ill—offering no comment when told Dolores was needed for a time in San Antonio. "One should be needed somewhere, especially if one is a woman."

I tried too soon, she thought, watching him move into the darkness of the patio. He has been under a great strain and shock and he is *triste*. He grieves over Alvaro and I made him more lonely for Susanita—. She had an impulse to follow him and sit beside him under the friendly stars, but she felt instinctively that he had a need of being alone. Head bowed, she walked slowly to her room and the redeeming habit, if not always the solace, of her rosary.

The yellow bloom of the huisache trees again poured its perfume over the wall into the patio, and swallows rebuilt their nests under the eaves. The blooms became tight green beans, the baby swallows stretched wings and flew, and day still followed upon day in dragging monotony. A rider, earning a precarious existence by dispensing news, brought word that the war was over. At which Don Santiago laughed in derision. "The war will be over, my friend, only when either the Mexicans or the *Americanos* are driven from Texas. The *río* will run red for many a year." And there he let the subject drop. The wind slowed to breezes and summer spread its cover of somnolence over Rancho La Palma.

Doña María Petronilla made an attempt to penetrate the wall around her husband, one peaceful evening when the moon spilled enchantment into the patio. She put a hand on his arm as she took the chair beside his and said softly: "Santiago, we are far from old, there are many years of life before us. Must we be alone through those years? And if we must, can there not be companionship between us? I was your bride, happy and proud of you, proud that you chose me when there were many others to be had. Can we not go back to that day, Santiago? At least, could we not try?"

His answer came at once, as if he had asked that question many time and knew the answer. His voice was flat and emotionless, like something inanimate held out to her on a tray. "You too, Petronilla, have betrayed the name I gave you. To me the *Americanos* remain all that is despicable, and I would rather my daughters marry in the homespun of a *peon* than in the laces and jewels of an *Americano*. Angela could not even wait for a period of mourning; I had believed you women would at least give the three months of seclusion in respect of Alvaro's death. It seems even that was too much in the haste to bring another *gringo* into the family. Our faith, customs, and traditions are rooted in our honor which I, at least, find to be my duty before God to treasure and uphold. You as my wife should have stayed by my side encouraging and helping me instead of siding with the enemy. Do you think I had no need of encouragement, Petronilla? You can go to those children who are no longer mine, if you wish, and should you wish to stay with them, your position and the courtesies of it will not be withdrawn from you. That is all I can offer you, to whom I gave the name of Mendoza.

She rose and stood with hands clasped, looking down at him. Leave him, leave this *hacienda?* That was impossible. She wanted to cry out in protest to him, wanted to drop on her knees and plead with him. That too was impossible, it would only embarrass and demean them both. She told herself fiercely that she could bear this also until he would change. In time he would change, surely. She would find a modicum of happiness by ministering to his comfort and keeping things as they should be. Dolores would come home soon and there would be more life in the *hacienda* and in the end—ah, in the end? What would be the end?

She took the chair again beside him, keeping her face down so the moon would not show her wet cheeks.

Don Gabriel del Lago was a man beset. A half dozen times he had walked to the big square stone house setting in the park of young trees, turned back again and wandered through the crooked narrow maze of the streets of San Antonio. His boots hurt his feet, his legs protested against the outrage of walking, his head was in a whirl, his conscience tore him one way while necessity tore him another. The day was warm and his jacket was hot, he was hungry and thirsty and afraid to enter the strange places. He wanted to go home again and knew he must stay to fulfill his mission. Added to all that a woman in a spread of skirts bore down on him, and he barely had time, in his dazed confusion, to step out of her way.

"Gabriel! Of all people, what are you doing here?"

"Dolores!" He grasped her hand as if it were a plank in the sea in which he was drowning. "I ask the same of you!"

Joy lit Doña Dolores's face as she gestured to a shiny carriage. "I wish you would come with me, Gabriel. That is if it is not against your feelings to come to the home of my nephew because he is an *Americano*. I am with Angela here."

That was his objective, he told her when they were in the carriage; ashamed, however, to tell her that old loyalties and prejudices had turned him back each time he had come close to the house. His neighbor Caleb Leeds, he said, had exhorted him to file his land grant and get definite boundaries set or he would surely lose it. "I remembered that Angela was married to the Señor McLane, and I thought he would help me. Then when I came here I discovered I was a stupid *ranchero* who knew only his sheep and for a city, only Matamoros, and I—I, Dolores, a grown man, did not know what to do."

At the stone house she led him to the huge, elegantly furnished living room. A few minutes later McLane came home, welcomed him heartily, declared he was to make this his home while in town and, noting his travel-worn condition, took him to a room, had hot water sent to him, and asked where he had left his horse so José could be sent after the animal. "Rest here or do what you will until dinner, Don Gabriel, the house is yours. I will meet you at dinner."

Doña Dolores took advantage of Don Gabriel's absence to put on her newest black silk and the amethyst earrings and pendant her nephew had given her, combed her hair in an elaborate knot, and set it off with the high latticed jet comb. With her best black fan in her hand she repaired to the living room to entertain the guest, the duty having seemingly fallen upon her.

They never knew just how they came to be sitting together on the frilly French sofa. Certainly Don Gabriel had had no previous intention of telling her about the loneliness of his ranch, when he knew he was not to marry Susanita. "But after the first shock I was glad, for I saw then that I loved her as a daughter, and marriage to an old man like me would have been terrible for her. It—"

"Old—but you are certainly not old, Gabriel! That would be saying I am old because we were children together, and when I married Anselmo—"

"I remember when you were married. You looked so forlorn and unhappy I could have wept. I did weep, I felt such grief for you, Dolores."

"I was such a homely bride. I felt—homely, too."

"You are not homely, Dolores. When I saw you today I thought you looked beautiful. You look beautiful now."

"Gabriel!"

She rose and stood away from him, as if to make room for this wonder which had so suddenly made its appearance. She was blushing like a girl, hands clasped over her breast. Why, they loved each other! They had always loved each other and were discovering it only now.

He rose and put her hand to his lips, waves of crimson welling over his round face. "Dolores, I know now why I was glad when Alvaro brought me the news about Susanita. All these years—and I did not see."

Old customs laid stern hands on her and she withdrew another step; flutteringly, like a shy young girl trapped and wanting to flee. She swallowed hard, smiled, and admitted, "I see now why I was so very angry about your marrying Susanita. But Gabriel, this is—is most—"

"Shocking, Dolores?" He laughed. "We are in a shocking and different world now. Look at us, guests in the house of an *Americano*. You must have defied Santiago to come here, can you not defy convention and listen to me ask you to marry me directly? We have wasted so much time, why waste more?"

"But—but women of my age do not marry. Our friends will hold me in scorn. This isn't—right, Gabriel."

She would not admit that the lack of the usual formalities of a round-about presentation of affection and proposal by proxy touched the individualism in her and exhilarated her. She knew her protests were only verbal, a concession to custom, and when he laughed again she laughed with him. "At least my nephew Alfredo would approve of the directness. Oh, Gabriel, I have longed for the quiet of the *rancho*. The city is nice for a time but—"

"I have money, we could live wherever you wished."

"The summer on the *rancho*, Gabriel." She blushed again and tapped his hand with her fan. "There will be grandnieces and nephews, and they must have a *rancho* to come to."

Red McLane came and asked Don Gabriel for his land grant; asking questions, marking boundaries on paper, exasperation in his voice. "From a rock shaped like a man to a clump of hills covered with small stones—*Dios mío*, Don Gabriel, I suppose that is a forty-fifty mile stretch! That's the trouble with these old grants, they wander all over the place and when we draw a definite line you people say we are defrauding you, that we took a league, or three or more, away from you. There must be straight lines, definite lines, do you understand? Do you agree to that? Meanwhile I shall record it as it is, but surveying will have to be done, at least to get corners and solid marks to go by."

Don Gabriel was bewildered, so few acres or miles had never mattered when there was so much land. "Well," McLane answered grimly, "they won't matter to most of the land-grabbers coming into Texas now—not unless the other fellow claims them, then they will matter a great deal. A greed for money may be satisfied, but when the greed is for land there is no filling it, it is like quicksand in a river. I advise that you define your corners and places between them to get some sort of line, marking with rocks, dead trees, whatever you have. If someone puts money before you and tells you to take it or leave but your *rancho* is theirs, let me know *pronto* and I'll attend to it. There will be much trouble for may years and much bloodshed, over land. Tía Dolores tells me your new neighbor is one of my countrymen, what manner of man is he?"

Don Gabriel shrugged. "He seems a nice enough man. He offered me friendship, and I have drunk wine with him."

McLane's eyebrows arched. He was not now the affable host but a man of business who knew where his profit lay, and he flattened a hand on the small table at which he was sitting. "Take his friendship and drink more wine with him but keep an eye open. Trust people, Don Gabriel, but always keep at least one eye open, understand? You'll be surprised at what you'll see with that open eye, sometimes."

An amazing man, thought Don Gabriel. If it was this type of men who were taking over Texas then indeed it would be built into a great state—it came to him in a small panic. How could a girl like Angela bring herself— Angela herself broke into his reflections, standing in the doorway. And then he saw his questions answered in the tenderness blotting the hardness from McLane's face as he rose and went to her, bending over her hand; in the softness of his voice as he said, "I am glad you have come. We have Don Gabriel for guest."

First, Don Gabriel noticed, the smile to her husband before she came forward. Angela—this poised, gracious lady in the modish dress and cluster of curls behind the ears? He could scarcely believe it, and greeted her awkwardly. How Santiago, he thought, would have appreciated all this elegance, approved proudly of his daughter and admired the efficiency of his son-in-law. (If he were as weak as I am. If he were a weather vane veering in the wind instead of the rock that storms cannot move. If he were not the true *caballero*.)

"And I am glad," Angela said sweetly, offering her hand to be kissed, "that tonight we have no other guests for dinner and can be informal. This is a pleasure indeed, *señor*."

It was Angela who urged an immediate marriage when she heard the news. "If *Tía* first goes home the wedding will be delayed. You have that new dress, *Tía*, and if you do not have everything else as it is supposed to be—"

"That is what I think," Don Gabriel agreed. "Now I do not wish to go to my *rancho* alone any more, she must go with me. What is a dress or a tablecloth, Dolores?"

Outwardly reluctant, she agreed on condition that they go to Rancho La Palma after the ceremony. Santiago would hold her in contempt for marrying at her age, particularly as its shameful haste would put in the category of an elopement. She herself, she admitted, would have raised an eyebrow at such proceedings not so long. Inwardly she was happier than she ever dreamed she could be, to at last have a place where she would not be secondary. Here she was treated like a queen, but it was Angela's place to reign; and this Angela was doing effectively by now, managing her charities and her duties of hostess in a nice balance. There was a big negress in the kitchen who needed no supervision and managed the rest of the servants besides, and with Tecla now being trained to be maid and companion to Angela, Doña Dolores felt she was no longer needed. At first it had been somewhat baffling when McLane told her: "Our women do not need an army of women around them unless they are weak and sick or need pretense of gentility. I do not intend for María de los Angeles to be smothered, like crowding six flowers in a pot where only one can bloom to perfection." But after a time she understood. She had been one of those six flowers all her life, and now it was already as if the leaves of her were expanding, the roots spreading and firming. The whole world was topsy-turvy and it was true that a dress or tablecloth mattered little. What mattered so many little things that only seemed important until one turned them over and saw they were nothing? As for such old friends who might cut her, she had plenty of new ones here in San Antonio. She knew she would not lack for friends.

The same austere *padre* married them at an early Mass, disapproving this marriage as much as he had disapproved Angela's. A widow should endure her lone state and make it a jewel for her crown and cling to her dignity. It was the influence of those *gringos* whom the Lord had sent as a scourge to His people. Doña Dolores bridled and stiffened in indignation; he asked the questions and pronounced them man and wife with such bad grace.

"Perhaps," Don Gabriel laughed, as the carriage was bouncing over the road to La Palma, "he thought me an undesirable bridegroom, I am so short and round." He was happy. He had never been so happy, and sang snatches of song all the way. And when they finally came to the *hacienda* he leaped out of the carriage like a boy.

Don Santiago took this latest and most unexpected development with no outward show of emotion, keeping the talk at dinner upon things concerned with the ranch. He had not seen his friend since the visit with him in February to escape Angela's wedding, and this was August. The truth was that the ride had been too far for Don Santiago, but Don Gabriel believed he had somehow offended him then. Even later in the starlit patio, when the women had much to discuss in the privacy of a room, Don Gabriel felt a strain even his good nature could not dispel.

"Are you well, *amigo?*" he finally asked, when silence thickened uncomfortably. "You are thinner, I notice." He had attributed the loss of weight, the gaunt prominence of the narrow Castilian features, the steady peculiar glow back of the eyes, to grief over Alvaro, but now he wondered if there were not also a bodily pain.

"Quite well, Gabriel. My appetite has not been as keen, and I have lost some weight, yes, but that is not of any consequence." Silence again, intensified by the call of a night bird flying overhead. It is as if our friendship is dying, thought Don Gabriel, and I can do nothing to save it. When Doña Dolores's laughter drifted out to them, Don Santiago said, somewhat harshly, "I find it strange that you married Dolores, particularly when she flouted our traditions by taking the hospitality of an enemy she helped to insinuate into my household. The—other one—had at least the manner of a gentleman so born, but this uncouth red one—God help Texas if men like that are its destiny! Did you stay in the house also, Gabriel? Do you too love them?"

"Love them, Santiago? If I had the gift of prophesy I would say that there would never be love between us as a people. Yet a repulsing of those who would bring us at least understanding, like this Señor McLane, will bring us nothing of advantage. I have concluded that unless we go to Mexico and stay completely Mexican we must conform in part. I have had Señor McLane record my land. It *is* men like him who will really build Texas, Santiago, though I fear many will be harder than he. He is amazing. Yes, I stayed in his house when I found that I—I loved Dolores, and I marveled at the efficiency of it as compared to our own; and the manner in which he is directing Angela's piety is surprising, you would not know her. If I have bent down from my pride, it is because I thought it wiser to have pride suffer a little rather than have all the rest of me suffer. I am only forty-three, Santiago. It may be that I live that many years again, and I prefer to live them in peace and with some pleasure if I can. My land, a wife, good will with my neighbors, they are things to enjoy even if one gives some pride in exchange for them."

Don Santiago rose, looming tall in the star-diffused darkness, and his voice brimmed with sorrow. "There are many, Gabriel, for which God be thanked, who still can distinguish jewels from glass. Life must have its jests, however; not a member of my family, except the one who died, but picked up the glass." He laughed, not restraining the mockery as he added: "I am sure you would like to retire, my brother. Surely your young bride awaits you with eagerness."

He walked up the portico to his room. Slowly, and it seemed to Don Gabriel as if each footfall was a hammer blow nailing a coffin in which lay their lifelong friendship.

In the house Doña Dolores, sitting on a chest and using her hands volubly, was telling about her stay in San Antonio. "Such a house you cannot imagine, Petronilla! Windows of glass, it is as if there were no space in the wall at all; one can sew inside without candles and see what goes by outside without opening the door and letting the wind come in. The house is built in one piece and without a patio in the center, the patio is on one side and more like a garden, and one goes to the rooms in the house through doors in the walls and not outside from the portico. There is what is called a 'piano,' which is like a harp around which a box is built, and one hits the strings by pressing pieces of ivory like a row of teeth on the front of the box. Angela can play songs on it already, and she and Alfredo sing together—. Oh, the people to whom Angela is hostess to, Petronilla! The governor, and generals—I must admit their General Houston gave me a fine deference and kissed my hand very nicely indeed. Angela has I do not know how many evening gowns, one more beautiful than the other and cut almost daringly low because her husband likes to see her perfect white shoulders—yes, and she wears them without complaint and most graciously, too. And she is already pregnant and attributes it as God's approval of her marriage, with the baby coming at Christmas time. You know Angela would, and she may be right about it. I must admit she is doing a great deal of good among our people who need help; they call her their Angel of Good, though Alfredo sees to it that they do not take advantage of her. But she never oversteps the time she should be at home and she gives deference to her husband's wishes. I would never have believed Angela could be made into such a splendid woman, Petronilla, though Alfredo says he saw it the minute he looked at her. It looks as though the marriage will turn into a success after all."

They left after a day's stay, as soon as Doña Dolores could pack such of her things as she felt would be immediately needed. Don Santiago's courtesy took on an ostentation which synonomized his displeasure and was far harder to bear than a direct voicing of it. Don Gabriel wanted to get the carriage back to San Antonio as quickly as possible. McLane had refused to allow either José or Estéban to drive the carriage so their former master would not be embarrassed, but Don Santiago did not know that. Nor would it have mattered to him had he known. He gave a single glance at the two strange Mexicans, the one holding the reins and the other a rifle, and lifted his lip in contempt of their neat *gringo* clothes. Doña María Petronilla, genuinely glad for the happiness of Doña Dolores, promised to visit them soon; knowing she would not, at least for some time to come. At least this, she thought, could not be laid at the door of the Americans— and corrected it immediately. Dolores would not have departed from custom and laid herself open to ridicule by marrying at her age. Not before the coming of the *Americanos;* not unless, as it happened, she had been in the house of one who put custom second if it served him better so, as McLane did. She wondered if Don Gabriel would have dared to propose as he had if the old ways were still with them—would have done so now, had not Dolores lifted a barrier.

The invaders had brought lawlessness. For good, or bad? Doña María Petronilla could only wonder. Yet—it did seem right for Dolores and Gabriel to marry, so very right.

She told her husband hesitantly that Susanita was going to have a baby, and courageously added; "Gabriel says if it is a girl he is going to give her his mother's rosary of matched pearls."

A gardenia suffered decapitation by Don Santiago's hand, its petals strewn like confetti on the *tipichil* floor of the patio. She watched a second flower being jerked from its stem, took a deep breath and went on: "At least God is not turning His face from our daughters. Dolores says that Angela will also be a mother, at Christmas."

Don Santiago looked at her, incredulously. "Angela? María de los Angeles to have a baby?" He laughed. He threw the petals in the air above him and let them shower on him and laughed. Laughed until a hundred devils were mocking each other from the walls, in an insanity of glee over this jest.

He was still laughing when he mounted the horse that always stood saddled for him by the gate. He rode like the wind past old Victorino watching his sheep, who crossed himself and muttered a prayer. When he got to the top of the bluff, he dismounted and sat on the stone slab at the foot of the big cross until the big bell over the well in the patio called him in faintest tinkle.

It sounded, today, like the toll of a requiem. He did not even see the crimson majesty of the lowering sun, nor the golden luminosity of the plains.

Chapter 36

The war was over. Santa Anna made the most dramatic ride of his career, passing in an open carriage through a lane of soldiers and Rangers. Gold braid, jewels, shell of pomp—aloetic palliative of defeat—. Hays, with Lane, at Sequalteplán, mowing down the guerrillas and taking no prisoners. Writing down the date, February 25, 1848, for the record, making good his promise to add the period. The war, said Washington, was over. Peace, said Washington was here.

War, Texas knew, is a fecund mother whose children spring from her full grown. Want, wrapped in tattered sheet; hunger drooling over bleached lips; disease, mouth open, hands spotted; contamination, dipping hot fingers in wells; despair, black and ugly, screaming curses; lust, the vile one, staling the innocent; misery, babbling senseless prayers; intolerance, which coined the words "*gringo*" and "greaser" and impregnated them with contempt; prejudice, the long-lived, driving new nails in the barrier of racial and religious differences. Revenge, and Hatred, and Murder, and Greed—ah, Greed!—the four that never slept.

The war. Yes, the war was over. So said the record.

Texas wrote its history with a scratchy, blotty pen, and called its southern line the "bloody border," and strove for peace inasmuch as its poverty allowed—in a chaos that Time alone could bring to a semblance of order. Texas had too few Stephen Austins, and did what it could without them. Texas got neither sympathy nor understanding from Washington, and licked and bound up its wounds as best it could.

At Rancho La Palma summer strung its somnolent days like a necklace of identical beads. Tomás reported a brush with Indians and a *vaquero* wounded, to the west. To the south a band of Mexicans, driving cattle across the río, had been routed, one of the men drowning in the water. "The old *escopeta* worked this time," Tomás said. "I think the noise of it scared them half to death. I brought the cattle back." Northward, a caravan of wagons and riders, all Americans, had stopped at a *vaquero* camp and asked about land to the west, but this time Tomás did not report; nor did he mention to anyone that these men had asked specifically where the Rancho La Palma line was, and explained: "We hear he has two sons-in-law of position of our countrymen and do not wish to encroach on his land." A good *caporal* used his judgment about such things, and it told him to be silent.

Doña María Petronilla took to spinning and weaving to keep the placidity she deemed necessary, now that the large *hacienda* was all echoes. There was another letter from Luis Gonzaga saying he was happy, earning his way, and would soon leave with Doctor Devlin for Spain. He loved her, "and if you can, tell *papá* I love him also, and hope some day to make a portrait of him to hang in the *sala*. I hope some day to make portraits of all of you—done by that famous painter, Mendoza. That is how I sign the pictures, with the *Z* large. Señor Devlin worked it out for me and I feel most important—" A small sketch of his mother was enclosed, well done but too youthful, with the name prominent in a corner. Doña María Petronilla left the picture and the letter, with one from Susanita, on a table in the *sala*, but Don Santiago looked only at the picture and remained impassive when she told him about the name and gave him Luis Gonzaga's message. When she left the room he stood and looked, long and intently, at the treasured old portraits brought from Spain, staring at him from the *sala* wall.

"Mendoza," he whispered. "The name Mendoza." And he drew it with a finger on the wall—with the *Z* large.

Old Victorino came and stood before the master seated in the patio, trouble clouding his kind face. "Santiago," he said firmly, "the *Americanos* have understood that only a Mexican understands the herding of the sheep, and they pay wages to good ones. Raymundo and Marcelo whom I so carefully trained and who know sheep better than the sheep themselves—which is not much for the good Lord knows He gave sheep no intelligence— both of them have gone, and they the best herders I had. I thought that if you paid my herders a little," the old man looked up at the pale sky and stroked his long white beard, "it might be for the best. The old days will be going, and I am glad I will not live to see more of the new than I see now. This *rancho* has always had the best help for they were treated well; that is why your father was rich and why you are rich, Santiago. If we lose our good help we lose everything. Look at the orchard, since Gregorio is gone—he works for Don Gabriel's neighbor if you did not know it—and look at the garden, and these last two we have at the *jacal* are worse than the rest. José and Tecla were fine workers and loyal, and already more has been lost to us since they went than a little wages would have cost, in corn alone on which the rats grow fat. José had a hand for a sick lamb, now what I cannot do there means more dead lambs. There is carelessness everywhere, and it is in my mind that after a time sheep and cattle will be turned over to the thieves that infest the land more and more; turned over by your herders and *vaqueros* for a few pesos.

"There is a feeling, Santiago, since Paz is no longer here and does not come home, and Susanita and María de los Angeles are as if dead—there is a feeling among the *peons* as you must surely have noticed yourself. Something will have to be done, Santiago, and very soon."

Don Santiago moved a little in his chair and Victorino noticed with a shock how deep the grooves were from the nose to the bitter, straight-lipped mouth. No emotion showed as he answered steadily: "If I must buy loyalty, I will do without it, Victorino. I have done what I believe right and will continue to do so, and I am surprised and shamed that you, too, argue your seditions. I am tired, Victorino."

The old man shifted from one sandaled foot to the other, looked at the implacability stamped on the set features of his master's face, answered, "*Sí, señor,*" and walked away. Had Don Santiago lifted his eyes he would have noticed that the old spring was gone from the faithful goatherd's step, his head drooped forward, his blithe good nature burdened with sorrow. Victorino was suddenly old, old.

Toward the end of October a letter came for Doña María Petronilla. An exciting letter that planted roses in her pale cheeks. There was a baby girl already two weeks old. "Paz prayed hard that it have blue eyes, for while all babies have pale eyes, she says, this one's are already like the deep spring sky. Paz is making the satin robe for the statue of Our Lady which she promised. The baby is blond and so white and the loveliest thing in the world to us. I believe that if *papá* saw her his heart could not resist her, and he would take me to his heart again and look with favor on Roberto. I have this plan: You come here to us if you can, and we will go back to Rancho La Palma with you. I am a little afraid to come alone. Surely *papá* will not deny you, for it is soon All Souls Day and you will want to burn candles for Alvaro and have a Mass read. Do come, *mamá*. Roberto is sending soldiers to guard the coach so nothing can happen to you."

Doña María Petronilla had never heard that he who hesitates is lost but she acted upon it now, knowing that if she waited until she got the upper hand of her joy and desire she would not have the courage to ask her husband. She found him seated on Alvaro's grave and said quickly: "Santiago, I have meant to ask if I may go to Matamoros to pray at a requiem Mass for Alvaro; you know I would feel better for it and that is the custom." She twisted her hands, repelled by the glow of his eyes fixed unwillingly upon her, further words failing her.

He raised an eyebrow. "I suppose there is a baby, Petronilla. At least I cannot imagine why else you should be so excited."

Now the words tumbled out. "A baby girl with her blond hair! Santiago, I know I am offending you by asking, but I would stay only a few days—if I could leave in the morning I would come back after All Souls. Santiago, I—I—"

"You are only a woman, is that it?" She wanted to believe there was a note of tenderness in the voice but the habitual flatness held no lift. It was as if he did not care, was too weary to care at all. He rose. "I will see Juan Bautista. I suppose it will be Nicolasa who will accompany you?"

Nicolasa? Old and trusted but a companion no, never! Why, there was not a woman to go with her and that struck her as so strange that she laughed. What could she do with one when she got to Susanita's, and then the room in the coach would be needed coming home? "I will find someone," she said, and walked to the house. It was of course unthinkable that she go alone. Finally she thought of Isadora, who made the desserts. The girl had wanted to go to Matamoros and her mistress knew why; the young Mexican who brought Susanita's letters. That might mean that the girl would not come back and in a sudden recklessness she decided it did not matter. Someone else could make the desserts or they would do without them. She ran to her room, pulling clothes from the chest. Santiago had not even hesitated, surely that meant his heart had softened. When he saw Susanita and the precious grandchild—ah, her prayers were being answered! Mother of Perpetual Help, thank you, thank you.

With an early start from Matamoros the party arrived at the *hacienda* while the sun was still in the sky. It was quite a retinue with the soldiers for guard, Warrener riding ahead. Juan Bautista driving the six white mules pulling the shiny coach, a soldier in the empty carriage behind driving the four nondescript mules. Their visit, this time, would be short, even if Don Santiago welcomes them. Manuel, against his pleadings and protestations, had been left behind. Inside the coach anticipation kept faces bright, even Paz shedding some of her years now that "home" was nearing. Doña María Petronilla glowed anew with the memory of her departure when her husband, after a stiffly courteous leave-taking, had suddenly put his arms around her and kissed her cheek. Now as she stepped from the coach her heart was beating in double time, a little fear creeping into her certainty of forgiveness for them all.

"I will carry the little one," said Paz, taking the bundle from Susanita. "I alone will have the courage to put her in his arms."

Nicolasa came running, servants began to gather; all smiles that their little beloved one was home again and more beautiful than ever. So Don Santiago had sent for them after all, they whispered. Strange, that he had said nothing and now was not even here. Their smiles faded after they had greeted the women and retreated to the kitchen. The *Americano* sitting at table in his uniform in this house, with the son of Don Francisco at its head. Dorotea rattled a pot. She would not believe it until she saw it, and then she would think the master suddenly gone insane. Had they seen how important old Paz was? As if *she* had given birth to the *niña* herself.

"He rode out this morning," Nicolasa told them, shaking her head. "Something is not right. He took no dinner last night, no chocolate this morning, only coffee at *merienda* yesterday, and then he did not complain about it. Tomás is out at the camps, but I do not think Don Santiago rode with him as he does not ride far any more. Not since—" Nicolasa checked herself when she saw shadow come into Doña María Petronilla's face; both of them conjuring the picture of Alvaro and Don Santiago running their horses before leaping on them, shouts and laughter drifting into the patio with the dust as they disappeared.

"There is nothing to worry about," Doña María Petronilla said quickly. "Only today—I told him I would be home today. Ring the bell, Nicolasa, he will come if he hears it."

"I think I know where he is." Susanita put a hand on her husband's arm. "You will ride with me and we will find him. You know the place we called *papá*'s altar, *mamá*, where he so liked to go. I am sure we will find him there."

At this the baby protested loudly, reminding her mother that her meal had been delayed unduly and she was hungry. It was finally decided that Warrener's argument prevail, that he and Simón the *vaquero* ride to the bluff. For Warrener, when Susanita gave him the location of the bluff, felt certain that Don Santiago would have come home, seeing the cavalcade, if he had been able to. They waited awhile after the bell was rung and Simón went up in the tower, then rode out on the empty trail. The women went inside, Susanita to worry over her reception now that the high wave of excitement had passed. Now Doña María Petronilla saw her husband's slow movements, the loss of weight and strain in his face, as something more than grief over Alvaro, and reproached herself that she had been blind to it before. Paz went to the kitchen, to worry over the dinner, the house, the patio, the servants, the soldiers loafing against the wall.

"We turn here," Simón directed. "See, there is the cross on the bluff. Don Santiago's father's father saw Rancho La Palma de Cristo in a dream from there, and when the dream came true he built the cross in thanksgiving to God. The family has been in Texas close to a hundred years, *señor*, if you did not know."

Warrener knew, for Susanita had told him. And already, he thought now, the men piling into the new state were asserting their rights as "Americans," wearing the rainbow of the pioneer as if it were new and theirs alone. Already talking loudly about running all Mexicans across the Río Grande from this "our" land.

"Look, *señor*; there is Negro!" Simón pointed to a saddled horse grazing at the foot of the bluff. "Don Santiago always rides to the top, it must be that he has been there so long that Negro grew impatient and came down. Let me ride quickly and—"

"No. I will walk up alone and you stay here with the horses until I call you." They loped to where Negro was grazing and Warrener swung out of the saddle hurried up the steep zigzag path.

It was a last irony that an American, and the man who took his most beloved child, should be the one to close the lids over the eyes of Don Santiago de Mendoza y Soría. Dying in the aloneness he had made, he lay on his back, arms outstretched, where Death had gently eased him from where he had been standing on the edge of the bluff. A smile lifted the lips set so long in bitterness, and peace smoothed the stern lines of the aristocratic face.

What, Warrener wondered, did Don Santiago see as he stood here and lifted his arms, on this day which he must have known was his last? Did he see the grandchildren, the guests, the activity and happiness that might have been? Did he hear laughter again, and song, and the trip of dancing feet? Did he feel arms about him, and touch the sweetness of love again?

336

Or had he held to the last to the staff of his traditions, speeding his soul with his head held high in the right of his convictions, to stand unafraid before the God whom he had worshipped and, he believed, obeyed?

Warrener noticed that Don Santiago's hand was tightly clenched. He stooped and opened the fingers to see what they held.

A scoop of earth, brown and dry, trickled from the palm and lost itself in the sandstones.

THE END

Hombres Necios: A Critical Epilogue

BY MARÍA COTERA

A critical reading of *Caballero*, situating it in the Chicano literary canon, would inevitably place it in comparison with Américo Paredes's foundational text, *"With His Pistol in His Hand"*.[1] In such a reading, *Caballero*'s collaborative creative process; the period in which it was written (a period which saw the birth of LULAC and other such organizations bent on the quick and easy assimilation of "Latin Americans" into mainstream culture); González de Mireles's education at the University of Texas at Austin, an institution which produced such racially biased scholars as Walter Prescott Webb; and the novel's message of cooperation with the forces of Anglo domination would lead many scholars to read the novel as an assimilationist text. However, if we place *Caballero* in the context of other works by women of color and Jovita González de Mireles as a precursor not to Américo Paredes, but to writers like Ana Castillo, Cherrie Moraga, and Gloria Anzaldua, the novel's trenchant critique of the patriarchal world view of foundational texts like *"With His Pistol in His Hand"* becomes clear. *Caballero* then takes on meaning as the ironic title of a novel that deconstructs the myth of the warrior-hero while politicizing the domestic sphere. As such, it presents an oppositional response both to dominant patriarchal culture as a whole and to elements of that culture in traditional Chicano texts.

Caballero is an early, and important, attempt to give a voice to the Chicana speaking subject during a historical period which witnessed the rise of nationalist movements among Tejanos in response to U.S. imperialism. In her essay, "And Yes . . . The Earth Did Part," Angie Chabram Dernersesian traces the development of the Chicana speaking subject as a response to the *poetas del movimiento*, whose nationalistic discourse leveled critiques at dominant culture, while positing a universal Chicano subject that privileged "male forms of identity or subjectivity."[2] Chabram Dernersesian contends that when Chicanas began challenging the authenticity of a monolithic Chicano voice, the "earth" did part under the feet of the universal Chicano subject, and "under the pens of not one but many Chicana poets and cultural practitioners."[3] This splitting of Chicana/ Chicano subjectivity along gendered lines resulted in cultural productions by Chicanas which deconstructed and even subverted nationalistic discourse and "entrust[ed] them with their own self-definitions and subject positions; [while combatting] male-oriented figurations of Chicanas."[4] Powerful examples of Chicanas reclaiming a subject position include *Loving in The War Years*, in which Cherrie Moraga calls for an understanding of identity which defies those boundaried designations of the self which nationalism and heterosexism construct, and the important historical and analytical work of Adelaida del Castillo and Norma Alarcón, which recontextualizes and challenges the traditional "male-oriented figuration" of La Malinche.

Caballero's revolutionary act is to give authority to voices which are often effaced in nationalist movements because of their challenge to "singular constructions of idealized, homogenous subjects of . . . identity."[5] Its multiplicity of voices provides a literary counterpoint to the emergent myth of the singular Chicano "warrior hero" who battles the forces of outside oppression "with his pistol in his hand," while maintaining a patriarchal code of oppression within the home. In its unflinching depiction of patriarchal values in Chicano culture, its deconstruction of the idealized male hero, and its thematic use of the issues surrounding Malinchismo, *Caballero* forecasts the cultural production of women of color that Chabram Dernersesian cites as emerging in response to the nationalistic male-centered discourses of the early seventies.

HOMBRES NECIOS[6]

Caballero opens on the eve of 1846 in a ranching community in Matamoros. It depicts early hacienda life with a curious mixture of vitality and meticulousness typical of González de Mireles's studies in folklore. The story centers around one hacienda, Rancho La Palma de Cristo, and its patriarch, Don Santiago de Mendoza y Soría. We are introduced to the inhabitants of Rancho La Palma as they gather together for *El Alabado* under the watchful eyes of the patriarch. His wife, Doña María Petronilla, with her "self-effacing meekness and the faded thinness," enters first, followed by his eldest daughter, María de los Angeles, dressed in "doleful nun's garb," as a sign of constant rebellion opposing her father's injunction against her entering the convent. The household servants, peons, and vaqueros also attend the evening *Alabado* and afford us a look into the hierarchical world of a working rancho, where servants wear "flat huaraches," peons shuffle about on bare feet, and vaqueros peer at the master from the periphery, aware that they must attend the service but afraid to come too close to the civilized realm of the hacienda.

Susanita, Don Santiago's second and favored daughter, and the picture of blond femininity and childlike submissiveness, enters next, followed by Doña Dolores, his widowed sister, whose strident questioning of patriarchal values is a constant source of conflict within Rancho La Palma de Cristo. Another source of conflict is Luis Gonzaga, Don Santiago's younger son, whose talent for drawing and love of art relegate him to the world of women. Unlike his elder macho brother, Alvaro, who loves to shoot and ride, and beds as many of the peon and servant women as possible, Luis Gonzaga prefers the company of his sisters to that of his father, who considers him an "insult to his . . . manhood! A milksop."[7]

The novel's conflict arises when Don Santiago agrees to move the family to their town home in Matamoros for the holidays. The decision is a result of planning by other Mexican hidalgos who wish to have a common place to meet and organize against the "Americanos." Matamoros, because of its proximity to Fort Brown, is ideal for this purpose. What the hidalgos do not realize is that prolonged exposure to Americano men and Americano values will have a profound effect on those people in their culture who are not insulated by power, and who are not included in their planning process; their wives, children, and peons. Slowly, as his children leave him to explore a wider range of possibilities in the world of the Americanos, and his peons reject the slave-like system of the hacienda in order to explore their identities as labor in a world of capital, the power base that Don Santiago has been consummately unaware of, yet which has held his hacienda together, begins to erode beneath him.

Unable to negotiate with the incoming Anglos, as many of his children and compañeros have done, Don Santiago and his savage son Alvaro isolate themselves on the rancho, spending their days riding and shooting. "Alvaro filled a need, a violence in Don Santiago, born from his frustrations. There was a need of something to cover the breach in the wall where a son and a daughter, and old nurse and valuable servants, had gone through" (p. 274). Although, ironically, Don Santiago looks to his macho son Alvaro to fill a violent need, the references to maternity are significant in that they point out the misguidedness of Don Santiago's formation of an alliance with the overtly masculine Alvaro in response to a maternal need for his children. Don Santiago's inability to mediate between the paternal/maternal is indicative of his narrow understanding of identity itself which is locked into essentially heterosexist designations of male/female. His is an "absolute notion of the self as an autonomous, independent entity" that denies possibility of understanding "the otherness within the self and the incessant presence of the self in the other."[8]

Don Santiago worships a fetishized and exclusive self that is the patriarch, a male of god-like proportions and power. He worships this image of himself at a natural altar, a secluded place at the uppermost region of his ranch, a spot that Don Santiago aptly calls his "rendezvous": "It was a rendezvous beloved by the master of Rancho La Palma. Here pride could have a man's stature, here he was on a throne. He stood beside the cross, monarch of all he surveyed" (p. 44).

The identification of this special place as Don Santiago's "rendezvous," a word typically indicating a place of meeting for two or more people, is important, for as Don Santiago looks down upon his domain, he is visited by a vision of power personified—the alter ego of the patriarch, who is its reflection in the material realm: "Power was wine in his veins. Power was a figure that touched him, and pointed, and whispered. Those dots on the plain, cattle, sheep, horses, were his to kill or let live. The peons, down there, were his to discipline at any time with a lash, to punish by death if he chose. His wife, his sister, sons and daughters, bowed to his wishes and came or went as he decreed" (p. 45).

The vision whispers to Don Santiago and points to the problematic nature of the patriarch's identity. The master's power is defined by his possessions, by his ability to "punish [them] by death if he chooses." When his possessions are stripped from him, his power is dissipated and his identity threatened.

Don Santiago's vision returns later in the novel, after his retreat from Matamoros to Rancho La Palma de Cristo. The move is an attempt by Don Santiago to escape the deleterious influences that Americano culture is having on his family by imprisoning them in the isolated domestic sphere. He is shocked to find that Anglos have invaded even this remote territory, and his servants have greeted them with smiles of curiosity instead of gunshots. Feeling violated by what he considers a breach of trust among people that he considers his possessions, Don Santiago vents his rage on Tío Victorino, an elderly goatherd, whipping him mercilessly. Don Santiago escapes once again to his rendezvous to seek comfort and justification for his violent act.

> The Master of Rancho La Palma stood beside the high stone cross which centered the bluff that was like the fragment of a huge stone wall. It was the first visit to his rendezvous since his return, and he galloped to it in a need to justify the morning. His kingdom stretched as fair as ever, but the magic of it refused to come and fill his soul. He had rationalized his deed to himself, but the gnaw of regret had not lessened; Tío Victoriano's grief-stricken eyes refused to leave. There was a flatness in his mouth as if he had drunk water long stagnant.
>
> And then a man with his own face came and stood beside him and looked at him with quiet eyes, pointed an arm and said, "listen to me Don Santiago" (p. 273).

The "man with his own face" points to the plain, but this time the vision offers a different reading of those "dark spots in the distance." Don Santiago's steers and cows, his sheep, and "galloping horses being driven to corral" are joined by the "oxen and mules and fowls you do not see but you know are safe at home" (pp. 273–74). Instead of affirming Don Santiago's figuration of power as total possession, the vision reminds the patriarch that to be the legitimate master of Rancho La Palma, he cannot rule over its inhabitants with his "heel on their necks" (p. 274):

> The man held out a hand and smiled. He had a warming, a sweet smile. "Your choice is now. You can be the man you are, or the one I am. You know me. I am the part given you by your splendid mother and I once lived with you."
>
> Don Santiago scooped up earth and looked at it, and as he looked, possession took him in the grip of its pride, and he gave himself to it as a shameless woman to a lover. He struck out with the empty hand at the man with the quiet eyes, and struck again and again (p. 275).

The "man with the quite eyes," the legacy left to Don Santiago by his mother, is the image of compassion and acceptance, the feminine locked within his masculine identity. It is the voice of "the other," a mediating force that allows the master to see himself as servant, the man to figure himself as woman. It is a voice that Don Santiago attempts to silence with his lustful grasp of the one element of a rancho that he *can* posses, the earth. This inability to negotiate the interior threat that the voice of "the other" poses to his identity reflects Don Santiago's limitations in negotiating exteriorized conflict, "because a fixed identity," like that of Don Santiago, "can be persuaded, coerced, and ultimately controlled."[9]

As his identity is increasingly threatened by the very real invasion of Anglo military forces into his territory and the encroachment of Anglo culture into his domestic sphere, Don Santiago's idealization of Alvaro grows. Alvaro, the patriarch's eldest son, is the consummate caballero and the image of patriarchal privilege: "Alvaro, spurs clinking, swaggered past the servant women, lustful, possessive eyes on the youngest and prettiest ones. Slender but powerfully built, the muscles revealed by the tight-fitting suit of buckskin moved with the coordination of a creature of the woods. Don Santiago watched his firstborn with approval, greeted him with a slap on the shoulder, and playfully shoved him beside his mother" (p. 5).

Alvaro's heroic appearance stands in contradiction with his swaggering and brutal demeanor. The idealized masculinity that Alvaro represents is demystified through the voices of the women that he claims to be protecting, but in reality victimizes. While he brashly joins a band of *guerrilleros* in response to the invasion of American troops into Mexico, he gains notoriety not only for his military skill but also for his prowess in using and discarding "camp women." In fact, it is one of these used women that betrays him to the Rangers, leading to his capture. Alvaro is brought to his home town of Matamoros, where the Rangers intend to make an example of him by hanging him in the plaza:

> This one was a prize, in a way, because his depredations were so— ah, manifold, if I may use the word, his evasion of our traps so clever that he achieved that high ambition of the desperado, a name. He is known as *El Lobo* and a wolf he is, too. He's a bad hombre, lieutenant, and I agree with the men that a public execution in a town where he is known would be very beneficial. The other two with him are harmless enough, I believe, and have evidently had their fill of war. Unfortunately a fourth of this gang whom we particularly wanted, one Cortinas, got away. *El Lobo* should be hanged—and high (p. 399).

The numerous references to Juan Cortina in *Caballero* are important. As a real historical figure, and, according to Américo Paredes, the earliest border *corrido* hero,[10] the references to Cortina place the character of Alvaro in the socio-historical context of the *corrido*. His prowess at eluding the law, his nickname of *El Lobo*, and his reputation as a lover all establish Alvaro as the consummate warrior hero.

When Susanita, his younger sister, learns of Alvaro's fate, she takes quick and decisive action, arranging to make the dangerous journey from Rancho La Palma to Matamoros on horseback accompanied by a male servant. Once in Matamoros, she contacts her Anglo lover, Lieutenant Warrener, and with his help, saves Alvaro from public hanging. Expecting her brother to be thankful for her sacrifice, she instead encounters the insolent gaze of a *guerrillero*:

> Susanita gave an involuntary gasp at the sight of him. Somehow he managed to shave, his trousers were brushed and his shirt at least half clean. He now wore a long mustache with twirled outstanding ends, sideburns ran down to his ears and his black hair lay black smooth and shiny. His black eyes traveled insolently over the Rangers, passed Warrener as if he were not there, and flung contempt at his sister so plainly that blood diffused her cheeks.
>
> . . . Alvaro grasped Susanita's wrists when she stretched hands to him. "No, don't kiss me," he snapped. "When I saw you, *you*, sitting alone in a room full of men—how did you come here? When?"
>
> She told him what happened from the time Pancho came to the *hacienda*, hurt to tears at his manner to her. She had scarcely finished when he flung further indictment at her. "Riding all night alone with a *peon*, you a Mendoza y Soría! Going to a soldier camp, riding with them, consorting with them, alone! Couldn't you let me die instead? It would have been an honor to our name, dying for my people and my country, now you have dishonored us forever" (pp. 402–403).

Like the figure of Gregorio Cortez in Paredes's *"With His Pistol in His Hand"*, Alvaro "becomes the typical guerrilla, the border raider fighting and fleeing, and using warrior's tricks to throw the enemy off."[11] These attributes alone would, had he been the central, unproblematic hero of *Caballero* (as the title implies), transform the novel into "a folk hero's tale of almost mythic proportions."[12] However, *Caballero* goes beyond retelling the traditional myth of the *corrido* hero by pointing out that a "man fighting for his right with his pistol in his hand,"[13] is fighting for *his* right and the rights of other men to maintain a traditional patriarchal order. By exposing this inconsistency, *Caballero* establishes Susanita as the true hero, a brave woman who risks her life and her honor to save the imprisoned *corrido* hero and suffers severe consequences as a result of her actions. Because she has "soiled the family honor" Susanita is banished from the hacienda. Her punishment reveals the contradictions inherent in a patriarchal code of honor which "protects" women, yet banishes them from the sphere of protection when they transgress its narrow limits. In one of the frequent eruptions of the female narrative voice in *Caballero*, the concept of "feminine honor" is revealed as a tool to keep women enslaved: "Honor! It was a fetishism. It was a weapon in the hands of the master, to keep his women enslaved, and his fingers had twisted upon it so tightly he could not let go" (p. 419).

Caballero reveals the *corrido* tradition, as represented in and through characterizations like Don Santiago and Alvaro, for what it is, an attempt of "patriarchal Mexican-American communities to retain their traditional culture in the face of advancing Anglo-American hegemony."[14] As such, *Caballero* represents an attempt, far before its time, to deconstruct traditional male-centered images of resistance and bring a multiplicity of voices to the Tejano experience.

Notes

CHAPTER 1

1. In MS-2 the bracketed passage is marked with a single line in the right-hand margin and a question mark.
2. Beginning here three pages are missing in MS-2, and we have substituted closely corresponding pages taken from MS-1. The social identification of Fulgencio is left unclear.
3. Here MS-2 picks up again.
4. The bracketed passage is marked with a question mark in the margin of MS-2.
5. This bracketed passage is marked "Omit" in the margins of MS-2.
6. Bracketed word is marked out by a single line in MS-2. We restore it here for the evident ideological import of this change.

CHAPTER 2

* The Lord is the master of this house (footnote translation in the original).
1. The singular "buena noche" is in the original MS-2.
2. Bracketed passage seems to be the authors' effort to condense in MS-2 material originally in the foreword to MS-1.

CHAPTER 3

1. Cf. Américo Paredes, *"With His Pistol in His Hand": A Border Ballad and Its Hero* (Austin: University of Texas Press, 1958, 1971), pp. 15–32.
2. Bracketed phrase marked out with single line in MS-2.
3. Reference to the Olivares ranch, the site and subject of González's *Dew on the Thorn*.
4. Typing illegible for short phrase here.
5. Typing illegible.

CHAPTER 4

1. Single word illegibly typed.
2. Bracketed phrase marked through in MS-2.
3. Probable allusion to John C. Hays, one of the first company commanders of the Texas Rangers, authorized by the new Texas Republic in 1836. In December of 1842, Republic of Texas forces—the Mier Expedition—led by Texas Rangers invaded Mexico near Laredo. After a fight with the Mexican army, 166 were captured at Mier and every tenth man put to death when they drew, by random lot, one of 17 black beans from a pitcher with 166 white and black beans. Also, Padre Pierre is probably modeled after the actual "French clergyman Abbé

Emanuel Domenech . . . who ministered to the religious needs of the Brownsville area from 1849 to 1855." Cf. David Montejano, *Anglos and Mexicans in the Making of Texas, 1836–1986.* (Austin: University of Texas Press, 1987), p. 31.

CHAPTER 6
1. Typing illegible for one word.
   * A legendary character in Spanish literature, prototype of the irresistible lover. (Original footnote in MS-2).

CHAPTER 7
1. Juan Seguín, the Mexican mayor of San Antonio in the early 1840s, fled to Mexico, along with many fellow Mexicans, in response to Anglo depredations.

CHAPTER 8
1. See Montejano, *Anglos and Mexicans,* p. 54 on trade between this area and New Orleans.

CHAPTER 9
1. Chapter 9 is missing in MS-2. However, chapter 8 in MS-2 is unusually long in comparison to other chapters, and its conclusion clearly and coherently leads into chapter 10 and is similar to chapter 9 of MS-1. The authors may have intended for the last portions of chapter 8 to be, in fact, chapter 9 but neglected to mark it formally as in MS-1. The end of the serenade scene and the church and dance scene of the following days seems a reasonable narrative place to now make this division, restoring, in our opinion, a reasonable chapter 9.

CHAPTER 10
1. Cf. the child character Chonita in Américo Paredes's short story "The Hammon and the Beans" in his collection *The Hammon and the Beans and Other Stories* (Houston: Arte Público Press, 1994). Paredes wrote his story circa 1939, although it was not published until 1963.

CHAPTER 13
1. In the mid-nineteenth century a Monterrey lawyer, Antonio Canales, led irregular border Mexicans in revolt both against central Mexican authority and the new Anglo-American invaders.
2. Obviously Mexico won its political independence from Spain in 1821. Here Canales is referring to what he sees as a still-influential and corrupting Spanish political culture exemplified by Santa Anna.

CHAPTER 14
1. Typing illegible.

CHAPTER 15

1. Typing illegible. Short phrase.

CHAPTER 23

* According to legend Saint James (Santiago) appeared on a white horse to the Spaniards and turned the tide of battle against the Moors. (Footnote in original MS-2).

CHAPTER 28

1. Bracketed passage crossed out by single line in MS-2.

CHAPTER 29

1. Bracketed phrase is crossed out in MS-2.
2. Here the authors take some literary license with history. In November, 1847, through early 1848, Jack Hays and his Rangers were in southern Mexico with the advancing U.S. Army. Possibly the authors are confusing (or taking advantage of) a town called Izúcar de Matamoros near Mexico City that Hays and the Texas Rangers did attack. See Frederick Wilkins, *The Highly Irregular Irregulars: Texas Rangers in the Mexican War* (Austin: Eakin Press, 1990), p. 143.
3. Here the authors use "alcoholics" in an unconventional sense, as synonymous to "liquors" rather than those addicted to them.
4. As in MS-2: Apparently Susanita has awakened and Inez is prattling on.
5. Word "sweet" crossed out by single line in MS-2.

CHAPTER 31

1. Drawing in part on Jovita González's M.A. thesis, David Montejano notes the not infrequent occurrence of such intermarriage between the landed Mexican elite and upper-class Anglo newcomers, such as the fictive Warrener, in which marriages were presumably based on love but also on economic interest, as McLane is suggesting. Indeed, through the name "Davis," the historically well-versed González may be suggesting a certain congruency between Lieutenant Robert *Davis* Warrener and the historically real Henry Clay *Davis*, an Army officer also discharged in South Texas after the war, who, according to Montejano, "married the daughter of a landed Mexican family and built a *rancho* and a mercantile house across the river on land belonging to his father-in-law. The Davis Rancho formed the beginning of Rio Grande City" next to Jovita González's childhood home of Roma and her later research field site. But in McLane's identification of Warrener as a potential future founder of a "new town" across from Matamoros, Warrener is clearly also a prototype for Charles Stillman, merchant and developer of Brownsville, Texas. See Montejano, *Anglos and Mexicans*, pp. 38–41.

HOMBRES NECIOS: A CRITICAL EPILOGUE

1. While it essentially a folklore study and not a novel, a case can be made for viewing *"With His Pistol in His Hand"*, as an originary text for much of Chicano fiction. Concerning the influence of *"With His Pistol in His Hand"* on Chicano literature, Ramón Saldívar writes: "[The text] became the primary imaginative seeding ground for later works because it offered both the stuff of history and of art and the key to an understanding of their decisive interrelationship for Mexican American writers. Paredes' study is crucial in historical, aesthetic, and theoretical terms for the contemporary development of Chicano prose fiction because it stands as the primary formulation of the expressive reproductions of the sociocultural order imposed on and resisted by the Mexican American community in the twentieth century." See Ramón Saldívar, *Chicano Narrative: The Dialectics of Difference* (Madison: University of Wisconsin Press, 1990), p. 27.

2. Angie Chabram Dernersesian, "And Yes . . . The Earth Did Part," in *Building With Our Hands: New Directions in Chicana Studies*, eds. Adela de la Torre and Beatriz M. Pesquera (Berkeley: University of California Press, 1993), p. 39.

3. Ibid.

4. Ibid.

5. Ibid.

6. Translation: Foolish Men. *Hombres Necios* is the title of a poem written in the late seventeenth century by poet and nun, Sor Juana Inez de La Cruz. This poem is considered by many to be a precursor of feminist thought because of its indictment of patriarchal culture's double standard of setting impossible goals of purity for women, while encouraging promiscuity as a proof of manhood.

7. Jovita González de Mireles and Margaret Eimer, *Caballero*, E. E. Mireles and Jovita González de Mireles Papers, Special Collections and Archives Department, Mary and Jeff Bell Library, Texas A&M University–Corpus Christi, p. 5 (hereafter cited with page numbers in parentheses).

8. Saldívar, p. 174.

9. Ibid.

10. Américo Paredes writes: "Cortina definitely is the earliest border *corrido* hero that we know of, whether his exploits were put into the *corridos* in 1860 or later." See Américo Paredes, *"With His Pistol in His Hand"* (Austin: University of Texas Press, 1958), 140.

11. Ibid., pp. 119–20.

12. Saldívar, p. 34.

13. Paredes, p. 149.

14. Saldívar, p. 38.